Under
Cedar
Shades

ᎤᏂ ᎨᏥᎢᏢᏙᏗ ᎠᏂᏣᎳᎩ
Trail of Tears National Historic Trail (Including Proposed Routes for

Springfield

Indianapolis

Dayton

Springfield

Illinois

Indiana

Cincinnati

Cape Girardeau

Kentucky

Hopkinsville

Clarksville

Nashville-Davidson

McMinnville
Shells Ford

Tennessee

Rock Island

Fort Cass

Chattanooga

New Echota

aw Bluffs

Muscle Shoals

Huntsville

Echota

Atlanta

ippi

Birmingham

Georgia

Alabama

Legend

The Bell Route
The Benge Route
The Round Up Routes
The Water Additional Routes
The Water Land Components
The Disbandment Routes
Designated Routes

UNDER
CEDAR
SHADES

A Novel

To Elizabeth
Best wishes
Your cousin
Helen Lavinia Underwood
May 2009

HELEN LAVINIA UNDERWOOD

To order additional copies of this book, contact:
Xlibris Corporation
1-888-795-4274
www.Xlibris.com
Orders@Xlibris.com
45270

CONTENTS

PROLOGUE 13

BOOK I—The Cherokee Removal 15

    1.   Greenberry and Analeha...19
    2.   The Cave..27
    3.   Fort Cass 33
    4.   Shells Ford on the Collins 41
    5.   Blood Law Vengeance...51

BOOK II—The Preeces of Wales and The Chickasaw Romans..............61

    1.   Fannie and John 63
    2.   Lillie and Elizabeth..69
    3.   Preeces or Romans..74
    4.   War Comes to Bone Cave 79
    5.   Watch on the Collins 84
    6.   Surviving...91
    7.   The Last Indian 96

BOOK III—The Fraleys of Ulster and Hannah's People 101

    1.   Henry and Clary 103
    2.   Hannah...108
    3.   On to Tennessee 114
    4.   Trouble on the Mountain 120
    5.   Life in Jonesborough 125

BOOK IV—Orpha in Hell 133

    1.   Orpha and Avery...135
    2.   Hallie 141
    3.   Taking a Gamble...145
    4.   Out of the Depths...149
    5.   The Prodigal Returns 153

BOOK V—The Spruills of Scotland 161

    1.   Orpha and William 163
    2.   Sadness Revisited..168
    3.   Between the Blue and the Gray 172
    4.   Henry's Last Stand..177
    5.   Yellow Daffodils 181

BOOK VI—Vennie and James...187

    1.   Vennie Meets James..189
    2.   A Special Place 195
    3.   Revelations...202
    4.   Marriage and the Mines 206
    5.   Vennie and Clara..212
    6.   Endings and Beginnings...218

BOOK VII—THE STRAWBERRY FIELD 223

    1.   On the Great Wagon Road..225
    2.   The Homecoming..231
    3.   The Outrage 241
    4.   Moore's Grove 245
    5.   The Secret 250

EPILOGUE 257

Author's note..261
Acknowledgments 263
Resources 267
The Trail of Tears Association (TOTA)..273

Dedicated to the memory of my mother,

Ruby Mae Talley Greenway

1920-1993

And to my grandchildren

Leigh

Addie

Maggie

Melissa

Paige

Sara

Angelica

And for Alexander

in memoriam

AUTHOR'S NOTE

This novel is historical fiction. It is based on some real persons, places, and events, but it also includes purely fictional characters and incidents. It includes some of what I know to be true and some of what I suspect to be true. In some cases, names have been changed. I have drawn on many sources and have done my best to be true to them all.

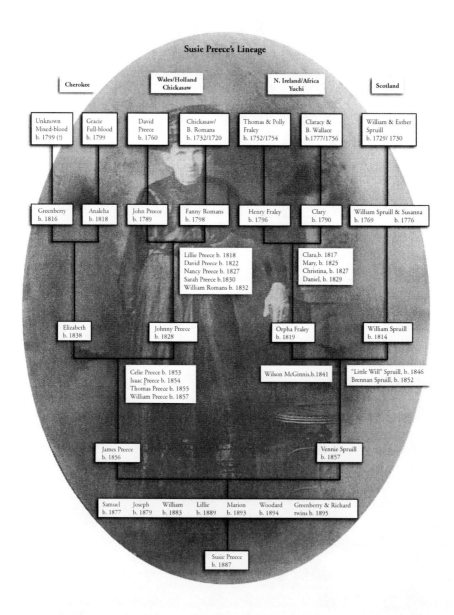

Susie Preece's Lineage

Cherokee

Wales/Holland Chickasaw

N. Ireland/Africa Yuchi

Scotland

Unknown Mixed-blood b. 1799 (?)	Gracie Full-blood b. 1799	David Preece b. 1760	Chickasaw/ B. Romans b. 1732/1720	Thomas & Polly Fraley b. 1752/1754	Claracy & B. Wallace b.1777/1756	William & Esther Spruill b. 1729/ 1730

Greenberry b. 1816	Analeha b. 1818	John Preece b. 1789	Fanny Romans b. 1798	Henry Fraley b. 1796	Clary b. 1790	William Spruill & Susanna b. 1769 b. 1776

Lillie Preece b. 1818
David Preece b. 1822
Nancy Preece b. 1827
Sarah Preece b.1830
William Romans b. 1832

Clara,b. 1817
Mary, b. 1825
Christina, b. 1827
Daniel, b. 1829

Elizabeth b. 1838	Johnny Preece b. 1828	Orpha Fraley b. 1819	William Spruill b. 1814

Celie Preece b. 1853
Isaac Preece b. 1854
Thomas Preece b. 1855
William Preece b. 1857

Wilson McGinnis,b.1841

"Little Will" Spruill, b. 1846
Brennan Spruill, b. 1852

James Preece b. 1856	Vennie Spruill b. 1857

Samuel b. 1877	Joseph b. 1879	William b. 1883	Lillie b. 1889	Marion b. 1893	Woodard b. 1894	Greenberry & Richard twins b. 1895

Susie Preece
b. 1887

PROLOGUE

I

From the dim mists of history
Books, DNA, and my computer
From memories of hushed whispers
Wake-up smiles, sweet nighttime lullabies
I search for thousands of long-ago lovers
To unravel the secret of who I am

II

Under cedar shades
I listen to the wind's song
Sometimes in shadowed stillness
I feel the sadness coming on
But I wait under cedar shades
Unafraid

BOOK I

The Cherokee Removal

1837-1839

As a result of the Removal, the Cherokee people were forced to leave behind their mountains, their land, their streams, everything they held sacred. How could this happen? We should know, and we should remember.

—Gayle Ross, great-great-great-granddaughter of John Ross, Principal Chief of the Cherokee Nation during The Trail of Tears

HISTORICAL SETTING

The Trail of Tears

Reprinted from the National Park Service
U.S. Department of the Interior

Early in the 19th century, the United States felt threatened by England and Spain, who held land in the western continent. At the same time, American settlers clamored for more land. Thomas Jefferson proposed the creation of a buffer zone between U.S. and European holdings, to be inhabited by eastern American Indians. This plan would allow for American expansion westward from the original colonies to the Mississippi River.

Between 1816 and 1840, tribes located between the original states and the Mississippi River, including Cherokees, Chickasaws, Choctaws, Creeks and Seminoles, signed more than 40 treaties ceding their lands to the U.S. In his 1829 inaugural address, President Andrew Jackson set a policy to relocate eastern Indians. Between 1830 and 1850, about 100,000 American Indians living between Michigan, Louisiana and Florida moved west after the U.S. government coerced treaties or used the U.S. Army against those resisting. Many were treated brutally. An estimated 3,500 Creeks died in Alabama on their westward journey. Some were transported in chains.

Historically, Cherokees occupied lands in several southeastern states. As European settlers arrived, Cherokees traded and intermarried with them. They began to adopt European customs, while being pressured to give up traditional homelands. Between 1721 and 1819, over 90 percent of the lands were ceded to others. By the 1820s, Sequoyah's syllabary brought literacy and a formal governing system with a written constitution. In 1830, the same year the Indian Removal Act was passed, gold was found on Cherokee lands. Georgia held lotteries to give Cherokee land and gold rights to whites. Cherokees were not allowed to conduct tribal business, contract, testify in courts against whites, or mine for gold.

In December 1835, the U.S. convinced a small group of Cherokees to sign a treaty ceding Cherokee territory east of the Mississippi to the U.S. in exchange for $5 million and new homelands in Indian Territory to the west. More than 15,000 Cherokees protested the illegal treaty. Yet, on May 23, 1836, the Treaty of New Echota was ratified by the U.S. Senate—by just one vote.

Every possible kindness . . . must be shown by the troops.

—General Winfield Scott
In charge of the Cherokee Removal
May 17, 1838

I fought through the Civil War and have seen men shot to pieces and slaughtered by the thousands, but the Cherokee removal was the cruelest work I ever saw.

—Confederate Colonel Z. A. Zele
Member of the Georgia Guard

ONE

Greenberry and Analeha

Cedar Mountain, Tennessee
December 1837

A thin blue mist hung between the hills. In the nearby fields, dead corn stalks and overripe pumpkins lay rotting under a light sprinkling of snow. Pieces of apples, dried and shriveled from the heat of the sun, clung to the roof. The underbrush, charred black at the edge of the woods, had been killed by the burning. Gunnysacks filled with nuts for winter oil leaned against the porch wall. Analeha and her mother, Gracie, had gathered and bagged them, as they had raided the bee trees to collect the sticky sweet honey. But all the winter preparations ended when Greenberry returned from the village council meeting and made his announcement:

"We must leave this place. And we must go at once."

At the meeting, Greenberry had listened while one of the elders read a warning letter from the United States government that had been distributed to every Cherokee council. In part, it said: "In the Treaty of 1835, it is stipulated that all Cherokees shall remove to their new homes in the west within two years of the ratification of this treaty, May 23, 1836. You have now, after wasting opportunities, only the short period of less than five months for the settlement of your affairs here and the removal to your new homes. Do not deceive yourselves. The treaty will be executed. As you value your lives, the lives of your families, and your existence as a nation, fail not to take the advice we now have given to you."

Several elders of the village council stood to denounce the threatening letter. One of them reminded the council that four thousand Cherokees, meeting in tribal council at Red Clay, had rebuked the treaty. "I think few Cherokees will honor that agreement," he said. Greenberry knew the elder was right.

He had heard about the Cherokee leaders John Ross and John Ridge, both wealthy mixed-bloods educated in the ways of the white man. Greenberry knew both had parlayed with the white leaders in Washington, but they had taken different paths concerning the removal of the Cherokees. Chief Ross said the government had no right to remove the Cherokees from their land. Greenberry was convinced he was right. Like most of the village council, Greenberry supported the decision made at Red Clay. But he doubted Chief Ross would be able to prevail in the end.

It was the other Cherokee leaders—John Ridge, Elias Boudinot, and Stand Watie—who started all the trouble. They went against Ross and signed the Treaty of New Echota to give over Cherokee land in the east in exchange for lands in the west. They had already moved their families to the Arkansas Territory, where they lived in fine houses and had plenty to eat and hundreds of acres for their slaves to farm. Despite the efforts of Chief Ross to overturn the treaty, Andrew Jackson, the white leader in Washington, had made it clear the Cherokees would be removed to the west.

The elders discussed the mistreatment of the Creeks in Alabama when the soldiers collected them for removal the year before. The Creeks were taken in chains and prodded at bayonet point to holding pens from which they were forcibly removed to the west.

"This will surely be the fate of the Cherokees as well," said one of the elders. "Already white people in other villages are stealing Cherokee belongings. Some are beating and abusing Cherokee families before stripping them of everything they have."

"I will not stay here and wait for them to come and plunder our home," Greenberry said. "We will go to the high mountains. If we do not go soon, the soldiers will surely come for us. We will not leave our home for some distant place in the west. We belong here in the mountains, among the rocky cliffs, waterfalls, and rushing rivers. We will not go where there are no deer and no bear, and where the laurel, oak, pine, and cedar do not grow. He broke a handful of small green twigs from the east side of the cedar tree and then piled on larger branches making a crackling fire. Maybe this would help chase away the *anis-gi'na*, bad ghosts who could not stand the smell of burning cedar. Greenberry squatted beside the fire waiting to hear Analeha's argument.

Analeha, her thin body covered with the woolen blanket her mother had woven for her, shivered on the cabin porch, watching him, trying to read what he was thinking. For days he had been telling her they must go to the mountains to hide. She knew he would not give in. How could he think they could leave their comfortable cabin and go to some cave and live like animals? She had given up arguing with him. He would not listen to her.

Analeha remembered days sitting around the loom listening to the older women. "Everything has changed since the white people came," they said. The eldest, Old Sollie, leaned forward and spit tobacco juice into the gourd cup beside her.

"Not so long ago," she said, "people in our village followed the ways of Kanati and Selu. They sit side by side in the Upper World. They bring peace and harmony to our people. Selu, our mother, is the giver of corn. So, like Selu, we women grew corn and beans and pumpkins for the people's food. Men hunted meat for the family because our father, Kanati, hunted meat for his family. Women and men had different ways then. Now everything has changed. Now our men are no longer hunters. The government told us to leave our towns where we lived together and to build separate houses for our families, and we did. We bought cattle, horses, and hogs, and we planted grain. Our men became farmers like the white man, and now our women sit by the looms all day weaving and making cloth. We have become like the white women. And our men now do women's work. They plow and plant seeds in the spring and gather the harvest in the fall. Many even carry water. In the old days, it was disgraceful for men to carry water.

"More and more the old ways are changing," Old Sollie went on. "In olden days, it was the women who made decisions about their families. Now that they have taken on white ways, they wait for the men to decide."

Analeha thought of the hunting trips Greenberry took when he was younger. Even now he sometimes went away for days hunting deer. But he also helps plant seeds in the spring and harvest food in the fall. Sometimes he even carries water from the spring.

Analeha realized that, until recently, they had allowed Gracie to make many of the decisions about the care of their small piece of land. Most women in the valley had been the keepers of the land. Analeha knew that task would fall to her when her mother died. What would happen to their home if they left to hide in the mountains? Who would see that the land was plowed and planted? Who would gather the first corn? Who would be the keeper of their land?

Yes, Analeha thought, the decision whether or not to leave should be made by all three of us. Analeha knew her mother trusted Greenberry and had always included him in decisions. So why, she wondered, had Greenberry now decided this by himself? What had happened to the old ways? Greenberry had always listened to her side of an argument. She had admired him for being patient with Gracie when Gracie sometimes became too overbearing. Now there was no harmony in their lives. She had agreed to marry Greenberry because she thought he would be a responsible husband. She had thought she could trust him to think clearly about his own actions, but now she wondered.

She liked the way he had pursued her before they married. He first went to Gracie and stated his intent. Analeha had feared her mother might not approve because Greenberry's grandfather had English blood, and some of the elders in his village raised their voices against mingling with the white race. She had heard Gracie say the only reason whites or mixed-bloods wanted to marry an Indian was so they could get possession of their land.

Greenberry's Cherokee mother had given him his name, *Ee-jeh-yoos-dee-oo-day-tah-nuh*, because he had been born when the young juniper berries were still green. His mother had released his father from their marital bond when she learned he was living with a Creek woman in another village. When Greenberry was two years old, his mother died of smallpox. Her sister Susanna took Greenberry as her own child and raised him, making no distinction between him and her own children.

Gracie had warmed to Greenberry. "He can never provide you with much wealth," she had said, "but he will work hard. He knows how to plow and plant seeds. Besides, I know you love him."

"It was his eyes that drew me to him," Analeha told her. "His dark brown eyes are like the bark of the hickory nut in the fall. He has strong arms and shoulders like a great warrior, but he is gentle. He is not like some of the other young men who only know about ballplay and hunting. He knows how to carve. I loved to listen to him play on his flute."

"Yes, and he is wise for his age," Gracie said. "He pays attention to the sun, the moon and the stars."

Gracie had decided when she first met him that he was a special person. "Greenberry has many skills," Gracie said. "Susanna taught him how to plow and plant corn, beans, squash, and pumpkins in the spring. The men of the village taught him how to build storehouses for the harvest. From the priests and elders, he learned how to tend the fire in the council house and to keep the pine knots burning through the night. The storytellers told him ancestral stories. The hunters taught him to use the blowgun, the tomahawk, and the bow and arrow. Older men showed him how to carve flutes from cedar branches. When he plays notes on his flute, I can see how he is different from the others. Yes, Greenberry will make a good husband for you."

Analeha watched as Greenberry threw more branches on the fire. "Our people's fate has been sealed," he told her. "The government has no intention of keeping the commitments made in the treaty. Every treaty the white man has ever made with the Cherokees has been broken. We ought to know by this time that the government cannot be trusted. It never gives. It only takes."

Greenberry knew Cherokees had been moving out west for some time, but until now, the decision had been theirs to make. Small groups had moved to the Arkansas territory and later into northeastern Oklahoma. Some had returned to visit family members and friends. Even the great leader Sequoyah, who developed the Cherokee syllabary, had moved on his own. "If people like Sequoyah choose to go west," Greenberry told Analeha, "let them. But don't try to force me to move to a place I don't want to be."

Greenberry thought with pride how Sequoyah's Cherokee syllabary had given thousands of Cherokees, including himself and his own village council, the ability to read and write in their own language. Even though Sequoyah had never learned to read, write, or speak English, he had proven Cherokees were just as smart as the white man. Still, as the government letter proves beyond a doubt, the white man continues to rule our lives.

He would like to meet John Ridge and ask him why he signed the removal treaty. He would ask him what he thought would happen to the Cherokee people stranded in a land not their own. The more he thought about it, the more his anger grew. "Where is the Great Spirit?" he wondered. "Where is your white missionary God?" He cried aloud to Analeha.

Analeha moved her body to and fro on the cabin steps, sobbing. She thought of the missionary school where her Moravian teachers had taught that God is love. Some missionary leaders had attempted to stop the removal. Some had even gone to jail in Georgia for trying to help the Cherokees. Greenberry had come back from the town council one night and told her about the missionaries taking the cause to the Supreme Court in Washington. Their hopes had been raised when the Court ruled in favor of the Cherokees and against the removal. But the efforts of Ross and the missionaries had ended in defeat, when President Jackson had said: "John Marshall has rendered his decision. Now let him enforce it." Neither the missionaries nor the Indian leaders had any power to stop the removal. Greenberry said that even their own leaders could not be trusted, and she feared he was right.

"We cannot remain on the land," he said, "because sooner or later, the soldiers will come and take us by force."

Greenberry moved to the end of the porch and sat bent forward, his head in his hands. He could never understand why Analeha went to the missionary church. She would return from the services telling him about sermons she had heard, mostly about sin. It seemed to him the missionaries believed that everything Cherokees did was sinful. Why was it sinful to dance? Dancing was an important part of Cherokee life. How could the green corn dance be evil? And how could ballplay be sinful? And what was this forgiveness they kept talking about? How could he be expected to forgive those who had signed away Indian lands and driven people from their homes?

Greenberry thought of the days of his youth when the elders had taught him that Mother Earth and Father Sky were watching over him. They said Brother Moon came up each evening to put a glow on the night and Sister Sun came up each morning to brighten the day.

"Give thanks to the Great One for all he has given you," the elders said. "And remember that all the animals, birds, and even the rocks are sacred. In the old days, there was peace and harmony in the mountains. We must see that peace and harmony return."

The elders had taught him he must keep his life in balance. It was from them he had learned the Cherokee prayer:

> *Great Spirit, you speak to me in the wind. Your breath gives life to the world. Let me learn the lessons you have hidden in every leaf and rock. Make me always ready to come to you with clean hands and straight eyes, so when life fades, like the sunset, my spirit may come to you without shame.*

Greenberry thought of the mountains he climbed as a boy. There among the wild laurel, he gathered hickory nuts and wild berries. Sitting in the shade of the cedars, he looked out into the great valley below. He could smell the sweet aroma of the cedar wood. He understood why the elders looked to the cedar for comfort and protection. Sitting with the elders around the fire in the council house on cold winter nights, he often heard the story about the tree that never loses its green branches. "The cedar is a sacred tree," the elders said. "In freezing rain, heavy snow, and winter wind, the cedar survives. Other trees may lose their leaves, but not the cedar."

They taught him how to use its wood for carving flutes. "Cedar would never warp, nor would it rot. This is why cedar is perfect for flutes." Alone on the mountainside, he whittled on a cedar limb for many days until he had carved out a small flute. Placing it to his lips, he blew a tentative note and held it as long as his breath lasted. Mingling with the whisper of a quiet wind, it lifted his spirit high over the mountains.

He listened to the note reverberate across the hills. It was a haunting, ancient sound, raising the hairs on the back of his neck. But it was more than the flute's sound that lifted him. He loved to rub his fingers over its smoothness. The mossy earth where he sat and the trees around him seemed greener. The wildflowers, purple, white, and yellow at the edge of the woods, looked brighter.

Greenberry's reverie ended when his thoughts could not shut out Analeha's sobbing. He wished he could stop her tears and make her understand. He felt for the flute around his neck. Since the day he had carved it, it had hung there on a deerskin string. He must not leave it behind when they departed for the cave in the high mountains.

He gathered twigs and stoked the glowing embers. Pulling fresh cedar branches from the east side of the tree, he threw them on the fire. If burning cedar can chase away the *anis gi'na*, the bad ghosts, he thought, maybe it will drive away thieving neighbors and soldiers, too.

"No more praying to the white man's gods," he said aloud to Analeha. It startled her that he broke the silence with such words.

"This is what I know," he continued, his voice hard and unyielding. "As long as soldiers can follow paths and ford creeks and rivers, they will hunt our people down. White people want our land. Already they are raiding Cherokee homes and taking whatever they can cart away. That is what the white Christians do to their Indian neighbors." Greenberry spat on the ground. "What happened to their God's rule to love their neighbor? Does the Christian's holy book say that Cherokee people cannot be neighbors?" The venom in his voice made Analeha shudder.

"There is no way to stop the white settlers from taking our home," he continued. "But we will not wait for the soldiers to take us. We will not become prisoners of the white man. I have decided. Tomorrow you and I will leave for the cave in the high mountains."

Analeha waited for his next words, but he seemed to have nothing more to say. "And my mother?" she asked. "What will happen to her?"

"She is too old," he said. "She can go to the missionaries. They will take care of her. She cannot climb the high mountain, and she will not survive the winter in the cave."

How could he be so cold, so cruel? Analeha buried her face in her lap and wailed. She loved him, but why could he not understand that she also loved and depended on her mother? How could they leave her behind, all alone with no one to care for her? Why had he decided on his own that Gracie could not go? Such a decision is for women to make. Greenberry was acting like a white man. At least he might have discussed it with her and her mother. Into the night she cajoled him, trying to make him see reason.

At length, he sighed and said, "She is too old to climb the rugged mountain. Go to sleep. We will speak of it no more."

By morning's first light, Analeha's mind was made up. She would not go with Greenberry. She had promised to take care of her mother. She thought of all they had done together—picking berries in the woods, planting and harvesting corn, making corn mush, working the loom, weaving baskets, making pots. On cold winter nights as they sat around the fire, her mother had told her stories about strong tribal women.

"The mixed-blood Nancy Ward stood in the counsel all by herself helping make life-and-death decisions for the tribe. Once, she took a letter signed by twelve other women to the big council and pleaded with them not to give up land."

Greenberry cannot make such a decision on his own, Analeha said to herself. How could he think I would leave my mother behind? I will not go.

TWO

The Cave

Cedar Mountain
December 1837-May 1838

By midmorning, Gracie had packed a small clay pot, a gourd dipper, deerskins, corn meal, beans, dried apples, and dried pork in one of the baskets they had made together. She wrapped the basket in deerskin and attached it to Analeha's back. Analeha watched in disbelief.

"You must go with him to the mountains," her mother said. "I will go to the mission station. The missionaries will help me. There is no need to worry about me. You must go with your husband."

"I will not leave you alone," Analeha said, her voice hoarse from crying. She tried her best to be forceful.

"You *must* go," Gracie said with finality. "Maybe there is still time for Chief Ross to secure agreement for some of the people to stay in the East." She looked away to avoid her daughter's eyes.

Greenberry had heard the argument. Gracie understands, he thought. At least they would have a chance to survive in the cave, and perhaps someday they could return to their cabin and grow corn and dance the green corn dance, and they could raise their children in the cabin. They would sit under cedar shades in the summer and hunt deer and turkey in the winter. Gracie understood.

Greenberry secured his knife and hatchet to his waist belt, and strapped his bow and arrows and his gun securely to his back. He felt around his neck for his flute. Then he waited. He knew he could not leave Analeha behind. "The soldiers' horses cannot climb the steep rocks," he said to Gracie, hoping to relieve her of worry. "If the soldiers dare come after us by foot, the briar thickets will stop them. We will be safe in the cave."

Gracie knew Greenberry was wise in the way of caves. In his youth, he had explored every cave in the mountains near the village. "As soon as this is over," Greenberry assured her, "we will come back."

Analeha clung to her mother on the cabin porch. "Don't worry," Gracie said, "I will stay close to the missionaries at the mission station." Gracie could see snow clouds gathering. "You must go," she said. "A winter storm is coming up."

She watched them trekking up the steep mountain trail and waited until they were out of sight before allowing her grief to give way to a mournful wail. What had happened to her people? Her one last hope was that Analeha and Greenberry could survive the storms and the howling winter winds. She had placed seven small ears of dried corn in the basket to make sure the new corn they planted in the spring would grow and flourish. Would Analeha and Greenberry ever again dance the green corn dance in the spring? She remembered how, before eating the new corn, they had joined other tribal members in the green corn dance to atone for wrongs done in the past year and to pray for prosperity in the coming year.

Gracie waited to begin her preparations until they were far enough away so they would not see, even if they looked back. I will not leave here. This is my home, and no white man will live in it. I buried my two youngest ones in the cemetery on the hill. I raised my beautiful Analeha here. We planted seeds in the spring and reaped the harvest in the fall. We planted apple trees and picked the fruit for drying. We fished the streams. She looked through the cedar trees to the river below and sighed deeply. The soldiers will come for me soon, and there is no one to stop the white settlers from taking my belongings.

She poured oil from the grease lamp onto the puncheon pine floor and spread cedar branches throughout the cabin. Stoking the fire in the fireplace, Gracie took a shovel of red-hot coals from the grate and spread them on the cedar branches. She moved to her rocking chair on the front porch and sat down. Her last memory was of Analeha and Greenberry becoming a tiny speck, fading gradually into the mountain.

If Analeha and Greenberry had looked back, they might have seen the smoke. But they did not look back. The winter sun cast long shadows from the tall cedars across the snowy path as they climbed higher. Greenberry hoped he had made the right decision. The cave he had found above the river as a boy should still be unnoticeable to anyone on the trail. He remembered it had several caverns and alcoves behind the small opening. It would be warmer there, and they could build a fire at the end of the day when the smoke would be less visible.

Perhaps, he thought, others seeking to escape the removal have already found the cave. "It would be a good thing if others are there," he said. "I would not have to leave you alone when I go hunting for food."

Analeha could not imagine being left alone in a cave.

"We'll live like our ancestors did before the white man came," he said.

Analeha knew Greenberry was making small talk to keep her from worrying about her mother. She remembered her mother standing on the cabin porch all alone. Maybe she should have stayed behind.

"We must reach the cave before dark," Greenberry said. "The storm will bring a deep snow."

"When they reached the cave at sunset, they were glad to find James Blackbird, a Creek, and his Cherokee wife, Sarah, already living there. "I am glad you have come," Sarah told Analeha. "We've been here all alone for four months. It will be good for us all to be together."

James Blackbird told them of the horrors of the Creek removal that had begun the year before. "They took my people in shackles like criminals and forced them at bayonet point to walk for miles to Gunter's Landing in Alabama. Then they forced them onto flatboats that took them west."

"How did you escape?" Greenberry asked.

"I ran away to a village on the Hiwassee in Tennessee and found refuge with the Cherokees. That's where I married Sarah. I had hoped the Cherokees would not suffer the same fate as my people, but I was wrong. Soon there was talk that Cherokees, too, were being removed to the west."

Sarah and James Blackbird had arrived in mid-August, when she was already four months pregnant. "I've done my best to make the cave as much of a home as possible," Sarah said. "We covered the entrance with branches so the opening could not be seen from the river trail. And there's a spring nearby where we can get water." Analeha thought how tired Sarah looked.

Greenberry and Analeha stored their food and belongings in one of the alcoves. At first Analeha was frightened about living in the cave, but Sarah reassured her. "We must keep a fire burning near the entrance so wolves and grizzlies and other wild animals won't bother us. But we have survived so far without trouble, with only the cave crickets and beetles for company." Analeha wished she could be as cheerful about their cave home as Sarah.

Like a woman in her tribal village proudly showing her new cabin, Sarah led Analeha through the parts of the cave she had explored. They stooped to walk through a narrow passageway that opened into a large cavern. "Step carefully around the gypsum needles," Sarah warned Analeha. "They can be as sharp as glass. Take care not to lose your footing and fall."

The torchlight danced across brown, orange, and white petals of gypsum roses, lilies, and other flowerlike protrusions on the cave walls. Analeha wondered how something so beautiful could grow in such a dark place. The torch flickered, and Analeha shivered, hoping they would not be left in the dark. She shuddered at the thought of being lost deep inside a dark cave.

In the dim torchlight, Sarah showed Analeha the cave pearls. "You can have this one to keep," she said. "It can be your special gift. It comes from the earth and the water. This one is the roundest and smoothest of all the pearls I've found, but you can only keep it while you are inside the cave. If you take it outside, it will crumble and run through your fingers like sand."

"Do you bring any news?" James Blackbird asked Greenberry.

"Not good news. Before we left, we heard about people being taken from their homes. White settlers were swooping down like vultures to take over their farms."

"There are many others like us hiding out," said James Blackbird. "They cannot find us all. But we must be careful not to give ourselves away. We must remain here inside during the day and hunt mostly by night."

Many times in the cold midwinter, when the wind was roaring through the pines and tall cedars on the ridge above them, Analeha wondered if they would survive. Long, jagged icicles hung from the ledge over the cave entrance. Greenberry and James, wading through knee-deep snow, managed to find a few rabbits and wild turkeys on their hunting forays, though bigger game was scarce. They made traps of sticks and rawhide to catch small game near the cave opening, but were hesitant to hunt in the woods below or fish the stream for fear of being seen.

When Sarah's baby came early one freezing night at the end of January, Analeha did all she could to help. She placed a deerskin wrap on the floor of the cave and tried to raise Sarah to a squatting position to deliver her baby. Sarah was too weak to sit up and had to deliver lying on her back. James had gone outside to search for slippery elm or wild cherry bark for a tea to make the delivery easier. When he returned, it was too late. The baby had been stillborn. Sarah had suffered a long, hard delivery. She died a few hours later without ever holding her baby.

They buried Sarah and her baby deep within the cave so the bodies would not be discovered. They placed them among the gypsum flowers she had so loved. Anahela cried for a long time, thinking how the cave burial was like a prison for the spirit of her friend. How sad Sarah would never have benefit of the sunlight on her grave, though perhaps, like the cave pearl, her spirit would glow in the dark among the gypsum flowers. Soon after Sarah was gone, Analeha began to wonder how much longer she could last in the cave.

In February, Analeha found she was pregnant. She had missed her bleeding time, and she knew a child was growing inside her. It was a frightening thought that she could lose her baby and die here in this cave as Sarah had. Who would help with the birthing? How she longed for her mother. She could almost taste her mother's warm corn mush and fried bread.

Sometimes at night when the last embers of the fire were dying, she remembered lying in the cabin listening to the whippoorwill and smelling the cedar wood fire. She remembered times she had felt Greenberry's body hard against her. She remembered hoping a baby would soon grow inside her, but now she dreaded what might happen here.

As the days passed, supplies dwindled. Hungry and tired, Analeha and Greenberry hovered with James Blackbird inside the cave, waiting for the spring rains to stop. By the beginning of May, most of their food supply was gone. They found game even scarcer now, as most of the animals had moved lower down the valley looking for food. The last of the corn Sarah and Analeha had pounded to make mush was nearly gone. Analeha boiled the roots of the *U-ni-ga-nas-ha* her mother had given her to make a tea to quell their hunger pangs.

In mid-May, when she thought she could stand no more, Analeha announced in a resolute voice, "We must leave this place. We must go down to the mission where I can get help delivering my baby. I will not survive in this cave. I will die like Sarah, and my baby will die. At least at the mission we can get food and blankets." She wanted no arguments. "Do not give me reasons why we should stay. I have made up my mind. We have to leave."

Greenberry feared they would be captured, shackled, and thrown into the stockade, but he was too tired to try to convince her otherwise. He did not want her to deliver their child here and die like Sarah, so he told James Blackbird he was taking Analeha down to the mission.

"You must come with us," he said to James. "I need you to help me. I cannot take Analeha down alone. She is too weak to walk all the way."

James Blackbird said goodbye at Sarah's gravesite, and then left with Greenberry and Analeha on the journey down the mountain. Most of the ice had melted and they noticed the spring buds on the trees along the path. They could see blackberry bushes bursting into white, and the wild laurel was beginning to bloom. Analeha was thankful the sun's rays shone through the cedars, bringing welcome warmth. They walked for hours down the mountain path, encountering no one. Analeha hoped she would be able to make it to the mission before nightfall. When she became too tired to walk, Greenberry and James made a bed from hickory poles and limbs to carry her over the steepest and rockiest paths. Her hopes began to rise as they moved farther down. Surely her mother would be there. How happy she would be to see them.

Greenberry moved down the mountain in despair. He dreaded what awaited them. He knew the deadline for the round-up was at the end of May. What if they arrived just in time for the forced removal? If only they could have survived a little longer in the cave, perhaps they would have missed it. All the suffering of the past few months was for naught, he thought. He loved Analeha. She had endured the horrible winter and in a few months would give birth to their child. He knew she needed food and care, but he feared there would be nothing left for them but to become prisoners, to be prodded along like cattle to new lands.

By late afternoon, they arrived at the mission station to find the school closed. They could find no missionaries, only a few black servants who informed them the reverend doctors and the ladies had all gone to the internment camp at Fort Cass to help the Cherokee people. To Analeha's queries about her mother, the servants said they knew nothing, but thought she might have gone with the missionaries to the internment camp. Greenberry knew if they were to find medical help for Analeha, it would have to be at Fort Cass. Analeha was anxious to go there to find her mother, but they were all hungry and tired. They would eat the food the servants put before them and wait until morning to make the trek to Fort Cass.

THREE

Fort Cass

Charleston, Tennessee
May-October 1838

When Greenberry, Analeha, and James Blackbird arrived at Fort Cass, they were escorted to the Rattlesnake Springs encampment. Analeha had never seen so many people all in one place. She began at once looking for her mother. Would she ever be able to find her among these hordes? An overwhelming odor of excrement and urine permeated the camp. Sixteen-foot-square roofless enclosures, filthy and overcrowded, extended for miles. Pieces of bark, blankets, and scraps of cloth had been draped over wooden poles. Many people were sleeping on the ground with no overhead shelter.

"I'm looking for my mother. Have you seen her?" Analeha went from one family to another trying to find Gracie. She got little response about her mother, but she was horror-struck, listening to anxious, miserable mothers and fathers tell their stories. One mother wept as she told how she had lost all four of her children to measles.

"The camp shaman took children with fever into the river to be cured," another man said, "but the cold icy stream caused them to shiver even more. Most of them died within a day or two. They don't have privies, and the water's not safe. Whole families have died of dysentery, and children are dying of whooping cough and measles."

Someone said General Winfield Scott, the white leader in charge, asked the federal government for doctors in every camp, but was told there were not enough to go around. One of the soldiers said, "Cherokees don't want white doctors anyway. They listen to the shaman, drink root teas, and wait for death."

A woman said she was snatched from her home by soldiers and was not allowed to gather up her belongings. "They came with their bayonets and rifles, and poked and prodded us down the path like we were hogs," she said. "They gave us no time to pack anything to bring with us. We had to leave with what we had on. When it turns cold, what will we wear?"

"They wouldn't even let me feed the chickens before we left," said another. "My husband had to leave his plow in the field. He couldn't even take his horses out of harness. My three little ones were playing in the yard, and a soldier told them they would be whipped if we didn't all do as he said. The children begged us to go with the soldiers. When one of them pushed my little girl, my husband hit him, and they handcuffed him."

"They whipped me," the husband said. "Look here at my back. A hundred lashes, that's what they give me." Analeha also saw his wrists were bruised black and blue from the handcuffs.

Another, wiping tears from her eyes, said, "They burned our cabin. It was all in flames when I looked back. The rabble set it afire after they stripped it. Why? What did we do to them? It was all we had!"

Analeha heard terrifying stories about young Cherokee women in the camp who were being coaxed into drinking and giving their bodies to soldiers. A girl she had known in the mission school cried while telling Analeha of being defiled by federal soldiers. "I was looking for roots and nuts in the woods. Now my family won't let me come near them. They say I do not belong to them anymore."

Greenberry found whiskey easy to get in the compounds, though he wondered who could afford to buy it at the prices the bootleggers were asking. Some Cherokee men who had brought ponies sold them for money to buy liquor. At night around the fires, many tried to drown their misery in "white lightning," so called, Greenberry thought, because the white man uses it to strike down the Indian.

"Perhaps we should have stayed in the cave," Analeha confessed to Greenberry. She could see life here was even worse than in the mountains. There was food here, but not enough. Women who had the strength were allowed outside the camps during the day to collect berries, wild greens, and other plants, but, she wondered, at what cost to their personal safety?

Looking for her mother had been in vain. She sought out people she had known in the mission school, but they had seen no trace of Gracie. She and

Greenberry searched the cemetery outside the compound, but there were no markers to identify the graves. At last Analeha gave up. She knew her mother would want her to save her strength for the baby. At night when half awake she drifted off into dreams, Analeha could hear her mother singing the song the bear mother sang to her cubs, telling them how to survive the hunters:

> When you hear the hunters coming down the creek,
> *Tsa gi, tsa gi hwi lahi,*
> Upstream, upstream you must go.
> If you hear the hunters coming up the creek,
> *Ge I, ge I, hwi lahi*
> Downstream, downstream you must go.

In June when, Greenberry and Analeha thought they were ready to begin their journey west, they were surprised that Chief John Ross made a visit to the Rattlesnake Springs encampment. Greenberry wondered if they could trust this John Ross, who, with his thin lips and bushy eyebrows, looked more like a white gentleman planter than a Cherokee chief.

Ross was only one-eighth Cherokee. His grandfather was a Scot named John McDonald who owned a trading post at Fort Loudon in Tennessee territory in the mid-1700s. His grandmother, Anne Shorey, was a half-blood. Their first child, Molly, married a Scots trader named Daniel Ross. John Ross was their third child. In his youth, John Ross was known as *Tsan Usdi*, Little John, and later as *Cooweeskoowee*, or White Bird. His early education was at the Brainard Mission School near Chattanooga operated by the Congregationalists. It was one of the eleven government supported mission stations aimed at Christianizing and civilizing the Cherokees. Some students where white, but most were mixed-bloods and full-bloods. Though John grew up in a white man's world, he identified with his mother's people, the Bird Clan.

In 1813 John married Elizabeth Henley Brown, better known as Quatie, whose mother was a full-blood Cherokee and whose father was a Scots trader. Early in their lives, they built a plantation on the Coosa River near Rome, Georgia. There they raised their six children. Their holdings included more than two hundred fruit trees, a blacksmith shop, a smokehouse, stables, and slave cabins. Nearby Ross established a warehouse and a boat landing on the south bank of the Coosa River.

The year 1828 was a landmark year for the Cherokees. John Ross was elected principal chief of the Cherokee nation at the Council of New Echota, and Andrew Jackson was elected president of the United States. That same year, *The Cherokee Phoenix*, using Sequoyah's syllabary, was published both in Cherokee and English. In 1828, the Cherokees adopted a new constitution modeled after the Constitution of the United States, formally declaring their intent to remain in their homeland and to govern themselves.

Ross argued against laws which forced major cultural changes on the Cherokee nation, and with more and more white people moving into Cherokee lands, he had many new laws to address. The time-honored Cherokee matrilinial system was being undermined. "Every day our Cherokee traditions are being attacked by more offensive white laws. What business does the government have regulating Cherokee marriages?" he argued. When the Georgia legislature passed the Anti-Cherokee Laws prohibiting Cherokees from digging gold on their own land and laws that prevented them from testifying in court against a white man, Ross protested.

Ross had spent his entire life trying to hold on to Cherokee land. On May 28, 1830, Congress passed the Indian Removal Act, and Andrew Jackson signed the bill into law. John Ross led several delegations to Washington trying to forestall the removal, but on December 29, 1835, while Ross was in Washington, a small contingent of Cherokee leaders met with United States officials and signed the Treaty of New Echota. Major Ridge and his son John Ridge, John Ross's brother, Andrew, and Elias Boudinot had signed over the bulk of Cherokee land in the east. An embittered John Ross presented a petition with sixteen thousand names to show the treaty was not backed by the Cherokee people. Yet the Senate ratified the treaty on May 23, 1836—by one vote. A few days later, while Ross was still away from home, the state of Georgia seized Ross's Landing and auctioned off all the farmland and buildings. They left one room on the ground floor of the Ross mansion for Quatie who was in poor health. Ross's ferry at the head of the Coosa River was taken over by the Georgia government.

It was here at Ross's Landing in June of 1838 that the first group of Cherokees was forcibly moved to the west. They embarked on eleven flat boats. The heat was so intense and the people's misery so great that Cherokee leaders petitioned General Winfield Scott to postpone the rest of the removal until cooler weather.

We your prisoners wish to speak to you. We wish to speak humbly for we cannot help ourselves. We have been made prisoners by your men, but we do not fight against you. We have never done you any harm. We have been told we are to be sent off by boat immediately. Sir, will you listen to your prisoners? We are Indians, but we have hearts that feel. We do not want to see our wives and children die. We do not want to die ourselves and leave them widows and orphans. We are in trouble. Sir, our hearts are very heavy. The darkness of the night is before us. We have no hope unless you will help us. We do not ask you to let us go free from being your prisoners, unless it would please yourself. But we ask that you will not send us down the river at this time of the year. If you do we shall die. Sir, our hearts are heavy, very heavy. We want you to keep us in this country until the sickly time is over, that when we get to the west we maybe able to make boards to cover our families. If you send us now the sickly time is commenced, we shall not have strength to work. We will be in the open air in all the deadly time of sickness, and we shall die, and our poor wives and children will die too. And if you send the whole nation, the whole nation will die. We ask pity. Do not send us off at the sickly time. Some of our people are Christians. They will pray for you. If you pity us we hope your God will be pleased and that he will pity you and your wife and children and do you good. We cannot make a talk, our hearts are too full of sorrow. This is all we say.

—Cherokee leaders to General Winfield Scott,
Fort Cass, June 1838

Ross approached Secretary of War Joel Poinsett about holding up the removal until cooler autumn weather. Poinsett agreed and designated Ross to be superintendant of the removal. Ross organized the Cherokees into thirteen detachments of about a thousand people, and assigned a leader and assistant to each. He hired wagon masters and commissary agents for each detachment and a dozen or so Cherokee men to serve as Light Horse Guards to keep order. He convinced Poinsett he could cover the costs of the entire trip for sixty-five dollars per person, including sixteen cents a day per person for food and forty cents for oxen and horses.

Chief Ross tried to recruit a doctor and an interpreter for each detachment. The doctors brought with them castor oil, Epsom salts, laudanum, worm seed oil, mustard, quinine, and camphor to help them contend with dysentery, fevers, measles, whooping cough, and pneumonia. None of these medicines, however, could cure a sick child of pellagra or tuberculosis. Greenberry suspected there were not enough doctors and that the ones they hired would be overworked and soon fall sick themselves.

At noon on October 10, 1838, after waiting in the stockade for more than five months, Greenberry, Analeha, and James Blackbird left Rattlesnake Springs in a detachment of nine hundred and fifty persons under the leadership of the Reverend Jesse Bushyhead, a mixed-blood Cherokee Baptist minister, and his mixed-blood assistant, Roman Nose.

Most of Bushyhead's travelers were Cherokee Baptist converts, missionaries, and slaves. Chief Junaluska, who fought with Andrew Jackson against the Creeks in Alabama was among them, as was the elderly Chief White Path who had fought for years to preserve Cherokee ways. Before the long line of wagons and reluctant travelers began their sad journey, Rev. Bushyhead said a prayer. The young and the old, the well and the sick, walked beside the wagons. Analeha walked as long as she was able. When she could walk no longer, Greenberry managed to find a place for her among the supplies on one of the wagons.

Greenberry was glad they were leaving the filthy camp behind—the urine smell, the unclean water, the lack of privacy, and, most of all, the sad hopeless faces of those who still waited. He was glad John Ross had convinced the government it was better for Cherokee leaders to move their own detachments. At least the Reverend Bushyhead had the concern of the people at heart. For detachments led by white soldiers alone, who could say?

A silence fell over the long line of travelers. Some people turned to face their beloved mountains, knowing they were leaving them for the last time. "Thank you for allowing us to live among your hills and valleys," they said. And then they turned their faces toward the west. According to ancient Cherokee belief, westward was the direction of death.

It was a bright, clear October day, not a cloud in the sky. Old Chief Going Snake trotted past Greenberry. "A cloud's coming," he said. "It's a spiral cloud and it's coming out of the west."

Greenberry listened intently. He thought he could hear the faraway sound of thunder, but as he peered into the west, he saw no funnel cloud. No wind blew, and no rain came. The sky was a cold blue. The old chief imagines he is seeing a vision, Greenberry thought. In olden times Cherokees listened to the sky, the sun, and the clouds. But today, what does it matter?

Analeha could feel every bump and lurch of the wagon. She knew she was fortunate to be riding, for there was little room in the supply wagons for the weak and the sick.

While crossing the Hiawassee River, a runaway wagon killed one of the drivers. The detachment stopped until the horses were captured. Greenberry and James Blackbird stayed behind to bury the dead man, and later hurried to catch up with the wagon train. That night, after the camps were set up and while the women were preparing food, Greenberry joined Chief Junaluska and his men hunting deer and turkey to supplement the meager supply of food. As they sat around a fire roasting meat they had killed on their hunt, Greenberry listened to Junaluska talk about his part in Jackson's victory over the Red Stick Creeks at the Battle of Horseshoe Bend.

"I did great deeds for this Andrew Jackson," Junaluska said, "but if I had known he would drive us from our homes, I would have killed him at the Horseshoe."

"I wish you had!" Greenberry said. "And John Ridge in the bargain!"

"Tomorrow I'm going back to the mountains. Come with me." Junaluska's invitation to turn around and head back east lifted Greenberry's spirit for a moment, but he knew he could not leave Analeha.

"Analeha will soon deliver, and she will need me beside her."

It had become clear the detachment could not haul enough forage for the horses and oxen so essential to the venture, as well as the food supplies needed to keep the people fed. The original plans had not taken into account the growing numbers of sick and infirm who took up more and more space in the wagons. Bushyhead wrote to Chief John Ross that the only solution he could see was to haul the forage and supplies to a designated camping spot each day and send the wagons back for the people.

A day or so into the journey, more people fell ill with dysentery, joining the ranks of those who had already been sick when they left Fort Cass. Most of the elderly had to walk, and one woman fell dead from exhaustion the second day out. The detachment stopped just long enough to bury her beside the road. She would not be the last.

Analeha had no tears left, but she could hear other women crying. They cried because their children had died in the encampment from dysentery, measles or whooping cough. They cried because their homes had been taken or burned by former neighbors. They cried because their livestock, their orchards, their fields, their looms and spinning wheels had been stolen. They cried because they were leaving their children's graves behind. What else could they do but cry?

The early sunset left Analeha shivering in the autumn chill. Treacherous roads and swollen creeks had slowed their progress. On the third day, two mothers buried their babies in a single shallow grave beside the road. Analeha tried to shut out the sounds of their crying. She tried not to think about what might happen to her own baby.

The journey was long and painful for Analeha. Every jolt of the wagon gave her reason to believe the baby was coming at any time. She could feel its hands and feet pushing and kicking. She clung to the hope that they would reach the next camp before the baby came. In a fitful sleep, as the wagon bumped and rolled across the mountains, she dreamed of sitting beside a stream, cooling her feet on the smooth stones in the shallows. The roaring waters cascaded over the rocks below. In her dream it was early morning, and the blue mist drifted across the hills and valleys. The sun's first rays shone through the pines and cedars with brilliant golds and yellows. She was alone and at peace. She watched the *Nun-ne-hi*, the Little People, dancing among the broom sedge and rocks. She could hear them singing. Then heavy clouds rolled in, chasing the *Nun-ne-hi* away.

Analeha woke to the sound of thunder. Lightning flashed. The detachment leaders stopped to cover the wagons, and people who were walking scrambled under the wagons for protection. For hours the rain poured, and when it finally subsided, everyone was soaked and cold. They built a fire in a meadow and spread their wet clothes on the grass to dry. "More people will die of the cough," Greenberry said as he and James Blackbird helped move the sick close to the fire. "There will be many more to bury along the way."

"Did you hear about Chief Junaluska?" James Blackbird asked Greenberry. "He left last night with fifty other Cherokees headed back east. Said he was going to find Thomas's Indians in North Carolina. I guess nobody tried to stop him. Bushyhead said it was not up to him to stop them."

"I hope they don't catch him," Greenberry said.

That same day, Greenberry and James Blackbird helped bury an old man who had sat down along the trail under a tree and raised his voice to those around him, "This is as far to the west as I will go." He lay down in the mud at the foot of the tree, placed his loaded gun at his side, muzzle toward his head, and discharged the gun with his toe.

FOUR

Shells Ford on the Collins

McMinnville, Tennessee
October 1838-February 1839

It was nine days before the detachment reached the Collins River at Shells Ford near McMinnville. Analeha was too weak to help the other women set up tents and prepare the evening meal. Her water had broken. She was bleeding, and her pains had begun. Greenberry made a bed for her under a tree near the river. Covering her with blankets, he sent James Blackbird to find a midwife among the missionaries. Analeha could hear the birds settling in for the night, and she thought she could smell the honeysuckle and the wild rose growing along the riverbank. She could smell the cedar and pine fires burning in the camps. She could hear the moans of the sick and the cries of children, and she could hear the shamans' songs mingled with the songs of the Christians.

"If I don't survive," Analeha said to Greenberry, "you must find a way for our baby to live." The labor pains were coming closer and closer. After each onset, she thought she could not stand another. If only her mother were here. Between the pains, she lay exhausted waiting for the next contraction. She remembered Sarah's agony in the cave, and the women who lost their babies along the trail. She wanted the pain to stop. Where was the help James Blackbird was bringing? By the time the midwife arrived, Analeha was too weak to raise herself to a sitting position to deliver her baby. The pain was almost unbearable.

When the baby came, the midwife quickly cut the cord and wrapped the baby girl in a soft deerskin coverlet. She tried to place it in Analeha arms, but realized Analeha was too weak to hold it by herself. Analeha thought she heard the midwife say it was a girl. She closed her eyes to a feverish dream of the *Nun-ne-hi*. The *Nun-ne-hi* would protect her baby girl. Presently, she awoke enough to hear Greenberry's voice.

"Can you hear our daughter's cry?" he whispered. He could see she could not hold the baby by herself, so he eased the baby to her side and held her there. Analeha felt the baby's warmth against her breast and heard its tiny cry.

"Promise me," she whispered. "Promise you will see that she lives."

The bleeding did not stop. Analeha lay dreaming of the cool, clear water in the river and of the *Nun-ne-hi* pulling her gently under. Greenberry sat helpless beside her until the sun fell behind the mountains, and he knew she had drifted away. He did not bury the placenta as some Cherokee fathers did. There would be no more children, so it did not matter.

They buried Analeha on the bank beside the river. Greenberry stood with the child in his arms as Jesse Bushyhead said prayers over the grave. James Blackbird placed an oblong rock at its head. By the river, Greenberry sat holding his baby girl. Why had the Great Spirit allowed this to happen? Where was the white god of love?

He wished his people had listened to the *Nun-ne-hi*, who had warned them long ago about wars and evil on the earth. The *Nun-ne-hi* had invited them to come live under the mountains and under the waters. Some had listened and had gone with them. He remembered the elders saying that, years later, the Cherokee could hear them under the river talking, and when the people dragged the river for fish, the *Nun-ne-hi* would hold on to the fish-drag. The elders said they held on because they wanted to be remembered.

Why didn't my people listen to the *Nun-ne-hi*? he wondered. He had a strong desire to pull himself up from the bank of the river and, with his baby girl in his arms, join the *Nun-ne-hi* under the water. My life is over, he thought, and there is nothing left for a Cherokee baby in a white man's world.

By sunset, Greenberry had made up his mind. He knew he must honor Analeha's wish. He wrapped the baby in the deerskin cover she had fashioned and placed it in Analeha's basket. He took from around his neck the deerskin string that held the small cedar flute, and placed the flute in the basket beside the baby. The moon was almost full when he found his way northeast from the Shells Ford encampment to the white settlement at Rock Island. The clouds moved swiftly across the moon, and a slight breeze was blowing. He knew he must get to the settlement before the clouds brought the storm.

Analeha, I promised you I would see our baby lives. The only way she has a chance, Analeha, is if I take her to the white village. I am doing what you asked me to do. I'm finding a place where she can survive. Can you see me taking our baby to the white settlement? My feet move me toward the village, Analeha, but my heart drags behind. See there in the distance the lights? The Great Spirit is surely displeased with what I am doing, Analeha, but I am doing what you asked me to do. The winds blow. The lightning strikes. The Great Spirit sends a storm.

The thunder rumbled as Greenberry rounded the bend on the Collins River. He could see the dim light from grease lamps burning in the cabins. When he reached the nearest cabin, he placed the basket on the porch and knocked at the door. Hiding in the bushes nearby, he waited to make sure the baby was found. Through the barely opened door, he saw the dark outline of a woman. He watched as she lifted the baby from the basket.

"Who's there?" she called into the darkness. She waited a moment before taking the baby inside.

Greenberry held his breath until she closed the door. The rain began. He had hoped to get a glimpse of the woman who had taken his baby. Now his grief gave way to anger. There was nothing left. Analeha was dead, and he had left their baby with a white woman. He ran back to the encampment in the blinding rain, the anger rising in his throat. Why had this happened? Never in all his days could he have imagined giving away his child to anyone, especially a white woman. Yet tonight he had done just that.

He thought of the valley where he had lived with Analeha. In their valley, the white settlers and Cherokees had lived side by side. Most of the Cherokees in the village were Christians. Many full-bloods and mixed-bloods had attended missionary schools with white children. While Susanna had not allowed him to attend, Greenberry had heard how the missionaries were teaching Cherokee children about a burning hell. The village elders had sent word to the missionaries they did not want Cherokee children taught such nonsense.

What hypocrites the missionaries are, Greenberry thought. He wanted no part in their religion. From the beginning, hadn't the missionaries willingly carried out the government's plan to civilize and Christianize the Indian? Why else had the government funded the missionary schools? Surely Cherokees and white people could have lived as neighbors but for Andrew Jackson's broken promises and John Ridge's treason.

Greenberry felt a white-hot rage rising in him. Did John Ridge understand what he had done? If he had not given in to the white government, Analeha would still be alive. We would be living with our baby in our valley home, growing corn and hunting in the mountains. His heart pounded as he approached the encampment. He had decided what he must do. He hated Ridge. Ridge must pay.

It was not hard for Greenberry to convince James Blackbird to agree to his plan. Since Sarah's death, James had moved through the days stunned and hopeless. Like others along the trail, he walked with his head down, his stone face void of expression. Now Greenberry's plan offered him a reason to live. He needed to act, to be a part of something important, something bigger than himself. The idea of retaliation appealed to him. Like his warrior ancestors who had struggled to protect the land from white settlers, he would do his part to punish those who had given the land away.

They approached the Reverend Bushyhead to volunteer as scouts, and Bushyhead sent them to his aide Roman Nose. The aide was delighted. Two volunteers had recently fallen ill with dysentery, leaving Roman Nose without two of his best scouts. Greenberry's plan had been successful. Now they must be patient and travel with the Bushyhead contingent all the way to the new land in the west where he could find John Ridge.

The Reverend Bushyhead was scheduled to preach at Shells Ford on Sunday morning. He was a powerful speaker, Greenberry knew, and white Christians from McMinnville, Rock Island and nearby villages would gather to hear him. While some of those who come may be sympathetic, Greenberry thought, most of them will come out of curiosity. What a sideshow it will be for them to watch a Cherokee half-breed preach the Gospel!

Greenberry thought it would be strange to see Indians and white people praying together under these circumstances. He wondered if the white woman who took his baby would come to the meeting. No matter. He would not be able to recognize her anyway.

*   *   *

Lillie Preece did not know what to make of the baby she found on her front porch. Since the coverlet was made of deerskin, she decided the mother must have been an Indian. She had heard about the Cherokees being forced to move west. Perhaps some young woman on the march, fearful her baby girl would not survive on the trail, had gambled on some family taking her in and raising her.

"You must be a little Indian baby," she said softly to the child. "You are beautiful and sweet, but what am I going to do with you? I have never been a mother. Since Frank died, I am alone in this house. Why were you left on my doorstep? I've never taken care of a little one. Did the person who left you know I am part Indian? Is that why you were left here with me?"

The baby cried. "You must be hungry," Lillie said. "I'll warm you some goat's milk. Maybe that will do the trick." As she had done before with baby animals, she dipped a finger in the milk and placed it to the baby's lips. Her first efforts were fruitless, but finally, the baby began to suck hard on her fingertip.

When the baby was asleep, Lillie examined the colorful deerskin quiver in the basket. It held a rough-hewn cedar flute. Taking it from the quiver, she gingerly put it to her lips and blew. She could hardly make a sound. After a moment, she put it back and hung it over the mantle. Another mystery, she thought. "Perhaps it is there for good luck. And with me, little baby, you'll surely need all the luck you can get."

Lillie knew about the temporary Indian encampment at Shells Ford. Perhaps she should try to find the baby's mother. If she were to go to the camp at all, it would need to be now. The soldiers might move the Indians out even today. She wrapped the baby warmly and walked across the clearing to her mother Fannie's cabin. She told Fannie what had happened and asked her to take care of the baby for a little while.

"I'm riding over to Shells Ford where the Indians are camped," she said. "I want to see if I can find who left this baby on my porch in the middle of the night. I think it must be one of the Indian women."

"I doubt you will ever find her," Fannie said. "Even if you do, what will you say to her?"

"I don't know," Lillie said. "I only know I must go and see. I won't be long. See if you can get her to take some milk while I'm gone."

She saddled her horse and headed for Shells Ford. She hoped the early-morning October sun would melt the heavy frost on the fallen leaves along the river road and lift the fog hanging over the river. It's too early for winter, she thought.

Lillie would not soon forget what she saw at Shells Ford that day. Wagons, some covered, some left open to the elements, encircled the camp on the hill above the Collins River. Men and women lay in, around and under the wagons, too sick to acknowledge her presence. Emaciated bodies lay as close to the fires as they could get. The rain had been cold and heavy during the night. Now people were trying to dry their wet, rancid clothes. The smell was almost too much for Lillie. Women's eyes silently begged for help as she passed. Others lay listless, unable to move. She had heard preachers talk about hell as a place of eternal suffering. Surely this was it. How could there be a worse hell than this? How could God allow such misery, here amidst the oaks and cedars, the fall wild flowers blooming on the riverbanks and the blue October sky?

Under a towering oak, surrounded by a natural brush arbor, Jesse Bushyhead stood at a makeshift pulpit preaching to the gathered crowd. His loud voice bellowed over the assembly. He said everything twice, once in English, which she could understand, and once in Cherokee, which she could not. At the end of each sentence, he made a loud grunting sound for emphasis. A hymn printed in Cherokee and English was passed out. The crowd began to sing in both languages simultaneously, making a kind of chaotic drone: "I am a poor, wayfaring stranger, a-traveling through this world of woe; there is no sickness, toil or danger in that bright land to which I go." The song dragged on verse after verse. Lillie looked out over the crowd in disbelief. She knew she would never be able to find the baby's mother here. She could take no more of the misery, the chaos. Turning her horse toward Rock Island, she rode home.

*   *   *

Greenberry listened to the babel of the singing. He looked out over the crowd gathered in clumps around the Reverend Bushyhead. How could people who have been driven from their homes be singing praises to the God of those responsible for their plight? What kind of God, he wondered, would allow such suffering?

He strolled along the river waiting to join the scouting party. Close to the river's edge, a sick man lay on the ground. A shaman stood over him. On the edge of the camp, a black conjurer hovered over a newborn baby. Greenberry wondered how the slave woman and her baby would survive. She'll need to ride in one of the wagons, he thought. But who will allow a slave woman to ride in their wagon? There's barely enough room now for supplies and sick Cherokees. How many black slaves will die on this journey? In another part of the camp Greenberry heard a doctor ask: "What name will you give your child?" The mother made no answer. Why give a name to the child? Greenberry thought. Tomorrow it will die and be buried with the others.

In the early afternoon, Roman Nose, Greenberry, and James Blackbird left the Shells Ford encampment with orders to find a place to make camp no more than fifteen miles west toward Nashville.

"Look for a place near a creek or river where we can obtain corn and fodder, cornmeal, and bacon," Bushyhead instructed them. "And find a good place for the animals to graze."

They found an ideal glade with a mill beside a creek near Centertown, a few miles outside McMinnville, where they negotiated with miller Tom Underwood to sell them sufficient corn to feed the oxen, cattle, and horses, as well as cornmeal for mush and bread. They arranged to pick up their purchases the next day when the contingent would come through. The miller warned them to use caution with other millers and storekeepers along their way to Nashville.

"Most folk in this county are sympathetic to your cause," he said. "They think the government has no business driving you out. But you have to watch out. Some people just don't care. If they think there's money in it for 'em, they'd just as soon cheat you as to look at you."

Greenberry had hoped to go further than Centertown. He had wanted to seek out a campsite nearer Woodbury. Roman Nose protested it was too far for the detachment to travel in one day. Greenberry tried to convince him they needed to move faster before the weather turned cold. James Blackbird knew Greenberry harbored another reason for wanting to forge ahead at a faster pace, but he said nothing.

The scouts arrived back at Shells Ford after midnight and rested for a few hours. Early the next morning, they helped load the wagons, placed the sick and elderly as comfortably as possible in the wagons alongside the supplies, and roused the malingerers. By ten o'clock, they were ready to lead the contingent on its way to Centertown. Just before they left, the Reverend Bushyhead sent a message to John Ross complaining they had been forced to leave for the west without the government's promises to the tribe having been fulfilled. There were not enough doctors, supplies were dwindling, and they needed more money. He also reminded Ross to make sure the Cherokee people were represented when decisions were being made about their future.

After Bushyhead read his communication to the detachment, the contingent left Shells Ford late in the morning, and proceeded through McMinnville to Centertown, arriving just before dark. The next morning, after loading the supplies from the mill, the detachment moved on in a driving rain through Woodbury and camped on Stone's River north of Murfreesboro near the village of Lascassas. On Sunday, they stopped a few miles south of Lebanon at a place called Cedar Hill to rest and to bury two children who had died of pneumonia. Some of the missionaries had refused to travel on

Sunday. Standing in the middle of the thick grove of towering cedars, they sang a hymn:

> *His voice, as the sound of the dulcimer sweet,*
> *Is heard through the shadows of death.*
> *The Cedars of Lebanon bow at His feet,*
> *And the air is perfumed with His breath.*

Meanwhile, some of the Cherokees, mourning their dead children, broke cedar branches and set them afire, filling the air with the pungent smell of burning cedar in hopes the smell would chase away bad ghosts.

Reaching the Cumberland River near Nashville the next day, they encountered the first of many toll houses that would hamper their way west. Bushyhead protested against the high toll assessed for ferrying the detachment across the river, but there was nothing to do but pay it. Once on the other side, they bivouacked in a field, again paying an exorbitant price. At first the owner insisted they move on after one day, but Bushyhead negotiated to stay longer.

"We need more time. Our people need time to wash clothes, repair wagons and shoe their horses," he told the owner, who acquiesced after much haggling and the assurance he would be well paid.

In another progress report to Ross, Bushyhead said their travel had been slowed because so many sick people, both young and old, had to be carried in the wagons, severely limiting the quantity of supplies they could take. He also reported they had been slowed because the oxen had eaten poison ivy, leaving them with little strength to pull the wagons.

Wherever the contingent stopped, white men came to the encampment to sell their whiskey, and drunkenness became a problem. People were kept awake at night by raucous laughter and loud yelling. The missionaries, in particular, were angered by the shouting of profanities. Since many were getting little sleep, Bushyhead asked Ross for more Light Horse Guards to fend off the rabble along the trail.

A few days later when two Light Horse Guards caught up with the Bushyhead detachment, Greenberry and James Blackbird learned that Chief Junaluska and twenty-five of his men had been intercepted, arrested, and placed in irons at Fort Cass. They were to be sent west in chains under military guard. Greenberry was disappointed to hear this.

"They can't make him stay out there," Greenberry predicted. "He'll go back to the mountains in the east."

From Nashville, the Bushyhead detachment went to Hopkinsville, Kentucky, arriving in mid-November. The weather had turned cold and bitter. Chief White Path died. After Rev. Bushyhead read from the Bible and said a prayer, Greenberry and James Blackbird helped with the burial.

After crossing the Ohio River at Golconda, they traveled through southern Illinois to Green's Ferry near Cape Girardeau, Missouri. They reached the Mississippi River in early January, three months after leaving Fort Cass in eastern Tennessee. There they spent a full month trying to traverse the frozen river at a point where several detachments had converged and were trying to cross at the same time.

A Baptist minister traveling with one of the other detachments announced: "We have now been on our road to Arkansas seventy-five days and have traveled five hundred and twenty-nine miles. We are still nearly three hundred miles short of our destination."

While Bushyhead's detachment waited to cross the icy river, a messenger arrived from the east. Around the campfire that evening, he related what had happened to an old Cherokee named Tsali back east in the mountains.

"Old Tsali," he began, "was being taken to the stockade along with his wife, his brother, his three sons, and their families. One of the soldiers prodded Tsali's wife with a bayonet. Tsali attacked him with his knife and killed him. The other soldiers, seeing Tsali's brother and sons ready to use their own knives, ran away, leaving their guns behind. Taking the soldiers' guns, Tsali and his family fled to the high mountains. When the soldiers could not find him, General Scott sent word that if he would give himself up and accept punishment, the others hiding out in the mountains would be allowed to stay. Old Tsali gave himself up. His brother and his two oldest sons came with him. The Federals lined them all up and forced other Cherokee prisoners to shoot them."

Greenberry was furious. "This might well have been our fate," he said to James Blackbird.

"Maybe so," said James Blackbird. "But Tsali saved all the others. Maybe if we had stayed in the mountains, we wouldn't be on this miserable march."

"Don't talk to me of what might have been," Greenberry said. "Do not forget why we are here. Besides we cannot trust the word of the white government."

Hundreds of people lay sick and dying in the wagons and on the frozen ground. Greenberry and James Blackbird stayed busy making sure the fires did not go out. Shortly after crossing the Mississippi, several children and Bushyhead's sister Nancy died. Bushyhead held a service for them, and each was buried in a shallow grave beside the trail. In the midst of all the misery, after crossing into Missouri, a daughter was born to the Reverend and Mrs. Bushyhead on January 3, 1839. "We shall call her Eliza Missouri," he said. On February 27, 1839, Bushyhead's detachment arrived in the Arkansas territory. In his report to Chief Ross, he indicated there had been thirty-eight deaths, six births, and one hundred and forty-eight runaways, who presumably went back to the east.

FIVE

Blood Law Vengeance

Double Springs, Arkansas
June-July 1839

One of Ross's last duties as superintendent of the removal was to report on the thirteen detachments under his command. He stated he had been in charge of thirteen thousand, one hundred and forty-nine persons. Another four thousand had been under the command of federal troops. All told, more than four thousand Cherokees and their slaves had perished during the removal, including those who died in the stockades before the march began. Ross knew that fewer people had perished under his command than had died under the command of the federal troops, but this knowledge gave him little comfort. By best estimates, one quarter of the Cherokee nation had perished during the removal.

If the Cherokees who had suffered and survived the removal under Ross's command had any thought of finding a place of refuge in the new land, they were bitterly disappointed. Already tired, hungry, sick, and without hope, hundreds died soon after arriving in the new land. Those who survived found the federal government had once more failed to live up to its commitments. They had been promised rations for a full year to allow them time to settle in and raise their own food. Hardly any food awaited their arrival. Distribution had been hampered because the government had allowed fraudulent contractors to control the bidding process. They simply did not deliver what they had promised.

Greenberry and James Blackbird along with the other Bushyhead contingent survivors waited at Breadtown, one of the many ration stations, to receive what the government promised. Greenberry observed that on many days, when people came to get their rations, drunken contractors told them they would have to wait for another two weeks. Most of the new arrivals came with few belongings. Even those who had left with mules and oxen had lost them along the trail, and they had no farming equipment to grow food. Besides, Greenberry thought, the best land has already been taken. How he longed to be back in his mountains where he could hunt deer and plant corn. His resolve to make John Ridge pay grew daily as he watched hungry orphan children suffer the cold in makeshift tents.

When seven thousand Cherokees gathered in council at Double Springs in Indian Territory in June of 1839, Greenberry and James Blackbird were among them. John Ross had hoped to bring about a formal union of the Old Settlers and the New Immigrants. Greenberry's goal was different. He had promised he would avenge Analeha's death, and he hoped John Ridge would attend the council.

Ross called for unity and for a new constitution that would affirm the agreement reached in the meeting back east, that though they were being forced to leave, the Cherokee nation still maintained ownership of the land they were leaving behind. He called for the support of the Old Settlers in pressing the United States government to reimburse those on the removal for property they had lost.

Trying to appease the Old Settlers was a difficult task for Ross. While the newcomers numbered around fourteen thousand, there were roughly only three thousand Old Settlers. There were also about two thousand Treaty Party members, most of whom had emigrated voluntarily before the forced removal. Greenberry could see that Chief John Brown wanted no part of a new constitution. After all, why should the Old Settlers jeopardize the relationship they had built over the years with the government by pressing the demands of the new arrivals? Greenberry doubted whether a new constitution would make any difference. By late afternoon, most of the Old Settlers had followed their chief John Brown and walked out of Ross's proceedings.

Greenberry could hear the rumblings in the crowd against the Treaty Party. He doubted John Ridge and his followers would dare show their faces here in the council, but he waited and watched. In the crowd, he heard the arguments from those who claimed John Ridge and the Treaty Party members had signed the New Echota Treaty out of selfish ambition. They had broken the ancient Blood Law that meant death to any Cherokee who gave over Cherokee land without tribal approval. Others said that removal had been inevitable, and that John Ridge's aim in giving over to the federal government had been to salvage a Cherokee homeland in a peaceful manner.

Greenberry wanted to hear nothing in Ridge's favor. "I wish Ridge *would* come," he said to James Blackbird. "If he does, I will do more than ask him why he signed the treaty."

*   *   *

John Ridge was the second child of Major and Susanna Ridge. Born in 1803, his features were more European than Cherokee, his white genes coming from his Scottish highlands great-grandfather. When he was seven, Major Ridge enrolled him in the Moravian missionary school at Spring Place in Georgia. His mother did not approve. She felt he was being sent off to live with foreigners who would give him only a white education. She was also concerned about his fragile health.

Neither John's mother nor his father was interested in the religion of the Moravians. Major Ridge told the missionaries he had already heard the story of God's sacrifice of Jesus, and, while he accepted the existence of God, his God was not the God of the Bible. John, on the other hand, became a Christian. Years later, however, when helping negotiate treaties with the federal government, his disenchantment with both the white government and what he increasingly came to view as the white man's religion resonated loud and clear in one of his speeches:

> *You asked us to throw off the hunter and warrior state. We did so. You asked us to form a republican government. We did so, adopting your own as a model. You asked us to cultivate the earth, and learn the mechanic arts. We did so. You asked us to learn to read. We did so. You asked us to cast away our idols and worship your God. We did so. Now you demand we cede to you our lands. That we will not do.*

In 1818 John and several other young Cherokee men left for Cornwall, Connecticut, to attend a school operated by the Congregationalists. There he fell in love with Sarah Northrup, a New England daughter of missionary teachers at the school. Neither his parents nor hers were happy with the love affair. John's mother Susanna feared it would make John less effective when he became chief of the Cherokee people. Sarah's parents were afraid that if their daughter married an Indian, financial support for the school might suffer.

When John and Sarah announced their wedding plans, the town was outraged. The liberal newspapers denounced it. Ministers demanded this white-Indian wedding not take place. The mission school was attacked, and its leaders took a stand against mixed marriages. Major Ridge asked the missionaries at the school if there was anything in the Bible that forbade the marriage of an Indian man and a white woman. They admitted there was not.

After the wedding, John and Sarah traveled to Georgia to live with Major Ridge and Susanna on their plantation overlooking the Coosa River. Through an arched glass window, they could view the river, the ferry, the store, and the toll road. Through the rear windows, they could see the stables, barns, hog pens, and cabins for thirty slaves. Sarah challenged the Ridges about owning slaves. Her religion had taught her that slavery was wrong.

"I find it hard to accept that so much of your parents' way of life depends on keeping slaves," she told John.

"We've always had slaves," John told her. "My father says that slavery is necessary to keep the plantation going. He insists that successful Cherokee planters, like the white plantation owners, have always had slaves. I don't agree with him, but I can see his point."

"It's still wrong to own slaves," Sarah insisted. "Keeping black people in slavery is bad enough, but how can Cherokees justify owning other Cherokees? And even if your father keeps slaves, does that mean you have to be a slave master as well?"

Major Ridge and Susanna insisted that if Sarah and John were to live with them, John would have to keep slaves. They assured her he simply could not be a successful farmer without slave help. This did not satisfy Sarah Ridge. With the help of her cousin Delight Sargent, who had married John's first cousin, Elias Boudinot, she continued to challenge the institution of slavery.

Despite Major Ridge's expectation that John and Sarah would live in the section of the house he had built for them, they quickly saw the need to have their own house. At Sarah's insistence, Major Ridge then built a small cabin six miles away. In the beginning it consisted of only two rooms, but soon more were added until the house was a two-story structure. Here they settled in comfortably until life turned ugly when the Georgia government wielded its power to remove all Cherokees from Georgia soil.

In February of 1837, Major Ridge, his wife Susanna, a son, and a granddaughter left their Georgia plantation for a new home on Honey Creek on the Arkansas-Missouri border. They were barely out of sight when their Georgia property was taken over by white settlers. Major Ridge had stocked his boat with a hundred and fifty bushels of cornmeal, seventy-eight barrels of flour, and twelve thousand pounds of salt-cured bacon, enough to get them to Honey Creek and then some.

They left Ross' Landing with a party of 466 Cherokees and slaves transported in eleven flatboats, and they arrived at Gunter's Landing, Alabama on March 6, 1837. At Gunter's Landing, the flatboats were attached to the steamer *Knoxville,* and they traveled to Decatur, Alabama. There they boarded the Tuscumbia Courtland & Decatur Railroad and traveled to Tuscumbia Landing on the Tennessee River.

Dr. Lillybridge, the contingent's physician reported a number of illnesses caused by the cold and rain along the route. They camped at Tuscumbia Landing until the steamboat *Newark* arrived to take them up the Tennessee River, down the Ohio to the Mississippi, and upstream on the muddy Arkansas to Little Rock. There they boarded keelboats pulled by a steamer, and finally, traveling overland arrived at their new home on Honey Creek in Indian Territory.

Major Ridge knew his signature on the New Echota Treaty would make him less than welcome among many in the Cherokee nation. "I did what I thought was best for the Cherokee people," Major Ridge told Susannah. He knew followers of Ross were accusing him of signing the treaty out of selfish ambition. He also knew that sooner or later he would have to answer to other Cherokee leaders. He had not forgotten the Cherokee Blood Law. Sooner or later I will have to answer to the Blood Law, he thought.

In fact, in a council meeting years earlier, it had been Major Ridge who had called for the strict enforcement of the old Blood Law. He remembered standing in the council and demanding the death of Chief Doublehead who had given over to federal agents the hunting grounds between the Clinch River and the Cumberland Mountains. "The blood law of the Cherokee requires us to kill Doublehead," he insisted. "He has made deals with the federal government only to benefit himself, and he deserves to die."

Surely my people will understand that my case is different, he thought. I tried my best to keep the government from taking Cherokee land, but at last I could see there was no other option for the Cherokee but to negotiate for removal. All my life I have tried to protect Cherokee territory from white settlers. Will my people understand that I did what I thought was best for them? Now I'm left wondering when my own people will come for me.

He wondered if his grandchildren would know the pain and suffering his people had endured, and how he had tried to hold on to the home in the East. Would they ever realize that when their grandfather was born in 1771, the Cherokees claimed territory that later became Virginia, Kentucky, North

Carolina, Tennessee, South Carolina, Georgia, Alabama, and Mississippi? Would they know about his efforts with the federal government to stop the removal? Would they ever know that as a young man he had represented his people at Pine Log and spoke at the Cherokee Central Council against anyone taking Indian land?

When the Ridges disembarked on the Arkansas River, they purchased wagons, horses, oxen, and supplies and moved north toward Honey Creek at the northeastern corner of Arkansas. They arrived at Honey Creek in the spring when the redbuds, the white dogwoods and wild plum trees were blooming. Busying themselves and their slaves in clearing land and planting fruit trees, they waited for their son John and his wife Sarah to arrive.

Major Ridge was in his late sixties in 1837. On his early-morning rides around Honey Creek, he would often think of his boyhood days. How had he come from his simple mountain village on the Hiawassee River to live here in the West?

Major Ridge thought about the great expanse of land that once belong to the Cherokee, the Choctaw, the Chickasaw, the Creeks, and the Seminoles. The Cherokee at least had tried to adjust to the white settler's culture, even allowing missionaries to teach their children. Many had intermarried with white people. He thought of his own bloodline, with his Scottish Highlands grandfather and his mixed-blood Cherokee grandmother.

Trying to stop white people from coming across the mountains onto Indian lands had meant one battle after another for as long as he could remember. When he was a young boy, he heard stories about the great warrior Attacullaculla who had negotiated with the French, the English and even the Spanish to save some of the land. He remembered the time Attacullaculla had come to Ridge's village with his warriors, telling how his braves had put on war paint and fought the settlers along the Holston River. Many whites were killed, he said. He did not add how the whites had retaliated, and that many Cherokees had been killed in that retaliation. The boy knew there were always retaliations.

Major Ridge thought of the days when, as a younger man, he had fought with Andrew Jackson against the Redstick Creeks in Alabama. On March 27, 1814, five hundred Cherokees, under the command of a Colonel Morgan, had fought to open a way for Jackson's men, including Sam Houston, to take the Creek fortification and exterminate their warriors as well as their women and children. Major Ridge knew the Cherokee warriors had saved the day for Jackson. By ending the Creek War, the Cherokees had virtually assured Jackson's popularity and his eventual election to the presidency, his annexation of twenty million acres of Creek land in Alabama and Georgia, and the success of his forced removal policy.

Susanna busied herself preparing for the arrival of her children and grandchildren at Honey Creek. Once she had not minded moving from one place to another, but she had loved their Georgia home on Oothcanoga Creek and hated to leave it for a new home yet to be built far away in the west. She remembered dreading the long trip. Now that she was here, she wondered if she would ever become accustomed to the new place.

Back in the east, in preparation for leaving Georgia, John Ridge and Sarah had sold their plantation at Ross's Landing. Meeting with Elias Boudinot and his wife Delight Sargent, they made plans for traveling to Honey Creek. Most of their slaves and horses had been sent by ferry earlier. Taking a different route, they traveled the southwestern Kentucky path in carriages. They stopped along the way at Old Hickory near Nashville to visit with the aging Andrew Jackson, who by now was nearly blind. At night around the campfire, they talked of plans for educating Indians and for helping missionaries translate the New Testament into Cherokee, using Sequoyah's syllabary. They reached Honey Creek in November of 1837, the year before the forced removal from the east began.

*   *   *

As the day wore on, Greenberry watched and waited for John Ridge to appear. He listened as Chief Ross and Chief Brown went back and forth over the issue of a new constitution. The Old Settlers had their own form of government, and they did not want Ross and the newcomers dictating how they would live.

Toward the end of the afternoon, Greenberry noticed a commotion in the rear. He turned to see a tall, slender man and an older, stouter gentleman entering the council meeting accompanied by several Treaty Party members.

Greenberry nudged James Blackbird. "They must be the Ridges, father and son. They are dressed like wealthy white men."

"Who are the other two walking just behind them?" James Blackbird asked.

"Probably Boudinot and his brother Stand Watie," replied Greenberry. "They all look more like white gentlemen farmers than Cherokee chiefs."

He watched as they slowly made their way toward the front of the gathering. All eyes were on them. "Let's work our way through the crowd," he said to James Blackbird. "I need to get nearer."

"You'll never be able to get near enough," James Blackbird said. "They're too closely guarded. Put your knife away. If you make any move toward John Ridge, they will kill you."

"What do I care?" Greenberry said. "He has already taken everything I hold dear."

Before he could make a move, Greenberry saw Ridge turn and lead his people out of the council meeting. They have sensed the hostility of the crowd, he thought, and no doubt fear for their own lives. Greenberry watched them go, vowing to forestall his revenge for another day.

The Ridges' concern about the Blood Law had been well warranted. Some days later, Greenberry managed to become friends with some of the Ross camp. He learned that a secret meeting had been held to invoke the Blood Law against the leaders of the Treaty Party. The Ridges, Elias Boudinot, and Stand Watie were among those accused. They were not present to face their accusers. From each of the seven clans of the Cherokee nation, three representatives were appointed to sit in judgment. John Ridge's own Deer Clan condemned him to death. Greenberry learned that executions were pending for John Ridge, Elias Boudinot, and John's father, Major Ridge. He knew what he must do.

On the night of June 21, 1839, he and James Blackbird joined the group of Cherokees ready to ride to John Ridge's house. In the darkness, the other riders would assume they were legitimate members of the execution party. Riding furiously until they reached Honey Creek at daybreak, Greenberry felt the hunter's exhilaration in anticipation of the kill.

The party quietly surrounded the Ridge home in the early-morning light. Greenberry's thought was of Analeha and the baby. Three of the assassins dragged John Ridge from his bed, and with Sarah and the children wide-eyed with horror, they stabbed him again and again. Sarah screamed and begged for mercy. Amid the cries of the Ridge children, Greenberry and James Blackbird joined twenty-five other assassins marching in single file to stomp on Ridge's body. Greenberry learned later that Major Ridge, on his way home from one of his vineyards, had been ambushed by Cherokee gunmen. Other assassins stabbed Boudinot in the back, and split his head open with tomahawks. Stand Watie managed to escape, having been warned by one of the missionaries. The Blood Law had been fulfilled.

After the assassinations, a contingent of Ross's followers, fearing retaliation, formed a cordon around his house. Ross denied any part in, or any knowledge of, the assassinations. At the suggestion of Jesse Bushyhead, Ross held another convention on July 1 to seek a compromise among the disparate parties. Not many Old Settlers or Treaty Party members attended, but those who came met again with John Ross on July 12 and signed an act of union with Ross's National Party. The first act was to declare amnesty for all crimes committed by anybody since the arrival of the late immigrants. However, in the aftermath of the assassinations, law and order broke down. The federal government sent soldiers onto Cherokee soil to arrest anyone involved, though no one was arrested. Bushyhead and Sequoyah again tried to bring peace, but to no avail. For many days after the killing of the Treaty Party leaders, retaliations continued. Corpses were found along trails, and there seemed to be no end to the killing.

Greenberry and James Blackbird had accomplished what they set out to do. What were they to do now? Most people had lost hope. Most did not have the strength to care about what was happening around them. Ross has money, Greenberry thought. Ross's family won't go hungry. Still, to be fair, he knew that Ross and most of the other wealthier Cherokees were trying to meet the needs of poorer Cherokees out of their own pockets. Since the assassinations, the government had stopped the payments promised the recent arrivals. Greenberry looked out over the makeshift tent homes where dazed, sick people cried to go back home and wondered where it would all end.

Many Cherokee men had turned to liquor to help dull their misery and pain. Greenberry and James Blackbird had both stayed drunk for days to deaden their own pain. The violence continued. Treaty Party members hunted down people involved in the assassinations. James Blackbird and Greenberry tried to stay clear of the camps, where suspects were being picked off daily. Treaty Party gangs attacked, robbed, and murdered members of John Ross's National Party.

James Blackbird's own Creek tribe, he learned, had suffered terrible times since their arrival in Oklahoma Territory. "I'm going back to Alabama to find my people. White plantation owners captured some of them, mostly children, and made slaves out of them. I'm going back to Alabama to find them."

"They'll hunt you down and kill you, James Blackbird," Greenberry warned.

Trying to sleep off the white lighting he had bought in camp, Greenberry camped in wooded areas. When he finally stayed sober long enough to regain his senses, he decided there was no place in this chaotic land for him. As he tightened his saddle, three black ravens circled overhead. They dived, then disappeared. He thought of the old tale of the Raven Mockers, horrid wizards who take the shape of the raven and dive down to take people's lives and eat their hearts. He felt uneasy. It's the liquor, he thought. With no idea where he was going or what he would do, he rode into the morning sun.

BOOK II

The Preeces of Wales
and
The Chickasaw Romans

1814-1869

Remember the sky that you were born under,
know each of the stars' stories . . . .
Remember the earth whose skin you are:
red earth, black earth, yellow earth, white earth,
brown earth, we are earth . . . .
Remember.

—*Joy Harjo, Creek poet*

ONE

Fannie and John

Chickasaw Bluffs, near Memphis, Tennessee
1814-1843

Fannie Romans never saw her father, but she had heard enough stories about him to imagine what he was like. Bartholomew Romans, a surveyor, had been sent by the British government to draw maps of Indian territory, and like other white traders and speculators, he wanted land and slaves.

"The way Mama told it," Fannie said to her daughter Lillie, "he also wanted women. My mama was a mixed-blood Chickasaw who grew up on the Lower Chickasaw Bluffs near Memphis. She told me Bartholomew Romans had come to survey Chickasaw country in Tennessee and northern Mississippi. She said she saw maps he had made of lands in Florida and all over. He asked her to be his woman, and despite the old men in the counsel who told my grandma she should keep my mama from living with a white man, she let him move in anyway. Mama had been taken with his blond hair and good looks. But as she said, he stayed just long enough to put me in her belly.

"When I was young," Fannie told Lillie, "I overheard women gossiping about him. They said he wanted a squaw to cook for him and many women to sleep with him. He came here to make maps, they said. But he made lots of mixed-blood children as well. You know," she went on, "Chickasaw full-bloods were resentful of us mixed-bloods. Still are, even though there are more of us every day. When I was younger, I used to wish I had no white blood. But no more. We owe much to Bartholomew Romans. We owe our Romans name to him, not to mention our light-colored skin. It means we can blend in. I remember, in 1840, after I came with your papa to White County, a census taker came to the farm at Rock Island. When he asked John the color of the people living in his house, John said, 'You damn fool! Can't you see they're all white?'"

"I wish I had known this Bartholomew Romans," Lillie said.

"I expect it's better you didn't," Fannie replied. "According to Mama, he was a mixed-blood within his own race. His mother was Dutch and his father English. I think he got the worst of both. I doubt if we would have liked him. I guess he was not the best of white men. He thought all Indians were no good, more like animals than people. She said he even put that down in his books."

"Did you ever see his books?" Lillie wanted to know.

"No, and I don't think Mama did either. She said he was always drawin' and scratchin' something on pieces of paper. But she never saw the books. She said one day he disappeared as quickly as he'd come."

Fannie Romans had met John Preece when he limped into her Chickasaw village near Lower Chickasaw Bluffs in western Tennessee in 1814. Fanny understood little English. What little she knew, she had learned from English traders who stopped at the depot near Memphis. Fannie was accustomed to seeing white land speculators, Scots and English, coming through looking for land, but John was not looking for land. He needed to recuperate from wounds he had received at the Battle of Horseshoe Bend. The only thing she could understand from John's gibberish was "Horseshoe Bend." Fannie dressed his wounds with herbal poultices, fed him corn cakes and mush, and helped him maneuver around the village. It didn't matter that John couldn't speak her language. She was drawn to him at once.

White speculators and traders had plagued the Chickasaws in the Mississippi Valley ever since the days De Soto's men had marched through more than two hundred years before. Even as far back as that, white men had been sleeping with Chickasaw women, making more mixed-bloods. Like me, Fannie thought. She knew the full-blood High Mingos had tried to stop intermarriage between white men and Chickasaw women, but they couldn't do anything about it.

John was immediately taken with Fannie's gray-green eyes, shiny black hair, and light oak skin. It wasn't just her appearance that impressed him. Though she was small in stature, he was amazed at her stamina. She worked from sunup to sundown, milking cows, plowing fields, taking care of her younger brothers and sisters, cooking meals, carrying water from a nearby stream, all without complaint. "That's what I'm supposed to do," she told John. And when she behaved shyly around John, and he teased her about it, she explained that when Chickasaw boys were born, they were placed on panther skins to ensure they would grow to be strong and smart. Newborn baby girls were placed on fawn or buffalo calves' skin to make them shy.

John liked her way of laughing when he did his crazy antics, like making faces, playing pranks, hiding in haystacks, and jumping out when she strolled by on her way to the fields. When she giggled, he thought it sounded like water rippling over rocks. She laughed when he mimicked the way some of the old women of the village walked with hickory sticks. Even the old women themselves found it funny.

Within a few weeks after his arrival in the village, John had so ingratiated himself with the village elders that when he stated he wanted Fannie for his wife, no one raised an objection. After all, Fannie herself was a mixed-blood. What some of Fannie's people did find odd, however, was the difference in their heights. Fannie was just five feet and John stood a lanky six feet-two. "What does she want with that tall skinny white stick?" they laughed.

When John's wounds were almost healed and he began to walk without his hickory stick, Fannie noticed a restlessness in him. She had loved his habit of whistling as they walked together, but these days there were more and more long, quiet stretches. She knew he wanted to go home. He had learned some Chickasaw words, and she had learned a little more English. John loved to hear Fannie talk in her language. It sounded like the singing of birds. When they were alone, they were able to speak with each other with growing facility. John would tell her about his little cabin in middle Tennessee, and when he finally asked her to go with him, she wished he hadn't asked. She was reluctant to admit even to herself that she would go with him anywhere.

"I don't want to leave here," Fannie told him. "Most of the white men who marry Chickasaw women live in the Chickasaw villages with their wives. I'll just be another Indian squaw in your village. Why would you want a squaw for a wife? That's what your people will say. They will say you married a squaw."

John tried to reassure her. "See that land?" He pointed to the flat grassy stretch along the Mississippi. "It's beautiful, isn't it?" She could only nod and smile. "Well, it's nothing compared to my place at Rock Island. I've built a cabin in the most beautiful valley at the foot of the Cumberland Mountains. It is surrounded by rolling hills and meadows where wild strawberries and blackberries and rhododendron and white roses bloom in the spring." He hardly stopped for breath. "Gushing streams pour over rocks into rivers full of fish. At the fork of two rivers, the Caney Fork and the Collins, I built my cabin. Cedar trees and big oaks give shade in summer. The soil is rich and will grow corn and beans and pumpkins, and anything else we want to plant. We can grow apple trees. And we can raise cows and pigs, and there will be plenty to eat in the summer and the winter. We can sit on the porch on summer nights and hear the crickets and frogs in the cedars, and in the fall we can watch the oak and maple leaves on the mountainside turn to bright reds and yellows. We can warm by the blazing fire in the winter. Best of all, we will be together."

Fannie didn't understand all the words, but she understood John's enthusiasm, and she believed he truly loved her. She wondered, though, how much he was exaggerating. She had a feeling he was good at that.

John seemed reluctant to talk about his family, but Fannie finally managed to get him to tell her a little about himself. She learned John was born in Virginia around 1789.

"My papa came from Wales," he said at last. "He was in some kind of trouble with the British government, and so he came to Virginia to keep from being thrown in prison. When the war broke out, he fought the British and ended up spending six months in irons in a British jail in Quebec. When the war was over, he was awarded 640 acres in eastern Tennessee, so when I was six, we moved from Virginia to his land in east Tennessee near the Watauga.

"I don't remember much, but I do remember we traveled in ox-drawn wagons. We passed small towns and farms where we would sometimes stop to buy food and supplies. My brothers and I would romp through the meadows when we stopped in the afternoons. We would swim in the cool creeks along the way and sit with Mama and Papa around the fire at night. Sometimes we would stop where other wagons of people were camping.

"When we reached the Nolichucky River, Papa took us to the place where our new home would be. Some neighbors came and helped Papa clear the land and build our cabin. It only had one room, with a loft where us boys slept. Mama and Papa and the girls slept below by the fireplace. We chinked the cracks with mud, and used split logs for the floor.

We used to play with the Crockett boys. Their cabin was just a mile away. We all loved to swim in the Nolichucky. And I remember we had to fight the Cherokees. They claimed we'd squatted on their land, but my papa said the land had been given to him for fighting the British."

That was about all John would tell her about his family. Mostly what she heard from him was about men taking land and more land and fighting wars.

She thought about her white father, Bartholomew Romans, and wondered if John would be like him. John never told her why he left his father's farm on the Nolichucky and came over the Cumberlands into Tennessee. What he did dwell on was what he saw at Horseshoe Bend in Alabama. At first he had bragged about fighting under General Andrew Jackson against the Creeks.

"I joined the United States Thirty-Ninth Infantry," he told Fanny. "We were about to lose against the Creeks when the Cherokees under Junaluska jumped into the Tallapoosa River and attacked the Creeks from the rear." In a more somber tone, he confessed to Fannie he had deserted when he saw Federal soldiers and Cherokees slaughtering Red-Stick Creek women and children.

"I just couldn't take anymore. Everyone they captured," John said in a whisper, "they cut to pieces. They had no mercy, even for the children." Fannie wanted to comfort him. She touched his hand and held it in her own. She could see the massacre had shaken him deeply.

When the time came for John to leave, Fanny went with him. She knew she could no longer remain in the village without him, and it was clear he wouldn't stay. As they rode away, Fannie hoped John's mountain home in East Tennessee would be everything he had promised. But even if it's not, she thought, being with him will be enough.

Years later, sitting on the front porch in her rocking chair on Laurel Creek near Rock Island, Fannie remembered how John had cajoled her to come and live with him. She had not been disappointed. He had been right in everything he said. There was no other place as beautiful. She loved to sit here in the spring when the apple and pear trees and the wild flowers were blooming. In June, when it was warmer and the chores were done, she loved to sit on the porch and listen to the children in the meadow arguing about what games to play. They would have her tie strings to June-bugs' legs so they could watch the tiny insects fly in circles. She could hear the boys, Johnny, David, and William, playing marbles, and she loved to watch Lillie, Sarah, and Nancy playing house and singing their dolls to sleep in the cradles John had made for them.

But to Fannie, the happiest sound of all was John's whistling as he returned home from his peddling trips. She would hear the jingling sound of the mule team pulling the peddling wagon over the hill and down to the cabin. If John's whistling rang out over the sound of the wagon, she knew he had done well selling his wares. He sold needles, thread, calico, chewing tobacco, salt, and any other household items he could manage to acquire. But his main feature was ripe apples, pears, peaches, and plums when they were in season. Fannie had helped him plant the seedlings in their first year of marriage. When the trees bore fruit, John loaded as much of the ripe produce as the wagon could hold, and sold it wherever he could find buyers.

After a few years driving the peddling wagon, it occurred to John they could make more money selling fruit trees than just the ripened fruit itself. Cutting buds from the trees that had borne the best fruit, they inserted them into the peach, apple, and pear seedlings, using strips of dried grass to tie them in place. When the grafts took hold, they trimmed away everything above the graft, and new varieties of fruit were born. Thus began the small nursery they called Preece Trees. John could now peddle quantities of the little grafted trees, producing new varieties for orchards across Tennessee. With hard work and good management, the venture was soon bearing fruit in ways they could scarcely have imagined in the beginning. John dubbed Fannie's favorite new variety of apple "Chickasaw Red." Not to be outdone, Fannie named one of her new apples "Sugarplum White."

At first John would be gone for only a few days, but as time went by, he traveled farther from home, sometimes staying away for weeks at a time. Fannie missed him, but she had plenty to keep her busy. Apart from maintaining the farm and the orchards, she had taken on a new job collecting feathers from the women in the community and storing them in a log building on the stagecoach road at Rock Island. John had agreed that, twice a year, he would take the collected feathers to Sparta to sell to small factories that made women's hats, pillows, and feather beds. With the proceeds from the feathers, the women would buy fine cotton thread. In the cold winters, Fannie loved it when they would work together at the church, quilting and crocheting fancy patterns on pillowcases and doilies.

John and Fannie put the children to work in the orchards, pruning in the spring and gathering apples and pears in the fall. As soon as they were old enough to use a knife safely, John taught them the art of budding the peach seedlings and grafting the apple and pear seedlings. He also taught them how to use the hoe to keep the weeds from choking out the rows of new little trees. When the trees produced, they all picked the fruit together. Yes, Fannie thought, on balance, life has been good to us.

TWO

Lillie and Elizabeth

Rock Island, Tennessee
1844-1848

Fannie was grateful when Lillie found the Indian baby on her porch. It had not been easy for Fannie to watch her oldest daughter suffer the loss of her stillborn child and then her husband Frank, who had died soon after in a logging accident. Lillie had been depressed for a long time.

"My life is over," Lillie had told Fannie.

"You'll find someone someday," Fannie told her. "You weren't meant to be alone."

The little baby girl had truly been a gift to both of them. Most of Fannie's children had been given biblical names: Isaac, John, David, and Sarah. "Let's name her Elizabeth," Fannie suggested. "In the Bible, Elizabeth was the mother of John the Baptist. The Bible says she had been barren for years, and God made a miracle and gave her the baby. I believe it's a miracle that this little Indian baby was left here on your porch." While Lillie did not know the Bible like her mother, she did like the name Elizabeth. She thought it was a strong name, so she agreed. Fannie took out her Bible and had Lillie inscribe: "Daughter, Elizabeth, born October 1838, Cherokee."

In the first few years, Lillie gave no thought to telling Elizabeth she was not her own. However, lately she and her mother had talked about telling her. One day, when Elizabeth was about six, she came home crying. The boys at church had laughed at her. "How come you got dark skin? And how come your hair is so straight? Are you a squaw? Or a darky?" they taunted her. "Where'd you come from anyway? Bet you're a Indian squaw."

Lillie knew she must tell Elizabeth the truth. But no matter how she tried to tell her how much she loved her, the damage had been done. Lillie told Elizabeth the story of finding her on the porch that stormy night. She told her what a miracle that had been, but she avoided telling her about the horrors she had seen at the internment camp the day she went looking for Elizabeth's mother.

"I don't wanna be a Indian," Elizabeth cried. She knew from the way the boys at church said the word, it was not something good. "Why do they call me a Indian squaw?" she asked. Lillie could see her explanation was not satisfying to Elizabeth, so as she often did when she was frustrated, she called on her mother Fannie for help.

"You're my favorite grandchild," Fannie told Elizabeth. "And do you know why? It's because we have ancient blood, Cherokee and Chickasaw blood."

Elizabeth's face brightened. She loved Fannie in a special way. Of course, she loved her mother, too, but it was her Granny Fannie she especially admired and looked up to.

"My people, the Chickasaw, and your people, the Cherokee, were here a long time before their people even *thought* of coming," Fannie told her. "The next time they make fun of you, you just tell them that."

Lillie decided it was time to give Elizabeth what they had found beside her in the basket. "Elizabeth," she said, "I have a surprise for you. Close your eyes and hold out your hands. And don't peek." Elizabeth knew this game. Granny Fannie and Lillie had played it with her often. She closed her eyes tight and held out her hands.

Lillie placed the cedar flute in Elizabeth's hands, and said: "Now open your eyes." Elizabeth stared at the flute.

"What is it, Mama?" She asked Lillie.

"It's a special gift we found in the basket with you when you came to us. Your mama and papa must have loved you so much, and it must have been very hard for them to leave you. But they had to go on a long journey, and they knew it would be a hard journey, too hard for a little baby like you. So they searched and searched for the best place to leave you. Isn't it a miracle they left you with you Granny Fannie and me? And they left this little gift for us to give to you when you were older."

It was then Granny Fannie spoke up. "It makes a wondrous sound. Let me show you. Listen." She lifted the flute to her lips and blew one soft high note.

Elizabeth brightened. "Oh, let me! Please," she said.

Granny Fannie handed the flute to Elizabeth and hung the deerskin string around her neck. "Now when them boys call you names," she said, "you just lift the flute and blow into it like I did."

Elizabeth blew until she was able to bring a sound from the flute. "They'll wish they had one, too," said Fannie, "but you must not take it from around your neck. Tell them it is your magic flute that chases away witches. I think it'll chase those boys away, too."

Fannie was willing to do anything she could to keep her granddaughter from suffering the pain of rejection. She understood what Elizabeth was going through. Elizabeth sat practicing the flute until Lillie called her to supper. Fannie thought of her own childhood when people in her Chickasaw village would remind her she was a "half-breed" and make fun of her lighter skin. Perhaps someday she could share with Elizabeth the pain she had experienced. She would not tell Elizabeth about her own childhood, anyway not today. She would wait until she was older. Today Elizabeth had enough problems of her own.

In the summer of 1845 when Elizabeth was seven, Lillie married Thomas Moore, a widower twenty years her senior. Thomas's children were all grown and married, so Elizabeth was raised as their only child. They both doted on her. She made their family complete. Soon after the marriage, Lillie decided it would be best if she went to court and legally adopted Elizabeth. She wanted to be sure no one could take Elizabeth away from her.

So, with Thomas and Fannie in tow, Lillie went to the Van Buren County court house in Spencer to seek legal guardianship of Elizabeth. Fannie put up an eighty-dollar bond to fulfill the court requirement. Lillie was nervous in front of the judge. She didn't like having to answer the questions the court clerk asked her because she feared she wasn't answering them properly.

"Who are her real parents? How did you get her? What evidence do you have she is an Indian? How do you know what tribe she's from? Why do you want to take legal guardianship of her? Does she have any legal rights to property? What's her real name?"

When the clerk finally asked, "What name shall be given to this child?" Elizabeth tuned in more closely to the proceedings.

"Preece," Lillie answered in a firm voice. Before she knew it, she had said, "Preece. Her name is Elizabeth Preece." Thomas looked surprised, but said nothing.

"Preece," Elizabeth said the name softly to herself. She liked the sound of Preece. It was like the wind whispering. She was no longer just Elizabeth. She was Elizabeth Preece.

Sometimes Lillie thought Fannie went overboard in trying to amuse Elizabeth. "You're spoiling that child," Lillie would tell Fannie. It was Fannie who insisted on taking Elizabeth to the traveling circus. The outing was one of the most exciting memories of Elizabeth's early childhood. Fanny dressed Elizabeth in her best calico dress and braided her long black hair into a pigtail. Lillie hitched up the mule to the small cart and the three of them were off.

Tents arranged in a large circle by the river advertised different sideshows. After seeing chattering monkeys, slithery snakes, and even a two-headed man, Elizabeth ran towards a baby elephant just outside the circle. A man dressed in Indian garb was giving children rides on the elephant. He wore deerskin, with a belt that had long tassels, and on his moccasins, bells that jingled when he moved. Lillie thought it didn't look safe for Elizabeth to ride, but Elizabeth begged, and Granny Fannie said she thought it was fine.

The elephant knelt to allow Elizabeth to climb onto his back. As the Indian lifted her into the saddle, she saw the elephant had a red-feathered headband just like the one the Indian wore, only bigger. "What's your name?" he asked Elizabeth as the elephant lumbered around the well-worn path.

"Elizabeth," she said. "Elizabeth Preece."

"Happy to meet you, Elizabeth Preece," he smiled. "Hold on tight."

Later when Elizabeth stood by the Collins River with Lillie and Fannie eating cotton candy and sweet popcorn, she thought what a wonderful day it had been. It was the last day of the circus, and workers were already beginning to break down the tents. They were moving from Rock Island to Sparta for their next engagement.

They watched the tall Indian man as he tried to coax the elephant to board the ferry. Elizabeth thought his big ears reminded her of the elephant's ears. He pushed and pulled, but the elephant would not move. Finally, the elephant plunged into the river, soaking the Indian and splattering the onlookers on the bank. The Indian tried slipping up on him in a boat, but the elephant would wait just long enough for him to come near, and then let him have it again with a trunk full of water. The elephant then aimed his trunk directly at Elizabeth and sprayed. Water went all over her and Mama Lillie and Granny Fannie as well. Elizabeth jumped up and down laughing. The Indian man laughed with her as he wrung the river water from his long braid.

"Did he soak your braid, too?" he asked Elizabeth.

"A little," Elizabeth giggled. "Are you a real Indian?"

"Yes," he laughed. "I'm a real Indian."

"Well, I'm an Indian, too," she announced proudly. She thought the Indian man was very nice. Later she told Mama Lillie and Granny Fannie she had never seen anything so funny in her whole life as that elephant spraying water all over everybody.

The sun was about to set, and as the air became cooler, the crowd began to disperse. The circus manager was on the verge of sending word to Sparta that the circus would be a day late, when the elephant decided to allow himself to be led on to the ferry. Smiling, the Indian waved goodbye to Elizabeth, who waved back. The ferry moved across the river, and as dusk was falling, Elizabeth could see him leading the elephant up the road toward Sparta. She watched until he disappeared around the bend. At last, Elizabeth, Lillie, and Fannie climbed into their cart and headed for home, laughing all the way.

The other event Elizabeth would always remember was when, at the age of ten, she and Lillie went to Shells Ford. It was then Lillie told her about the contingent of Cherokees that had come through Shells Ford in great numbers heading for the new territory. Walking past the little log church, they went beyond the marked graves to the back of the cemetery. Under a grove of tall cedars near the bank of the Collins, they found several small slabs of rough rock markers, some standing upright, others fallen flat on the ground. It was a hot August day, and thunderclouds were beginning to gather. Amid the nameless markers, Elizabeth and Lillie stood in silence. Lillie wondered how many of the Cherokees who left Shells Ford on that day had actually reached their destination. Had Elizabeth's parents survived the journey? It had begun to rain. This will be good for our corn crop, Lillie thought. Lillie and Elizabeth retreated under the cedars and waited for the downpour to end.

THREE

Preeces or Romans

Rock Island, Tennessee
1853-1856

When Elizabeth turned fifteen, she fell in love with Johnny Preece, the eldest son of John and Fannie. He was ten years her senior, and she had always known him as Uncle Johnny. He wasn't really her uncle, she would try to explain to anyone who seemed interested. Soon after her birthday, when Johnny came back from one of his cave-exploring expeditions, he said he wanted to marry her.

Elizabeth was sure she had always loved Johnny. Even as a child she had admired him. He had chosen her to be on his side whenever they played Annie Over or Whiplash or hide-and-seek. He had always bought her entries at the community cakewalks and pie-supper auctions. Elizabeth and Johnny had regularly eaten together at Fanny and John's table. They had worked together in the fields and swam together in the river.

People were accustomed to seeing them together, Fannie knew, but lately she thought she detected some raised eyebrows at church. Fannie thought she'd better speak to Lillie about it. "People are gossiping about Johnny and Elizabeth getting married," she told Lillie. "And it's not because he's her uncle, which they know he's not. It's because Elizabeth is Indian." Nobody had ever raised a question about Fannie's heritage, since the day John had brought her home with him. Hadn't the census takers always listed everybody in the family as white?

Fannie had been the backbone of the Rocky River Methodist Church for many years, volunteering to prepare the bread and grape juice for communion and making certain the coal oil lamps were clean and ready for use on Sunday mornings. She was the one asked to be in charge of the monthly all-day singings and dinners-on-the-ground, and she was the one who kept the minister informed and in line. When she sat with the other churchwomen around the quilt frame, she had ignored stories about Indians that had caused everybody to laugh. Then someone would apologize when they remembered Fannie's granddaughter was Indian. Fannie had ignored their meanness because she did not want to be ostracized. She had worked hard to belong, and she could see no reason why that should change.

After Elizabeth and Johnny announced in church they were getting married, Fannie was sure she sensed a coldness among the church members.

"I caught little bunches of my friends huddled together talkin' when I went to market, and as I approached, they quit talkin'," she told Lillie. "Some actually turned around and stared at me."

"You're seein' something I don't," Lillie said. "Not everybody disapproves of Johnny and Elizabeth marryin'. Maybe you've misjudged your neighbors."

"I haven't misjudged my neighbors. I know how they feel," Fannie said.

"I think Elizabeth is too happy to pay any attention to them," Lillie said. "Besides, it's none of their business anyway. If she can ignore them, why can't you? After all, that's what you've always told her to do."

On Sunday morning a week before the wedding, with the entire family sitting on the front pew, Fannie stood up and confronted the congregation. "I understand that some of you have concerns about my son and my granddaughter marryin'. What right do you have to raise questions about them tyin' the knot? You know they're not blood kin. But that's not what you're riled up about, is it? It's because Elizabeth is Indian. I want you to show me where the Bible says it's a sin for an Indian woman and a white man to marry. Some of you people are livin' in sin, and everybody knows it. Men sleep with other women besides their wives, and wives pretend it don't happen. People steal other people's pigs, cows, and horses. Families fight over inheritance. You gossip about each other, and everyone knows gossipin' is a sin. Some of you even make up lies and pass them along to your neighbors as if they were the truth." Fannie paused.

"Some of you married first cousins, blood cousins," she went on. "I don't remember anyone raisin' a question about that. Well, now I'm gonna give you something you can really gossip about. You think just because my man John is a white man, I must be white, too. Right? Well, let me tell you something you don't know. I'm a mixed-blood Chickasaw, and proud of it. I guess you can figure out that makes all my children mixed-blood Chickasaws. All except Elizabeth, of course. She comes from the Cherokee.

"What about that, preacher? Do you think we're livin' in sin? Is there anything in the church rules that says you can't marry two Indians?"

Fannie looked at the preacher sitting in his chair behind the pulpit. His head was bowed, his hands clasped together in his lap. He seemed unable to respond. Fannie signaled to her family, and they all marched out of the church behind her.

Johnny gave Elizabeth's hand a reassuring squeeze, and she smiled as she returned it. She was proud of her Granny Fannie that morning. She would not soon forget the courage it took for her to stand before that congregation and tell them what hypocrites they were.

Lillie, on the other hand, resented her mother making a public spectacle of their Indian heritage. Why couldn't Fannie just let it be and not make a fuss? If she hadn't told everybody, she thought, most people would never have known. Nobody needs to know we all have Indian blood. And why did she have to remind everybody Elizabeth is not mine? Why did she have to announce it to the whole community?

Later, when some of the church members came calling to say they were sorry and they hoped the family would come back to church, Fannie invited them in, but with a certain wariness in her dark Chickasaw eyes.

*　　*　　*

Fannie worried that John's trips selling fruit trees were taking him farther and farther from home. She knew he was staying away longer, sometimes for weeks instead of days. When he was at home, it seemed he could hardly wait to leave again. He had become aloof and distant with her and the children. She had heard gossip he had taken up with a woman in McMinnville, so she was not surprised when, one day, a young woman, obviously pregnant, struggled up the road to their cabin.

"Ah'm a-lookin' fer my man," she said as she drew near. "Have you seed him?"

"Depends on who he is," Fannie replied. "Has he got a name?"

"Calls hisself John."

"Does he have a last name?"

"Ah think hit's Price or Pease or somethin' like that."

When Fannie confronted John, he tried to explain. "Aw, Fan, she don't mean nothin' to me. She tricked me into gettin' her in a family way. I swear I didn't set out to do it. She used her wiles on me. Anyway it didn't happen but once, and besides, I was drunk when it happened."

Fannie didn't want to hear any more. "You go live with her," she told John. "You can't live here anymore."

The boys took their mother's side. "I never want to hear the name Preece again!" William spat out at his father. "I'm changing my name to Romans. I'd rather be a Chickasaw Romans than a bastard Preece." The other children agreed, all except Lillie, who tried her best to calm them. Fannie made John sign over all the land to her.

A year later when John came home and begged Fannie to take him back, she refused. "Why can't you just forget what happened and take him back," Lillie begged. "He's old and tired and has no place to go."

"He has you," Fannie countered. "That'll have to be enough."

Lillie understood her mother's anger, but the other woman had turned him out. He had no money and was no longer able to work. Lillie could not leave her father without a place to live, so she and Thomas took him in. Until his death, John lived next door to Fannie. He saw her at a distance nearly every day, but she never spoke a word to him, nor did she acknowledge his presence in any way. For years after, many of the children went by the name "Romans" instead of "Preece."

Why must her mother be so cold? Lillie wondered. What was it in Fannie's Chickasaw background that made her so unforgiving? She knew her mother harbored resentment against her own father, Bartholomew Romans, for his disrespect and hatred of Indians. But Lillie suspected there were other memories her mother had never shared and she wondered if she ever would.

When John died in 1854 during the typhoid epidemic, Fannie made all the children attend the funeral. She shed no tears, but with her children gathered around his gravesite, she had Lillie read a Bible passage, and then said goodbye to him, speaking the words in Chickasaw. Lillie often wished she had known enough Chickasaw to understand what her mother had told her father that day.

Fannie died of pneumonia two years later. They buried her next to John in the woods at the back of the farm. The night before the burial, while the mourners were talking quietly together in the hall, Lillie moved to Fannie's coffin to say a last goodbye to her mother.

She took Fannie's Bible from the mantel. Looking down at her mother, Lillie whispered, "I remember how you always took this Bible with you to church and how you used to ask me to read it to you almost every day. And I remember how proud you were when Elizabeth's name was recorded there next to mine. I remember how you told me to write the word Cherokee beside her name. Well, it bothered me then, and it still bothers me now. Everyone knows having Indian blood can make a person's life harder. Who would know that better than you? It's nobody's business how Elizabeth came to be my child, and no one ever needs to know she's Cherokee. For that matter, we don't need to keep reminding people you and I have Indian blood either. People may suspect, but they can never prove it if it's not written down somewhere. So I want you to take this Bible with you, Mama. I don't want you to make this last trip without it."

With that, Lillie leaned forward to kiss her mother's cheek, and, dry-eyed, slipped Fannie's Bible under the folds of her burial gown.

Johnny was named executor of her will. Fannie had bequeathed Falls Mill Farm and Preece Trees Orchards to her six children. When they couldn't agree about who would get which piece of land, they went to court to determine how the farm would be divided. The judge decided the land would be sold and the proceeds shared equally. In the court proceedings, John and Fannie's youngest child, William, submitted his last name as Romans. A few months later, at the age of eighteen, he went back to court and legally changed his name from William Preece to William Romans.

"I got married by the name of Romans," he told the judge. "That's what I want my name to be."

Lillie had never considered changing her name. She saw no sense in it. Elizabeth found it sad that the name Preece she had thought so beautiful was now a name some members of her family didn't want to be called.

Fannie's death was the saddest day of Elizabeth's life. Fannie had been the one to hold the family together. She was Elizabeth's rock. The morning Fannie died, Elizabeth searched for the little cedar flute. Finding it in the bottom of the trunk, she took the flute from its deerskin quiver, and, standing on the porch overlooking the valley, she played the one Chickasaw tune Fannie had taught her. Granny Fannie understood what it's like being Indian, she thought.

FOUR

War Comes to Bone Cave

Van Buren County, Tennessee
1857-1864

In 1857 Johnny inherited enough money from the sale of Fannie's property to purchase a small piece of land just east of Rock Island in the little community of Bone Cave. With the help of his neighbors, he built a two-room cabin with a loft not far from the Bone Cave crossroads on Rocky River. He and Elizabeth, with their five children, Celie, Isaac, Thomas, James, and William, moved in and tried hard to make a living. But for all their trying, it soon became clear that the family couldn't make it on what they could produce on their forty acres. Johnny was soon hiring out as a day laborer on neighboring farms to help make ends meet. Still, despite dwindling income, they managed to keep the family clothed and fed. However, neither they nor any of their neighbors were prepared for what was about to happen.

On November 6, 1860, when Abraham Lincoln was elected president of the United States, the people in the Bone Cave community were faced with hard decisions, some of which separated families and tore neighbors apart. Few local farmers kept slaves, and most of them felt no loyalty to the plantation owners who did have slaves. But when word came that South Carolina had seceded from the union, followed quickly by Alabama, and Georgia, Tennessee had to decide whether or not to follow suit. Elizabeth and Johnny tended to agree with neighbors who argued that Tennessee should stay with the Union.

"Why should Tennessee secede?" one asked. "Let the rich plantations owners in South Carolina, Georgia and Alabama go to hell!"

"Nobody we know keeps slaves, except for a few big landowners over in White county," Elizabeth told Johnny. "They're just causing trouble for the rest of us."

"There are a few slave owners in this county," Johnny countered. "Not everyone thinks like you, Elizabeth. Some people are claiming that Lincoln needs to be hanged or thrown in jail. I think most people don't care. They just want to be left alone."

When Fort Sumter was fired upon, President Lincoln called for volunteers to suppress the rebellion. The Tennessee legislature voted in favor of secession. There would be no more peace in this valley, Elizabeth thought. The people of Bone Cave continued to work their farms, waiting to hear what the secessionists and the unionists were planning.

In 1861, many men in Bone Cave responded to the Confederate call to arms and marched off to war. Others kept quiet and went about their business as if nothing had changed. Like most of the small farmers around Bone Cave, Johnny had no interest in fighting a war. As he told one of the recruiters, "I have no Negroes to defend, and I see no reason to go to war."

Elizabeth admonished him to be careful about stating his views so openly. "It's better not to say too much right now," she said. "It could sound like you're not being patriotic, and that could get you in a lot of trouble with the secessionists."

They had heard the Confederates were mining saltpeter in Big Bone Cave to make gunpowder, and Elizabeth thought that might be a solution for Johnny. "They're looking for men to help with the mining," she said. "You wouldn't even have to join the army, so you wouldn't be forced to go and fight. You can stay home with the family." By the time conscription began in April of 1862, Johnny was working full-time in Big Bone Cave for the Confederates.

When fifteen-year-old Solomon, Johnny's nephew, lied about his age so the army would take him, Johnny's sister, Sarah, was distraught. "You could have waited a year or two and then signed up," she told her son. "Right now, you have no idea what this war is about. It's all them Confederate soldiers in their fancy uniforms comin' through here wavin' the flag that's got all you young men rarin' to go to war. You just want to sign up because the other boys are doin' it."

Despite Sarah's pleas, Solomon joined the Confederate Company E of the Twenty-fifth Tennessee Infantry in July of 1861. By 1862 most men around Bone Cave between the ages of eighteen and forty had joined the

Confederate regiments. A few joined the only Union regiment in the area, but many others headed for the hills.

When in December, Lillie's husband Thomas contracted pneumonia and died, she moved in with Elizabeth and Johnny. The two-room cabin was already overcrowded. Lillie shared a small wooden bed with Celie. Isaac and Thomas slept in the loft on feather pallets, and Johnny, Elizabeth, and the two younger boys, James and William, shared the other larger room.

Johnny's salary from the cave was not enough for eight people. With most of the men in the community gone, Elizabeth wondered how anyone could survive. Why couldn't the government listen to those East Tennessee lawmakers who wanted to suspend the draft in the rural mountain areas? They argued it was too hard for families to live with all the men away at war, but the leaders of the Confederacy said the South needed soldiers too desperately to allow such a thing. The request was denied.

At the beginning of the war, the family went about its days as usual. While Johnny worked for the Confederates at Big Bone Cave, Elizabeth struggled to work the farm. The children helped as best they could, but Elizabeth missed having Johnny at home to coordinate the farm work. She put Isaac in charge. He was only nine, but he had a good head on his shoulders. His job was to assign specific chores to the other children and keep an eye out to make sure everyone followed through. Celie complained she should be in charge, since, at thirteen, she was the oldest. So Elizabeth put her in charge of the barn. Celie gathered the eggs and fed the chickens twice a day. She helped Elizabeth milk the six cows every morning and night and churn the milk to make butter. When the spring came, Isaac plowed the forty acres, and all of them, including James and Thomas, planted pumpkin and corn seeds. Yet it was becoming harder and harder to provide for the family.

Before the war, the peddlers had come regularly enough to keep them in molasses, coffee and tea. But they never came anymore. Salt was hard to find. Most of their salt had been purchased from Kentucky, and it had all been taken by the troops. Soon soldiers and bushwhackers from both sides begin their forays through the county, taking whatever food they could find. Among the first things they took were the chickens. Chickens were especially hard to hide. Johnny, with the help of the boys, built a chicken coop in the woods a good distance from the house. They used thin logs and pieces of wire Johnny had found around Big Bone Cave, and they covered the coop with branches and sticks to make it more difficult to spot. The boys collected worms and bugs to feed the chickens, but they found the foxes were as apt to steal the chickens as the soldiers.

"Somebody has to keep an eye on the chickens," Isaac said. "James gets the job." The plan was for James to warn the others if he saw marauders coming, and then the other boys would grab the chickens and run for the coop in the woods. One day James waited too late to alert the others. Before he knew it, the marauders were upon them. James grabbed a hen and ran into the house. Elizabeth told him to stash it in the secret cellar they had dug under the floorboards in the main room.

The chief marauder demanded that Elizabeth and Lillie make food for them. Elizabeth explained they had none. James watched as the men stationed themselves within a few feet of the hiding place. The hen began to scratch and cluck, and Elizabeth, Lillie, and the children stood frozen.

"Who are you, little boy?" one of them asked four-year-old William.

"I da baby," replied William, smiling from ear to ear.

"But don't you have a name?"

"I da baby," William said again.

"Well, Ida Baby, do you like chicken?"

William nodded his head up and down and then quickly moved to stand on the plank just over the chicken. Both men roared with laughter as they pulled the hen out. Their laughter was short-lived. Isaac stepped from behind the door with his rifle aimed at the intruders. "Which one of you wants to be shot first?" he said in a calm, even voice.

The men backed away. "We was awful hungry," one said. "We didn't mean to cause no trouble."

"Take enough corn for the two of you to eat and then leave," Isaac said. The men took the corn, thanked them, and left. Isaac stood on the porch with his rifle at the ready, and Elizabeth stood on the other end of the porch aiming her rifle at the men as they hurried away.

"That'll teach you not to mess with the Preeces!" James hollered after them.

Elizabeth worried about Johnny working in the cave. "When Union soldiers come through and ask questions," Johnny had told her, "don't tell them anything unless you have to. And don't ever tell the children what we're doing in the cave." That presented a problem for Elizabeth, since the children, particularly the two oldest, were always asking what their father was doing. Isaac had seen the guards posted at the roads leading into and around the cave, so he suspected something important was taking place.

One night as they lay in bed, Johnny told Elizabeth: "I wish they hadn't put me in charge. One of 'em said yesterday that Big Bone Cave could make the difference in winnin' the war. He said we have to turn out more saltpeter, and we have to do it faster. I don't know how I can make three hundred men go any faster. Most of 'em are not soldiers, and some of 'em don't even believe in the cause. I don't know how much longer I can do this."

Elizabeth could see the work was taking its toll on Johnny. After spending twelve to fifteen hours a day stooped over, at times crawling along the cave floor, he would come home many nights barely able to walk. He told Elizabeth his eyes were bothering him, and she noticed his cough was getting worse from working in the damp caverns day after day. He would often come home late with applejack brandy on his breath, eat the meager supper she had prepared for him, and then fall into bed exhausted.

FIVE

Watch on the Collins

Tandy's Knob, Bone Cave, Tennessee
Spring 1864

Not all of the workers at Big Bone Cave were mining saltpeter. Some, too young to work in the caves, kept the workers supplied with food and firewood. Others were stationed as guards on the mountain to watch for Federal troops. They needed young agile runners to work with the guards, so Johnny wanted ten-year-old Isaac and nine-year-old Thomas to work as runners. "We need the money," he said.

Elizabeth wasn't happy about the idea. "I need Isaac to stay here to work the farm," she insisted, "and Thomas is not over the fever yet."

"Then James can do it."

"He's too young. He's only eight."

"He's old enough to take some responsibility," Johnny argued, "and you know we need the money."

So during the spring of 1864 when James was eight, he served as a runner for a lookout scout on Tandy's Knob. On the first morning while James readied himself to go, Elizabeth had second thoughts. "James is too young," she protested again. "He could get lost on the mountain."

"I'm not too young," James chimed in. "I can take care of myself." Johnny wondered how long it would be before Elizabeth could let go of James. William should be the one she clings to, he thought. He's the youngest. But it's always

James. James, with his light copper skin and his straight coal black hair, looks like her, and he's every bit as stubborn as she is.

Elizabeth left the room and returned with the cedar flute. "James," she said. "Take this with you. Hang it around your neck, and don't take it off. If you're ever lost, blow hard like I showed you. It'll help us find you."

James had discovered the flute a year before the war when he was rummaging through the trunk at the foot of the bed, and he had asked his mother if he could have it. He was fascinated with the smell of the red cedar wood, and the smooth feel when he slid his fingers down it. When Elizabeth showed him how to make the high-pitched sound, he could hardly contain himself. "Let me blow on it," he begged.

"Hold it this way," she said, placing his index finger on the first of the six notes. "Now hold it tight and blow." The first time he blew, the sound was wavering and weak, but he kept trying until he could produce an even note. James was hooked.

Isaac, with a twinge of jealousy, taunted James. Mimicking his mother's voice, he said, "Blow your horn, James, if you run into the boogey man!" Johnny gave Isaac a hard look, and admonished him to stop his teasing. James didn't care. He was off to do something important, and the flute was his.

At first James was afraid of the odd-looking scout in charge of the lookout. He's tall like a giant, James thought, and his ears are too big. He stared at the scout, whose long black hair was pulled back and tied with a leather string. He's scary, James thought. He wasn't at all sure he wanted to be a runner for this man.

"We must watch," he said to James. "If we see blue soldiers coming, you must run as fast as you can to tell the workers."

It was hot on top of the knob, but James found a large rocky overhang under which he could shade himself. He was fascinated with the scattered clouds that cast dark shadowy patterns over the small farms. He could see where the Collins River and the Caney Fork merged and all the roads that met the Kentucky Road. The scout stood with his hand on his forehead shielding his eyes from the sun. He moved his head from side to side, scanning all roads leading into Bone Cave.

Sometimes James caught the guard looking at him in a funny way, taking quick sidewise glances at him. A few days into their watch, the scout asked James where he got his flute.

"My mother gave it to me," James said.

"Can you play it?"

"I can blow it loud."

"Let me show you how to play it," the scout said.

James removed it reluctantly from around his neck. He remembered his mother telling him not to take it off, but he decided he liked the scout and thought it would be nice to hear him play it. He watched with curiosity as the scout ran his fingers over the flute's smooth surface. The scout placed his fingers over the six holes on the top and played a high-pitched tune that sounded to James like the wind whistling through the cedars. When he was finished, he replaced the flute string over James's head.

"When I was about your age, I carved a cedar flute just like this one," the scout said, continuing his watch over the valley.

"You made a flute?" asked James in surprise. "Sometimes I whittle with Papa's pocket knife, but I could never whittle out anything as good as a flute."

James looked forward to his days on Tandy's Knob with the scout, but one morning he arrived in a grouchy mood. Isaac had been needling him, and he couldn't do anything about it.

"What's wrong, James?" the scout asked.

"I hate Isaac!" James shouted. "I could kill 'im! He always makes fun of me, and calls me a runt. He thinks he's so big and he thinks he knows everything."

"James," the scout said, "we must do our job watching the valley for soldiers, but while we watch, I will tell you a story."

James welcomed the chance for some diversion. "I like stories," James said.

"Once," the scout began, "the animals challenged the birds to a great ballplay. A day was set for the game. The animals and the birds always danced before the game. The animals danced on a smooth grassy bottom near the river and the birds danced on the treetops over by the ridge. The captain of the animals was the Bear who was very, very strong. He bragged he was so strong he could pull down anyone who got in his way. The Terrapin said that his shell was so hard that the heaviest blows could not hurt him, and he kept rising up on his hind legs and dropping hard again to the ground. This is the way I will crush any bird that tries to take the ball from me, the Terrapin said. The Deer chimed in that he could outrun all the other animals.

"The captain of the birds was the Eagle. The Eagle and the Hawk were both swift and strong in flight, but they were afraid of the animals. When the dance was over and the birds were preening their feathers and waiting for the captain to give the word to start the game, two little things hardly bigger than field mice climbed up the tree. They crept on a limb near the Eagle captain. Let us join in the game, they said."

"Did they let them play?" James asked.

"Yes, they did," Greenberry said. "But let me tell you the rest of the story. The Eagle Captain asked: Why don't you play on the side of the animals? They are four-footed. The little things answered: We asked the animals, but they made fun of us and said we were too small. The Eagle captain took pity on them, but the other birds wanted to know how they could play on the birds' team when they had no wings. Then some of the birds met and came up with a solution."

"What was it?" James wanted to know. "What did they do?"

"They decided to make wings for the little ones. They cut off a corner of the ground hog's skin drum and made wings. Then they fastened the wings to the front legs of the first small animal and called it the Bat. The Bat practiced throwing and catching the ball, and, by dodging and circling about, he kept it from falling to the ground. They knew he would be one of their best players. But now they had used up all the leather for the Bat and they couldn't fix wings for the other little animal."

The scout paused and glanced at James to see if he was listening. "Can you guess what happened then, James?" he asked.

"What happened?"

"Two large birds took hold of each side of the little animal and pulled as hard as they could until the little animal became a Flying Squirrel."

James's eyes widened. "What happened then? Who won the ballplay?"

"When the signal was given to start the game," the scout continued, "the Flying Squirrel caught the first toss and carried it up the tree, and then threw it to the birds who kept it in the air for a long time until it dropped. The Bear rushed to get it, but the Martin darted after it and threw it to the Bat. By his dodging and doubling back, he kept it out of the way of the Deer, until he finally threw it in between the posts and won the game for the birds. Because the Martin had saved the ball when it dropped, the birds gave him a gourd to build his nest, and he still has it today."

James smiled, knowing the next time Isaac called him a little runt, he would know something Isaac didn't know. He had learned he didn't have to be the biggest to be a winner.

"Tell me another story," begged James.

"Maybe another day," the scout said, looking all around, scanning each road into the valley for unwelcome travelers.

The next day, James came ready for another story. "Please," he begged. "You tell good stories. Where did you learn such good stories?"

"When I was a boy," replied the scout, "I would sit with the elders in the council house and listen to them tell stories, sometimes all the night long. It was from them I learned how to tell stories."

"Where is this place, this council house?" James wanted to know.

"It is over there farther to the east in the higher mountains. Would you like to hear how those mountains came to be?"

"Oh yes!" replied James.

"We must not forget why we are here on Tandy's Knob," said the scout. "If you will help me keep careful watch, I will tell you how the mountains came to be."

"Oh, I will, I will," said James. "Nobody will get past me!"

"The earth is a great square island floating in water," began the scout. "It hangs down by a cord from the sky vault of solid rock, just like that rock you sit on every day. Before this, when all was water and the animals lived above, it became too crowded. They wanted more room, so the little water beetle volunteered to look for a solid place in the water for the animals to live. When the little water beetle could not find a solid place to rest, it dived to the bottom of the water and came up with some soft mud. The mud began to grow and spread, and it became the island we call the earth. It was then fastened to the sky with four cords."

"Who fastened it?" asked James.

"Nobody remembers," said the Scout. "At first the earth was flat and very soft and wet. The animals were anxious to find a place to live on the earth, and so they sent out different birds to look for dry places, but none were found. Finally, they decided to send the Great Buzzard, the father of all buzzards. He flew all over the earth, but it was still too soft. When he reached our country, Cherokee country, he was very tired. His wings began to flap and strike the ground. Wherever the Great Buzzard's wings struck the earth, there was a valley."

"Like that valley below?" James asked.

"Yes," said the Scout, "Like that valley."

"How did the Great Buzzard make a mountain?" James asked.

"Well, when the Great Buzzard's wings turned up again, there was a mountain. When the animals saw this, they were afraid the whole world would be mountains, so they called him back and asked him stop making mountains. But our home remains full of mountains to this day." When the scout finished, he glanced at James who stood transfixed, awed by the undulating hills and mountains in the distance.

Every day James wanted another story. Every day thereafter, while he kept lookout, the scout told a different story. He told James about the *nun-ne-hi*, who watch over children. "The *nun-ne-hi* are little people," he said, "no more than knee-high, and they live in caves and laurel thickets. Sometimes they even live under the waters of rivers and streams. They like to play tricks, but they like to help people, too."

"I would like to see these little people," James said.

"They will not let you see them," the scout said. "But if you do see them, you must look away or they will disappear and not return. And you must never speak about them after the sun goes down."

The scout also told him the story of *ka-la-nu*, the raven that flies with the Raven Mocker, a horrid wizard who takes the shape of the raven and dives down to take people's lives and eat their hearts. James shuddered, a little frightened by that story. He had noticed two or three big black birds swooping and diving over the Knob. "Do you think they might be Raven Mockers?" he asked.

"They are just black birds," said the scout.

James was intrigued by the scout's stories, especially the scary ones. Despite his fear, he wanted to hear more. They made the time pass faster. "Please tell another story," begged James.

"Can you write, James?" The scout asked.

"I can write my ABCs," he said.

The scout smiled and said, "Once there was a great Cherokee leader named Sequoyah. One day he was sitting beside a stream and the wind blew a paper across his face. As he looked at the paper, he saw it had writing on it. Some white man has put talk on that paper, he thought. Of course, he couldn't read it. Then he decided if the white man can put talk on paper, so can the Cherokee. So he worked and worked, until he had made a mark for every Cherokee sound. His wife thought he was crazy, and she kicked him out of the house. But he kept working. He built a little cabin a ways down the creek, and he worked there for two years. One day, his wife set his cabin afire, burning all his papers."

"She burned the cabin?" James asked.

"Yes, but he still kept working. And finally, after twelve more years he was ready, so he called the village elders together and told them he had made a way for the Cherokee to put talk on paper. They laughed. Then he said, I tell you what we'll do. Send my daughter out into the woods and then tell me what you want me to write on paper. They agreed, and when she was out of earshot, they told him a few words and he wrote them down in Cherokee.

"When the girl came back in, he handed her the paper and told her to read it to the council. She read it, and it was word for word what they had told him to write. They were amazed and wanted Sequoyah to teach them to write in Cherokee. Soon, hundreds of Cherokee people had learned to read and write in Cherokee."

"Can you read and write in Cherokee?" James asked.

"Yes, I learned when I was a boy sitting with the elders in the council house. They all were learning, too."

"Can you show me how to write Cherokee?"

"It won't be easy for someone who does not speak Cherokee. The best thing you can learn from this story is, when you set out to do a thing, keep on trying and never give up."

"Then let me try to write in Cherokee. I can learn. I know I can."

The scout took a piece of slate rock and made some marks on it with another rock. "Do you remember the story of the *ka-la-nu?*"

"Sure," said James. "The *ka-la-nu* is the raven that flies with the Raven Mockers."

"Well," said the scout, "This is how the word looks in Cherokee."

"Looks like chicken scratching," laughed James. "But, here, let me try to copy it." Taking the slate, he copied the marks the guard had made and announced, "Didn't I say I could do it?"

SIX

Surviving

Bone Cave, Tennessee
Summer 1864

At the supper table that evening, Elizabeth asked James what happened during the day on Tandy's Knob. "Nothing." James replied. "I watched the shadows on the fields."

"Does the scout talk to you?" Elizabeth asked.

"Sometimes."

"What do you talk about?"

"He just tells me stories while we watch."

"What kind of stories?"

"I don't remember," James said.

His mother shook her head. It was like pulling teeth to get James to tell anything. James, on the other hand, was afraid to tell Elizabeth he had taken the flute from around his neck and let the scout play a tune on it. He also wanted to keep his newfound writing skill a secret, at least until he had learned to do it better.

Finally, late one afternoon, the scout spotted Union soldiers crossing the Collins River at Rock Island. He told James to run as fast as he could to warn the workers. James literally flew down the hill. Within minutes, all work stopped in the cave. The vats and paraphernalia outside were covered with tree branches cut to camouflage the entrance. The workers waited in silence, and the Confederate guards stood poised behind trees along the road with their rifles at the ready.

The young Union scouts rode jauntily. The only sounds that broke the dead stillness were their voices and the bees buzzing. "Can you believe how beautiful this place is? So quiet and peaceful," one soldier said. "I'm going to bring my gal here to live in these rolling hills after this war. I'm going to build me a little cabin by that stream we passed. And we can plant pumpkins and beans and my gal can plant flowers of all kinds. Do you smell them honeysuckles? The Rebs don't deserve to have this place all to themselves."

Rifles cracked. "We got 'em!" one of the Confederates reported. "They won't be bringing back any Yankee platoon now." Alongside the graves of the men who had died working in the cave, graves were dug for the Union soldiers. How would families of the men buried there ever know what happened to them? The miners went back to work, nervous other Union scouts could come upon them at any time.

Elizabeth put her foot down after the events of that late afternoon. James would not be allowed to go back to Tandy's Knob. "It's too dangerous," she told Johnny. "Besides, it's too much responsibility to put on a child."

"But they need me up there," James protested. "The scout said I saved the day."

Johnny rubbed James' head, telling him how proud he was. "You have done your job well today," he told James. "You need to stay off Tandy's Knob for a while. Maybe later you can help the scout again."

By 1864, even though there had been no major battles fought in the county, life had become more difficult for the families left behind by their soldier husbands and fathers. Food was scarce. Pickled or salt pork had become the main meat staple for the Preeces. Before the war, they would kill hogs in the fall and eat all winter from the hams and bacon curing in the smokehouse. Now soldiers and hungry deserters had taken most of the hogs. By the end of the growing season, soldiers from both sides would strip the cornfields, and carry away all the garden vegetables.

Johnny and Elizabeth had to find ways to hide food. They instructed the children to bury sweet potatoes, turnips, pumpkins, and dried corn under the house. They filled gourds with dried field peas and beans and buried them in the woods. They tried preserving the apples, but by the time the apples were ripe, marauders would strip the trees, leaving only rotten ones.

The leaves of the pokeberry plant became a main staple for the family in the spring. Elizabeth, Lillie and the children would search for the poisonous pokeberry plant near the edge of the woods and strip off its tender green leaves. They would boil the leaves through multiple waters until the poison was leached out, and then with a little hog lard, they would scramble the green leaves with chicken eggs, or with wild turkey eggs when they could find them.

Elizabeth remembered stories Fannie told her about how her Chickasaw mother had helped people in their village survive times of hunger. "We made hickory nut groat," she had said. So Elizabeth had the children collect hickory nuts in the woods and pick the sweet kernels from the thick hulls. She then crushed dried corn she had hidden away and mixed it with the crushed hickory nuts.

The children stayed sick most of the winter with colds and dysentery. Elizabeth treated them with Fannie's recipe for bitter tea made from the red berries of the wahoo bush and with hot sassafras tea. When William developed a large sore on his leg that would not go away, Elizabeth treated it with poultices of mustard powder wrapped tightly with strips of white sheeting. When anyone had croup, Elizabeth used Fannie's polecat grease recipe. To cure chills and fevers, she steeped snakeroot in hot water mixed with applejack brandy.

Before the war, looms and spinning wheels had been put aside and store-bought material had replaced homespun. Now, if the family were to be clothed, most of it had to be done by hand. Elizabeth and Lillie and the other women returned to looms and spinning wheels. Elizabeth had learned from Fannie how to spin wool, but she had never made cotton cloth. She quickly figured out how to cut patterns to make petticoats for the women and girls, and she made shirts of coarse homespun for the boys. Fannie had taught her how to make brown dye by boiling walnut bark, and purple dye from sumac berries. Thus she was able to add a touch of color to the family's garments.

Even before the war, the children went barefoot in the summer. But every year in the fall, the family went to Sparta to buy leather shoes. After the first year of the war, the children wore hand-me-downs until there were no shoes left. They no longer had money to buy shoes, even if they could be found. The shoe factory in Sparta was now making leather army boots for the Confederacy.

Elizabeth knew Johnny was smart in finding ways to solve problems, but she couldn't believe her eyes when he showed her shoes he had made for the children. He had carved wooden soles to fit each child, and wrapped each sole in dried deer skin, using deerskin strips to hold the wood and the deer skin together. "Maybe," he said, "these will keep little feet from freezing this winter."

Elizabeth was glad she and Lillie had spent long winter days and nights before the war using old dress pieces to make quilts, but by the end of the war, most of them had been stolen. Keeping the family warm in the winter was a challenge. Elizabeth kept the children busy cutting small trees and scavenging for firewood. Sometimes they would take a cord or two to Spencer to sell to people who had no way of getting fuel. More than once, Elizabeth instructed the children to give the firewood to an elderly couple down the road.

By late 1864, Elizabeth noticed more and more Union troops were coming through Bone Cave. Johnny came home one night and announced he thought the Yankees were getting too close. Everyone at the cave was on alert.

"A squadron of Federal cavalry and a wagon train is camped at Burritt College in Spencer," he said. "The soldiers are using the buildings for barracks, and the dormitories to stable their horses."

Johnny, Elizabeth, and Lillie, like everyone in Bone Cave, were weary of the war. Johnny struggled to hold his own at the cave. They were thankful no one in the family had been harmed. They had been able to protect themselves and the farm from hungry soldiers on both sides and drunken mountain marauders who would swoop down to take whatever they could find.

Johnny had taught Elizabeth and Lillie to shoot a rifle, and Isaac had practiced until he was an excellent marksman. Everybody in the family had a job to do. Isaac and Thomas were to keep watch for anyone approaching. Elizabeth and Lillie were to keep guns ready. James was back as a runner with the scout on Tandy's Knob, and was doing his own watching from there.

It was little William who, on one hot July day in 1864, came running into the house screaming and pulling at Elizabeth's apron. "Bad men! Bad men!" Elizabeth's heart raced as she watched two filthy men with long dirt-matted beards ride up to the edge of the porch. Lillie had latched and bolted the cabin's two doors, front and back. Isaac and Thomas had taken a rifle and hidden in a clump of trees behind the house.

"Celie," Elizabeth said, "take William with you up in the loft. And William, be as quiet as a mouse."

Elizabeth stood near the door with a butcher's cleaver in her hand, and Lillie stood beside her with a carving knife. A heavy fist pounded on the front door. The women stood frozen. Then a heavy foot kicked the door. The door held firm. Elizabeth held her finger to her lips to signal them to make no noise. They could hear the men move off the porch and then, in a instant, a large log Isaac had cut for firewood early that morning came through the door, making a hole big enough to get an arm or a leg through. Elizabeth brought the cleaver down hard. The first arm that came through the hole received a quick slash near the elbow. The wounded man swore and backed away, nursing his bleeding wound.

When the second intruder stuck his arm through the broken board trying to reach the inside latch, Elizabeth came down hard with the butcher's cleaver, cleanly taking off the end of his fingers. She watched from the window as he pulled back screaming. Maybe now they would go away. But no sooner had the thought crossed her mind than a thunderous blow sent the door flying, splintering it into pieces on the floor.

There was no time to aim rifles. One of the men hit Lillie across the face, knocking her to the floor. The other dragged Elizabeth by the hair to the side room and threw her across the bed. Celie and little William screamed from the loft above. Then Elizabeth heard a shot ring out in the main room, and another a second or two later. The man on the bed beside her jerked back and lay still. When she was able to focus, she saw Isaac frozen, his rifle still pointed at the man on the bed.

"It's okay, Isaac." Lillie said. "Let me have the gun."

By the end of the day, when Johnny and James came home, the bodies had been buried in the woods, and most of the blood had been cleaned away. Elizabeth suspected they would never be able to remove all the bloodstains, just as they would never be able to forget this terrible war. What a horrible thing for children to have to remember!

The family seldom attended church anymore. With most of the men away fighting the war, the women in the community saw no use in going to church. It was a long buggy-ride, and most of the community's horses and buggies had been conscripted for the Confederacy.

"I don't know why we should go to church," Lillie said to Elizabeth. "All the preacher does is talk about how evil the Yankees are, and how God is going to give the glorious Confederacy victory. I find no comfort in that. Somehow I get the feeling their God is not my God."

"I do think people are meaner since the war," Elizabeth said. "Don't you?"

SEVEN

The Last Indian

Bone Cave, Tennessee
1864-1869

In the fall of 1864, Johnny was barely able to work. He dragged himself from bed every morning, and Elizabeth wondered if he could make it through the day. She begged him to stop work and stay home. He was coughing constantly and losing weight, and his eyesight was so bad he was barely able to see.

Late one afternoon, while Elizabeth and the children were scouring the woods behind the cabin for hickory nuts, they heard a thunderous noise. "What was that, Mama?" Isaac asked. "Sounds like somebody shooting off a big cannon."

Elizabeth knew in an instant what it was. "It's the cave," she said. She had long dreaded this day. "Dear God, I've got to get down there. I've got to find James and Johnny. Hitch up the wagon, Isaac, and be quick about it."

Isaac hitched the mules to the wagon, and they all headed for Big Bone Cave. Even before they arrived, Elizabeth knew it was over. The Union soldiers had set off dynamite at the back cave entrance. How had they managed to escape the lookouts? Good Lord! She thought. James went up on Tandy's Knob this morning! Please God, let him still be up there!

When they reached the top of the hill overlooking the cave, they could see workers pouring out the entrance, gasping for air. The miners emerged, coughing and spitting. Union soldiers arrested them and put them in chains. Elizabeth strained to see if Johnny came out, but she couldn't see him.

"Lillie," she said. "You and the children stay up here. I've got to go in."

"Be careful!" Lillie admonished.

"Just keep the children away," Elizabeth said. "Isaac, you come with me. I may need you." No one tried to stop Elizabeth and Isaac as they plowed through the smoke and the confusion. They entered the cave and made their way through the rubble among the broken vats and twisted pipes. In an alcove near the back entrance, they found Johnny. One of his men knelt beside him.

"He was a brave man," he said to Elizabeth. "He stayed behind to make sure we got out safe."

They found James near the foot of Tandy's Knob. He was sitting against a tree on the path in tears. "It's all my fault!" he said over and over. The scout was with him, trying to reassure him.

"There was nothing you could do," the scout said. "It wasn't your fault. We both tried. There was no time. Besides, how could we know they would come in from the rear? Look, your mother has come for you."

Weeks later, Elizabeth and the children, exhausted from grieving, took flowers to the entrance of the cave and stood for a long time in silence. The scout stood with them. Elizabeth had been comforted that first day when the tall Indian had come to speak to her of Johnny's bravery in the cave and about James being a good boy. She surprised herself by inviting him to stay a while with them. He seemed so familiar. Where had she seen him before? He agreed, as long as he could work to earn his keep. "I will sleep in the barn," he said. "I will stay until it is time for me to leave."

"What should we call you?" Elizabeth asked.

"Greenberry," he said.

*   *   *

When the war ended in the spring of 1865, no brass bands or cheering crowds greeted the shabbily dressed soldiers returning home. Solomon had come home a few months before the end of the war with a leg missing, and like most of the returnees, he tended to keep to himself. People began looking for places to live outside the valley. Their farms and businesses had been destroyed.

Greenberry helped the boys keep the farm operating. James, in particular, spent every waking moment with him. In 1866 when the spring plowing and planting was finished, Greenberry told Elizabeth the time had come for him to leave. James was crestfallen. "Why are you going away?" he asked.

"It is time," Greenberry replied.

"Will you ever come back?"

"Yes, I will come back."

"When? When will you come back?" asked James

"When you see me coming over the hill," replied Greenberry.

"You promised to tell me more stories," James reminded him. "And you said some day you would take me to Cedar Mountain where you lived when you were a boy. You said you would take me with you and show me all about caves."

"When I come back," Greenberry said.

James watched him until he disappeared over the hill.

Greenberry, true to his word, returned every fall for the next five years. He would work over the winter and into the spring, and then disappear again until the next fall. He came to be known to some as the last Indian in the county. Some called him "the vanishing half-breed."

Bitterness and anger about the war permeated the Bone Cave community. Many held grudges against the few freed slaves, most of whom left the area, fearful of what the Ku Klux Klan might do to them. Elizabeth tried to help the children understand why the war was fought. It was not an easy task, as she wasn't sure she understood it herself.

"Here in Bone Cave," she told them, "we didn't know much about slavery. There were few big plantations that used slave labor in the whole of the county. People here were too poor to afford slaves, even if they thought they needed them. But around Sparta and McMinnville, some people did keep slaves. Slavery is wrong, and now that the war is over, there can be no more slavery. That may be the only good thing to come out of this war."

"Why did the soldiers come after us, if we didn't have slaves?" James asked.

Elizabeth knew James did not always hear the entire message—just bits and pieces. "All we need to remember," said Elizabeth, "is that President Lincoln has freed all the slaves. Now we need to get on with our lives."

"It's not fair," James said. "We didn't keep slaves, so how come we got beat?" He couldn't understand why they had to be punished because someone else did something bad.

"Life is not always fair," she replied. "War hurts everybody, not just bad people."

It seemed to Elizabeth that everywhere she went, someone was complaining about something. Some men resented that former slaves were now allowed to vote when they themselves couldn't. Farmers complained they couldn't work their farms because they were forced to rebuild roads. Money was scarce. If people had been poor before the war, they were even poorer after.

Lillie died of pneumonia in January of 1869. Celie married and Isaac left home looking for work. Thomas found a job mining coal on the mountain at Ravenscroft, a few miles east of Sparta. He continued to live at home. Even though his income was meager, he gave it to his mother to help the family manage. With James, Thomas, and William still at home, Elizabeth had three to feed besides herself, and, for months at a time, four with Greenberry.

When Robert Shelby, who owned the next farm over, proposed marriage to Elizabeth, she agreed. His wife had died in childbirth three months before and left him with three children to raise. He offered Elizabeth more security with his farm and a larger house. She felt she had little choice. She hoped that merging their assets would mean a better life for them all.

"He promised he would take care of all of us," Elizabeth told James.

"All he wants is somebody to take care of his own young'uns," James said. James wanted no part of Robert Shelby and his brood.

James turned fifteen that spring. He remembered the days when his father was alive. His mother was happy then, he thought. Now she was sad and tired-looking all the time. He knew it was because of his father's death. If only he had warned them in time, maybe his father would still be alive. Since his death, a nightmare about running down the mountain to warn his father had plagued James. In the dream his legs moved, but they moved too slowly. A loud explosion in the dream always woke him.

He felt the need to get away. "When the spring planting is done," he told his mother, "Greenberry has promised he will take me with him to explore caves. He says we'll go over the mountains to the place where he was born."

When the day arrived, Elizabeth offered no resistance. She knew how much James had come to depend on Greenberry. She knew she could rely on Greenberry to keep her son out of trouble. She also knew James was leaving home for the last time. She kissed him and pressed a few coins in his hand. Taking the flute from its peg over the door and placing the deerskin string around his neck, she said, "Keep safe, and come back soon."

"I will, Mama," James promised.

BOOK III

The Fraleys of Ulster
and
Hannah's People

1800-1833

One must never accept injustices as commonplace, but must fight them with all one's strength. This fight begins, however, in the heart.

—James Baldwin
Notes of a Native Son

ONE

Henry and Clary

Rutherford County, North Carolina
The early 1800s

As early as 1705, the Virginia Assembly had decreed: "The child of an Indian and the child, grandchild, or great-grandchild of a negro shall be deemed, accounted, held, and taken to be a mulatto." North Carolina and Tennessee soon followed with similar laws, dividing people into two colors: black and white. By the time Henry Fraley and Clary had their first child in 1817 and announced their intention to marry, it was a well-established rule in Virginia, North Carolina, and Tennessee that a white person could not marry a person with black blood, even one drop.

Henry was the second son of Scots-Irish parents, Thomas Fraley and Polly Wilson. His Quaker grandparents, Alexander and Catherine Fraley, had migrated to Virginia from Ulster with their children in 1774, finally settling near Jonesborough, Tennessee, on the Nolichucky River. Despite his parents' objections, Henry's father Thomas had signed up to fight with the Overmountain men against the British. When the war ended, Thomas received a 650-acre land grant in North Carolina and settled there with his wife Polly in what later became Rutherford County.

Clary was the daughter of the mixed-blood slave woman Claracy and the Scots-Irish plantation owner Buncombe Wallace. In her veins flowed the blood of an Indian woman from the Yuchi tribe in middle Tennessee, a Portuguese sailor who came to Tennessee with De Soto, an African tribesman sold as a slave in South Carolina, and more than one white Southern planter.

During her early years, Clary lived partly in the big house with the Fraleys and partly in the slave quarters. By the time she was ten, Clary was helping Polly take care of five children, one of whom was Henry, born in 1796. Henry was Clary's favorite. She became more of a mother to him than Polly, who had become tired and disinterested in children after her sixth child was born. Clary was the one who rocked Henry to sleep at night, and often when she tried to put him in his cradle, he would cry for her to pick him up. "Ah, child," she would sigh. "You spoiled."

When he was hungry, he would nuzzle her breast searching for milk. "I'm not your mammy, honey," she whispered, "but I love you better than your own mammy does. And I ain't got no milk, but I'll take you to Lucinda. She won't mind nursing you."

Henry clung to Clary constantly. No matter what she was doing, she had him with her. For most of the day while doing her chores, she carried Henry, his legs wrapped around her thin hips, his arms clinging to her shoulders. When Polly taught her children what little she knew about reading, Clary sat beside Henry and the rest of the children. Henry often slept with Clary on her pallet in the cabin she shared with the slave girl Selina, and sometimes Clary slept with Henry in the big house. They moved easily between the farmhouse and the slave cabins without much notice.

By the age of ten, Henry was learning the skills of blacksmithing and wagon-making from Isaac, one of the seven slaves owned by Henry's father. Patiently, he showed Henry how to cut and cure the long, straight hickory saplings to make wagon tongues and how to make the spokes and, using the intense heat of the smithy fire, he showed him how to shape the metal tires for the wheels. In a few years, Henry absorbed most of what Isaac could teach him, and became almost as proficient as his mentor.

When Polly overheard her two kitchen slaves gossiping about Henry and Clary, she decided it did not look quite right for a sixteen-year-old girl to be sleeping with a ten-year-old boy, so she decided to separate them, at least at night. She told Clary to sleep in the slave quarters, and made Henry sleep in the house. The separation didn't work. Henry would slip out of the house at night and end up on the pallet with Clary in her cabin. At last Polly gave up trying to separate them. Instead, she opted to ignore the relationship, hoping Henry would "grow out of it."

By the time Henry was seventeen and Clary was twenty-three, they were still living together in the slave cabin. When their first child, Clara, was born in 1817, neither Polly nor Thomas wanted to acknowledge the birth. But by the time the second child, Orpha, was born in 1819, they had given up trying to separate Henry and Clary. As they had come to accept Clary as part of the family, they admitted their love for their two little granddaughters, Clara and Orpha. Still, they couldn't help wondering if things might have been different if they had acted earlier.

"It was our fault that we let it happen," she told Thomas.

It was when Henry announced he wanted to marry Clary that Thomas and Polly realized how complicated life had become. "We love Clary, but you can't marry her," Thomas told his son. "By law she's a mulatto, a squaw."

Clary had warned Henry they wouldn't be allowed to marry, and even if they did marry, no one would accept them as husband and wife. But Henry was determined. When he approached the preacher about it, he was informed it would be not be possible under any circumstances.

"Even if I wanted to marry the two of you, I couldn't," the preacher said. "I am prohibited by law from performing interracial marriages, and even though she may not look it, she's black."

"But Clary ain't black," Henry insisted. "She's mostly Indian and white."

"That don't make no difference. In the eyes of the law, she's still black. She counts as a mulatto, and there's nothing anybody can do about it."

The preacher dismissed Henry with a doleful look.

On the next Sunday morning, Henry waited until his father and mother and brothers and sisters had left for the church. "Let's go to church, Clary," he said.

"You know we can't go to church together," Clary protested. "We'll be throwed out. You go on. I'll stay here with the children."

"Put on your best dress and get the children ready," Henry told her. "We're going to church together."

Clary washed Clara and Orpha's faces and had them put on the identical yellow flowered cotton dresses she and Polly had made for them. She then pulled out an indigo dress Polly had given her on her birthday. She brushed her chestnut-colored hair back, trying to make even the slightest curl go away. Today she knew the church members would be staring, trying to figure out just how much black blood she had. Henry insisted she wear a pair of Polly's shoes. "You can't go barefoot to church," he told her.

At the door of the church, Henry, in his father's hand-me-down black frock-tail coat, took Clary's hand and led her and the children to a pew midway down the aisle. The preacher was leading the congregation in a song, and by the time they had reached the last verse, the parishioners in the back of the church had begun to whisper. Those in the front turned around to see what was going on, and soon the whispering spread throughout the congregation.

The preacher looked at Henry and Clary for a long moment, and was about to instruct the congregation to rise for the benediction, when Henry stood up. "I have something to say," he announced.

Startled, the preacher managed a smile and said, "You go right ahead, Henry." A hush fell over the congregation.

"This morning," Henry went on, "I want you all to witness a marriage. The preacher won't perform it. The government won't recognize it. But I want you to know that, in the eyes of God, Clary and me are husband and wife. We always have been. We always will be. Nothing any of you can say or do can change that. Soon we're leaving this place and going across the mountain to Tennessee. We can't live here anymore. I know some of you think we've been living in sin, but where is the sin in these two beautiful little girls God has blessed us with? I defy any one of you to say otherwise. Who wants to cast the first stone?"

"This is all your fault, Thomas Fraley!" came a voice from the congregation. "And yours, Polly Fraley! You should have put a stop to this years ago. The sin is upon your head!" Thomas and Polly sat frozen to their pew. A part of them knew the woman was right. The congregation was abuzz again, whispering, nodding agreement, wanting to see Henry punished.

"Listen!" Henry called over the hubbub. "Listen to me! Clary, the children, and I will be waiting at the door to receive congratulations or whatever else you want to offer.

"Come, Clary. Come children." Hand in hand, they walked to the back of the church and stood waiting. Most walked past them without a word. Two or three shook Henry's hand, kissed Clary and the children, and wished them all well in Tennessee

Thomas and Polly waited until the church was empty before they stood to file out. As they passed, Henry could see the rage on his father's face. Polly remained speechless, her expression a mixture of disbelief and heartbreak. Never would they have thought this could happen.

Clary thought about how Polly had always been kind to her, maybe even loved her. Now that love seemed to be waning. How could the world turn around so suddenly? Clary knew she and Henry couldn't continue to live on the farm. Henry was right. If they were to live together, they would have to go somewhere far away. Maybe in Tennessee, things would be different.

It was not only white people in the community who had objected to their relationship. For years, Clary had endured the disapproval of the other slaves on the farm. They taunted her with, "You a half-breed mulatto squaw and your daddy's white. Jes' because you look white don't make you white. Ain't nothin' good gonna come of you keepin' on livin' with Master Henry." She could handle their disapproval, but she couldn't live with Polly's rejection. She was also sure Polly and Thomas knew where she came from. She must make them tell her. She had to know.

"The only thing I know," Polly told her, "is that Buncombe Wallace brought you here from his plantation just across the state line in South Carolina when you were only a few days old. He wanted us to take you. I wanted you the moment I saw you. I had just lost my first child, and you were such a beautiful baby. I've loved you since that day, and I still love you now. You're like my own."

"I want to know about my mama," Clary said. "Who was she? I need to know before we leave for Tennessee. Please, I need to know now."

Polly squirmed in her chair. "I don't remember anyone telling me about your mother." Clary looked at her for a long moment. Clary knew she had to know more. Then Polly said, as if the thought had just occurred to her, "Yes, I do recall that Buncombe Wallace told us your name was Clary, and I believe, if I remember correctly, he said your mama's name was Claracy."

TWO

Hannah

Cowpens, South Carolina
May 1823

Clary told Henry she could not go to Tennessee until she went to the Wallace plantation. If her mother was there, she wanted to see her. Henry knew the one person who would know more about neighboring plantations than anyone else was Isaac. Isaac had been with the Fraleys for years. He had built the two wagons that had brought the Fraleys to North Carolina. Not only had he served as their blacksmith, he had often shod horses for people traveling through the area. If anyone knew who to ask about Clary's mother, it would be Isaac.

"Mistress Wallace die a few years back," Isaac said, "and the master married a younger woman. The one you want to hear from is a slave woman name of Hannah. She know everything about the goings-on at the Wallace plantation. She been the Wallace's kitchen woman from way back. If I's you, I'd go there without Master Wallace knowing it. Something ain't right on that plantation. They say Mistress Wallace touched in the head toward the last. Some say she didn't die a natural death. Some say she kill herself. Some say she was poisoned."

At sunup, Henry hitched the mules to the wagon, and he and Clary headed south to the Wallace plantation, a full day's journey from the Fraley farm, across the line in South Carolina. The sun was setting beyond the mountains as they neared the Wallace place. Henry stopped the wagon in the woods near a creek a good distance from the house and waited until dark.

Finally, when all was still except the crickets and frogs, and the big house was dark, Henry and Clary crept to the slave quarters. There were fifteen or so slave cabins, but only one had a dim light coming from under the door. Henry waited in the dark while Clary tapped lightly. A young woman came to the door.

"I'm looking for Hannah," Clary said.

The door opened wide enough for Clary to see a candle flickering on the table.

"She down a ways. Four cabins down."

Clary hoped Henry was staying near. She certainly did not want to run into Buncombe Wallace. She approached the darkened cabin and knocked, at first timidly and then a little harder. This must be the right cabin, she thought. She had begun to doubt it when the door opened, and she heard a woman's voice, "What you want?"

"Are you Hannah?"

"What you want to know for?"

"I'm looking for a woman named Claracy."

"Who are you?"

"My name is Clary, and I stay at the Fraley farm over in North Carolina. The Fraley's smithy Isaac said you might know about my mother."

The woman whisked Clary into the cabin. "Lawsy, child, I do believe you my grandbaby! I *knows* you is! Bless Jesus! My prayers been answered!"

Hannah lit a small candle and moved it up and down Clary's body. "Law, child, you look the spittin' image of you mammy. Are you as light as she was? I can't see good in this light."

Clary could hardly believe her good fortune. For a moment, she felt unable to speak. Then her questions came pouring out. "Can you tell me about my mama? Where is she? How come I was taken to the Fraleys when I was a baby?"

"Whoa, child! I too old to cipher all that at once." Hannah stopped talking for a moment and placed her finger over her lips. "Shh," she whispered. "Somebody might hear."

She guided Clary to the small pallet in the corner and blew out the candle. "Lay down, child. Lay here beside me, and let me tell you where you come from."

Clary lay beside her grandmother in the dark.

"Our peoples go way back," she began. "Our grandmammies and grandpappies were here a long time before these white folks come. One of you grandmammies was a Yuchi Indian and one of you grandpappies was a Portugee sailor."

"How do you know that?" Clary whispered.

"Well, my mammy tole *me* her mammy tole *her* about this man called Soto. He come from way yonder in a foreign land. He had some Portugee sailors with him and they was all a-lookin' for gold. They stopped off in this Indian village in Tennessee to rest a few days. When Soto ready to leave, some of his Portugee sailors didn't want to go, so Soto left 'em with their women, and after a while they had little Portugee and Indian babies. One of them babies was our way-back grandmammy."

"That story happened too long ago," said Clary. "What I want to know is how come I ended up at the Fraley place?"

"Well," said Hannah, "I'm a-comin' to that. But first you need to hear the whole story. Many, many years after Soto, one of our grandmammies was still a-livin' in this same Indian village in Tennessee. Them people, the Yuchi, was the first people here, even before the Cherokee. They got attack by the Cherokee, and the story tol' me was that them peoples in that village all decided to kill theirselves to keep the Cherokees from taking them prisoner. All but this one woman, our kin. She didn't want to die, so she taken her baby and run as hard as she could."

"Where did she go?"

"Well, she hid from the slavers for a week or so afore they caught her. She were too weak to run. The slavers sold her to a South Carolina planter name of Long, and he took her to work on his plantation. For many years, my own mammy and her mammy and me lived on the Long plantation. We stayed 'til after I had Claracy. The Longs didn't have no children, and the plantation was gettin' all run-down. Most of the good bottom land had done been sold off. When the master died, the mistress sold all the slaves, all 'cept my mammy and grandmammy. She let my grandmammy stay in the little cabin 'cause she was too old to sell. They let my mammy stay to take care of the mistress, but they wouldn't let Claracy and me stay.

"That were a sad day when we had to leave them there. It jes' break my heart to know it'd be the last time I'd ever see them. Your mammy Claracy was just a young girl when they put her and me on the auction block. At least they let us be sold together. Most of the time, they don't care. I was glad to leave the Long place. It'd been a terrible time, 'specially when the old master could still get around. He was about the meanest man I ever seen. He would make us women do things we didn't want to do—bad things. Everybody on the plantation was afraid of him, and we was all glad when he died."

"Was he my grandpappy?"

Hannah's voice dropped almost to a whisper. "Yes," she said. "You got to understand, child, some masters want womens with light complexions, and some don't. But Long, he did. An' so did Buncombe Wallace. The lighter, the better. That was my downfall, mine and your mammy's. We both got slim noses and light color like you."

Clary understood. She knew she had that slim nose and light complexion, and she had hazel eyes—blue and green and brown all mixed together.

"So Buncombe Wallace is my pappy?"

"Honey," Hannah said, "Maybe we just plain unlucky. Buncombe Wallace spotted you mammy when she was thirteen on that auction block in South Carolina. He was willing to pay any price for her. He bought us both for twenty-five hundred dollars, the highest bid any slaver made that day. I was glad he bought us together. I didn't want my Claracy tooken from me. I knowed my child would need somebody to protect her. But in the end, there wasn't nothin' I could do when Buncombe Wallace come to our cabin at night and make me leave. Claracy beg him to leave her alone, but he wouldn't.

"I think Mistress Betsy suspected what was going on, but she didn't say anything at first. She weren't right in the head, you know. Sometimes she ack like she sweet as sweet could be, and sometimes she the very old devil. She would fly into hissy fits and chase us around the place with a broom or whatever she could find, even the poker. She'd slam us over the head iffen she caught us. One time she purt' near kilt me. She whup me with a razor strop 'til I lost my breath. When I begged her to stop, she just went at me harder. Law, she could be the very old devil hisself. A few days after it was over, she come puttin' grease on my cuts and bruises and sayin' she was sorry. She was pure crazy!"

"What's that got to do with my mama?" Clary asked.

Hannah hesitated, drew a long breath and said, "Ah, child, you gittin ahead of me. At first, Mistress Betsy liked yo' mammy. She knew you mammy was smart, and she make her the head of the weaving room over the two other weavers. You mammy got to be a real good weaver. She taken the cotton and the wool and her and the other two womens wove blankets and cloth for winter clothes. The weavin' room was full of looms and spinning wheels, and the mistress herself would sit at a loom some days all day long. Course she didn't do no spinnin' or weavin', but she told you mammy she loved to hear the clackin' sound of the loom and to watch the way the shuttles run in and out carryin' their long tails of colored thread. She said she loved to hear you mammy and the other women a-singin' with their feets a-peddlin' and their hands a-workin' the bobbin.

"Sometimes the mistress could ack like she jes' as sweet as sugar. One time she even throwed a big wedding party for one of the slave girls. She had me and Sukie bake a big white wedding cake. She had us set tables out in the yard under the trees and spread 'em with white sheets. An' she invite everybody on the place. It was Saturday and the field hands' had the day off. It was all a-goin' fine 'til she spied Master Wallace talkin' with you mammy, and she jes' blew up. Before it was over, she was yellin' and screamin' and rippin' that dress off that woman and smackin' her in the face. Then she turn on me, claimin' I was tryin' to poison her. She sent for the razor strop, and right there in front of everybody, she beat me black and blue an' wouldn't quit 'til Master Wallace stop her."

"What did you do?" asked Clary.

"What *could* I do? She the mistress. She can do anything she want to, and I hafta take it. But don't you worry none. She got hers. She dead and gone, and she can't hurt nobody no more."

"How'd she die?" Clary asked.

"She was jes' too mean to live. When she find out you mammy big with you, she figger Master Wallace the daddy. She throw Claracy out the weaving room and make her go work with the field hands. She tell Master that if you come out lookin' like him, she gonna sell you both. And that jes' what she did.

"I won't never forget that day they come to the cabin to take you away from us. You mammy holler and scream and hold you tight against her breast. I fall on my knees and pray to Jesus. I beg the master not to take you away from you mammy. It took the master and the mistress and two field slaves to pull you away from her. I was afraid they'd kill you trying to pull you apart. Then the master took you off in the wagon and didn't come back for two days. The next day after he come back, they sell you mammy to a slaver from South Carolina. Not long after that, the mistress took to her bed and died. Some say she couldn't stand to live and killed herself. Some say somebody poisoned her."

There was a long silence. Clary broke it with, "Do you think she was poisoned?"

"It's a-comin' daylight," Hannah said. "You'd best be goin' before that sun come up. You wouldn't want to run into Master Wallace. No tellin' what he'd do if he found you on the place. Buncombe Wallace a bad man, but don' you never think his bad ways rub off on you. You yo' mammy's chile, and she the sweetest and the best that ever drew a breath. Right up to the time they took her away, she thought of nothin' but you. She wouldn't say nothin' to nobody but me, and she wouldn't eat a thing. She sat on the bed in the cabin, holdin' her arms tight against her chest, jes' like she was still holdin' you. She sho' did love you, child. We never did know what happened to you. Some said the Mistress had you killed, but I knowed in my heart you still alive somewheres. And, now, bless Jesus, I can meet my Maker knowing you's all right."

Dawn was breaking as Clary and Henry set out for the Fraley farm. They rode a long way in silence. Finally, Henry asked, "Did you find out what you wanted to know?"

Clary began to cry. "I met my granny, and she told me lots of things, some I wanted to know, and some I didn't." She wiped her eyes with the hem of her dress. "Before today, I didn't even know I had a granny. I still don't know where my mama is, but I know she loved me, and that's enough. Now I'm ready to go to Tennessee!" Henry smiled, put his arm around her, and gave the mules free rein.

"Henry, what did you do all night waiting for me?"

"Aw, I just lay in the wagon hoping you were all right. Once or twice I dropped off, but I was afraid the horses would make too much noise, and we'd be found out."

"Did you ever wonder if it wouldn't have been better for you if we had not ended up together?"

"No," he said. "I knew from the beginning we was meant for each other."

"And my mixed color don't matter to you?"

"Never has, and when we move over the mountain, nobody needs to know. It'll be easier for everybody that way."

Clary leaned toward him and said, "Henry, I learned something else today."

"What's that?" Henry asked.

She smiled up at him with fresh tears in her eyes. "How very lucky I am to have you."

THREE

On to Tennessee

Rutherford County, North Carolina
May 1823

Henry and Clary had no doubts about their decision to leave for Tennessee. After the episode in the church, they knew they could no longer live in the community. It was not just the church people making life uncomfortable for the Fraleys. Outsiders were beginning to cause trouble as well. The crowning blow came with the burning of one of Thomas's cattle barns. They awoke one night to the whooping and hollering of drunken marauders who had swooped down from the nearby hills swearing to rid the county of "nigga luvahs." The young heifers Thomas had recently purchased were rescued, but the barn was completely razed. Will it be the house next time? Thomas wondered.

That night in the light of the torches, Thomas recognized some of the sheriff's men, and he knew it would do no good to report the burning. He remembered hearing how corrupt the early county governments in the Carolinas had been. The Tory-run government had appointed all the county officials, including the sheriff and his deputies. Answering only to the English crown, they had quickly become corrupt. They levied high taxes, collected the money, and pocketed it. A group of frontier farmers calling themselves the Regulators had banded together to address citizen complaints, but they soon became just as corrupt as the county officials, and were finally chased over the mountains into Tennessee by irate citizens.

Thomas had real reservations about their future on the farm. "It's hard enough to raise corn and get it to the mill," he said to Polly. "It's hard enough to drive cattle south to Charleston, and everything else I have to do without having to deal with backward-thinking barnburners and closed-minded religious bigots. It's nobody's business how I run my life!" In the end he knew it was something he would simply have to contend with. He found himself wishing he had taken his family over to middle Tennessee three years before when his brother Alexander went there to buy some of the good, cheap land they had heard was available.

Isaac helped Henry load the wagon. The items they selected to take along included an axe, two Kentucky rifles, and one of every tool on the place, including blacksmithing tools. With Thomas' blessing, Isaac helped Henry load the smaller of the two anvils from the smithy shop. Clary and Polly packed salt, corn meal, flour, fatback, corn, dried apples, and other staples. To maximize sitting space, pots and pans were suspended from the bands that held the canvas across the top of the wagon. Henry took two sacks of dried corn for the two wagon mules and the two riding horses. Clary packed two trunks—one for the girls and one for her and Henry. She used the clothing to wrap the dishes Polly had given her.

Thomas gave Henry one hundred dollars, and said, "Maybe you can make a living 'smithing and making wagons somewhere in Tennessee. If that fails, I guess you can always farm."

When faced with the finality of Henry and Clary's decision, Polly decided it didn't really matter what people thought. She just didn't care anymore what those old biddies in the church said behind her back. Gossips! She was sure there was a verse in the Bible that condemned gossips, but she couldn't remember where it was. She knew she was very tired of kow-towing to them, and she knew she didn't want Henry, Clary, and the girls to leave, no matter what anybody thought.

Clary was like one of her own. She had raised her from a baby. "When all is said and done," she told Thomas, "they are our children, *both* Henry and Clary, and I love them." Polly couldn't imagine them taking her little granddaughters way yonder across the rugged mountains. "There are panthers and bears and who knows what else," she said to Thomas. "I've heard about entire families being killed in those mountains, and others who've had everything they owned stolen by bandits."

Polly realized she might never see Clary and Henry and the girls again. She begged them not to go. "We've made it together this long," she told them. "We can survive if we stay together. I beg you please, stay here with us."

Thomas remained quiet as Henry and Clary prepared to leave. He knew it was the right thing for them to do. The longer they stayed, the more likely other nastiness would happen. He also knew that, whether they stayed or left, things could get pretty dangerous for everyone concerned. He took the hunting rifle down from the wall pegs above the fireplace, made sure it was loaded, and placed it under the bed.

The next morning, May 10, 1823, there were no tears shed and no fanfare. Even the horses stood in silence as if they understood the seriousness of the occasion. Isaac made a kissing sound signaling the mules to pull the wagon out of the barn. Recognizing the inevitable, Polly had baked fresh biscuits, corn bread, and teacakes for the journey. She hugged each of her granddaughters an extra long time, and told them not to eat the teacakes all at once. Six-year-old Clara promised she wouldn't, but four-year-old Orpha giggled, and Polly knew the teacakes wouldn't last long.

After Polly said goodbye, she ran to the garden behind the house to cry alone. Life is so unfair, she thought. Whoever or whatever designed this world gave no thought to the suffering mothers and grandmothers must endure. Mothers carry and give birth to children. They feed and clothe and care for them. They are allowed to have them for a little while, but then must watch them fly away, like the nesting hummingbirds in the spring. Do bird mothers feel the same pain when their fledglings fly away? There does seem to be less singing after the little birds have gone. What will I do now that the children have left? At least, I can hold my memories close. I'll remember the antics of my little granddaughters. I'll miss them, even if they sometimes go too far. Orpha, especially, seems to know no boundaries. Polly listened for the noise of the wagon on the road.

Orpha yells beyond the barnyard, "Please, Granny! Help us! Grandpa is after us with a switch. He's gonna whup the daylights outta us. He said so!"

"Law child, what have you done this time? No matter. Just run as fast as you can for the smokehouse. Maybe he won't look for you in there."

Thomas' eyes blaze, his voice trembles, "Where are they, Polly?"

Can't tell on the girls. "What did they do, Thomas?"

"They done gone and ruint durn near all the watermelons in the patch—more than fifty of 'em. Ever last one busted wide open. They gonna get it now!"

Can't protect them this time. This time they've really gone too far. "Aw, Thomas, let 'em be. They're just children."

"I'll find them, so you might as well tell me where they are."

He stomps down the path towards the smokehouse. Orpha and Clara peek through the chinked cracks and watch him.

Clara whines, "It's all your fault, Orpha! You all time getting us in trouble." Orpha puts her hand over Clara's mouth as Thomas comes nearer.

Orpha's watermelon party hasn't turned out as she expected. They hadn't meant to bust every watermelon. "Honest, Grandma, we didn't mean to bust up all them melons, but they was all green. We just knowed the next one had to be ripe, so we just kept on."

The girls squeal now. Thomas has found them. Peach tree switches hurt, but not as bad as his old razor-strop.

The rattle of wagon wheels jolted her from her reverie. She could hear the sound of the clanging pots and pans getting farther and farther away. "I wish I'd been a better mother—and a better grandmother," she said to Thomas that night.

"Nobody could ever say you didn't take care of your family," he said. She was glad Thomas was there to give her solace, though she knew Thomas in his own quiet way was just as sad and worried as she was. He, too, must be wondering how long the rest of the family can hold out in this place.

Henry had no map to guide them north over the mountains into Tennessee, but Thomas had given him general directions. Describing the route he had taken across the Blue Ridge with the Overmountain men, he reminded Henry he must follow the trail in reverse. "Remember, Henry," he said, "I was coming from Jonesborough, same as your grandpa did. You'll be heading in the opposite direction."

Henry was drawn to Jonesborough, in part, because of his Quaker grandparents. They had been at odds with Henry's father, not only because he had run off to the war, but also because he kept slaves. "I wish I had known my grandparents," Henry said to Clary. "I think we would have seen eye to eye on many things."

Just before they left for Tennessee, the preacher gave Henry a dog-eared copy of a an anti-slavery newspaper, the *Emancipator*. A Quaker named Elihu Embree had published it four years earlier in Jonesborough. With great excitement, Henry read the paper from cover to cover, delighted to see his own anti-slavery convictions reflected there. It told how Embree had come as a boy from Pennsylvania with his father. As a young man, he owned slaves until 1812 when he underwent a change of heart and joined the Society of Friends at Fairview, near Jonesborough. Shortly after, he became an ardent worker in the cause of abolition. Henry was also pleased to see an advertisement for Embree's Iron Works. "If they're still there, maybe they can use a man with my skills," he told Clary. "I want to meet this man Elihu Embree."

Except for stops to relieve themselves and to water the mules and horses, the first leg of the trip had been uneventful. By midday they had reached McDowell's Station, and Orpha was complaining of stomachache. When Clary asked about the teacakes Polly had sent along with them, neither Orpha nor Clara would comment. Orpha didn't feel like talking, and Clara remained tight-lipped, afraid of incurring Orpha's wrath. Clary wished she had kept a tighter watch on the teacakes. That Orpha, she thought, is going to be something to contend with!

By noon, the road had taken them down the Catawba River Valley past Linville Mountain to their right and Black Mountain to their left. Bypassing the village of Linville, they stopped for the night just outside the town of Marion. Henry dreaded the next several days crossing the mountainous terrain. Thomas had warned him about the narrow, steep, and winding mountain roads. They would need a good night's rest before undertaking the next leg of the journey.

During the long laborious hours over the Blue Ridge, Clary found herself thinking about Thomas and Polly back on the farm, especially about Polly. Clary wished she had told her how much she appreciated her. Did I thank her enough for the spinning wheel? There was precious little space for it in the wagon, but Clary had been glad to get it. "Teach the girls how to spin and weave," Polly had told her. "They need to learn how to make their own clothes. Here, take this pair of wool cards, too."

Many nights she and Polly had worked at the loom after everyone else was asleep. Polly had taught Clary how to dye the thread to get just the right color. Clary remembered her grandma Hannah saying her mama Claracy had been the best weaver on the Wallace plantation, and Clary wondered if she could ever be as good a weaver as her mother.

She would always cherish the quilt Polly gave her as they were about to leave. One of her most comforting memories was of working with Polly around the quilting frame with the children sitting underneath, playing Little Mary Mack. "Put your hands straight up facing my hands," she remembered Orpha telling Clara. "Clap your hands together and then slide them down. Now do that at the same time you say the story. You have to say it fast, though."

> *Little Mary Mack dressed in black*
> *Silver buttons up and down her back*
> *Combed her hair with Mama's comb*
> *I'll tell Mama when she comes home.*

Yes, she would someday tell Polly how much she loved her, that is, if her little family survived this journey, and if she were fortunate enough ever to see Polly again. She could see Clara and Orpha in the wagon, their little hands clapping together in rhythm. How sad it was neither of them would ever see their great-grandma Hannah. She couldn't imagine what it must have been like living on the Wallace plantation. After hearing her grandma's story, she wondered how they had all survived.

"You're sayin' it too slow!" she heard Orpha cry. "You can't do nothin' right!" Clary knew before the game was over, Clara would be in tears, and Orpha would pretend to feel sorry for her. Where did she get that little sassy, mean streak?

Clary wished she had not left her grandma so soon that morning on the Wallace plantation. It had all been unreal, a dream, that night she had lain beside Hannah in the dark listening to her story. She had heard about the mistreatment of slaves on other plantations, but she had never witnessed it on the Fraley farm. They only had seven slaves, and they prided themselves on being good masters. How could there be such a thing as a good master? Slavery is wrong, she thought. No one has a right to own another person. She was glad they were headed over the mountains to Tennessee, where Henry said there were people who wanted to see all the slaves freed. Life has got be better over the mountain, she thought.

FOUR

Trouble on the Mountain

Roan Mountain
May 1823

Clary was glad they had waited until the middle of May to set out. Blackberry winter was almost over, and it was getting warmer. Still, the roads in the mountains would likely be muddy and harder to travel with all the spring rains. They passed blackberry canes blooming along the edge of the road and stopped at meandering streams and water falls for fresh water. As they climbed higher, the trees seemed to grow taller. Oaks, hickories, pines, and maples dwarfed the wagon.

Henry noticed some places along the way where hunters had used fire to clear the underbrush, making it easier to find wild game. Perhaps that was a good omen for his own hunting. He would keep a close lookout for rabbits and squirrels. Henry felt a strange uneasiness. Perhaps he was simply over-reacting to unaccustomed surroundings, but he dreaded facing the mountain ahead of them. On the farm, he could see for miles down row after row of rolling cornfields. If a storm came up, he could see the clouds gathering in the distance and be prepared for the wind and rain. Here in the mountains, dark clouds seemed to appear suddenly from nowhere, and there was no time to prepare for the flashes of lightning, the rumbling thunder, and the pelting rain. Henry dreaded nights in the mountains.

Henry and Clary agreed to take turns sleeping, and they kept a fire burning each night of their journey. On the fourth day they stopped to camp in a meadow near Yellow Mountain. Henry shot a quail in the afternoon, and Clary cleaned and cooked it over the fire. Orpha and Clara played under the wagon until Clary called them to supper. After supper, without protest from the girls, Clary pulled the quilt around them in the wagon and they fell asleep. Then she volunteered to stand watch the first part of the night. Henry spread his bed near the fire and drifted off to sleep. Clary sat by the fire with the rifle. She was pleased to be sitting on this mountain keeping watch for her family. She stared into the surrounding darkness for a while, then placed more wood on the fire. It cracked and popped. She could hear Henry's faint snoring, and the movement of the wind in the top of the tall trees. Before she realized it, she had dozed off.

A frenzied movement of the horses and mules startled her awake. She heard a low guttural growl in the darkness. Readying the gun, she pointed it in the direction of the sound. Then against the glow of the flickering firelight, she saw the panther's shadow as he leapt. A horse screamed and whinnied piteously.

"Shoot into the air." Henry shouted. "You might hit the other animals." She aimed the gun high, held it steady and pulled the trigger. The panther fled. Clary ran to the wagon where Clara and Orpha sat screaming. By the light of the lantern, Henry could see one of the horses had been badly mauled.

"Clary, keep the girls in the wagon. I'm gonna have to put him down. He's hurt real bad." The horse lay panting on its side. "Don't worry old boy, it won't hurt long," he said. Henry raised the rifle and pulled the trigger. The horse lurched and lay still.

"I'll stand watch the rest of the night," he said to Clary.

Each day Clary doled out the food they had brought with them. Along the way, she and the girls looked for sprouts of fresh young poke and dandelion greens while Henry went looking for game. In the evenings, she boiled the poke greens to leach out the poison, and then mixed them with dandelion greens, a piece of dried salt pork, and a small amount of the remaining corn meal to make a thick soup.

Orpha and Clara noticed little of their parents' worry about finding food. They loved playing among the wild black-eyed susans in the meadows. Picking the white, pink, and yellow moccasin flowers, they made them into bouquets and gave them to Clary. Years later, Orpha would tell her children stories of crossing the mountains into Tennessee, but her stories would not be the same as the stories her parents told.

Late one afternoon, as they turned a sharp upward curve in the narrow road, they saw ahead of them a wagon with a broken wheel. An old man sat beside the road. He had unhitched his two mules, and they were hobbled and grazing along the roadside. Having met few other travelers on the road, Henry was pleased to offer the man his help. Even if he had not been so inclined, the broken wagon was blocking the narrow road and there was no way around it. To the left was an interminable wall of rock. To the right was a precipice, a sheer drop-off to the valley below.

"You're in luck, sir," Henry announced. "I'm a wagon-maker. Maybe I can help."

"I knowed if I set here long enough, the Lord would send somebody to help me," said the old man. "Praise the Lord! Looks like you're the one he sent."

Henry assessed the damage, and announced, "It's pretty bad. I'm afraid there's not much I can do. You not only have a broken wheel, but the axle's gone, too. Looks like it was already worn out, and a good jolt just cracked it. It's beyond anything I can do out here to put it right."

"I just can't see how I'm gonna git by without my wagon," the old man said. "My wife died a while back, and I just couldn't make it on the farm by myself, so I'm headed to Tennessee to look for my son. But still and all, without a good wagon, how am I gonna haul this stuff?" He motioned to a few wooden boxes and gunnysacks in the wagon. "Besides," he added, "my boy is expecting me to bring him a wagon."

Henry looked the situation over and said, "You don't have a big load. Since we're going to Tennessee ourselves, maybe we could make room for you to go along with us."

"That shore would be mighty kind," said the old man. "I'm much obliged to ye." After supper, Clary bedded the children down and sat by the fire with Henry and their guest. She noticed he had become inquisitive, asking one question after another. She began to feel uncomfortable.

"Where y'all come from?" he asked.

"Back in Rutherford County," replied Henry.

"Where 'bouts in Rutherford?"

"We lived with my ma and pa on their farm."

"Where ye headed?"

"To Jonesborough, over in Tennessee."

"What ye gonna do in Jonesborough?"

When he noticed the old man had picked up his rifle and laid it across his lap, Henry began to worry. Thomas had warned him about thieves and murderers, and now he was feeling more and more uneasy. After a little while, Henry announced he had to relieve himself.

When he stooped to pick up his rifle, the old man raised his own gun and said, "Just leave it be."

Clary stiffened. She thought of the children asleep in the wagon.

Henry knew they were in trouble. "What do you want?"

"Now what do ye think I want? I want ye wagon and ye guns and whatever else ye got." Nodding in Clary's direction, "I hate to leave y'all here in the middle of the night with the wild animals, but I cain't hep it." His voice took on an angry tone. "Git over here!" he barked at Henry, "Unload my stuff onto your wagon, and tie my mules on behind. Move!" Henry saw no choice but to do as he was told.

Then the old man hollered to Clary, "Get them babies outta there. *Now!* I don't need no squallin' younguns in my wagon." Clary shuddered, convinced now he was intending to kill them all. She thought of the other rifle in the back of the wagon. Lifting the children down, she told them to shut their eyes tight and stay close behind her. The old man was ranting and raving at Henry about how life had treated him mean, and how he had every right to take whatever he could get his hands on to make up for it. "They all think I'm just a crazy old man," he said. "I reckon I'm gonna hafta show 'em!"

Reaching in the back of the wagon, Clary carefully raised the gun. Without hesitating, she took aim and shot the old man in the chest. The impact of the shot knocked the old man off his feet and threw his body backward to the ground. There he lay looking up at Henry with sightless eyes.

"Is he dead?" Clary wanted to know. She couldn't believe she had done such a thing. It seemed to her she would never stop trembling.

"Yes, he's dead," Henry said.

"Dear God, what have I done?"

"Hush, Clary," Henry said. "It was either him or us. You did the right thing. I just thank God we're all safe."

The children were clinging to each other under the wagon. Orpha was crying. Clara sat dry-eyed, staring straight ahead. Clary pulled them close and held them. Orpha gladly returned her mother's embrace, but Clara did not respond.

As soon as light appeared over the valley, Clary helped Henry load the old man's body onto the broken wagon. Summoning all their strength, they pushed it over the cliff. Henry hitched the old man's mules to his wagon and harnessed them with his own. A four-mule team will pull better and make the trip faster and easier, he thought.

"I think we're not too far from Roan Mountain," he told Clary. "Perhaps we can make it by midday tomorrow. We'll all feel safer there."

That afternoon, as they passed the towering tulip trees on the side of Yellow Mountain, Clary and Henry began to feel a little more at ease. They set up camp for the night, careful to keep the guns close by.

"Don't wander out of sight," Clary told the girls. "We have to be more watchful now." She worried about Clara, who still refused to speak.

On June 6, on the twenty-fifth day of their journey, they reached Roan Mountain in the early afternoon. Clary thought she would never in a million years be able to describe what she felt there at the top of Roan Mountain.

Henry brought the wagon to a halt in the middle of a heavy fog. "We'll have to wait for the fog to lift," he said. He warned the girls not leave the wagon. "If we lose you in this fog, we might never be able to find you again." He remembered seeing the early morning fog hanging over the fields on the farm in North Carolina, but he had never seen any fog as thick as this.

Clary strained to hear sounds through the thickness, but all was still. Sitting with the girls in the back of the wagon, she could barely see Henry at the front. The fog teased them for a moment or two, offering quick glances at their surroundings, then thickened up again. Clary shivered, and pulled a quilt from the bedding box to cover the girls.

When at last the fog lifted, she sat awestruck. Trees stood like ghosts in the rising mist. A brilliant sun burst over undulating ridges strewn with purple and pink rhododendrons. Dewdrops on the grass glistened in the sunshine. Clumps of flaming orange azaleas and patches of tiny wild yellow hawkweed grew in profusion across the meadows. Clary marveled at the layers of dark blue mountains fading into a lighter blue beyond, and beyond that, in the distance, still lighter blue mountains rising into the clouds.

She couldn't forget shooting the old man on the mountain. She would likely never forget, but here at the top of Roan Mountain, her heavy burden was lifting along with the chill, at least for the moment. Still, in a tiny corner of her mind, she wondered if Clara would ever get over the sight of her mother shooting a man to death. She didn't worry about Orpha, who went on as if nothing had happened. Little Orpha, perhaps too young to understand, hardly skipped a beat in her play and her mischief.

Henry broke her reverie. "We have to go," he said. "We'll need to get a move on if we aim to get to Jonesborough before dark. We still have a long way to go, and who knows what trouble we might run into before we get there."

FIVE

Life in Jonesborough

Washington County, Tennessee
1823-1833

During their first two years in Washington County, life was not easy for the young Fraleys. Indeed, it was not easy for any of the small tenant farmers. Nonetheless, Henry and Clary were able to scrape together enough to live on. They moved into a little log cabin on Avery McGinnis's place. Besides share-cropping on thirty acres of McGinnis's thousand-acre farm on the Nolichucky, Henry worked part-time as a blacksmith for McGinnis and part-time repairing wagons for the Embree Iron Works, a ways down the road in Telford. What a disappointment to learn he had come too late to meet Elihu Embree.

According to Elihu's brother Elijah, "You're about three years too late. My brother died back in '20." It was even more of a disappointment to learn that the *Emancipator* had died with him. The issue the preacher had given him in North Carolina was apparently the only issue ever published. Elihu Embree had been a partner in the Telford Iron Works with his brother Elijah, who became sole proprietor upon Elihu's death.

Henry was surprised to learn that both of them had owned slaves. When he queried Elijah further, Elijah told him, "When my brother became convinced that slavery was wrong, he didn't free his own slaves right away. He didn't want to set them loose with no financial support. When he knew he was dying, he wrote a will stipulating that all of them be legally emancipated and provided with sufficient funds for their immediate support and their education. I've made a will that takes care of my slaves the same way."

Henry wished he had known Elihu Embree. He hoped he would meet others who felt as he did. He was sure if slavery weren't ended, it would mean the death of the nation.

Elijah Embree liked this young man from North Carolina. When he learned Henry was skilled in wagon-making and blacksmithing, he agreed to take him on part-time. The foundry was hard on wagons, given the weight of the products that needed transporting. Soon Henry had more work than he could handle, especially with his responsibilities to McGinnis. In the early morning hours, after feeding the animals, Henry would hitch the mules to the plow and turn the fields for planting. With what was left of the hundred dollars Thomas had given him, he bought a cow, two sheep, and a brooder of twenty-five baby chicks. He still had his one riding horse, the two mules he had brought from his father's farm, and the two he had appropriated on the mountain.

Clary and the girls planted rows of corn in the newly worked land Henry had turned. When the tiny shoots came up, it was their job to chop the weeds out. Clary worked in the fields until noon, and then spent the rest of the day cooking, tending the garden, churning butter, and taking care of the younger children. By 1828, Orpha and Clara had two sisters, Christina and Mary, born two years apart, and by 1829 a brother, Daniel, was born. Given all the work their mother had to do on the farm, it fell to Orpha and Clara to take care of the babies. Orpha regularly complained that she never had any free time just for herself. She hated taking care of babies!

She also hated when her father sent her and Clara to replant corn. "You can tell where you need to replant by the empty spaces in the rows," he said. "Just drop three or four grains into the empty spaces and cover them like this." He scraped some dirt over the kernels with a hoe.

"How many rows do we need to replant?" Orpha asked.

"You need to replant wherever the first corn didn't come up," her father told her. "It will probably take you all day, and, if you don't get finished today, you can come back tomorrow, and the next day after that 'til the job is done."

In all of her ten years, Orpha had never heard anything so ridiculous. "We don't need to take all day," she told Clara. "Come on, I'll show you." She dug a big hole in the first row and dumped in the whole sack of corn kernels. Then she covered them up with as much dirt as she could pile on top.

"You gonna git us into trouble agin," Clara said. "What'll Papa say?"

"He don't have to know, does he? I ain't gonna tell him, and you shore as shootin' better keep your mouth shut!"

Two weeks later, Henry was puzzled that there were no new corn sprouts from the replanting, that is, until he caught sight of the mountain of sprouts shooting up in abundance where the bag of kernels had been dumped. "Bring them girls out here to me," he said to Clary. "And cut me a keen peach-tree switch."

Over the years, Clary and Caroline McGinnis had developed a satisfying friendship that extended beyond the difference in their social stations. Caroline never felt herself above Clary, and Clary never saw herself as inferior to Caroline. Clary wondered if Caroline might turn away from her if she knew about her mixed-blood. Perhaps she knows it, Clary thought, and it doesn't matter.

Caroline had found more than just a tenant farmer's wife in Clary. They had developed a companionship that came close to that of sisters. When Caroline learned Clary had skills in weaving, she asked if she would like to help her make linen. Avery had bought Caroline a patented flax spinning wheel on one of his trips to Baltimore. She had learned from one of her slave women how to process the flax, but she knew little about weaving it into linen cloth. She promised Clary that if she would help process the flax and instruct her in weaving, she would let Clary use some of the linen to make clothes for her children.

In the weeks that followed, Caroline and Clary became patient teachers and good friends. Caroline showed Clary how to soak the flax stems. "We'll keep them in water for several weeks," she said, "so that the inner core rots and the tough bark dissolves. This leaves the gummy material that binds the flax fibers to the rest of the stem." After about five weeks, she announced they were ready for the next step. "Now we beat the core and outer parts. Let me show you. We'll break and remove the chaff with this knife, and straighten the fibers over the teeth of the hackle to remove any chaff that's left. As soon as we remove all the short coarse fibers, we can arrange the long fibers on this distaff, and we're ready to spin."

Clary was amazed! Linen thread created from this tough flax plant! As she worked with Caroline to teach her what she knew of spinning and weaving, she remembered with gratitude how Polly had patiently taught her. And she recalled how Hannah had said her mother Claracy had been the best weaver on the Wallace plantation. She wondered what Caroline would say if she knew her mother and grandmother were mulatto slaves.

Clary loved working at the spinning wheel and seeing the results of her labor. She was able to make clothes for the children, and she also enjoyed working with Caroline to create patterns for beautiful bed coverlets. She loved the colors they were able to create for dyeing with indigo, madder, and logwood, and they made their own brown dye from butternuts and walnuts. To make green, they used yellow flowers and indigo, and they used alum to fix the colors.

Caroline often wondered when Clary had time to take care of her own family. Beyond the time they spent together, Clary's church duties required a good deal of her time. Of course, Clary has two older girls at home to help with her younger ones, she thought. She wished she knew more about Clary. She had come to appreciate their friendship, but when they talked, Clary always seemed reluctant to share much about her life before she came to Jonesborough.

On the western outskirts of Jonesborough under the sign of the Green Tree stood Barkley's Tavern, a favorite gathering place for locals. Henry often stopped by the tavern on his way home from Embree's Iron Works. There he heard comments and jokes that made him uneasy. Most of the comments were about a mixed darker-skinned people called Ridgemites living in the next county over. According to the tavern revelers, soon after the first settlers had arrived, these people had come from the border areas of southwestern Virginia and western North Carolina to escape color discrimination and taxes. This area in East Tennessee had become a kind of no-man's land generally ignored by the law.

"They claim they're not black," said one. "They claim the reason their skin is that color is on account of Injun blood. They claim white folks just wanted the best bottom land for theirselves, so they accused them of being black so's they could take it over."

"Yeah," spoke up another. "I hear that when they passed the law sayin' nobody with black blood could vote, or hold office, or testify in court, some of them Ridgemites had to go to court to see if they could vote. The judge made 'em take off their shoes to see if they was flatfooted. If they was, that meant they was colored, and so they couldn't vote. If they wasn't flatfooted, even if they just had a little bit of arch, the judge figgered they had enough white blood to let 'em vote."

This tale led to a stream of loud guffaws from the drinkers.

"After that," the tavern owner chimed in, "the white squatters went to court and kicked them flatfooted Ridgemites off that good bottom land and took it for theirselves."

More laughter ensued.

Hearing all this, Henry couldn't help being apprehensive. The question of Clary's mixed-blood had not emerged since they arrived. He had seen no reason why the issue need come up, but given their experience in North Carolina, he had begun to worry.

"Where is this place exactly?" Henry asked the proprietor.

"It's off over yonder on the other side of Clinch Mountain."

"Where's that?"

"Why, it's up there just northwest of Jonesborough, across the county line. And as long as they stay up there in their place on the ridges and in the hollows and don't come down here a-stealin' and raisin' a ruckus, we git along fine. But one thing's for sure, and don't you forget it, them people is a different breed from us. One thing I have to say for 'em, though—they do make the best whiskey around here."

"You oughta know, Tom," said an old man wiping his beard. "They furnish you with the stuff we're a-drinking right now." The crowd laughed again.

Ignoring the old man, the proprietor continued, "They don't pay no taxes on their whiskey. They don't always get away with it, though most of the time they do. Sometimes the law hauls 'em over to Knoxville to the federal court and they get fined anywheres from ten to a thousand dollars a pop. It ain't exactly fair, though. It's about the only real way they have of supportin' their families."

Henry found himself thinking about Clary and wondered how she would feel hearing this conversation. Henry's thoughts floated above the Irish jig the fiddler was playing and the loud nasal singing of the rough-clad cloggers dancing on their toes, their bodies held stiff and straight as sticks. Applejack spilled over on the tables as everybody clapped their hands in rhythm to the music, and Henry began to forget about corn crops that had failed, livestock that had not survived, and color discrimination laws that kept some people in their place.

In the early hours of the morning, Henry lay awake beside a sleeping Clary. He was thinking about how Jonesborough had been a hotbed of political thought since the time of the earliest settlers. Hadn't most of Jonesborough's citizens, like my papa, done their part to send King George's men back where they came from? Yes, he reflected, Jonesborough draws all kinds of people. He thought of the Quaker Embrees leaving Pennsylvania to start an iron works business that was now keeping the Fraley family from North Carolina in food. He wondered if there were other Quakers who might start up the *Emancipator* again. Henry knew there weren't many people who were willing to speak out on the subject of slavery, and he hoped he could sort them out from the ignorant yahoos he found himself drinking with in the tavern.

Elijah Embree had mentioned he was a member of a Quaker meeting at Fairview just outside Jonesborough. He had invited Henry to go along with him, and Henry went, hoping to meet others who shared his anti-slavery convictions. Henry had invited Clary and the children to go, but Clary declined saying she had to attend the Methodist church with Caroline.

Henry arrived at the little log meeting house just before the meeting began. He noticed the interesting seating arrangement—hand-hewn wooden benches arranged in a square around the room, with men and women sitting in separate sections. The worshipers, Henry noticed, settled quietly into silence. There was no leader, and nobody spoke for the next three-quarters of an hour

At last an elderly man stood up. He hesitated, waiting for the words to come. "I know the evil in me is weakening," he said, "and the good is being raised up." He sat down. Silence ensued. Then Elijah Embree stood up. "Let us hold our African brothers and sisters in the light," he said, "as we endeavor to bring an end to the terrible blight of injustice brought upon them by the slave trade." Henry was moved, both by the silence and by the sentiments expressed. He must get to know more about these Quakers.

He was aware that most of the slaves here in Washington County belonged mainly to a few large landowners like Avery McGinnis. It's too bad religion can't make people see that slavery is wrong, he thought. He had heard that some of the itinerant preachers were quoting the Bible to prove that God intended slavery to exist. They preached that black people were meant to be subservient to the white race. Some preachers even quoted the apostle Paul's advise for slaves to obey their masters.

Henry saw what a powerful impact religion could have on a person when Clary, after attending a revival meeting held by a circuit-riding preacher, announced she'd been saved. Henry could see the hand of Caroline McGinnis in Clary's change. He knew she had been wooing Clary for some time to join her church. She seemed genuine in her stated affection for Clary. She probably feels it her duty as a good Christian to take the young family from North Carolina under her wing, he thought.

Henry tried to tell Clary about his experience at the Quaker meeting, but she seemed uninterested. Instead, she chastised him for not going with her and the children to the Methodist church. "You don't even know what we do at our church."

So Henry agreed to attend the service with her and the children the next Sunday. Unlike the Quaker service he had attended the week before, he found it to be a loud and at times boisterous affair. The people were noisy as they entered the church, and it seemed to him the preacher did a lot of unnecessary hollering.

And the people sang. Oh, how they sang! It seemed each one was trying to sing louder than the other. The service began with a hymn, lined out by the song leader. He would sing a line or two, and the congregation would repeat it in unison. It reminded Henry of the way slaves would sing as they worked in the fields.

The preacher's sermon was based on the Ten Commandments. After quoting each commandment, he proceeded to catalogue the many ways the people were breaking it. Henry thought the preacher missed several good opportunities to point out some real evils, such as war and slavery. When the preacher had finished with the tenth commandment, he prayed an exceptionally long prayer, and, wiping his brow with a white cloth, sat down. After four or five more hymns, the song leader brought the service to a close by lining out a final hymn, "When we all get to heaven." Can *everybody* make it to heaven? Henry wondered. What about slaves? What about mixed-breeds and mulattos? What about Clary? Can she get in?

If Clary had simply accepted her newly found salvation and not forced it on the rest of the family, Henry and the children could have ignored it. But for good or ill, Clary became a changed person. Nowadays, when Henry went to the tavern after work, she admonished him, "It's a sin to sit in a tavern and drink alcohol." It seemed now whatever he did and wherever he turned, sin was involved. "You can't work on Sunday. The Bible says so."

He worried about the girls. Whatever they did or wanted to do prompted a sermon from Clary. Orpha in particular, was having a difficult time. When all she received from Clary was a stream of Bible verses, she began to rebel.

They had been too busy to see what was happening to Orpha. When she announced she wanted to take a job outside the house to help the family, they were delighted. Recently they had begun to worry about how Orpha was spending her time. She would sometimes say she was going to spend the night at Mandy's house, and that she and Mandy were going to the church pie supper. Clara would always confirm Orpha's story, although she resented having to do so. Sometimes, Orpha would come home wearing a dress her mother had never seen. "Mandy gave it to me," Orpha would say. Clary suspected Orpha was not telling the truth, but she dreaded confronting her because she knew Orpha would win out in the end.

Orpha knew she loved her mother, but at times, she also hated her. She paid less and less attention to Clary's harangues, closing her ears to them whenever she could. When she announced she was going with the other young people to a hoe-down in Jonesborough, her mother countered with: "Oh no, you're not. Dancin' is a sin, and sinners go to hell. Do you want to go to hell? You're not goin' to that dance."

"Well, I guess we'll see," Orpha said, and went to the dance anyway.

BOOK IV

Orpha in Hell

1834-1844

All this the world well knows, yet none knows well
To shun the heaven that leads to hell.

—William Shakespeare
Sonnet 129

ONE

Orpha and Avery

The Owl's Nest, Snake Hollow, Tennessee
Spring 1834

The change in Clary's attitude was more than Orpha could stand. At least, until her mother had gotten religion, she and Clara had been able to do things with their friends—join in cake walks, taffy pulls, pie suppers, and box socials. At least they had been able to meet other young people at such events. Now, every time they turned around, Clary was preaching about how they must not succumb to the evils of smoking tobacco or dipping snuff or drinking liquor. Worst of all, according to Mama Clary, was the evil of fornication. Both Orpha and Clara had experimented with tobacco, but knew little about fornication.

Once they took dried tobacco leaves from the shed, crushed them, rolled them in brown paper, lit one end with a match, and inhaled. They both became deathly sick, and Clary vowed to punish them for smoking. She cut a peach tree switch and began to use it on their bare legs. Orpha was fourteen when she grabbed the switch from her mother and started hitting back. Clara begged her to stop, and her mother stood in disbelief.

Clara said she was sorry for smoking the tobacco, but Orpha remained tight-lipped and defiant. Clary went inside and fell on the bed in tears. She realized she had lost control of Orpha. She would refrain from trying to save her anymore. She wished Henry would do something, but he claimed he was too busy.

Though Orpha at fifteen wanted no part of her mother's religion, she would often go with Clary to church meetings just to get away. She never went inside the church. Orpha would simply wait outside in the wagon until church was over. Other young people were doing the same. Some of the boys played marbles for money at the back of the log church, and Orpha sometimes cajoled them into letting her play. Few boys could turn Orpha away when she wanted something. "No" was simply not a word she was willing to accept. Besides, they liked having her around. She was fun. She laughed at their antics and encouraged them in their gambling.

One night, when she was feeling more restless than usual, she spotted Avery McGinnis leaning against a tree watching her. At forty-five, he always had his eye out for a pretty girl. Sitting there in the wagon, half in light and half in shadow, she became his damsel who needed rescuing. Would he have time to rescue her tonight? His wife would surely be in church at least another hour.

Whether Avery seduced her or she seduced him, they were a pair for the next ten years. Avery was a man thirty years her senior, her family's landlord, and her father's employer. He looked every bit the roving horseman Orpha knew from a song she had heard, and like the horseman in the song, she wanted him to ride up, sweep her onto his steed, and take her away from boredom and her mother's constant nagging. It was not just a physical attraction that drew her to him, though she knew some women would think him handsome. At forty-five, he had a boyish, carefree look that defied age. His whole demeanor radiated a worldly wisdom, and his quick smile evidenced a sense of humor.

With Avery, Orpha felt alive. Life with him promised much more than the drudgery and despair she saw in most women, including Avery's wife, Caroline, and even her own mother. He told Orpha wild, fantastic stories, some of which she knew he had made up. "Well, I declare, Avery, are you sure that really happened?" It really did not matter to Orpha whether it was made up or not. She was ready to dive into life with Avery in whatever manner he suggested.

If Orpha was charmed by Avery, an older man, Avery worshipped Orpha's youth. Her unusual beauty, her honey-colored skin and her long black hair attracted him, and he was drawn to her need to be wanted. She's different, he thought. She's not like anyone I've ever seen before. Once when he had visited Philadelphia or Baltimore, he couldn't remember which, he had noticed a life-size painting on a tavern wall of a beautiful nude woman lying on a couch, her thighs propped up on pillows. Around her neck, a rose was attached to a thin black velvet ribbon. He never forgot that painting. Perhaps he was ever after hoping to find such a woman, and now she had risen from her couch and found him.

When he gazed into Orpha's bluish-green eyes, outlined by her thick dark lashes, he was held captive. Her puckered lips raised a wild desire in him and challenged him to give her whatever she desired. Her unrestrained carnality and innocence lured him. That was what he had seen in the painting of the young woman on the tavern wall. That was why he had been drawn, almost against his will, and certainly against his better judgment, to Orpha.

He wanted to dress her in the finest silks and calicos and the best feathered bonnets, and parade her on the streets of Jonesborough. But that was the one thing he knew he could not do. People around Jonesborough knew him, and it would certainly not be good if Caroline found out that he was entangled with a young girl the same age as his daughter.

He thought how Caroline had ignored most of his escapades with women. She would do nothing that would put her standing in the community at risk. She would continue to turn a blind eye to whatever he did. She had borne him six children, one every year since the marriage, and she would ignore his peccadilloes for the children's sake and for her own. Avery did wonder, however, what Caroline would do if she found he was sleeping with Orpha, the teenage daughter of her friend Clary. Orpha and Avery had been able to elude Caroline's eye, meeting secretly since that first night at the revival service. From early on in their marriage, Avery had never stayed at home with the family, and Caroline had become accustomed to his announcing he had business in Knoxville, or Wytheville or even as far away as Philadelphia. So when he was gone, she thought little of it, or, if she did, she simply ignored it. That was just the way he was, and she had long ago given up hope of doing anything about it.

When Avery took Orpha over Clinch Mountain and into the hidden valley at Black Water Springs for the first time, they stopped along a creek, tied up the horses and made love. It was just after Orpha's fifteenth birthday, and Avery had promised her an adventure she would never forget.

"You have to be plucky and daring to do what we're doing," he teased. "This is a real adventure. Nobody goes where we're going over the mountain unless they are running away from the law, or anxious to experience something really different."

As their horses struggled over Clinch Mountain, Orpha began to wonder if she had done the right thing. When they neared the Owl's Nest at Snake Hollow, she could see the lights and hear the loud music. She was excited, but she felt something was about to happen she couldn't control. "Take me back to Jonesborough, Avery," she begged. "This place is scary."

He laughed. "You'll be fine. Believe me, there's nothing to worry about."

They tied their horses to a tree and unsaddled them. Avery pulled her through the door and into a large, smoky room filled with people. Orpha could smell fish frying in burning lard, and a cheap, sweet perfume mixed with body sweat hit her nostrils. She thought she would have to vomit.

Everyone's attention was focused on a tall swarthy woman singing in the corner. She was singing about a woman, who, finding her husband in bed with another woman, shot them both to death. The song's words made her shiver, reminding her of a song she had heard Grandpa Thomas sing. She remembered him strumming his dulcimer and singing about a woman and her lover in England who had been stabbed to death by her husband, a lord of high degree, when he found them in bed together. The words were similar, but the tempo and the music were new to her.

The woman in the corner, accompanied by a fiddle player, was plucking an instrument Orpha had never seen before. The music was not doleful or slow like the ballads her grandfather had sung. This new music had a definite beat, and. she found herself tapping her foot in rhythm. The onlookers clapped their hands and swayed back and forth.

"What's that thing she's playin'?" she asked Avery. "It looks like a gourd."

"It's a banjo. You never seen a gourd banjo before?"

No, she thought, but it won't be the last time I see one. Before I've lived much longer, I'm gonna learn how to play that thing.

Despite the smells and the unfamiliar surroundings, it didn't take long for Orpha to settle into this strange world of music and dancing. Corn whiskey flowed, the bow flew across the fiddle strings and the banjo broke loose in a fast dance tune. The woman in the corner sang as she picked her banjo:

> *Mama don' allow no banjo-pickin' 'round here.*
> *Mama don' allow no banjo pickin' 'round here.*
> *Well, I don' care what Mama don' allow, I'll pick my banjo anyhow.*
> *Mama don' allow no banjo-pickin' 'round here.*

The room became a frenzied movement of men and women dancing, crisscrossing, flowing in and out of lines, stomping, hollering. The dancers stopped only long enough to swig down a little whiskey. "Mama don' allow no whisky drinkin' 'round here . . . ."

Nobody seemed to care who had come to the shindig. Orpha had never seen such a mix of people. People with straight hair, kinky hair, curly hair, blond hair, brown hair, people of all skin hues, with eyes of all colors, black, dark brown, blue, blue-gray, deep purple, hazel, a strange shade of yellow gold, people of all ages, uncouth, unshaven, unclean, and surely most unacceptable to people on the other side of the mountain.

Old Virgie, who owned the Owl's Nest, kept whiskey and apple brandy flowing. Fried fish, beans, and hard corn pone were available at a reasonable cost. Those who'd had enough of drinking and dancing could retire to one of the several log huts built alongside the main lodge, or they could just camp out under the stars.

As the night wore on, Orpha noticed an unusual couple dancing together. The woman weighed at least three hundred pounds, and she was dancing with a string bean of a man right in the middle of the floor.

"Who's that?" Orpha couldn't believe her eyes.

"That's Hallie the Huge and Skinny the Thin. They're husband and wife."

"She sure is a big woman," Orpha said.

The two stopped dancing only long enough to refresh themselves from the open-mouthed clay jug. About midnight, Orpha heard Hallie challenge Skinny to a fight outside in the yard. Old Virgie tried to stop it, but by the time he got there, Hallie had pinned Skinny to the ground and was threatening to kill him. Her three hundred pounds stretched over Skinny's bony body like some massive whale, smashing and smothering the life out of him.

"I can't breathe!" yelled Skinny. "Git offa me, you black bitch!" Orpha stood amazed as Hallie the Huge began pounding his face to a pulp.

"Not 'til you take back what you just said!" she screamed in his face. "I ain't black! I may be a little dusky, but I ain't black. I come from the Portugee! An' my pappy was a Indian chief! Don't you ever call me black again!"

"I won't, Hallie! I won't, little darlin'!" he whined. "Just let me loose." It took four men to pull Hallie off.

Orpha had crossed over Clinch Mountain with Avery without considering the consequences. She had trekked into this strange valley—this no-man's land—and danced the night away. How had the time slipped by so quickly? If I never have another moment like this one, Orpha thought, I won't have a thing to complain about, no recriminations, and no thought of guilt. This night, this moment, is mine.

Later, she would have to face the consequences of her actions. Her mother, quoting Scripture, would "heap coals of fire on her head" for straying off the straight and narrow. Orpha thought "straight" could just as well be said of laces and "narrow" of minds. Life's not just about *this* right way, or *that* wrong way, she thought. Life is about facing the cold in winter and the sun in summer, and living the best one can through both seasons. Orpha knew her mother would not like this kind of thinking. Since she got religion, Orpha thought, she's become harder and harder to live with.

"Mama wants me to repent my evil ways," she said aloud to no one in particular. "No matter what I do, she sees it as sinful. But I can't live my life the way she wants me to. I love Mama, and someday, when the time is right, I won't hesitate to tell her so. But not now. Not yet."

TWO

Hallie

The Ridge, Hancock County, Tennessee
1834-1838

Hallie Hollins made the best whiskey on the Ridge. Everyone knew that. No one on the Ridge would dispute it. Without making and selling whiskey, most people on the Ridge would have starved to death. Skinny supervised the growing of corn on the hillsides and in the hollows, and helped Hallie with the running of the stills. The whiskey was carried off the steep ridge in gourds on pack mules. Hallie was a savvy businesswoman. She used the bartering system to best advantage, exchanging liquor for pots, knives, food staples, guns and ammunition, and whatever else she needed.

Since the night Avery had introduced Orpha and Hallie at the Owl's Nest, they had become fast friends. Hallie was twenty when she hired sixteen-year-old Orpha to help with her children. "I can't pay you," she said, "But you can have a place to stay. Ain't much, but I'll feed you." Orpha jumped at the offer. It had become harder and harder to live with Clary and Henry. She needed a place to stay, and Hallie had made her feel needed.

Avery didn't like the idea at all. "You don't want to live with these people," he said. "They barely make a living in this God-forsaken place. And they live like pigs. They're all right to raise hell with, but not to live with."

Orpha was beginning to think she was seeing a side of Avery she wasn't sure she liked. Maybe it was a need to control, combined with kind of haughtiness.

He had insisted he would take care of her and had even promised he would buy a little piece of land over in Hawkins County and build her a cabin. But so far, that had only been talk.

When Orpha moved in, Hallie already had three children of her own and four orphans she had adopted. Hallie and Skinny's extended cabin had an elevated floor that served as a roof for rabbit pens and chicken coops. By keeping them under the house, they could be sure no one would steal them. "We got to keep 'em safe from gypsies and thieves," Hallie told Orpha. "If we hear a noise at night, we shoot first and ask questions later. So you'll have to listen for noises under the house at night. And you'll have to sleep with some of the younguns up there in the loft."

Orpha climbed the ladder to a six-by-eight-foot loft above the main room. Most of the space was taken up by a bed with rough-hewn posts and wood railings, corded from end to end and side to side with ropes of flax. A straw bed tick lay on top. The only other furniture in the room was a log bench. A pallet of old quilts lay on the floor.

Downstairs, a rock fireplace four feet wide by six feet high commanded the end wall of the main room, and an iron rod extended across the fireplace three or four feet above the fire from which a pot hung suspended on a hook. Over the fireplace was a wooden dowel placed horizontally for drying pumpkin, meat, and the like. A rough-hewn log table and benches with bark still attached had been placed in the middle of the room. There were no openings for light.

"Sometimes we go to bed at dark." Hallie said. "Saves candle wax."

Orpha learned later that during the cold winter months, they did indeed go to bed early, keeping the fireplace embers burning until morning. "If the fire does go out," Hallie told her, "Skinny fires a cotton rag out of his gun to get it going again. If worse comes to worst, somebody goes over to the neighbors two miles away to borrow a chunk of fire." A pine knot was glowing in the back of the fireplace, and a lighted wax candle on the table gave off an eerie glow.

People on the Ridge pointed to Hallie as their idea of goodness. "It is good she takes in orphans," they said. "It's good she never turns anyone away when they come to her door. If they are hungry, she loads them up with vegetables from the garden—whatever's in season." When wells went dry, as they often did on the Ridge, they called on Hallie. Before she became too heavy to walk, she would go around with her forked stick and witch for underground water. The stick would begin to shake and twitch when it was over an apt spot. Hallie's stick never failed. She could always find water.

From time to time, she was also called upon to rid people of warts or moles. She would rub the offending protuberances with a thin hickory stick, chanting quietly something nobody could understand. "Now don't touch it," she would say. "Let it be. Before you know it, it'll go away." People would often come back within a few weeks to tell her how grateful they were she had witched away their warts and moles. Women of the Ridge looked to Hallie when their babies came due. Until Hallie was too heavy to travel in a wagon, she would go at all hours to deliver a baby.

Most people on the Ridge believed in witches, or at least they said they did. To appease witches that might make milk turn sour, they would put a coin in the milk, or use a butcher knife to cut though it before drinking it, or throw salt in the fire to keep witches away from the churn.

Hallie was a storehouse of knowledge about witches and ghosts. At bedtime, when the last candle was snuffed out and the cabin became still, everyone would wait for Hallie to tell a story. One particular story Hallie told was a favorite with the children. They would cover themselves from head to toe and lie there shivering, dreading the ending they all knew by heart.

Hallie began: "There was this man whose big toe was cut off when he was plowin' in the garden, and when his woman collected the vegetables, she picked up his big toe and cooked it in her green beans and potatoes. The man died that night, and they say that every night after, he comes a-lookin' for his big toe. He comes a-knockin' at the door, crying 'Who's got my big toe?' But nobody answers. Then he opens the door and comes in the cabin, sayin', 'Who's got my big toe?' Still nobody answers. Then he climbs the ladder to the room upstairs, askin' agin, 'Who's got my big toe?' Agin nobody answers." Hallie's voice would became a growling monotone, lingering and quivering on every word, "Who's—got—my—big—toe?" Then she would grab someone's toe and yell, "*YOU'VE* GOT MY BIG TOE!" Everyone would shriek and laugh, and Hallie would say, "Now go to sleep."

Life on Newman's Ridge with Hallie was hard. Orpha was beginning to wish she had not agreed to accept Hallie's offer. If she had thought life with her mother and father in their cabin in Jonesborough was hard, she was having some second thoughts.

Orpha had never before thought about the differences that separate people. Even though Henry and Clary are poor compared to Avery and Caroline, she thought, they are rich compared to Hallie and her friends on the Ridge. As she considered her own plight, she realized that as a hired hand, a servant to Hallie, she could, but for Avery, be seen to be even a rung lower on the social ladder than Hallie.

Still, she enjoyed being around Hallie. The more she got to know her, the more she liked her, as, indeed, she had come to like most of the people on the Ridge. While they had little, they were generous people. She thought they were the most accepting, least judgmental people she had ever met, although she had noticed some tended to disparage others whose skin, they reckoned, was a shade darker than their own.

After a while, she adjusted to the routine of day-to-day living on the Ridge. On Mondays, they built a fire under Hallie's big round cast-iron kettle to heat water for washing clothes. By the time the clothes were wrung out and ready to be dried, Hallie would be huffing and puffing, unable to finish. So she would sit in her rocking chair and watch Orpha hang the clothes on the line. During the rest of the week, she was busy cooking and taking care of the children. Hallie managed the cousins she had hired to keep the stills operating in the nearby caves.

Hallie declared every Saturday and Sunday holidays for everyone, except for four cousins who had to keep watch at strategic points to protect the entrances into the valley. They watched not only for Federals searching for stills to break up, but also for potential buyers looking to get themselves a quart or two of Hallie's good moonshine whiskey.

Saturday was a bath day. Orpha would take the children to the waterfalls nearby, stand them naked under the falls, and with a bar of lye soap, make them scrub and wash their shivering bodies. Hallie had long since given up making the trek to the falls, so she appreciated Orpha taking on the task. Hallie managed to get her own bath in the kitchen.

"Whatever else they may say about us," she told Orpha, "they'll never say we was a dirty bunch." On Saturday nights most of the valley, including Hallie and Skinny, turned out at the Owl's Nest to drink and to gamble until morning.

On Sundays, Orpha would sometimes accompany Hallie and her seven children when they went fishing up at Zur Pond. Even with her three hundred pounds of fat, she would take her walking stick and grunt her way to the top. When any of the children had to answer a call of nature, she would remind them to be careful of poison ivy. "I've already tended to too many itchy bottoms," she told Orpha. "And watch out for copperheads. I don't want to have to suck the poison out of your legs!"

When Orpha needed someone to talk to, she found a willing ear in Hallie. She talked incessantly about Avery. At last, Hallie ventured to give her a piece of advice which, of course, Orpha proceeded to ignore. One Saturday sitting on the bank of the pond, Hallie, out of the blue, had turned to her and said in a quiet deliberate voice, "Avery ain't no good for you. You better stay away from him."

THREE

Taking a Gamble

Rogersville, Tennessee
1838-1839

Orpha paid no attention to Hallie's warning. She continued her trysts with Avery at the Owl's Nest every Saturday night. In the course of their time there, he taught her to play poker, and soon she became an expert. Hallie played a decent game as well, but poker was rapidly becoming an obsession with Orpha. Avery noticed she had become especially adept at bluffing. She could tell who had good hands and who had lousy ones, and she could bluff her way to a win with nothing in her hand. Avery was impressed, and he kept staking her to whatever money she needed to keep playing. He enjoyed watching his protégé manipulate the Ridgemite gamblers.

As long as Avery and Orpha limited their gambling to the Owl's Nest in Snake Hollow, there seemed little reason to worry about running into people who might know them. Few of Avery's friends were likely to venture over the mountain to the Owl's Nest, and it was certain no one in Orpha's family or circle of friends would come to Snake Hollow to gamble. However, Orpha's appetite for poker challenged Avery to find higher-stake gambling establishments in town. Rogersville, the county seat of Hawkins County, while no frontier metropolis, boasted several saloons and gaming establishments that drew professional gamblers passing through the area.

If gambling had been their only vice, perhaps they could have managed to avoid trouble. However, both Avery and Orpha now seemed to throw all discretion to the wind. One night in Rogersville, they drank too much and quickly became boisterous and unruly. Before the night was gone, both were drunk and barely able to keep themselves upright. Orpha danced on the bar tables, laughing uncontrollably, and Avery started a fight over a comment by one of his fellow gamblers that he thought impugned Orpha's good name. Orpha awoke the next day in the local jail. She was unable to remember anything that happened the night before. Avery came for Orpha and paid the fine for her release.

"Who bailed *you* out?" Orpha wanted to know.

"My money," he replied. Yes, she thought, money can buy almost anything, including freedom.

They laughed all the way back to Hallie's about being arrested and spending the night in the jailhouse. "But Avery," Orpha said, "I didn't like the way that jailer kept looking at me, and it made me mighty mad when he called me a Ridgemite slut."

Their downfall came when they ventured into the Globe at the Sign of the Eagle in Jonesborough. It was one of several inns and taverns near the Great Stage Road that offered passengers a "table plentifully provided with all the necessities of life."

Later when Orpha was able to think back on their antics, she realized how much Avery was willing to gamble not only with his money—of which he seemed to have plenty, but also with their reputations—of which there seemed to be less and less. She hoped Caroline wouldn't find out about her and Avery. And what would Mama and Papa say?

In the back room of the Globe, men gawked at Orpha's card-playing prowess, and even though women were not usually welcome in such places, the men quickly accepted Orpha as part of the landscape. One night, as the evening wore on, both Orpha and Avery drank too much whiskey. The more they drank, the more Lady Luck seemed to abandon them. They began a losing streak that depleted their ready cash, and Avery became loud and abusive, insisting he had plenty of resources he could draw on to keep them in the game if only the others would take his marker. When they were thrown out of the game, Orpha was too far-gone to care. They were both ordered off the premises and pushed out the door of the Globe and onto the street. Not to be outdone, Avery drunkenly approached passersby about joining a poker game right then and there.

"This little lady," he shouted, his arm around Orpha to hold her erect, "can whip all comers. Ante up and see if she don't!"

It didn't take long for the sheriff's men to arrest them for disorderly conduct and throw them in jail. The sheriff, who knew Avery as man of position and money, and one who had supported his bid for sheriff, sent for Caroline. It was on November 2, 1838, that Avery and Orpha were charged with illegal gambling and "debauching the public morals," and a court date was about to be set when Caroline arrived in her buggy. She managed to talk the sheriff into dropping the charges, and they were set free.

Caroline ignored Orpha, and acted as if such behavior on the part of Avery were a common occurrence. Orpha knew Caroline would tell Henry and Clary soon enough, and she didn't want to be around when they found out. She begged Avery to get her back to Hallie's at once, and, over Caroline's protestations, he hired a coach to take her back to the Ridge.

Orpha was surprised when, a few days later, Henry and Clary showed up at Hallie's place. When she left home three months before, she told them she'd taken a job as a maid-housekeeper for Hallie Hollins over in Hancock County. Since then, she had not been home even once. The visit of the previous night to the Globe in Jonesborough was the closest she had come.

"We've come to take you home," Henry said.

Clary was crying. "Caroline came to the house last night and told us what happened," she said. "If we'd had any inkling you'd been foolin' around with Avery, we would've come long before now."

"We're leaving the farm," Henry said. "I won't work anymore for a man like Avery."

"Caroline ordered us off the place," Clary said. "She said we had to take you with us, or she'll have you thrown in jail. We're leaving Jonesborough in a day or two, and you have to go with us."

"Your Grandpa Thomas and Grandma Polly have sold their farm and left North Carolina," Henry said. "They stopped with us a few weeks ago on their way to White County. They've gone over there to a place called Lost Creek where they aim to buy some land, and they want us to come and help them work it. I'm going to keep up my wagon-making trade, and I'll keep working as a blacksmith. You and your sisters can help your Mama set up housekeeping. After that, you can help Daniel and me with the farming."

"I can't come right now." Orpha said. "Hallie needs me here. I'll join you later when you get settled."

A few days later, Hallie, Orpha, and the children were sitting on the banks of Zur Pond fishing. Hallie knew Orpha was upset about telling Henry and Clary she couldn't go with them to White County, and she knew the real reason Orpha had refused to go. Orpha had been complaining of feeling bad recently, and Hallie figured she was pregnant. "I can't eat much without throwing up," Orpha complained. "What am I gonna do? God knows I couldn't go with

Mama and Papa in this shape. Besides, when I told Avery, he said I should stay here, and he would take care of me and the baby."

"I could give you somethin' to help you end it right now," Hallie told her. "But if I was you, I wouldn't do it. I helped Mattie Childress once after she had borne six children, one right after the other. She couldn't hardly feed the six she already had, and she was afraid the next one would kill her."

"I don't think I could do away with my baby," Orpha said.

"I think we'd both regret it if I helped you get rid of it," Hallie told Orpha. "It's not a problem for me, if you really want it. I just love taking care of children. My children are all I have to live for. When I'm old, they'll take care of me, just like I'm taking care of them now. You're welcome to stay here as long as you like, and when it comes time, I'll help you deliver it. But you'll have to stay away from whiskey until after the baby is born. You ought to stay clear of Avery too. But I guess that's too much to ask."

After Caroline collected Avery from the Jonesborough jail, she told him to keep away from Orpha, or he would have to leave. "You're too old anyway to be gallivantin' with a younger woman. She'll tire of you and then where will you go? You have grandchildren you haven't even seen. It's a shame," she said.

Avery listened to Caroline's admonitions, but he had no intention of staying away from Orpha. He bought a few acres in the woods near Rogersville and built a two-room log cabin for her. "You can't ride over to Hallie's on horseback in the shape you're in," Avery said to Orpha, "but anytime you want to go, I'll take you over in the buggy."

FOUR

Out of the Depths

Hawkins County, Tennessee
1839-1843

The baby was born seven months later. Orpha named him Wilson. She had no time for drinking or gambling anymore. She planted a small garden and took care of the baby, and as long as she was able to ride, she took him by horseback over to the Ridge to help Hallie.

Caroline softened her attitude somewhat towards Avery when she saw he was making regular visits to see their married children and grandchildren. She knew he was still seeing Orpha, and Avery knew she knew, but they carried on with their pretensions, keeping life on an even keel as much as possible.

When in 1841, at the age of fifty, Avery became ill and took to his bed, it was Orpha, not Caroline, who took care of him. At twenty, Orpha was taking care of Avery and their two-year-old child in the cabin he had built for her. Caroline wanted no part of him by then. At first he would have occasional bouts of coughing, but then the cough became almost constant. For months he lay in bed barely able to breathe.

In late 1842, Avery asked his brother Asa to bring a solicitor to help him write a will. Asa was to sign as a witness. Avery left twelve hundred acres to his wife Caroline, along with horses, cattle, and personal household furniture. He ordered that at Caroline's death, everything be divided among their six children.

Asa was surprised by a codicil Avery insisted on adding. Asa wondered what Caroline would say when she learned Avery had left property to Orpha. This will not be easy for Caroline to swallow, he thought. Avery stipulated in the codicil that Orpha was to receive fifty acres of land, the cabin he had built for her, an old mare, six head of cattle, twenty-three head of hogs, and all the household items. He also left her one sidesaddle and six beehives. What surprised Asa even more was that Avery named Caroline as executrix of the will.

"Whatever possessed you to do such a thing?" Asa asked Avery. "What in the world do you expect to accomplish by such an action? Do you really think Caroline will abide by this codicil without protest? Do you actually trust the court to uphold your wishes over Caroline's objections?"

Avery made no reply.

Asa reluctantly signed his name as witness to the will and the codicil, wondering as he did so if Avery's illness had left him unable to think clearly and make rational decisions. Had he lost his mind? Asa left thinking that if Avery thought Caroline would abide by his wishes, he really did not know Caroline at all.

Avery died in October of 1843 at the age of fifty-three. Orpha didn't attend the funeral. Caroline had forbidden her attending, and Orpha hadn't wanted to create a scene. After the funeral, it didn't take Caroline long to contest the codicil. She employed one of the many lawyers in Jonesborough and went to court to have it rescinded, stating that Orpha had unduly influenced Avery when he was too ill to know what he was doing. She told the judge that Avery had committed bigamy, living with Orpha in the next county. The judge declared that since Caroline was "an upstanding citizen, who paid her taxes and had contributed most generously to the town, while her husband had disgraced and deserted the family," the codicil was null and void.

The most crushing blow to Orpha was the argument that Avery's son should not be raised, as Caroline said, "by this immoral woman who has moved in with those low-life, thieving Ridgemites over the mountain. She's lived among them so long, she's become one of them. And, Your Honor," she told the judge, "like most of those shiftless people, this woman has no means of supporting Avery's child."

The judge decided that four-year-old Wilson would be taken from Orpha, and bound over to Caroline. "Who will take care of this child?" the judge asked Caroline. "Will you be raising him yourself, or do you have some other plan?"

"My cousin and his wife over in Arkansas have no children," Caroline answered. "They have the means to raise a child, and have expressed the desire to adopt him."

Orpha couldn't believe Caroline could be so cruel. She knew Caroline was not concerned about Wilson. She only wants to punish me for taking Avery away from her, she thought. It was clear to Orpha that everything was stacked against her. She had nothing. Caroline had money and power. "Please don't take my baby," Orpha pleaded. "I will take him to my mother's, and you'll never see either of us again."

No amount of pleading moved Caroline. She whisked Wilson out of the courtroom so fast, Orpha never even had a chance to tell him goodbye.

She made her way back to her cabin. Orpha knew she was alone now. She was numb. How could any mother take away another mother's child?

What could she do? Where could she go?

When she managed to pull herself together, she knew there was only one place she could go—to Lost Creek Valley and find Mama and Papa. Caroline has stolen my baby, she thought, but she won't keep me from finding him. Someday I'll find my baby if it's the last thing I do.

Orpha made one last visit to see Hallie before she left. "Hon, I shore do hate to see you go," said Hallie. "I'll never forget you."

"Hallie, I've lost my baby," Orpha cried. "They've taken him off to Arkansas. Caroline said I would never be a fit mother to my son, no matter what I did. Maybe she's right. I've made a pretty sad mess of my life."

"Honey, we both know you've been a good mother to your baby," Hallie said. "But you gotta move on. You can't let it git you. When you've done all that you can do, that's all that's required of you."

"You have been the best friend I've ever had," Orpha said. "I don't know what I would have done without you."

"Honey, you're gonna make it," Hallie said.

"I want you to have my mare and saddle," Orpha said. "That's all Caroline left me with. She took everything else. Can't you just see me galloping across them mountains on that old gray mare, getting saddle sores all over my bottom?" They laughed together at the thought.

"You don't have to give me your mare," Hallie said. "If *you* can't ride her, imagine *me* trying to climb up in that saddle! Talk about sway-backed horses, why, I'd crack her backbone right in two."

"I know you can't ride her, but she's all I got left to give you," Orpha said. "Maybe one of your children can use her. I got no use for her. I'm going by stagecoach."

Hallie took Orpha's hand. "I'm much obliged to you. An' don't fret. One of the boys will take you over to the stagecoach stop in Jonesborough." Then she reached behind her chair and brought out a bulging flour sack. "I got somethin' I been meanin' to give you. I had a man over in Snake Hollow make it for you. See, it's just like the one Leeler plays at the Owl's Nest."

She reached into the sack and brought out a gourd banjo. "You said one time you wanted to learn to play it. So now's your chance. And when you've learnt to play it, you can come back and play it for my funeral."

Orpha gave Hallie a big bear hug and said, "Hush up about funerals. I'll be coming back to see you one of these days, and you better still be here." Hallie leaned forward to plant a kiss on Orpha's cheek. Orpha wondered how long Hallie could last with all that weight and with a right leg and foot swelling twice the size of the left.

Putting a few clothes in the sack with her banjo, Orpha bought a stagecoach ticket to Knoxville with the money she had saved from her winnings at poker. At Knoxville, she bought another to get her to Sparta.

FIVE

The Prodigal Returns

Lost Creek Valley, White County, Tennessee
Spring 1844

"Some folks call this place Sunset Rock," the coachman explained. "Everybody wants to stop here and look." After crossing over the winding mountain road into White County in the spring of 1844, the coachman stopped near a massive rock outcropping on one of the highest peaks. The passengers stepped down to admire the view. Orpha could see for miles and miles across the valley and to the hills beyond. It was breathtaking.

If Sunset Rock had lifted her spirits, Orpha's arrival at the Rock House Inn just before sundown left her less than elated. When she tried to hire a buggy to take her to Lost Creek, the local coachman refused to take her.

"It's too dangerous to go tonight," he said. "These strange birds flew in here to roost yesterday around sundown and stayed until about ten o'clock. They covered everything inside an area about a mile and a half wide and just about as long. The preacher said they're pigeons, but they didn't look like no pigeons I've ever seen. No sooner had the first covey arrived than another one flew in. There wasn't enough roostin' room for the new batch, so they just lit on the backs of the first ones and set right there. I'm afraid they're coming back agin tonight. Some say it's witches a-doin' it, and if it *is* witches, I don't want no part of it."

He waved his hands to make his point. "See them branches broke down all over the road? Well, they was so many birds roostin' up there they broke the limbs right off the trees. People been shootin' at 'em, tryin' to kill 'em, but I ain't seen no dead birds yet! The guns are ready for tonight, I reckon, but I ain't gonna wait around to see if they kill anything. I'm goin' home and shut my door."

Orpha thought of Hallie. She would say it was an omen, but Orpha refused to believe in such things. People conjure things up to find a way to lay blame, and if they're doing it for my benefit, she thought, they can just stop. There couldn't be anything worse happen to me than what's already happened. She knew it was no use arguing with the coachman. With what little money she had left, she paid for a bed in the women's section at the Rock House Inn.

Orpha would never have imagined the welcome home she received from the family. They were all there waiting for her—Henry, Clary, Clara, Christina, Mary, and Daniel. But where were Grandma Polly and Grandpa Thomas? Hadn't they come to Lost Creek Valley from North Carolina?

"Papa and Mama are gone now," Henry told her. "Mama died the year after they came, and Papa died just last year. They talked about you a lot. They would have loved to see you all grown up."

How sad, Orpha thought. I remember waving goodbye to them when we left for Tennessee. I guess I thought they would always be there. I remember Grandma Polly telling me not to eat all the teacakes she had baked for us. Life changes fast, she thought.

It seemed Henry and Clary had invited everybody in Lost Creek Valley and all the Fraleys in Big Bottom to the welcome home party for Orpha. Pigs roasted on spits over a large outdoor fire. White cotton sheeting covered tables of rough planks, quickly built for the occasion. Women brought green beans cooked with ham hocks, diced boiled potatoes mixed with chopped onion and pickles, johnnycake and sweet potato pie. Even though many of the neighbors were church-going people, Orpha noticed most of them didn't hesitate to drink a touch of Henry's homemade apple brandy. Henry's wagon served as a platform for the fiddlers and the banjo players.

The celebration started midafternoon with eating, singing, and dancing. Orpha joined the musicians and strummed on her gourd banjo. "I really got to learn to play this thing," she told one of the fiddlers. Orpha couldn't understand her swirling emotions: elation, surprise, confusion, and a sense that she didn't deserve such a homecoming.

In the first few days in Lost Creek, Orpha realized time had brought change to all of them. Clara was the one who surprised Orpha the most. She was close to thirty and still at home. Orpha had seen her in nothing but her long black skirts and brown, high-necked blouses since she had come home. She noticed Clara's hair was pulled tight against her head and tied in back, making her look stern and unattractive. It seemed to her Clara almost never smiled.

"I thought you'd be married by now," Orpha said.

"Ain't found me no man I want to marry," Clara said. "Guess I'll just be an old maid." Then, quickly changing the subject, she looked at Orpha and asked, "What did you do all those years after you left us?" Orpha detected a hint of bitterness in Clara's question and wondered if Henry and Clary had ever told Clara anything about her life in Hawkins County.

"Well, I worked for a woman named Hallie over the mountain from Jonesborough." Orpha said. "I did whatever had to be done around the place, but my job was mainly taking care of her children."

"Did you meet any men?" Clara asked.

"No, not any to talk about."

"Did you live with this Hallie?"

Clara's questions were becoming uncomfortable for Orpha. "Yes," she said.

"Must have been a big place for you to live there," Clara said. "Did you have any fun while you was there?"

"Some," Orpha said.

"What kind of fun?" Clara asked, a slight pique in her voice. "It shore ain't been much fun around here. The most fun I've had since you left was at that party they throwed for you when you got back."

Orpha decided it was time to end the conversation. Maybe later she could share her secrets with Clara, about losing Wilson and all the misery it had brought her. Maybe when the time was right, she could even tell Clara about her life with Avery. But for now, she thought, it's my secret to keep.

It didn't take Orpha long to see that Henry had prospered in his wagon-making business as well as with his farming. He had cleared trees and high grasses on the land he bought in Lost Creek, and planted corn, wheat, and a little tobacco. The weather had been kind and the harvests had been bountiful.

"I'm even raising turkeys," he told Orpha, chuckling. "Come on out here and see my brooders and pens."

Orpha followed her papa to the barn and to the turkey pens beyond. "You should have seen me and Daniel herding turkeys to market in Georgia last fall," he said. "I hired a couple of hands to help us, and we drove five hundred big fat turkeys from Sparta, Tennessee, to Sparta, Georgia, about three hundred miles each way."

"That's really some story," Orpha laughed. "I can't imagine you drivin' three hundred turkeys all that way. Are you trying to tell me there really is a place in Georgia called Sparta?"

"Yep, there really is a Sparta, Georgia," Henry told her. "It took us nearly three weeks to make the trip. We smeared tar on the turkeys' feet to keep 'em from becomin' too tender to walk."

"I'm glad life has been good to you in Lost Creek." Orpha told Henry.

"Well, it weren't in the beginning. When we first arrived," he said, "we had to clear away all this low-laying brush. It was thick and twisted. There weren't that many trees, just brush. We built a one-room cabin. We all slept in that one room until we could add on three more. Now that you're home, I'm thinking of addin' on another room just for you and Clara, so the two of you won't have to sleep with the other girls."

It seemed to Orpha that her mother had changed less than any of them. Except for her slightly stooped shoulders and her graying hair, she still looked the same. Same old Clary, Orpha thought, especially when it comes to religion. One Sunday, soon after Orpha's homecoming, Clary was complaining to Orpha that Henry and the children never went to church with her. "Clara is the only one who goes with me," she said. After a slight pause—for my benefit, thought Orpha—Clary added, "Of course, they all go to the church socials. That's where they meet all the young people. Henry never goes to any of it. He won't even go to the all-day singings and dinners on the ground."

Orpha remembered Henry never had much use for the church. "As long as the church refuses to speak out against slavery," he said, "they won't catch me attendin' their meetin's. It's nothing but hypocrisy to say you love your neighbor on Sunday and then sell him on the auction block on Monday."

Orpha had little interest in what went on at the church. She certainly agreed with her father about the hypocrisy, and she paid special attention when she heard him ask her mother, "Don't you care that two of the biggest slavers in this county are members of your church? They sell anywhere from a hundred to two hundred slaves a year, and nobody in the church speaks out against it. You, *of all people*, should be outraged that your fellow church member Murphy does a brisker business sellin' slaves on his auction block of a Monday than the church ever does savin' souls of a Sunday."

Clary gave Henry a withering look and walked briskly out of the room. Orpha suspected Henry had almost divulged something he was not supposed to, and she could see he regretted it. She wanted to know more, but for now, she decided, it might be best just to let things be. She felt sorry for her mother that day and volunteered to go to church with her.

If nature had been kind to the Fraleys up to the time Orpha joined them in 1844, the drought that followed came near to wiping them out. Drought had left the corn crops dry and stubbly, and the wheat fields didn't produce. Food was hard to come by. Even the animals were suffering. Most of the turkeys had died. The family never seemed to have enough to feed themselves, much less the livestock. And good water was getting scarce. The well Henry had dug when they first arrived was yielding mostly mud. The creek had almost dried up, although they were still able to get enough water from there to take them through each day. The water they could spare for the animals was increasingly limited. At last the rains came in torrents, filling the rivers and springs and overflowing onto the lower lands.

"When it soaks in and drains off," Henry told the others, "we will start again and plant seeds."

Orpha decided it was time she found a way to contribute to the family's dwindling resources. When she announced she wanted to get a job working at the Bon Air Hotel and Health Resort on Bon Air Mountain, Henry said nothing, but Clary made no pretense about how she felt.

"You don't want to work as servant girl to them rich people," she told Orpha. "They come there from the big cities to 'take the waters' as they say, but all they do is laze around and practice every kind of sin there is—drinkin', gamblin', carousin'. We don't need money bad enough for you to sell your soul to the devil up on Bon Air Mountain." Later, reweighing the family's need against the moral risks of working on Bon Air Mountain, Clary said pensively, "It's a good distance away. How would you get there?"

"I'd manage," Orpha replied.

Orpha had first learned about the resort hotel from gossip at the welcome home celebration. "Rich folks come to Bon Air from all over to get away from the heat," someone said. "I didn't know until just the other day," said another, "that there are three different springs near the hotel flowing within thirty feet of each other—one with sulfur water, another with free stone water, and a third one heavy with iron. Between them, they are supposed to cure just about anything that ails you."

Another person said she used to go there before the hotel was built. "It was so beautiful to look out over the mountains. You can see three counties and two states from up there. It's such a quiet, cool place. I really loved going there."

"But it's different now, with all them rich foreigners takin' over the mountain in the summertime," said another woman. "Since they built that place in '42, none of us local folks feels comfortable goin' up there anymore. We used to go all the time on picnics. Now they come in their fine carriages from as far away as New Orleans. They come from all over the country—Memphis, Huntsville, even North Carolina and Virginia. I won't go up there anymore. I don't aim to have them fancy women struttin' around and lookin' down their noses at me."

"On the other hand," said another, "it ain't been all bad. There's lots of ways we benefit from the rich foreigners. For instance, my man makes pretty good money supplyin' them with meat, milk, eggs, and vegetables."

"That's so," Clary had chimed in. "I don't hold no truck with how they carry on up there, but I have to admit that my man Henry has got some good work because of the hotel. Them foreigners are always needin' wagon and coach repairs after travelin' over them rough mountain roads."

"See there, Mama," Orpha spoke up, "There's some good in everything. Papa told me he had sold lots of turkeys up there, too. I do believe I need to go up there and look around and see if there ain't something I can do they're willin' to pay for."

From the middle of 1845 until the outbreak of the war in 1861, Orpha worked every summer for the Bon Air Hotel and Health Resort, first as a housemaid, and later as supervisor of housekeeping. During her early days at Bon Air, Orpha met Leonard Seeley, a mixed-blood Chickasaw, who worked in the stables as a groom. It soon became clear to Orpha that they had a special affinity for each other. On an afternoon in late May, he convinced her to go riding with him over the ridge and through the valley. Orpha thought she had never seen anyone who could ride a horse like he could. She found herself liking him for his stolid, quiet manner, as well as for his superior horsemanship.

Leonard Seeley was the son of a Scotsman, Bennett Seeley, and a full-blood Chickasaw woman, *Wa-mon-ee*, who lived in the Mississippi Territory in West Tennessee. Leonard was handsome with dusky skin and long straight black hair that blew in the wind as he rode. Leonard spoke English well, having been taught in a mission school near his village. Like many Chickasaws, Leonard had adopted the ways of white settlers, and he seemed comfortable in their midst.

In 1830, Chickasaw leaders met with government representatives, including President Andrew Jackson, at Franklin, Tennessee. They were persuaded to sign an agreement that would result in their removal. On the day set for the removal, July 13, 1837, Colonel Upshaw, the government official-in-charge, had rounded up only three hundred Chickasaws and their black slaves, though others joined them as they marched through the Chickasaw nation. The Chickasaws had paid for the removal out of their own pockets from the sale of their lands to the government. When the detachment passed through Memphis, onlookers did not see the misery behind the well-ordered Chickasaws in their tribal dress astride their princely horses.

By 1843, most Chickasaws had migrated to Indian Territory. But some rode east toward the mountains of Tennessee to hide out. Leonard Seeley had done just that. When his family joined the Chickasaw removal, he headed east across middle Tennessee bound for the Cumberlands.

"I spent the first year hunting and fishing and hiding away from the authorities," Leonard told Orpha. "Most Indians had been driven out of this area, so no one was threatened by the few of us who were left. I worked for short periods of time for farmers and lumber mills, doing whatever work I could get. I even hired out to help a man and his son drive five hundred or so turkeys from Sparta, Tennessee, to Sparta, Georgia. I was afraid to stay too long in one place, afraid I might get caught and sent west."

"I'll bet you don't know who it was you helped drive them turkeys to Georgia," Orpha laughed. "That was my Papa and my brother Daniel. Ain't life funny?"

"Maybe so," he said. "Life may be funny in some ways, but mostly it can be pretty hard, especially when the government won't let you own even an acre of land to build a house on for your family."

"But you don't have to worry about that," Orpha said. "You don't have a family."

"Not yet," he said with a twinkle in his eye, "But I might have if a certain pretty lady would agree to marry me."

Orpha blushed. She found herself wondering what it would be like to wake up every morning with Leonard beside her. Still, she wasn't sure they could ever be legally married. If they were to be together, it would probably have to be in a union unblessed by either church or government. Yet, after Avery, she thought, I shouldn't let that little worry stand in my way.

Orpha liked Leonard Seeley. Often at the end of the day, when the inn workers would gather around the campfire behind the hotel, Orpha would join Leonard in making music. He played the fiddle, and she played her banjo. He had a favorite song he liked to sing over and over, changing one important word.

It's Orpha in the springtime, Orpha in the fall!
If I can't have my Orpha, I'll have no gal at all.
Git along home Orpha, Orpha! Get along home I say!
Git along home Orpha, Orpha! I'll marry you some day!

"It's you better git along home, Leonard. I ain't a-marryin' nobody," laughed Orpha.

"Maybe not today," he said. "But you never know about tomorrow."

They sat quietly gazing into the burning embers long after the others had gone in. She wondered what it would be like to be married to Leonard Seeley.

"Do you believe in signs?" Leonard interrupted her thought.

"I don't know," she responded. "What kind of signs?"

"Well, my old mammy was a great one for signs," he said. "She always told me that if I could learn to read 'em, signs could tell the future. And I believe that turkey drive I went on with your papa is a clear sign you and me were meant to be together." Laughing, Orpha allowed as how it didn't seem to her much of a sign at all. Still, she found herself considering the possibility of a life with Leonard.

But that was before she met William Spruill.

BOOK V

The Spruills of Scotland

1845-1870

We all come from the past, and children ought to know what it was that went into their making, to know that life is a braided cord of humanity stretching up from time long gone, and that it cannot be defined by the span of a single journey from diaper to shroud.

—Russell Baker, Journalist
From *Growing Up*

ONE

Orpha and William

Lost Creek Valley, Tennessee
1845-1857

Orpha had heard about a new road beginning construction from Sparta across the mountain to Crossville. When completed, the road would go through Bon Air by the hotel, following the old Indian path. By the middle of June, she began to encounter road workers breaking up gravel in the new roadbed. They were a loud and raucous crowd who hollered and hooted as she rode by. She tried to ignore their stares and whistles. She liked working at the Bon Air Hotel and Health Resort, and she generally liked the early morning ride to get there. She certainly wouldn't let a few hoots and whistles spoil her day.

She loved the exhilaration of waking up in the morning to roosters crowing and cowbells clanging. When the first streaks of the sun's rays filtered through the thin fog across Lost Creek Valley, she saddled her horse. Henry and Clary were always up before dawn and busy with their farm chores. Henry was up first to build the fire in the cook stove, and then Clary prepared breakfast. Nobody spoke much at the breakfast table. Sometimes it occurred to Orpha that breakfast would be a good time to tell them about Wilson, but she kept putting it off.

On this June morning, very much like other June mornings, she felt a sense of satisfaction about riding off to Bon Air. She felt needed. She had been accepted back as part of the family, and she intended to show them how grateful she was. How interesting life is, she thought. Every day there's something new. Nothing ever stays the same, and I'm glad.

The road leading out of Lost Creek Valley was rough, almost too rough for travel, and when she turned off onto the new road, her horse had an even more difficult time plodding through muddy holes and over rocky terrain. But progress was being made. Men were putting through a road that would make travel easier and bring people from everywhere.

Sometimes, as she rode, she would think about Little Wilson and wonder whether he was happy and being taken care of. One day soon she would have to go to Arkansas and find him. Her daydreams ended abruptly when suddenly the horse struggled to maintain its footing through the newly dug earth. Orpha pulled on the reins in an effort to steady him. "Whoa!" she said. The next thing she knew, she was on the ground, lying flat on her back in the mud. You really never know what's just around the next bend, she thought.

Men's faces appeared above her. "Is she all right?" one said. "Here, I'll help her up," another snickered. "I think I'm just the one she needs. Stand back and get outta my way. I'm coming, Honey!"

Among the raucous voices, she heard one she thought showed real concern.

"Are you okay?" he asked. "Can I help you up?" She stretched out her hand and he pulled her to her feet. She brushed off the dirt and mud from her dress.

The others taunted her rescuer with, "Sweet William found him a girl!" He ignored them. "I'm sorry," he said. "I should have stationed someone around the bend to warn people."

Orpha was more humiliated than angry. She responded to the hecklers with: "Idiots! Leave me alone!"

"My name is William," he said. "William Spruill."

William Spruill knew he was named for his father William, who was named for his grandfather William, and when he had his first son, he knew he would call him William. What he had no way of knowing was that the first Spruill was not a William but a Walter.

Born about 1198 near Loch Lomond in Scotland, Walter had not yet acquired a family name. His family belonged to a settlement of fishermen and hunters who lived at the head of Loch Long. Walter was a member of an extended family, the Clan MacFarlane, whose members dominated and terrorized the surrounding countryside for six hundred years. Walter's father eked out a living on a small plot of land on the northern shore of Loch Long at the foot of the Arrochar Mountain range, but he was best known for his skill as a guide and hunter. He was frequently asked to lead the hunting party of Alwyn, Second Earl of Lennox.

When Walter was about the age of twelve, he was sent to the Benedictine monks to be educated at the Abbey of Paisley. There, he became friends with Gilchrist, the seventh son of Earl Alwyn. It was at Paisley that Walter, at the age of nineteen, finally acquired the name of Spruill. The monks who were his teachers referred to him disparagingly as "Spreuille," meaning in Middle Scottish, "to sprawl." It was conjectured that the name arose when his teachers continually tripped over his long legs. What is a matter of historical record, however, is that about this time, he married and began to beget more Spruills.

In 1221, Earl Alwyn's son was granted the barony of Arrochar, and in that autumn, Gilchrist and his father, the earl, visited Arrochar to meet the inhabitants and to hunt. Walter and his father led the hunting party. During a rest period, the hunting party was attacked by a band of outlaws. Because Walter felt responsible for leading the party into danger, he distinguished himself by fighting fiercely and driving the outlaws away. Several of the earl's men were so badly wounded they were unable to return home; and having observed Walter's bravery, to make up for the holes left in his entourage, the seventy-year-old earl offered him a job. When the earl died, Gilchrist became the first chief of the Clan MacFarlane, and for the next forty years, Walter served Gilchrist as his right-hand man. In 1306, Walter was given charter to lands in a place called Cowden, an estate in Renfrew near Glasgow that remained in the Spruill family until 1622, by which time most of the Spruills had migrated from Glasgow to Northern Ireland for political reasons.

Orpha's William was descended from one William Spruill, an elder in the Presbyterian Church in County Donegal. William's great-grandfather, born in 1729, was one of the first Scots-Irish settlers to cross the Blue Ridge into the Shenandoah Valley of Virginia in the mid-1700s. By 1784, five more Spruill families had moved into the area.

William's grandfather, William, obtained a grant of 168 acres on the Cowpasture River and lived there with his wife, Jane, until 1761. Unable to protect themselves from Indian uprisings, they worked their way south into the headwaters of Moffatt's Creek where, in 1772, they bought 470 acres and built a log cabin on their new land. Grandfather William fathered fifteen children, one of whom was William's father, who was born in 1769 and came to be called Squire Billy. He married Susannah Beard in 1804, and their third child, William, was born in 1814. This William migrated from Augusta County in Virginia in 1838 to White County, Tennessee, and, indeed, was the very William who caught Orpha's eye and heart.

How could she have known on this spring morning in 1845 that someone special would be waiting for her around the bend in the road? She wasn't sure she believed in providence, but the minute he said, "My name is William Spruill," she knew their lives were destined to be intertwined. She was certainly not looking for a man. She'd had enough of men with Avery, but here was this tall, lanky man, his head and face mostly covered by dark hair, standing in the middle of the road gazing down at her with sympathetic blue eyes. Yes, she thought, I must definitely get to know this man.

As he helped her remount her horse, she asked, "How long have you been here in these parts?"

"Since '38. I've only been on this job for a year now."

"Do you know my papa, Henry Fraley?"

"Sure, me and him served on a jury together a while back, and I saw his family at the Fourth of July picnic."

The first time Orpha took William home with her to Lost Creek, Clara was not kind in her opinion of him. "He's the ugliest man I ever saw. Who can tell what he looks like with that heavy beard? Is he hidin' a ugly Adam's apple? He's too skinny. He needs somebody to fatten him up." Orpha wondered why Clara had nothing good to say about William. Would she be this critical about any man I brought home, or did she really think he's not the man for me?

Orpha could only agree William was nothing great to look at. But to Clara's criticism, she replied, "He's gentle and kind, and he has a quiet way about him that makes me feel good. He's not like some of these loud-mouthed men here in Lost Creek and Big Bottom, or like those rich, self-centered men at the Bon Air Hotel. He's something extra special. "Besides," Orpha went on, "I'm not askin' for your approval or anyone else's for that matter."

Through the summer, Orpha worked at the resort while William continued as overseer for the building of roads in the county. In August, William asked Orpha to marry him. Clara insisted Orpha should think about marrying Leonard Seeley instead of William Spruill.

"Even though Leonard's a half-breed," she reminded Orpha, "he'll make you a good husband."

"What did she have against William?" Orpha wondered. She paid no attention to Clara, and the next day she told Leonard Seeley she had accepted William's proposal of marriage. Leonard began to sing:

> Git *along home, Orpha, Orpha! Git along home I say!*
> *Git along home, Orpha, Orpha! I'll marry you some day!*

He kissed her hand, wished her well, and said, "I do intend to marry you. Not now, but someday. I'll come for you one day when you least expect it. Until then, git along home." Leonard left White County soon after.

After the wedding, William moved in with Orpha at her parents' home in Lost Creek. As a wedding present, Henry further expanded the family cabin so the newlyweds could have a room of their own.

In 1846, their first child, William, was born. Clara volunteered to take care of him during the summer while Orpha worked at Bon Air. "It's my way of contributing to the family," she said. Little did she know over the next ten years, she would be nursemaid to all three of the Spruill children—Little Will, Brennan, born in 1852, and Lavinia, born in 1857.

Orpha loved her three children and was thankful they were healthy and happy, but there had not been one day in her life since Wilson had been taken from her that she had not thought about him. She had told William early on about Avery and her child Wilson, but she had never told Henry and Clary. William was a good listener, and his advice to her was to let go of the past. "There's nothing you can do about it," he said. "So you need to accept that Wilson is happy somewhere in Arkansas, and you need to love the children who are here."

TWO

Sadness Revisited

Jonesborough, Tennessee
1858

On Wilson's seventeenth birthday, Orpha told William she was going back to Jonesborough to see Caroline. "Maybe she'll tell me where he is," she said. "I have to know."

As they approached Jonesborough, Orpha began to have doubts about seeing Caroline again. "Maybe I shouldn't have come. Maybe we should just turn around and go back," she said to William.

"You might as well go ahead," he told her, "What can it hurt? If it helps settle your mind, it'll be well worth the trip."

Time had not been kind to Caroline. She looked older than her years and she was almost blind. "Who's there?" She asked, tapping her cane.

"It's Orpha," she said. "I know you think I have no right to ask you, but I need to know where Wilson is."

"He's in Arkansas," Caroline said.

"Where in Arkansas?"

"He's with my cousin George and his wife, Molly. He's happy with them."

"It was wrong for you to take him away from me," Orpha said. "You did it out of spite."

Caroline stood, shoulders bent, her eyes closed. Orpha could see that Caroline's pain, like her own, had never gone away. At last Caroline spoke.

"They love him like he was their own," she said. "They've raised him and given him a good education. He's doing just fine. You'll only ruin it for him if you try to find him. He thinks you're dead. You've got to let him be." Her voice took on a soft pleading tone. "Just let the past be. We all have to get on with our lives."

Deep down, Orpha knew Caroline was right. She also knew she would have to carry the burden of her betrayal of Caroline with Avery for the rest of her life. Orpha wondered what life had meant for Caroline after she sent Wilson away. What would Caroline have done if her own child had been taken?

"Tell me about your mother," Caroline said suddenly. "Is she well?"

"She's fine, I guess," Orpha said, surprised.

"Clary and I used to be good friends," Caroline said. "Tell her I miss her."

Orpha and William left Caroline standing on the long porch of her big farmhouse looking sad and alone. "What must I do now?" Orpha asked William.

"Be a good mother to the children who are with us," he said.

Orpha had one more place she had to visit before they headed back to Lost Creek. She wanted William to meet Hallie. On many evenings, after their work was finished, Orpha had told William stories of Hallie. Now he would be able to meet her.

Hallie's guards greeted them as they reached the top of the ridge. They were taken as intruders and would have been summarily escorted back down but for Orpha's insistence they ask Hallie first. Once convinced Orpha was an old friend of Hallie's, they relented and let them pass.

"We hafta be mighty careful," one of the men said. "The revenuers is always after Hallie, and you never know what tricks they'll come up with to get at her."

As they approached Hallie's cabin, they could see through the front door she was sitting in her rocking chair. That's the same chair she was sitting in when I last saw her, Orpha thought. It's like I never left.

Hallie leaned forward as if to get up, but found it too great an effort. Sinking back laughing, she said, "I don't believe it! You look just like you did when you left twelve year ago. I reckoned I'd never see you again."

"I told you I'd be back, didn't I?" Orpha said. "Well, here I am!"

William couldn't believe his eyes. Orpha had told him Hallie was a big woman, but he had no idea she would be this big. She must be at least five hundred pounds, he thought. Her huge, flabby body looked as if it had been poured into the rocking chair, the fat bulging through the rungs and hanging in folds over the arms of the chair.

"I picked up this here disease," she said to William. "They call it elephantiasis. Makes my leg swell up somethin' awful. Trouble is, the swellin' won't go down again. I just have to live with it and hope it won't just keep on a-growin'."

William listened as Orpha told Hallie how they had met, how she was working at Bon Air, and how he was cutting new roads over the mountain. She went on, all about their marriage and their three children. She told Hallie how she had passed on to her children the tales Hallie had told years ago. She talked about her visit with Caroline. When she finally stopped to catch her breath, she asked Hallie, "And what about you? What have you been up to since I left?"

"Law, child," Hallie said, "there's too much to tell. I been married three times since I seen you. Two died of too much alcohol and one just up and left me. I have eight children now, all healthy and doin' well. Ever'body's gone fishin' up at Zur Pond today. I'm too big to go up there anymore. My leg won't let me. I lost my last baby a couple of years ago. And I've had to fight the revenuers for some time now. I've had seven warrants for my arrest, but every time they come to get me, they can't get me out the front door. They just smash my stills and leave."

She broke into a hearty laugh. "And then they elected that Wally Earl Eards, and he come up here smart-aleck-like and bragged he was gonna arrest me. When he couldn't get me out the door, he said he was gonna tear down the house. I laughed and told Wally Earl the law wouldn't let him tear down the house. He went back to town and told 'em down at the jailhouse that Hallie Hollins could be caught but not brought."

Orpha and William went into gales of laughter.

"Then they sent for federal revenuers from Washington," Hallie went on. "And I reckon they thought they could arrest me. One of 'em says: We aim to put you in this big rope sling and let you down the ridge to a wagon that'll haul you off to the Knoxville jail. Well, now, I tole him, that sounds like a real smart idea. I asked him if it was his idea, or did somebody else think it up? Well, ma'am, he says, it was mostly me. Some of the little details was thought out by other folks, but it was mostly my thinkin'."

William bent over laughing. "Well, did he try it?"

"He knowed better! When they come to arrest me now," she laughed, "I just offer 'em a sip of my best liquor outta my gourd, and they leave a-shakin' their heads."

William had thought Orpha must have exaggerated her descriptions of Hallie, but now he knew she hadn't. Everything she had told him was true.

"I'm glad I got to meet you," he told Hallie as they left. "Don't let the revenuers get you."

She laughed. "Life ain't easy, but we been put here, so we have to make whatever we can out of it. Don't you worry about me," she said. "They ain't a-gonna get me."

Orpha was glad she had made the trip to see Caroline, and she was glad William had been able to meet Hallie. Orpha realized she would never be able to do over what had been done earlier in her life, and even though deep down she still despised Caroline for taking her baby boy, she knew he was better off living in Arkansas with people who cared for him and could give him what she could not. And William is right, she thought. We need to get on with our lives.

THREE

Between the Blue and the Gray

Lost Creek Valley, Tennessee
1862-1864

L ife changed drastically for the family one morning in 1862 when Confederate soldiers arrived at the Bon Air Resort and began to tear it down. Guests were given one hour to get their things and get out. By day's end, the hotel and its outbuildings had been totally demolished.

"What a waste!" Orpha fumed. "Why couldn't they let things be? Just because the owner is a Unionist is no reason to destroy the place, is it?"

"That's reason enough, I reckon," William said, "given the mood of the people hereabouts. We both know there's been a lot of resentment among folks around here. People don't like foreigners, especially rich foreigners, comin' in and takin' over."

"I know that," said Orpha, "but did they have to take my job right out from under me? I don't know what we're gonna do for money after this. The family's gonna miss what I've been bringing in. A lot of people are gonna suffer because of this stupidity."

"And it won't be long before there won't be any more money from road-building, either," William said.

The family had watched the election of 1860 closely. Henry, who had just celebrated his sixty-fourth birthday, was taken aback when the state of Tennessee refused to list Lincoln on the ballot. "I'm voting for John Bell," he said. "He wants to keep the Union together."

After Fort Sumter, many who were previously pro-Union now favored secession. William was particularly vocal after that. "Lincoln called for seventy-five thousand troops to whip the seceded states," he pointed out. "I ain't gonna be one of them. I'm fightin' on the Rebel side."

"Surely, you can't do that," Henry argued. "You'd be supportin' slavery."

"You can't trust the Yankees," William countered. "They'll tell you one thing and do another. I just don't like them comin' down here and pushin' us around."

Henry stayed home on Election Day. He did not want to be drawn into a brawl with his neighbors. When some of his Unionist friends returned from the voting place claiming the secessionists had taken control and refused to let them vote, he knew he'd made the right decision.

"They threatened us," one man told Henry. "They said if we weren't for 'em, we was agin 'em. They said if we tried to vote, they'd make us pay."

"I don't understand it," one of the farmers said, shaking his head. "Most of them don't even own slaves. They just barely make it from year to year like the rest of us. Why do they want to fight on the Rebel side?"

Henry knew why. Like William, they resent Northerners coming down here and telling us what to do. They're convinced Lincoln is trying to take away their independence. Henry also thought many were spurred on by promises that their social standing would be raised, and they would be given good pensions after the war. Secessionists had spread the rumor that the Yankees wanted to put Negroes on an equal social standing with whites. That scared many of his neighbors.

When White County residents of both persuasions organized their own local companies, William joined the Twenty-fifth Regiment of Tennessee Infantry, one of nine full companies of the White County Confederacy. Orpha couldn't believe how her family was now divided over a war none of them really understood. Her husband was riding off in a Confederate uniform, and her brother Daniel was headed to the north of the county to sign up for the only Union Company raised in White County. It was hard to listen to her own brother and her husband arguing the right and wrong of the war, but when the two left, they parted friends. Little Will, now sixteen, decided his father was right about the war. He lied about his age and ran off to join the Rebels.

Henry was disappointed that more did not support the Union cause. Couldn't they see there was no future in secession? No future in slavery? When Henry did not show support for the Rebel side, he was threatened.

Many of his neighbors who supported the Union had fled to Kentucky. Henry considered going as well, but he didn't want to leave the family behind. He tried to convince the women to pull up stakes and go north with him.

"This is our land," Orpha said. "We've worked hard to raise our family here. We've come through hard times before, and we can't just let them chase us off our land. We're all neighbors in this valley. Nobody's gonna let good friendships be ruined by politics."

Had she known the chaos, the devastation, the pain that was coming, she might have agreed to take the family north. Little Will would lose his life at Fort Donalson a few months after he joined up. She and Clara and the children would suffer untold misery and deprivation in the farmhouse at Lost Creek before the war finally ended. And Henry would have his Quaker convictions put to the test as never before.

Christina suggested her mother and father move in with her and her husband, Michael O'Connor, in Sparta. "Papa can keep on repairin' wagons," Christina volunteered. "People are gonna need their horses shod, no matter which side they're on."

Michael, who worked as a White County surveyor, knew people with money and influence who might help. "For the safety of the family," he told Henry, "you'll have to promise you'll keep your Unionist sympathies to yourself. It would even help if you let it be known you hate Yankees."

Henry found the idea hard to swallow. He was not accustomed to letting other people dictate what he believed, whether it had to do with politics or religion, and he detested having to lie, no matter what the circumstances.

On the issue of slavery, Henry was convinced it was wrong to own another human being, just as it was wrong to separate people because of color. He and Clary had struggled for years because of color laws. Could a Union victory in this horrible war really bring about a difference in people's attitudes? Can anyone ever justify all the killing? It was wrong to kill another human being, in war or otherwise. It was also wrong to pretend allegiance to a cause he abhorred. What would Embree and his fellow Quakers say? At last, he decided he would keep quiet about his views so his family would not be harmed, and he and Clary would move in with Christina and Michael in Sparta.

The cabin in Lost Creek, like most of the farm homes in White County, had become a fortress. The Knoxville to Nashville turnpike that converged near Sparta with the Old Kentucky Road had become a military highway for both Confederate and Union troops. Both armies used the roads to move troops and supplies. That meant soldiers made foraging trips through White County, taking horses, hogs, cattle, chickens, and other produce. Orpha,

Clara, Brennan, and Vennie found themselves living in a hell they could never have imagined even a year ago. Though their cabin was not on a main route, not a single day or night passed from late 1862 until the war ended in 1865 that they did not live in constant fear. It was not the regular armies, either Confederate or Federal, they feared the most, but the bushwhackers. They would swoop down from the hills like vultures taking whatever they could find. Orpha and Clara had tried to hide what they cherished. Orpha wrapped her banjo in sheeting and buried it far away in the woods.

Orpha became a lieutenant in the household, giving orders about what to do if attacked. She and Clara kept a rifle near the front door and another beside the back door during the day, and at night they laid the guns beside their beds. Whether the weather was hot or cold, they kept the windows shut. At night they hung cowbells above the outside doors so if anyone tried to get in, they would know it.

By 1864, they had been robbed dozens of times. Sometimes in a single day, marauders and soldiers from both sides raided the cabin for food, blankets, clothing, farm tools, and anything else they could find that hadn't already been stolen. Orpha and Clara had tried raising vegetables in the garden and even planting a corn patch, but before they could harvest anything, marauders would come and strip the fields.

As the war neared its end, fewer bushwhackers and Rebel soldiers came by, and while there were still many Yankee soldiers in the county, they now seemed in too big a hurry to stop. Orpha and Clara began to relax their guard, and even returned to their prewar practice of doing laundry outside in the backyard.

One day, as they were building a fire under the big black wash kettle, three drunken men came upon them unawares. Vennie was playing with her doll nearby, and Brennan was gathering firewood in the woods behind the house. The leers on the men's faces told Orpha they were interested in more than pillaging. She knew it was too late to run for the guns. They had been left inside by the back door. Clara screamed, and Brennan, hearing the scream, came running from the woods. Orpha began trying to bargain with the men. "Take what you want, and leave us alone," she said.

They laughed. "We don't want nothing but you and this here other'n."

Clara began to cry. "I'll make a deal with you," Orpha said, "if you'll let my sister take the two children into the woods. I can handle all three of you."

"Why settle for one when we can have both?" said one with a lewd laugh.

"I promise you won't regret it," Orpha coaxed.

"You must be something else," one of them sniggered. "Tell you what I'll do. I'll throw this here penny up in the air and if it comes down heads, you got a deal. If it don't, she ain't going nowheres."

Clara stopped her sobbing. "You can't do that Orpha," she insisted.

"Hush, Clara. It ain't the first time I've ever gambled." It seemed an eternity before the penny hit the ground. "It's heads up." Orpha said. She turned to Clara and said, "Take the children up to the woods and don't come back 'til I holler for you. Somebody's got to take care of the children, and right now, you're all they got. So go."

Inside on the bed, Orpha closed her eyes tight and clinched her fists until her fingernails cut into the flesh and brought the blood. She bit her lip to keep from screaming. The only thing that was keeping her from passing out was thinking of Clara, Brennan, and Vennie safe in the woods. She knew she had to make sure the men kept their bargain. It seemed an eternity before they finished and left.

Afterwards, Orpha threw herself into the creek and scrubbed her body until it ached. What she couldn't wash away was the memory of that awful dog-in-heat smell mixed with rancid sweat, filth, and liquor. Later, she went into the woods and retrieved her banjo. When Clara, Brennan and Vennie returned, they found her sitting under the cedar tree behind the house playing "Wildwood Flower" over and over.

"Mama, are you all right?" Brennan asked.

"I'm fine. Don't you worry about your mama, honey," she said. "I'm fine. We're all fine, ain't we Clara?"

Clara couldn't bring herself to respond. What words could she ever say that would be worthy of the sacrifice Orpha had made for her today?

FOUR

Henry's Last Stand

White County, Tennessee
1864

Families in White County were sick of the war. Starvation was widespread even among the wealthy. Slaves were gone. Rich people who had never hoed a garden in their lives were forced to learn how. Like most other White Countians, Orpha was making coffee from parched oats and using molasses for sweetening. Clara and the children were digging up the floor of the smokehouse and boiling the dirt to get salt because there was no salt to be had in the stores. Besides, even if salt had been available to buy, Confederate money was worthless.

No one had heard from Daniel since he joined the Union's Fourth Regiment of the Tennessee Mounted Infantry. In January of 1864, his unit was sent to clear out Rebel guerillas in White County. It was not just luck that Daniel was assigned to his own county. Andrew Johnson, appointed by Lincoln as military governor of Tennessee, thought Rebels could best be controlled by their own kind. Daniel was elated that he could return home to Lost Creek. He could hardly wait to see the family.

"And you ain't never tasted anything as good as my mama's biscuits and gravy," he told his two buddies.

It was not altogether a joyous homecoming. He was saddened to find Henry and Clary gone from the farm, but he determined he could see them when he got back to Sparta. He could scarcely believe the way his sisters and the children looked. They were skinny and ragged and tired, and when he sat down with them at the kitchen table to the meager meal Orpha and Clara had prepared, he remembered happier times when his mother had served more sumptuous fare.

Clara had planned to attend a service at Fraley's Chapel down the road that evening, and Daniel, hoping to meet his sweetheart there, invited his buddies to go along. It was against Orpha's better judgment because she had heard rumors that Champ Ferguson and his men were in the area, but she reluctantly gave her tacit approval when one of the soldiers agreed to remain at the bottom of the hill to raise an alarm if guerrillas came anywhere near, giving them plenty of time to escape.

The preacher was in the middle of a prayer when a gunshot rang out at the bottom of the hill. Before anyone knew what was happening, Ferguson's men had surrounded the church and entered the sanctuary. Three of them stood with their rifles at the ready. Seeing the Union soldiers, one of them opened fire. Then the other two fired. The preacher's prayer ended abruptly when he fell to the floor mortally wounded. Five others had also been hit. Daniel, unhurt, ran out the back door with all three of Ferguson's men in pursuit. His friend, also unhurt, had fallen to the floor between the benches, where Clara and another woman stood over him, hiding him in the folds of their long dresses. He survived to report the slaughter to his superiors. Daniel was not as fortunate. The guerillas soon overtook him and shot him. He lay dead near the body of his lookout friend at the foot of the hill. Despite the continuing danger, Orpha decided Daniel and his friend would be buried in the cemetery beside the church. When Clary learned her only son had been shot and killed, she would not be consoled. She cried for days. Henry sat with her in silence, staring straight ahead.

Henry despised Champ Ferguson. Not only was Ferguson shooting and killing anyone even rumored to be a Union sympathizer in the county, his men had fired upon unarmed women and children in the church, killing five of them in cold blood. Hardest of all for Henry to bear was the knowledge that because of Ferguson, he would never see his only son again. Every Unionist in White and surrounding counties lives in dread of Ferguson's approach, he thought. How can my secessionist neighbors call him a patriot? Some of them even excuse his atrocities by claiming he's wreaking revenge for his own son's death and the rape of his wife at the hands of Union soldiers. Even if that's true, Henry thought, it doesn't excuse the horrors he commits. Henry knew that neither Ferguson nor any of his men ever joined the Confederate army, and when they fought alongside Confederate soldiers, they followed no rules of civilized warfare, bragging they never took prisoners.

It was during one of their many forays through White County that Henry came face to face with one of Ferguson's men. Henry tried to serve all comers in his blacksmith shop on the outskirts of Sparta, whatever their sympathies. Usually, soldiers were in too big a hurry to care what Henry's allegiance was, but this time it was different.

"He's throwed a shoe," the man began. "I want you to put another shoe on him, and I don't want you to take all day. I don't have time for this. I gotta get busy and root me out some Yankee lovers."

Henry said nothing, but the marauder could tell from Henry's startled look he'd already found what he was looking for.

"You wouldn't be a Yankee lover, now would you?" Ferguson's man snarled.

"If you want me to shoe your horse," Henry said, holding the shoe with his tongs in the blazing forge, "you better let me get this shoe hot enough so I can beat it down to size before I nail it on his foot." He kept his eyes focused on his work. He could smell the liquor on the man's breath.

"Well, are you? A Yankee lover, I mean."

Henry said nothing as he watched the horseshoe turn a bright red in the forge.

"I asked you a question!" the man insisted. "Are you a Yankee lover?"

Henry kept at his task.

"You better answer me," the man said. "I don't want no damn Yankee sympathizer shoein' my horse. You hear me?" He kicked Henry hard in the back, almost knocking him into the fire.

Years of pent-up misery and anger swept over Henry. In an instant, he had regained his composure, and with his hammer in his right hand and the red-hot horseshoe firmly clamped by the tongs in his left hand, he lunged at the marauder. The man screamed like a stuck pig when the horseshoe seared a brand into his stomach. Screaming and clutching himself, his eyes wide with disbelief, the man fell on the ground. In another instant, Henry raised his hammer, ready to swing it at the marauder's head.

"You go straight to hell!" Henry said.

Dazed, the marauder felt for his gun. The last words Henry ever heard were: "Damn Yankee sympathizer, that'll learn you!"

Christina and Michael arranged for the burial. Given the danger of travel between Sparta and Lost Creek, they did not send for Orpha and

Clara. Clary would not attend. Henry's death was more than she could bear. Already stricken with the killing of her beloved Daniel, she retreated too far into herself ever to return. She completely stopped eating and simply waited for death. It was not long in coming.

FIVE

Yellow Daffodils

Lost Creek Valley, Tennessee
1864-1870

Orpha had heard from William only once since he left. When two soldiers dressed in Union blue came riding up one afternoon in the summer of 1864, Orpha and Clara readied themselves for the worst. But to their surprise, one of the soldiers dismounted a good distance away and, waving a white handkerchief, shouted: "I have a message to deliver to Orpha Spruill."

"I'm Orpha Spruill. What do you want, Yankee?"

"We're not Yankees, Ma'am, we're Southerners, Rebs. We're friends of William Spruill." Orpha lowered her gun and invited the two soldiers in. Clara stood in the back of room with a gun pointed as they approached the porch.

"How come you're dressed in Yankee clothes?" Orpha asked.

"Yankees are all over this place," he said. "It's the only way we could get here. Your man's been wounded at the battle of Chickamauga," he said. "A bullet grazed one side of his head, but before I could get to him, the Yankees took him prisoner. He'd already told me all about you and Lost Creek before the battle. I think he was sent to one of them Yankee prisons. I was just passing through, so I thought you'd want to know."

Orpha invited the soldiers in for a meal of dandelion and poke greens.

"We ain't got much," Clara said. "But you're welcome to what we got."

"I appreciate you bringing me news of William," Orpha said. "I reckon being in a Yankee prison is better than being shot at on the battlefield."

"Where y'all from?" Orpha asked.

"Over yonder at Rock Island on the Collins," the soldier said. "But we couldn't git there. Too many Yankees. They dynamited the Big Bone Cave where our boys were makin' saltpeter for the Confederacy, and now they're swarmin' all over the place on both sides of the river."

"Where you goin'? "Orpha asked.

"Anywheres so we don't have to fight."

"Ma'am?" the other soldier asked as they were leaving. "Who planted them daffodils on that hill over yonder? I've never seen so many. I could see all that bright yellow, like sunshine, for miles as we come up the valley. I can't believe they are just growing wild."

"They're not wild," Orpha said. "We planted 'em, my mama, my sister, the children and me. We spread 'em around the hillside by breakin' up the clumps and replantin' them in other places. The daffodils are the only things the soldiers and the marauders don't steal."

"They just keep on a-comin' back every spring," Clara said. "We couldn't get rid of 'em if we wanted to."

"They're the only things that hold promise," Orpha said. "They'll be a-bloomin' long after this awful war is over. Just you wait and see."

For the next several months, Orpha waited and hoped for some word from William. Surely he had survived the Yankee prison and, any day now, would be coming home. But that was not to be. A neighbor boy from the same prison told her William had contracted pneumonia in the camp and died two months after the Yankees arrested him. Orpha couldn't imagine she would never see William again. Yet she had nothing left inside her for mourning. She found little consolation in knowing that so many other women in White County had lost their husbands.

Not many had stayed to endure the last throes of the war. They had left the county to stay with relatives or to try to find work. By the time the war was over, many people in Lost Creek Valley had gone somewhere else. Some people had been forced to leave because of their loyalty to the Union government, but others went simply because they had nothing left to stay for. Some were just too tired, unable to pick up the pieces. Lee's surrender only deepened the bitterness.

People began to notice the Ku Klux Klan was becoming more and more active. They claimed they had organized to help people in the community, but Orpha had heard they had murdered a free Negro and now most of the Negroes were fleeing the county. Unionists, both white and black, tried to organize the Union League, but it never gained strength. Most churches had closed their doors, and camp meetings were no longer held. No banks were operating, and there was no money to pay teachers. Even if there had been money, children had to remain home to help work in the fields. Education in White County was brought to a standstill.

When the war ended and there were no more troops coming through, the people left in White County dragged themselves back to planting and cultivating. They had little hope that things would get better. Orpha and Clara and the children worked hard to grow food. With two old broken-down mules and a hand-plow, they were able to turn a plot for a vegetable garden. At least they did not have to worry about bushwhackers stealing what they raised. When the beans, corn, and potatoes were ready for harvest, Orpha went to Sparta to barter with the two stores that were struggling to survive. She exchanged the vegetables for milk, butter, and corn meal. Young Brennan took a job working on the Covington farm near Bone Cave, and for his work, he was given milk, butter, and other staples.

By spring of 1870, Orpha had begun to think they could make it on the farm. Then forces of nature intervened. Early one morning, she awoke to a dead stillness outside—no animal or bird sounds, no movement of the trees, just silence. She knew a funnel cloud was not far away.

"Get up!" she yelled. "Get to the storm-pit. It's a-coming up a storm." They all huddled in the storm-pit. Henry had reinforced it with planks and built three steps leading downward and a heavy door that closed tightly. Inside he had placed wooden benches enough for six people. Over the top, he had built an earthen mound. It had not been used for some time, except to store fruit. Thirteen-year-old Vennie huddled in a damp corner, complaining of dripping water, and the snakes and bugs she feared were in the pit.

"You stay put!" Orpha told her. "You hear that wind blowing? It's like a monster coming to get us all. But we'll be safe if we just sit tight." Finally when the wind stopped and they could see daylight around the door, Orpha carefully opened it and stepped outside. "It's all over," she said. "The storm has moved on."

They were alive and well. The storm had not been able to touch them, at least not physically. Part of the cabin was still standing, but the windows were broken out and most of the roof was gone. The barn had been completely leveled, and they couldn't find the two old mules they had managed to keep through the war. Some days later, they heard about two mules that had been picked up by the storm and deposited on the other side of the county. Could they be Old Rock and Old Mandy?

A few apple trees in the orchard were still standing. "Thank God!" Clara said to Orpha. "At least we're all still alive."

Orpha didn't respond. She stood frozen, gazing up in horror at the big oak behind the house. A child's body was hanging naked from an upper limb. Her instinct was to find some way to keep Vennie away, but, even as the thought occurred to her, she knew it was too late.

"No!" Vennie screamed. "Get her down, somebody! Get Rosie down! Maybe she ain't hurt. She can't be dead! Not Rosie!" But Rosie was dead. Her friend from the next farm over had been picked up by the tornado and left hanging in their tree.

"Why did this have to happen?" Orpha wondered. "Haven't we all suffered enough already?" It seemed life had been bearing down on them for a long time now and she wished the misery would end.

"What are we gonna do?" Clara asked.

"There's nothing to do but to leave," Orpha said. "It would take months to make this place livable again. Maybe the Covingtons will take us in. Brennan said they need more help since all the slaves left. We can't move in with Mary or Christina. Neither of them has enough room. And we need a new start."

"But we can't just leave all our things," Clara protested. "Look. There's Mama's trunk. It ain't hurt at all. And most of our clothes are still hangin' on their pegs. And lookee here! Your banjo is still in one piece!"

Orpha couldn't believe it had survived. "Lordy mercy!" she exclaimed, picking it up and strumming it. "It's still in tune. I never would have believed it."

Vennie cried for days. Orpha and Clara tried to console her, but nothing they said or did seemed to help. How long would it be, Orpha wondered, before Vennie can forget?

"What about our things?" Clara asked again. Orpha was simply too tired to think about it now. Later she would get Brennan to come back with her in a wagon to get what was left of their belongings.

"And what about the land?" Clara asked. Orpha was sure that somewhere in the county records there was proof that this land belonged to Henry Fraley. She said as much to Clara, mainly to pacify her. She wondered, however, if records really did exist in the wake of the war's devastation.

"We'll go to the courthouse to reclaim the home place after we settle in somewhere," Orpha promised. "Even if there's not much left, it's still our property. We'll sort all that out later."

With little more than the clothes on their backs, they set out afoot towards Rock Island. When Orpha looked back up the road, she saw the daffodils in full bloom. The tornado had skipped right over them. Yes, she thought, the daffodils will be waiting for us when we come back to claim the land.

BOOK VI

Vennie and James

1871-1899

There is nothing to save, now all is lost,
but a tiny core of stillness in the heart
Like the eye of a violet.

—D. H. Lawrence

ONE

Vennie Meets James

Bone Cave, Tennessee
1871-1872

So it was that Orpha, Clara, and Vennie joined Brennan on the Covington farm near Rock Island. Since the slaves were long gone, they moved into two of the empty slave cabins. Vennie, at thirteen, became the surrogate mother for two children whose mother had been declared insane. No one had an explanation for Anne Covington's malady, except to say it happened during the war. Unable to cope alone, John Covington had come to Orpha for help.

"She refuses to prepare meals for the children," he explained. "She even claims they are not her children. Yesterday, she locked herself in her room and refused to come out. When I had the door busted in, she hardly seemed to notice. She was sitting in her rocking chair by the window saying over and over, 'Not my babies.' I don't know what I'm gonna do if you don't help me."

Anne lived out her days unaware of the happenings around her. She ate when food was put before her, and spent most of her time rocking in her chair by the window. After feeding the children each morning, Vennie helped dress Anne, who never seemed to see the children at all even when they played around her rocking chair. It was as if they were invisible. When her daughter Lucy would try to show her doll to her mother, Anne simply stared out the window, repeating "Not my baby, not my baby." It was a mystery to Vennie how any mother could be so insensitive to her own children.

One night when everyone was asleep, Vennie went to the cabin to talk with her mother and Aunt Clara about Anne. "It's because she depended on slaves to do everything for her," Clara said. "Without them, her mind simply closed down."

"She's so far gone," Orpha said, "even her husband can't comfort her. All that man knows how to do is to give orders. That's what he did when he had slaves."

Orpha thought of William. He had been right there at her side when each of their three children was born, and he had always been a good father to them. How lucky she was to have had William. She missed him terribly.

Vennie liked taking care of the two Covington children. She didn't even mind helping with Anne's care, but sometimes she found herself wishing for others her own age.

When James came to the Covington farm looking for work, Vennie was the one who answered the door. "I'm looking for Mr. Covington," he said. "Are you the lady of the house?"

He's trying to be smart, she thought. "Do I look like the lady of the house?" When he didn't answer, she said: "Nope, just work here. Mr. Covington ain't here. He's gone to town to buy seeds and supplies."

"When's he comin' back?" James asked.

"Don't know, maybe late afternoon."

"Can I just set out here on this bench and wait for him?" he asked.

"Don't make no difference to me," she said. Vennie shrugged and walked back into the house.

James sat watching for Covington's arrival. While he waited, he thought back to his travels with Greenberry. They had explored caves throughout Tennessee, and even gone over into Kentucky to see the Mammoth Cave. In the Great Smoky Mountains, Greenberry had taken him to Kituhwah, the first Cherokee town built thousands of years ago. At the top the mound, a fire was burning.

"This is a sacred fire," Greenberry had said. "It never goes out. It reminds the people the Great Spirit keeps us as one, no matter how far we are scattered."

Greenberry had taken him to Cedar Mountain to the place he had lived as a boy. Pointing toward a stream at the foot of the mountain, Greenberry had shown him the spot on the hillside where his cabin once stood. All James could see in the distance were farmhouses and barns with fences.

"Here is where I whittled out my flute," Greenberry had said. Reaching up to touch his own flute, James remembered wondering who had carved it.

"What happened to your flute, the one you carved?" he had asked Greenberry. A long silence followed, and James remembered it was at that moment the truth had begun to dawn on him.

"It is hanging around your neck, James," Greenberry had said softly. "Do you want me to tell you more?"

"Yes, I need to know. I need to know everything." He remembered the feeling that came over him when Greenberry told him. I guess that means I'm Indian too, he thought. Or at least part Indian.

The day they returned to White County, Greenberry had taken him to the cemetery at Shells Ford to see where his grandma was buried. There, among the fallen tombstones, he had stood with Greenberry under the shade of the cedars. On the riverbank, Greenberry had claimed he could hear the *Nun-ne-hi* singing under the rippling waters of the Collins. James remembered trying very hard to hear them, but the only sound he could remember was the metallic whine of a sawmill.

"You want a drink of water?" Vennie's voice shook him out of his reverie. James took the dipper and drank deeply. "Thanks. I'm much obliged. What's your name?"

"I ain't a-telling 'til you tell me yours," she said.

"I'm James, James Preece. Now, what's yours?" James liked the way she responded in her teasing tone. There hadn't been much time for that sort of thing in the last few weeks. He had been looking for a job, and mostly what he'd heard from people was, "Nope, ain't looking for no help. Can't afford to hire you."

"Go on," he said smiling. "Tell me your name."

"Vennie," she said.

"Where did you get a name like that?"

"Lavinia's my name, but they call me Vennie. My name is Vennie Spruill."

"How old are you?"

"I just turned fourteen. How old are you?"

"Sixteen."

"Where do you come from?"

"Over yonder near Bone Cave. It's where my mama lives, but I been gone from there for awhile. Been cavin'." James hesitated. "With a friend. We went all over the country lookin' for caves."

"Whatcha doing here?" she asked.

"I'm a-lookin' for a place to be and a job that will pay me some money. You reckon Mr. Covington can hire me?"

"What's that thing around your neck?" she asked.

"That's my flute."

"What's it for?"

"For playin' music."

"What's it sound like when you play it?"

"Like this." He placed the end of the flute to his lips and blew gently.

Vennie liked the sound of the flute. The notes lifted on the wind and died away softly. "What a sad song," she said. "Can you play a banjo?"

"Nope."

"I can't either, but my mama can. She said she would show me if I wanted to learn how."

"Banjo's too loud." James said.

"You can dance by the tune of a banjo." Vennie said teasingly. "You can do a real fast dance." The conversation ended when they saw the dust from John Covington's wagon in the distance.

"I'm James Preece, sir, from over Bone Cave way," James said as Covington stepped down from the wagon, "and I've come to see if you need some help on your farm here."

John Covington looked him over and said, "You don't look like you could do what I need done. Can you work behind two mules and a plow? I need somebody to help me plant these corn seeds right now, and then I need somebody to help me keep the weeds down when they come up, and then I need a hand to do general farm work. The pigs and sheep and horses and the cattle need feedin' every day. And my barn needs fixin'. The Yankees almost ruint it, and I ain't had time to fix it. My slaves all run off during the war. Durn Yankees and the war ruint just about everything."

James was beginning to wonder if he really wanted to work for Mr. Covington. It did sound like more than he could handle, but he saw Vennie playing with the children on the porch, and he quickly accepted John Covington's offer.

"I can't pay you until the fall when the crops bear, but you can have a place to stay and I'll feed you," Covington said.

"It's fine with me," James said. He knew he was lucky to find work at all.

For the next two years, James worked for John Covington, hardly three miles from Bone Cave where his father had mined saltpeter during the war. Sometimes in the late afternoon, he would ride over to the cave entrance and sit peering into the darkness. Grass had grown around the wrecked vats and the machinery that had once made saltpeter, and the entrance to the cave was covered with vines.

He remembered the good times when his family was together before the war, and wondered what it would have been like if the war hadn't happened. If my father hadn't been killed, he thought, if only I had done my job better on Tandy's Knob, if my mother hadn't married Robert Shelby. James felt alone, except when he saw Vennie laughing with the children in the front yard. On Sundays when she put on her best dress and bonnet and took the children to church, James watched, wishing he could take her some place where they could be alone and talk. But she's always with the children, James thought.

Vennie decided she liked James a lot. She liked his looks, his coal black hair, and his skin the color of ripe corn tassels. There was something sad about him, though, that made her want to know him better. Perhaps she could help him get beyond his doleful moods. She would often slip out to the back of the barn or to the field where he was working. She found James was not much of a talker, but he always had a smile for her and seemed genuinely glad to see her.

One morning during breakfast, Vennie mentioned his name, and Aunt Clara made it clear she didn't care for him. "Why don't you like James, Aunt Clara?" Vennie challenged her. "You don't even really know him. Mama seems to like him. Don't you, Mama?"

"Well, I don't really know him that well," Orpha said. "He's a good worker. He's always ready to help out when we need him."

"What have you got against him, Aunt Clara?" Vennie asked. Sometimes she thought she had one too many mamas. She loved Aunt Clara, but she wished her mother would take her part with Clara more often.

"He's just not the one for you," Clara replied. "You won't have nothing but trouble if you keep hangin' around him. He looks to me like one of them dusky people over in Scott's Gulf. You don't want to get mixed up with them. Didn't you notice how much darker his skin is? And that straight black hair and them big ears. Yesiree, I'll bet you anything he comes from over at Scott's Gulf. They's lots of mixed-blood people over there, mixed Indian and white, and I hear tell some of them even have black blood! And when he plays that flute he carries around his neck, what comes out is downright depressin'." Vennie was half listening. That's what she liked about James. His sad music gave him an air of mystery. He seemed to have a passion for two things—his flute music and exploring natural places. He cared about something more than going hunting and sitting around with the boys, seeing who could spit tobacco juice the furthest.

She had seen James earlier that morning on her way to feed the pigs, and in his awkward way, he had asked if she wanted to go with him to find the disappearing creek and the falls that poured down the side of Pine Mountain. "I'm goin' to the falls tomorrow," he said. "You wanna come with me? I'll show you where Lost Creek runs under the mountain."

The next morning, after the farm chores were done and the Covington children had gone with their father to visit relatives in McMinnville, Vennie announced she was going to the store at Bone Cave crossroads to get supplies for the Covingtons.

"Make sure you go right to the store and back, and if you meet up with that Preece boy, don't pay him no attention," Aunt Clara warned. "You're too young to be thinkin' about boys anyhow, much less about him!"

Clara turned to Orpha who was kneading sweet dough for teacakes. "I'll bet you anything she's goin' to meet that James Preece! She's been noticin' him more and more here lately," Clara said.

"He seems like a nice boy to me, Clara." Orpha said. "But you're right. Vennie is too young to be noticin' any boy."

TWO

A Special Place

Scott's Gulf, Tennessee
Spring 1873

Vennie hitched the horses to the wagon, and rode to meet James at Bone Cave crossroads. She had promised Aunt Clara and her mother she wouldn't be long at the store, even though she knew better. She passed the reins to James. He said they would take the wagon only so far and then walk the rest of the way. Earlier, Vennie had sneaked some of Orpha's teacakes and wrapped them in a cloth. There would be plenty of good cold water to drink at the falls. James had said so. Aunt Clara wouldn't approve of what she was doing, but she knew that whatever preaching Aunt Clara might do when she got back wouldn't compare with the joy of spending the day alone with James.

For the first few miles, they spoke little. From the Bone Cave crossroads, James headed east along the Caney Fork until they came to the Big Bottom Road. As long as they were on the main road, the wagon rolled along smoothly, and Vennie had no thoughts about turning back. But by the time they passed through the gap at the foot of Pine Mountain, Vennie was having second thoughts. She had never really been alone with James before.

As they went further down the valley, she could see tall trees and tall grass clearings on the slopes. James told her Indians had burned some of the clearings in earlier times to flush out deer and wild turkeys on their hunts.

On the lower bottomland, they passed cabins and plots of freshly tilled soil. In the distance, she could see a farmer plowing.

"Somewhere out here in Lost Creek Valley," she told James, "is my grandpa's land. Actually, now it belongs to Mama and Aunt Clara. We left it after the war, and some day soon we're going back." She had heard her mother say that after this year's crops were laid by, they would go back and fix up the place.

They had been riding in silence for about an hour when James announced, "We need to go the rest of the way on foot, and we gotta watch out for copperheads." Leaving the wagon and horses tied in a grove near a small stream, they headed up a steep hill covered with thick underbrush.

Vennie was scared of snakes, and she knew a copperhead bite could kill. Maybe I should've said no to James, she thought. She wasn't happy about wading through underbrush where snakes could be waiting. She shuddered at the thought of a copperhead bite. And what would she tell Aunt Clara and her mother when she got home? But she knew it was too late to be wondering whether or not coming on this trek with James was the right choice.

"Be careful now of them briars," James cautioned, taking her hand. His touch calmed her. Walking hand and hand with him, she forgot her fears. She began to notice the landscape had changed. They had left behind the open valley with its cedars and pines that cast long, slow-moving shadows on the hillside. Now they had moved onto a more rugged mountainous path with sentinel oaks, beech, maple and walnut trees towering above them.

James kept assuring Vennie they were almost there. If she had wondered about the wisdom of coming here with James, that thought had now evaporated. They had come upon a sloping sunlit meadow. The daffodils near the cabin at Lost Creek were beautiful, but they were nothing compared to this.

"They call the pink ones ladies' slippers, and the purple ones are wild iris," James said. "Over there are little yellow and white orchids, and that is the wood lily."

"How come you know so much about flowers?"

"I learnt it from a Indian man."

"I've never seen anything so beautiful," Vennie said. "Mama and Aunt Clara have to see this place." She bent to pick a flower, but James grabbed her arm.

"That's just where the copperheads like to hide," he told her. She jerked her hand back. James was right. He knew this place, and she trusted him.

She thought of the snake in the preacher's story about Adam and Eve, how the snake had convinced Eve to bite into the apple and make Adam take a bite, and how God had thrown them out of the garden. She couldn't understand why the preacher put all the blame on Eve, and let Adam and the snake get off scot-free.

"We only have a little ways to go," James said. "Just wait 'til you see what's ahead."

Flaming red azaleas encircled the meadow. White and pink mountain laurel and wild rosemary grew in abundance. Wading through ferns and briars, she was glad she had worn her high brogans. She struggled with her long dress and petticoat, trying to avoid the little sticky brambles that attached themselves to her clothes. She would have to pull the brambles off one by one when she got back. But no matter. James was holding her by the hand, gently pulling her along.

Finally, he announced they had come to the place where Lost Creek got its name. On a large limestone rock above the creek, they sat and watched the fast-flowing water below.

"This is where the creek goes underground and then reappears on the other side of the mountain," James told her. "There, it flows into the Caney Fork."

"So the creek's not really lost," Vennie said, untying her bonnet. "It just hides for awhile, and then comes rushin' out the other side. I'm amazed by how much you know, James." Vennie smiled as a broad grin spread across his face.

"This is my special place," he said. "I wanted you to see it. It can be our special place, yours and mine."

He leaned over and kissed her. She returned his kiss. It was everything she had imagined. He began to explore her body, touching her in places nobody had touched her before. He took her to him, holding her, making love to her until their breath came in gasps.

Later, as they lay quietly in each other's arms, she knew this was indeed their special place, their special time, their own garden. Suddenly she laughed out loud.

"What's so funny?" James asked.

"I was just thinkin'," she giggled. "What would Aunt Clara say if she could see us now?"

"Vennie Preece," he laughed, "You're a mean'un, you are!"

"How did you find this place?" Vennie asked.

"Me and Greenberry explored all of White County lookin' for caves," he said. "And one day we just happened upon this place."

"Who is Greenberry?" she asked.

He hesitated for moment, cleared his throat, and said, "This is the place where Greenberry told me how he left my mama on a white woman's porch in Rock Island."

Vennie waited for James to say more. She knew he was trying to put something into words for the first time, and it was not easy for him. After a moment, she ventured: "So your mama was left on somebody's front porch? How come?"

"Do you remember hearin' about the Indians who came through here walkin' all the way to Oklahoma years ago? Well, my mama was left as a baby when her mama died on the trail. Greenberry was her papa."

"So this Greenberry is your grandpa?"

James hesitated and then said, "Yep. Greenberry took my mama to Rock Island and left her with the Preeces. He buried my grandma over at Shells Ford."

"Did your mama know?"

"I don't know. She never told me." James remembered how his mother had given him the flute and said it was special and that he must never take it from around his neck.

Vennie knew James had brought her here because he needed to tell her. Aunt Clara was right after all about him being part Indian, but she was wrong about him being from Scott's Gulf. He's a mixed-blood Cherokee, she thought. But what does it matter?

"Let's not tell Mama and Clara," she said. "They don't need to know everything."

"Yep," James agreed. "It'll just be our secret." He was glad he could share this secret with Vennie. It made him feel less alone. He positioned his fingers on the flute and began to play, as if to say he was finished with the conversation.

"Is that the flute your grandpa carved?" she asked.

"Yep," he answered. James removed the flute from around his neck and placed the deerskin string over Vennie's head. "Here, I want you to have it," he said.

"But it's your special flute," Vennie protested. "You should keep it."

"I want you to keep it for me. Always," he said. "Greenberry says the music from a cedar flute will drive away bad ghosts."

"Will you teach me how to play it?" she asked.

"Sure," he said, placing her fingers over the first two holes.

At first, neither James nor Vennie noticed the dark clouds gathering. They were too intent on simply being together. A distant rumble of thunder jarred Vennie.

"Looks like a storm's a-comin' up," she said. "It's gonna be really bad!"

Since the tornado that had left her friend dangling dead on a tree, Vennie was convinced that every dark cloud, large or small, would bring a storm to blow everything and everybody away. She would pace the floor, and if it were in the middle of the night, she would insist that everyone get out of bed and dress, shoes and all. She hoped her mother and Aunt Clara and Brennan had run to the storm pit.

James was measuring how close the lightning was striking by counting the time between the claps of thunder. "It's gettin' pretty close," he figured. The coal-black clouds were rolling in fast. "It's too late to make it back to the wagon. Come on! I know where there's a cave a little ways off."

He pulled her along a ledge to an opening in the craggy rock face. They huddled inside. The wind roared furiously, followed seconds later by pounding rain. From the cave opening, they watched the wind whip the tall trees on the hillside, bending them almost to the ground. Vennie could hear the water roaring into the stream below. She wished she hadn't come.

When at last the storm was over, Vennie sat wet and shivering, wrapped in James's coat. We weathered the storm, James and me, she thought. She felt for the flute. James smiled.

"Let's see if we can get a fire going," he said. "We need to get out of these wet clothes."

He found some dry sticks and twigs near the front of the cave at a spot where an earlier fire had been laid. He managed to light the twigs from a matchbox he kept in his coat pocket, and soon a warm fire was burning.

James stripped naked and laid his wet clothes near the fire. He motioned for her to do the same. Vennie had never seen a man completely naked before, and she had certainly never stripped in front of a man, but she found she really liked being naked with James. She couldn't help seeing he had become all excited again. Clearly, James liked being naked with her!

"We're just like Adam and Eve," she laughed.

"Yep!" he said, "Before the fig leaves!"

He pulled her to him, kissing her, first on the lips and then all over her body. When at last he entered her for the second time that day, she was ready to receive him. Later, when the storm had subsided, they lay in each other's arms for a long time, until Vennie said, "Don't you think we should start back?"

They giggled as each tried to dress the other, pulling on clothes that were only slightly drier than before. As they leaned into one last embrace, they heard a loud voice coming from the cave entrance.

"I do believe you people are settin' in my parlor."

Startled, Vennie emitted a little scream.

"Don't be scared, Vennie," James said. "That's only old Ambers. He's harmless. This here's where he stays."

"Well, you could have told me that before," she said, a little miffed.

"There wasn't time. Besides, he wasn't here when we come in, and so I figured he'd gone out and got caught in the storm somewhere else."

"Hey! I knows you, boy!" said old Ambers, bringing a lighted torch with him into the cave. "Didn't you come here a while back with a tall, lanky Injun? I 'members 'cause I don't get much company up here."

"That's right," said James. "You fed us some possum stew. You told us about your wife and the man she left you for, how they found 'em both dead in a ditch, and how nobody never blamed you."

"Did I tell you all that?" Old Ambers chuckled. "Some folks thought I done it, but reckoned maybe I had a right to. Anyways, I come up here to stay where I wouldn't be no trouble to nobody. What happened to your Injun friend?"

"He went on his way."

"Who's she?" Old Ambers nodded toward Vennie.

"This is Vennie," James said. "She's my girl."

Vennie felt her face flush and wondered if James was blushing, too. She was glad Old Ambers hadn't arrived a few minutes sooner!

"Well, young lady, I'm glad to meet you! You ain't bigger'n a minute. With him so tall and all, y'all just don't match. But you're prettier'n anybody I've seen lately. Where'd you get them big green eyes? Aw, don't pay no attention to Old Ambers. Everybody thinks I'm crazy. But I ain't crazy. Been here for forty year, nigh on. They all lets me alone, and I lets them alone. 'Cept I steals me some roastin' ears sometimes. And I eats whatever varmints I can kill—coons, possums, rabbits, squirrels, skunks. My favorite dish is blacksnake soup. Y'all want some?"

"Guess not," said James.

"Not me," said Vennie. I'm not puttin' anything in my mouth that a snake's been in, soup or whatever, she thought. "Is roastin' ears and varmint meat all you eat?"

"Oh, anything else I need, I buy at the general store. I makes a little money sellin' trays and plates and spoons I carves out of buckeye wood. 'Course I saves some back to give to pretty girls like you."

He handed her a buckeye kneading bowl. "It's a weddin' present. It'll come in handy when y'all set up housekeepin'."

Vennie and James smiled at each other, a little embarrassed at Old Ambers's suggestion they might get married.

When the rain stopped, they headed back to the wagon. Vennie dreaded going home. What would she tell her mother and Aunt Clara? The truth, she decided. It wouldn't matter what she told them. They'd be angry about her slipping off for the day with James without telling them. She was too happy riding along with James right now to worry about it. Whatever they do to me, it's been worth it. I love James, she said to herself, and that's all that matters.

"We've weathered one big storm today and we can weather another," she said to James. It was Aunt Clara she dreaded most. Aunt Clara did not like James. Whatever she did with James would be wrong in Aunt Clara's eyes.

THREE

Revelations

Bone Cave, Tennessee
Spring 1873

They were standing on the porch—all of them, even John Covington, Anne, and the children. James helped Vennie down from the muddy wagon, took her hand, and they walked together to the porch.

"Thank God you're alive!" said Orpha as she hugged Vennie. "Let's get those wet clothes off you." Orpha quickly walked Vennie off the porch toward the cabin.

Brennan stood on the end of the porch spitting tobacco juice and waiting for Aunt Clara to start her preaching. He sometimes thought Vennie got away with too much, and most of the time he sided with Aunt Clara. Still, he wished James and Vennie had invited him to go with them.

Clara began: "Do you mind tellin' me where you and Vennie have been? And if you think I aim to let you get away with anything, you've got another thought comin'."

"M-ma'am," James stuttered. "Vennie and me got caught in the storm over near Scott's Gulf. I was a-showin' her where Lost Creek goes under the mountain."

"You ain't got enough sense to pour piss out of a boot! Can't trust a Injun with nothin' or nobody! What was you a-doin' over at Scott's Gulf where them mixed-breeds live? Was it your idea not to tell any of us you was a-goin'?"

James wanted to run. He couldn't remember being called an Injun before. He felt like a child. He hadn't felt this way since Isaac had made fun of him when he was little.

He was embarrassed, standing here in front of Mr. Covington. He was trying to think how to respond when Orpha appeared with Vennie.

"James," Orpha said, "Why don't you stay for supper? Don't pay no attention to Clara. She's been so worried about Vennie that she's takin' everything out on you." Clara glared at Orpha. "Vennie says y'all had a great time lookin' for Lost Creek until the storm hit. We're just glad you're both all right, ain't we Clara?"

"I'm sorry we didn't tell you we were going," James said.

"I'm sorry, too," said Vennie. "But Mama, you and Aunt Clara have gotta see this place James took me to. It's like a great big flower garden, like the Garden of Eden. I never seen anything like it. Tall, tall trees, and all kinds of wild flowers bloomin' in open meadows. And we met a man livin' in a cave."

"Don't tell me you run into old Ambers!" Clara said. "He's a murderer. Did you know that James?"

"Look what he give me," said Vennie, pulling out the wooden biscuit bowl. "He carves bowls and spoons out of the buckeye tree and sells them or swaps them for food."

"I know," said Orpha. "I gave him twenty-five cents for the wooden spoons we eat with."

"Well, I didn't know that," Clara confessed. "I didn't know I was eatin' out of spoons a murderer made. I declare, Orpha I wonder sometimes what goes on in that head of yours."

"First of all, Clara, nobody knows if the story about him killin' his wife and her lover is true. It's all hearsay, and if you believe what they teach you in that church over in Big Bottom, everybody can be forgiven. Do you believe that, Clara?"

"Well, yes, of course I do. But some things is hard to forgive. Still, I guess we don't really know for sure if he kilt 'em or not."

"There's nothin' else to say then," Orpha said.

That night after supper, Vennie put the Covington children to bed. When all the nightly chores were done, they all sat on the porch with the Covingtons. Mr. Covington took down his fiddle and played a lively dance tune. In a high, twangy voice, he sang:

If it hadn't a-been for Cotton Eye Joe,
I'd a-been married a long time ago.
Where did ye come from, where did ye go?
Where did ye come from, Cotton Eye Joe?

Orpha brought out her banjo and joined in with Mr. Covington. Together they played other fast mountain tunes. When they played a jig, James and Vennie began to dance. When Mr. Covington switched to a waltz, Orpha laid her banjo aside, and took Clara by the hand. They waltzed together, each woman holding up one side of her long dress as if on a ballroom floor. Even Anne Covington in her rocking chair patted her hand on her lap in time to the music. Then Vennie handed James the flute, and he began to play softly.

Orpha took Clara by the arm and led her down the path toward the orchard. "Clara, I need to tell you somethin'. I've kept this to myself for a long time, but sometimes secrets need to be told, and I think now's the time."

"Lord, Orpha, what in the world have you done now?"

"It ain't nothin' I done," replied Orpha. "It's somethin' Mama told me."

"What is it?"

"You're gonna find this hard to swallow, but we have mixed blood. We're mostly Scots-Irish, but one of our grandma's had Indian blood and black blood. Her name was Claracy, and she was a slave on a plantation in South Carolina. Mama even said she named you Clara because it was almost the same as hers."

"You're makin' that up! What made you come up with such a story? Mama never told you any such thing. I don't know why you're doin' this, but I don't believe a word of it."

"It's true, Clara." Orpha put her hand on Clara's arm.

Clara pulled away. "I'm not gonna stand here and listen to your tales. Why are you bein' so mean to me after all I've done for you?"

"I don't aim to be mean to you, Clara," Orpha said. "But there's more you need to know. Did you know that Mama and Papa were never married? They couldn't get married. She was considered colored, and it's against the law for white and colored to marry."

"I don't believe a word of it. If Mama did tell you, when was it? And if it's true, how come she only told you?"

"You remember when I first came from Hawkins County? Well, one morning I overheard Mama and Papa arguin' in the kitchen. I heard Papa tell Mama, "You of all people should be against slavery." Well, a few days later, I asked Mama about it, and she broke down and cried. That's when she told me. She told me it wouldn't do any good to tell the rest, so I didn't."

"Well, if that's true, how come you're tellin' me now?"

"I want you to let James alone. I think Vennie's set her cap for him, and, like it was with Mama and Papa, nobody can keep them from bein' together."

Clara walked ahead of Orpha for a little way, saying nothing.

"Don't you see?" Orpha said softly, putting her arm around Clara's shoulder, "If James is a mixed-blood and we're also mixed, that makes it perfectly all right for Vennie to marry him. And besides, what does it matter? Everybody is a mixed-blood, one way or another. And there's no reason to tell the children. It would just make their life more complicated than it already is. They don't need to know."

Clara never spoke to Vennie about what Orpha told her, and she stayed clear of James for a long time after. Vennie knew her mother had told Aunt Clara something that made her stop nagging James. She didn't know what it was, but she was glad her mother had come to her rescue.

At the end of the summer of 1875 when Covington's corn crop was harvested and most of it sold to local distilleries, Orpha, Clara, and Vennie decided it was time to move back to the farm in Lost Creek Valley and fix up the cabin. Anne Covington was somewhat better. She was responding more to her children and was even doing some cooking and cleaning. Brennan had gone to West Tennessee to look for a job.

When Vennie announced she wanted to marry James, Clara threw a fit. "You gotta put a stop to it," she said to Orpha. "Vennie's too young to get married, and if she marries James, her life will be nothin' but drudgery and trouble." While Clara had seemed to warm to James since they had moved back to the farm in Lost Creek Valley, she still didn't think him good enough for Vennie.

"Clara," said Orpha. "I declare I believe you'd be against any man who wanted to marry Vennie." She had often wondered why Clara felt this way. She remembered their conversations when she first arrived from Hawkins County. She had asked Clara if she had met any men while she was gone, and Clara wouldn't say anything. But then, thought Orpha, I didn't tell her anything about my life in Hawkins County either.

FOUR

Marriage and the Mines

Lost Creek Valley, Tennessee
1876-1890

Vennie and James were married in the fall of 1876 in the orchard behind the cabin in Lost Creek Valley. James was twenty and Vennie eighteen. They were married by a traveling cleric Clara referred to as a jackleg preacher, suggesting that he was connected with no church in particular and that his credentials with any church at all were questionable. The apples were ripe, and Aunt Clara served apple cider and apple pie to everyone, including all the Fraley relatives who had come from Big Bottom and the Preeces and Romans who had come from Rock Island and Bone Cave. She rationalized supporting the wedding on the grounds that since Brennan had left for Memphis, they had no man around to help with the rebuilding of the farm.

James was sad his mother Elizabeth hadn't lived to see him married. She had died just the year before. She'd had nothing but misery, thought James, since she married Shelby. Shelby had treated her like a slave, bragging to his friends that he'd found himself a squaw to raise his children. He'd seen to it that his mother was buried alongside his father Johnny in the Laurel Creek Cemetery near Bone Cave. He was glad Vennie had been there to comfort him.

The daffodils on the hillside would bloom again in the spring. They were about the only thing that didn't have to be replaced or repaired. James cut logs and hauled them to a sawmill on the Caney Fork. With the help of neighbors, they were able to use the lumber to replace the framing and the walls, and they trimmed out hundreds of cedar shakes to replace the roof. They worked seven days a week from sunup to sundown until the house was livable and the farm was producing. James and Vennie's first child, little Sam, came in April, just six months after the wedding. Even Clara seemed pleased to have a baby to care for once again.

That summer, Leonard Seeley came back, just as he said he would. "I've come back to marry you, Orpha, Orpha," he sang. Before she could find words to protest, he said, "William's gone now, and you and I are still young. We can get married over in Oklahoma, where it'll be legal. I can take care of you and you can take care of me. We can have a good life together. I know a mingo who can say the words over us in Chickasaw style, and the government can't do nothin' about it."

Surprisingly, Clara came to Leonard's defense. "You go with him," she said to Orpha. "I'll take care of Vennie and little Sam. Raisin' children is what I do best."

"You go on, Mama." Vennie said. "Aunt Clara's right. You've been doing for the family for a long time. It's time you do something for yourself."

So in 1876, at the age of fifty-seven, Orpha left the farm in Lost Creek Valley to marry Leonard Seeley. They lived together in Oklahoma until Leonard died seven years later. She was a widow again at the age of sixty-five. She considered going back to live with Vennie's folks, but she thought it might complicate things for everybody. So she lived with Brennan and his family in Memphis. Every year, she returned to Lost Creek Valley for a visit, until it became too difficult for her to travel.

When James realized the farm could not support the family, he got a job digging coal for small local companies that worked the mountains around Ravenscroft. At first he dug coal from the side of the mountain near Sunset Rock.

All in all, the years had been kind to the Preece family and to Aunt Clara. By 1888, James and Vennie had four children—Samuel, Joseph, William, and their first daughter, Susie, born in 1887. James's brother Thomas had asked him to come work with him at the Bon Air Coal, Land and Lumber Company, and James saw this as a good opportunity to increase his income.

His first job with Thomas was in Old Number One drift mine, a horizontal tunnel on the western slope of Bon Air Mountain just east of Sunset Rock. Later when two shaft mines were sunk at Bon Air, James spent most of his daylight hours almost two hundred feet below the earth's surface. Every time he stepped into the cage that took the men down into the mine, James wondered if this would be the last time he would ever breathe the mountain air. He wondered how long the mules would survive being lowered into the bowels of the earth. Even though the company boasted it had suffered very few cave-ins, there were still horrible accidents that left miners maimed for life.

At first James rode the six miles every morning from Lost Creek Valley and six miles back from the mine at night, but as the work hours increased from seven or eight to ten or twelve hours a day, he stayed in Bon Air in makeshift housing—a four-by-six-foot room with a canvas roof. "It ain't the best for sleepin', but it's cheaper than livin' in a boarding house," James told Vennie. For a while, he traveled back to the farm on Saturday nights and left on Sundays. Vennie worried when James came home covered in black coal dust. Sometimes when he had time, he would shower before he left work in one of the bathhouses provided by the company. But when the showers were all in use, he would wait until he arrived back at the farm. Vennie would heat a large kettle of water, and help him soap up and scrub away the black soot. "Just call me chalk eyes," he said. He didn't have to explain, since only the whites of his eyes were visible in the soot.

Like most of their neighbors, James and Vennie tried hard to make the arrangement work for the family, but as time passed, it seemed to Clara that she and Vennie and the children were coming out on the short end of the stick. More and more, James was staying away on the weekends. His explanation was that he was working longer hours to bring in more money, but as Clara said: "We ain't a-seein' more money. What's he a-doin' with it?" By 1889, Vennie realized they needed more income. Clara agreed. Sam who was now twelve, and Joe, ten, were old enough to run the farm.

"If you can take care of Little Will, Susie, and Lillie," Vennie said to Clara, "I can get me a part-time job at the woolen mill near Sparta." So Vennie went to work as a weaver in the mill on the Calfkiller River, making yarns, blankets, trousers, overalls, and pantaloons.

Clara seemed happier than Vennie could remember. James came home less and less, and it was only when he came home that Clara became morose and sullen. "I simply do not understand why you don't just tell him to stay away," she said to Vennie. "All he ever does is get you in the family way."

"He needs me." Vennie told Clara. "The mines are an awful place to work." Vennie hoped things would get better, and James promised her they would.

On Christmas Eve 1890, James came home bringing tops, yo-yos, and candy to the boys and rag dolls for Susie and Lillie. It was the night of the annual Christmas program at church, organized by Aunt Clara. In passing out the Bible verses the children were to learn for the program, she assigned three-year-old Susie to recite, "Jesus loves the little children." She gave Sam and Joe the responsibility of teaching her to recite the verse in a loud, clear voice. They thought what fun it would be to play a trick on Aunt Clara. It seemed the whole community had turned out for the Christmas program. Sam and Joe stationed themselves at the back of the church in the very last pew. When Susie stepped forward to say her line, she beamed and proudly said in a high little voice that was loud and clear: "Jesus loves the little monkeys!" The congregation broke into gales of laughter. Clara turned slowly and glared at the boys at the back of the church with a look that promised future retribution. But it was Christmas, and as they trimmed the tree James had brought in, all seemed to be forgiven.

It was the happiest Christmas Vennie could remember. Popcorn was strung and hung on the Christmas tree. Clara helped the boys cut out paper strips to make chains. On Christmas morning, Vennie brought out the flute she had stored in her trunk and asked James to play it. At first he refused, saying he had nearly forgotten how. The children begged and pleaded. Finally, James placed it to his lips and played the only tune he knew. Little Susie reached for it, and James let her hold it for a minute. Then he retrieved it and handed it to Vennie. "Don't ever forget I gave this to you," he said. Vennie placed the flute back in the trunk.

That night, James asked Vennie to move to Bon Air with him. "The company has built pretty little whitewashed renthouses with front porches and fenced-in yards. There's enough room for flowers in the front yard and a vegetable garden in the back. There's a company store right there in the town that sells all you need for staples. You could stay at home and take care of the children. The children can go to school there.

"On Saturday nights, we can listen to the bagpipes and learn to dance the highland fling. The company has brought in these coalminers from Scotland to teach us minin' techniques. Sometimes, you can hear them singin', 'My Heart's in the Highlands.' And they bring in fiddlers to play for the hoedowns. We could go dancin' every weekend."

What James did not tell Vennie was that the company literally owned the miners. They had little control over the money they earned. They were given scrip, a type of paper money printed by the company redeemable only at the company store. When a miner had change due him, he was given "clackers," metal money minted by the company. James also neglected to mention that prices at the company store were ten to fifteen percent higher than in Sparta. The company did not allow privately owned stores in its town, so there was no competition.

While the miners lived in small houses with few amenities, the bosses lived in big houses on the outskirts of town, and the owners lived in even larger houses, some with as many as fifteen rooms, including ballrooms and servants' quarters. On the main street were the company store, school, and church. Across the street stood the company's hotel, a doctor's office, and a post office, all of which the miners were required to use. Off the main street were alleys, and on one remote alley, black people lived in what was called "The Quarters."

James was not concerned with how others organized their lives. His thoughts were about keeping the family together, just Vennie, the children, and him. They didn't need anyone else, especially with Vennie staying at home to take care of the children. Vennie was almost convinced by James' argument—until she realized he had not once mentioned Clara. Then it hit her that James wanted them to live in this company town without Clara.

"What about Clara?" Vennie asked.

James had been dreading the question. He had hoped Vennie would read between the lines and find a solution about Clara. He knew Clara had never liked him. She had never accepted him as part of the family. He remembered overhearing her say to Vennie just before the wedding: "You've made your bed, now lie in it."

Clara had made it difficult for him to be a father to his children. "They have their chores to do," she would say when he came home from the mines and wanted to play with them. "And don't bring home candy. It's makes them sick." Once, when James had given Sam a lollipop, she jerked it away. "He can't have that. It'll give him the bellyache." It seemed to James that Clara thought he couldn't do anything right where the children were concerned.

His resentment of Clara heightened when she made insinuating remarks in front of Vennie and the children. "Just what do you think he's a-doin' when he stays away so long? He doesn't really care about you and the children. And when is he gonna start bringin' some money home?"

James didn't answer Vennie's question about Clara, so she asked again. "And what will Clara do when we move to Bon Air?"

"She could work for the company and live in one of the boarding houses," he said. "She can get a job there. The big bosses hire women to work in their homes and take care of their children."

Vennie couldn't believe James was so straightforward in his plans for Clara. She knew he had never cared for her, but surely he wouldn't turn her out, not after all she had done for the family—taking care of her and Brennan while Mama Orpha worked at Bon Air Hotel, helping them all survive the war, and then taking care of Sam, Joe, Will, Susie, and baby Lillie. Vennie could never agree to such a thing.

"It's not fair of you, James, to ask me to throw Clara out of the family," she said.

James lay next to Vennie in silence. He felt helpless. He knew Vennie would not go to Bon Air without Clara, but he couldn't bring himself to give over. All he really wanted was to be with Vennie and the children. For the first time, he felt the gulf that had been widening between him and Vennie had become too great to bridge. All those years waiting for Vennie to come over to his side were gone. Clara had won. What was it about the Fraley women that made them so loyal to one another, even to abandoning good sense?

FIVE

Vennie and Clara

Rock Island, Tennessee
1891

Clara had overheard Vennie and James talking in the middle of the night. She was horrified to hear James suggest she could get a job and live in one of the boarding houses. It's always James who tries to ruin our lives, she thought. So when Vennie announced she was going over to the Falls City Mill in Rock Island to look for a better paying job, Clara was pleased. She would no longer have to worry about James taking Vennie and the children off to Bon Air.

"You go right ahead and work at that mill in Rock Island," she told Vennie. "I don't mind takin' care of the children."

Though the overseers at Falls City Mill were all men, most of the weavers and spinners were widowed women and orphan girls who worked long hours to turn out cotton sheeting. Vennie quickly found many friends among them. Every morning she would rise early, hitch up the mule to the small cart and ride the few miles to Rock Island, arriving just before the opening bell sounded. Each evening she would leave work in time to arrive home just before dark. Most days, there was little time to talk to the children before she fell in bed.

Soon after she began her work at the mill, she found she was pregnant again. "After this child is born," she told Clara, "I'm not goin' to bed with James again."

James stopped coming home every weekend, and sometimes didn't show up for weeks. When at last he did come home, he brought a gallon jug of moonshine and spent most of his time drinking and sleeping it off. After each binge, he would ask Vennie to forgive him, promising he would never drink again. She knew it was an empty promise.

Vennie was glad Clara was there to help with the children. She often wondered what she would have done if Aunt Clara had not been there. Mama must have felt the same way, she thought, when Aunt Clara took care of me and my brothers. Still, Clara had increasingly become a thorn in Vennie's flesh where James was concerned, and there were times Vennie thought Clara had gone just a little too far in keeping the boys in line. Sam was forever complaining about her.

"Aunt Clara is just too mean," he said, "like the time she washed out my mouth with that awful tastin' lye soap just because I said damn. Why, damn ain't nothin'. All the boys at Sunday school say damn when they lose playin' marbles."

Vennie didn't always approve of Clara's methods of punishment, but she realized she didn't have much choice. Sometimes she wondered if she had done the right thing not going with James to Bon Air. Maybe with the family there, he would have stopped his drinking. But she knew that wouldn't happen, since he kept bringing jugs of liquor to the farm and staying drunk in front of the family the whole time he was home.

"Aunt Clara wants to punish me for the least little thing," Joseph said. "She's always screamin' at me not to spill any milk when I strip old Bessie. She says if I do, she'll cut a switch and streak my legs til it brings the blood. She ain't done it yet, but I think she would if she got mad enough."

It was tiresome for Vennie to hear the children complain about Aunt Clara, and most of the time she only listened with half an ear. But she couldn't abide Clara constantly enumerating James's faults in front of the children: "Your daddy's never been worth his salt. He's a good-for-nothing, half-breed drunkard, and that's all he'll ever be."

One night when Clara knelt with the children for their bedtime prayers, she wouldn't let them ask for God's blessing on their father. "You can say God bless Mama and Aunt Clara and all the aunts and uncles and cousins, but not your pa." When Will told Vennie about it, she decided Clara must be losing her mind. So Vennie, who seldom prayed, took over the task of helping the children say their bedtime prayers.

But it was still Clara who dressed them on Sunday mornings and made sure they went to Sunday School. Vennie seldom went with them. Her work at the mill was long and taxing, and she chose to use the quiet time on Sunday morning for some extra rest. She was disturbed, however, when the boys came home from church one Sunday saying Aunt Clara had told them they were sinners, and they had to go down to the mourners' bench and get prayed over.

"I was afraid," Joe told Vennie. "They were shoutin' and cryin'. And Aunt Clara said Sam and me was sinners, and when we die, God will throw us in a burning fire unless we get saved. What's gettin' saved mean, Mama?"

Joe's fear brought a hard realization to Vennie. Enough of Aunt Clara's religion, she thought. I don't like her telling the children they're sinners, and I've let her get away with her nastiness about their father too long.

"Aunt Clara," Vennie began, "The boys ain't goin' back to church unless they want to. They don't understand, and they're scared by it all. If you want to go, that's fine, but don't make them feel they're doin' something bad by not going."

Clara was only half listening. There she goes again, she thought, telling me how to raise the children. She has no right to tell me what to do. She's the one at fault. After all, I warned her about James, but she wouldn't listen. Now the chickens is comin' home to roost. And every time that rooster comes home, he gets her pregnant again, and, like always, I'm the one who has to take care of it.

"Clara, are you hearing me?" Vennie demanded.

Sullen and angry, Clara looked away. Vennie knew this wouldn't be the end of it. But at least, she thought, I've said my piece.

For days, Clara gave them all the silent treatment. The boys wanted to know why Aunt Clara wasn't talking. "She don't feel well." Vennie told them.

Clara's silence ended when the letter came from Brennan. "Mama is awful sick. She may not last much longer," he wrote. "She's asking for you. You better come soon." Vennie and Clara clung to each other sobbing. Each one begged forgiveness of the other for hurtful things they had said or done. Quickly, they readied themselves and the children to catch the locomotive for Memphis. It would take every penny they had saved to buy the tickets. They rode by stagecoach to Nashville, nearly a day's ride, and then caught the evening train.

This is the longest, saddest journey I'll ever take, thought Vennie. Somehow I thought Mama would be there always. Even when she went to Memphis, I never imagined I wouldn't see her again. Mama's the one who kept us alive during the war. She could somehow make us laugh, even in the hardest times. She can't be dying. What will we do without her? We just got to get there in time.

But they arrived too late. Orpha died the day before they reached Memphis. After the burial, Brennan asked Vennie and Clara to sit down with him to talk about what to do with Orpha's belongings.

"I don't want to talk about this now," Clara said.

"Neither do I," said Vennie, "but we don't have much choice. We have to leave tomorrow."

"Aunt Clara," Brennan said, "After Grandpa Henry and Grandma Clary died, you and Mama owned the farm together. Mama told me that her share was to go to me and Vennie, but I want Vennie to have my part. The two of you have worked hard on the land and kept the farm goin'. So it's only fair that the two of you share it."

"Well, I don't know what's fair about it," Clara stated. "I think your part oughta come to me. All Vennie deserves is a child's part."

"Aunt Clara," Brennan said. "Don't be that way. You and Vennie's family will have fifty acres between you, as well as the milk cows, the pigs and chickens, the wagons and the buggy and horse. Y'all can share all the household items too. All I want is that old gourd banjo Mama kept with her through thick and thin."

"Well, you can have that, as far as I'm concerned," Clara said. "But somehow it seems I ought to have more than Vennie."

"Aunt Clara," Brennan went on, "Do you remember that time when the soldiers hurt Mama, and afterwards, she sat for the longest time by that tree pickin' her banjo and singin' Wildwood Flower? That's the way I want to remember her. She was always givin', and I don't want us to be arguin' about her things before she's cold in the ground."

"Clara," said Vennie, "you can have whatever in the house you want. The only thing I want is the trunk Papa gave Mama when they got married."

The trunk contained two items Vennie cherished—the cedar flute James had given her and the quilt Clary, Orpha, and Clara had made during cold winter nights when she was very small. Vennie remembered playing with her rag dolls under the quilting frame. During the war, Orpha had buried the trunk where marauders would never find it.

When they returned home from the funeral, Clara pulled the quilt from the trunk and declared it was hers. "I worked real hard on that quilt," she declared, "and you ain't got no right to it."

Vennie was startled at Clara's vehemence. "If the quilt means that much to you, Aunt Clara, just take it. It's settled. The quilt is yours!"

"You're mighty right it is!" Clara sputtered. All her venom began to pour out. "You're just a spoiled child, Vennie, and Orpha wasn't a good mother, anyway. She went off with that Chickasaw Injun and left you and your young'uns here for me to take care of. All I've ever done is take care of other people's young'uns. I never had a chance to meet anybody and get married."

"Did you ever try, Aunt Clara?" asked Vennie.

"Yes, but your mother married the only man I ever loved!"

Vennie was puzzled. "What do you mean? You were in love with Leonard Seeley?"

"No, not him! I mean your daddy. I'm talkin' about William Spruill. I knowed him before she did, and he would've married me if she hadn't come back here when she did."

"Had my papa asked you to marry him?" Vennie asked.

"No, but he would've if she hadn't showed up and made up to him. She always got whatever she went after, and when she set her cap for your papa, he didn't have a chance. Of course then, neither did I!"

"Did either of them ever know you loved him?"

"Course not. I wasn't about to fight her for him! Let her have him, I said. But I always knowed him and me was meant for each other. I coulda give him good children, not like them mean and spiteful children of yours!"

"What do you mean, Aunt Clara? How are my children mean and spiteful?"

Clara's voice became a pitiful whimper. "Your boys are mean to me. I know they don't like me. None of you like me. They hide my snuffbox and brush where I can't find them, and they hide my bonnet, and sometimes at night, they crawl under my bed and make strange noises so I can't sleep. And you know how they ruint my Christmas program at church. I'm too old to put up with such shenanigans."

Vennie listened, and when she thought Clara had finished, said quietly: "What do you want me to do, Aunt Clara?'

"I want 'em whupped," she demanded. "They need a good switchin' with a good strong peach tree limb."

"Would you like to do that, Aunt Clara?" Vennie asked.

"No, it's your job. They're yours."

"Sam," Vennie said, "Get me a good strong peach tree switch. And make it a long one. Y'all are gonna get a good switchin' for treatin' Aunt Clara bad. And Aunt Clara's gonna watch you get it."

Sam went into the yard and came back with the switch. "We didn't do nothin' to her," he said. "She made it up. I don't know nothin' about her snuffbox and bonnet."

The other children began to cry.

"Sam, you're first," Vennie said. "Step up here." Clara began to walk away. "Clara, stay where you are. I want you to watch them being punished. But before I whup 'em, they're gonna say they're sorry for mistreatin' you."

"But Mama, we didn't do nothin' to her," Joe protested. "She made it all up. She's crazy. Aunt Clara, tell her we didn't do it." Clara's mouth was clinched into a tight scowl. It looked to Vennie as if she were retreating into one of her long silent spells.

Sam leaned forward, holding onto the porch post, and waited for the first strike of the switch. Just as Vennie raised her arm, Clara screamed and fell to her knees. "Don't hit him! They didn't do nothin'," she sobbed. "I'm sorry. I'm so sorry."

"It's okay, Aunt Clara," Vennie found herself saying. "Mama wouldn't want us to be angry with one another, would she? Aunt Clara, we've been depending on you too much, and sometimes we don't show you how much we care. Do we?" Vennie looked at the children who were watching in consternation. Sam realized his mother wanted them all to show Aunt Clara they cared. He signaled the others, who moved in closer, stretching to reach their arms around Aunt Clara and their mama as much as they could.

SIX

Endings and Beginnings

Lost Creek Valley, Tennessee
1893-1899

James continued his pattern of coming home every once in a while bringing some money, but it was never enough, especially after the seventh child, Marion, was born in 1893. It was a difficult pregnancy and Vennie couldn't work for most of the nine months. In 1894, she gave birth to her eighth child, Woodard, and in 1895, Vennie delivered twin boys, Greenberry, named for James's grandfather, and Richard, named for his great uncle.

Clara stopped saying bad things about James. She found it no use. It was the older boys who told their mother to send him away when he came back.

"All he does is drink hisself to death," Sam said.

Vennie had long believed that James would change. She still loved him, and hoped he would stop drinking. What had happened to the James she had loved when they were young? What was it that made him drink? Was it the war? A lot of people lived through terrible times during the war. Some got over it and some didn't.

James had never really told her much about his early childhood, and whenever she had tried to ask questions about his life, he would lapse into tales about exploring caves. She knew his father had died during the war, and that his mother had remarried and lived near Rock Island. Maybe I should have tried to spend more time with her, Vennie thought. Maybe between us, working together, we could have put his demons to rest. But it's too late now.

Maybe if he had not gone to work in the mines, things would have turned out better. If she needed a reason to explain James's drinking, she decided, maybe it was the mines. It's too much to ask someone like James, who loves the woods and the streams, the sky and the light of day, to work in a dark and damp underground cavern. I could never do that, she thought. James had tried. His intentions were good, but the black monster coal fueled by demon rum, had swallowed him up.

Joe and Sam left the farm and headed for Madison County, Alabama, in 1898 to look for work in the cotton mills. A year later, Sam returned to beg them all to follow them to Huntsville. He told them about how they could live in the Dallas Mills Company town. "They have housing and schooling and stores and doctors. We can all work there and make more money. Nobody can make it here on this farm—not enough to live on."

Two things happened to make Vennie decide to follow Sam and Joe to Huntsville. Vennie had been worried about Clara lately. She had not been feeling well. Susie, who shared a bed with Aunt Clara, woke one morning to find her still in bed beside her. When Susie leaned over to touch her hand, she found it cold and stiff, and she knew Aunt Clara was gone. They buried her in the cemetery at Fraley's Chapel over in Big Bottom with all the other Fraleys. At her funeral, the preacher spoke of Clara as a pearl of great price. Vennie and the children could never have imagined how much they would miss her. She might have been hard to live with at times, but she had been their solid rock. Vennie wished she had told her how much she loved and appreciated her.

The other thing that happened to convince Vennie to leave for Huntsville was something none of the children knew about. The last contact Vennie had with James was when he came to Falls City Mills and called her to come outside. He had been drinking.

"They arrested me and throwed me in jail for drinkin'," he told her. "Then they took the jail fine out of my wages. I owe the company store and they won't let me come back to work unless I pay off the debt."

"I ain't got no money for you," Vennie said. "Even if I had it, I wouldn't give it to you. You've let liquor rule your life too long. You've taken food out of the mouths of our children to buy your liquor."

"Well, if you can't give me the money I need, then I'll sell that farm, and you can move to Bon Air." James was hardly able to stand.

"You won't sell the farm. I will. Did you forget it's mine? I intend to sell it and use the money to take the children to Huntsville."

James had seldom been mean while he was drinking, but when he pulled his rifle from his saddle, and pointed it at her, she knew this was not the James she married. Actually, he was not so much pointing the rifle as waving it at her. *He's too drunk to know what he's doing,* she thought.

"You're not goin' nowhere! I'm your husband! You and the children are comin' with me."

Vennie was glad when two of the men from the mill slipped up behind James and relieved him of the gun. They put him on his horse and threatened to beat him to a pulp if he ever showed up there again bothering Vennie.

"I got rights!" James insisted, mumbling as the horse took him up the road, "She's my wife, and she took all my money and she won't give me any. It ain't fair. I'm her husband, and she oughtn't treat me that way."

That was the final straw for Vennie. She went inside to get her pay, placed the rifle in the cart, and headed home to Lost Creek Valley for the last time. "Tomorrow," she told Joseph, "I want you and the others to help me put everything in our two wagons. Then we'll strap on the canvas and hitch up the mules. We're goin' to Huntsville."

*   *   *

What have you done to yourself, boy? It is cold in this cave. Why didn't you build yourself a fire of cedar branches? Now a cedar fire is burning. I'm hot, Greenberry. I'm burning up. Can you chase away the Raven Mockers? They fly over the entrance to the cave, mocking me and waiting for me to die. I see Greenberry breaking a cedar limb and brushing it across the fire to chase away bad ghosts. He is standing over a blazing fire of cedar logs. In one hand he is holding a cedar branch and with the other he is pouring demon rum on the blazing fire. He is chanting. Warriors dancing in a circle around the fire. Drums beating. Leg rattles shaking slowly. Faster and faster. Stomp right. Stomp left. Stomp right. Stomp left. My heart is beating fast and hard.

Papa says I must go to Tandy's Knob and help the guard watch over the valley. I am watching, Papa. The blazing fire is burning, scalding, searing. I did not do a good job, Papa. The Federals found the cave. I didn't stop them. They killed my papa, Greenberry, and I didn't stop them. Not your fault, James. Oh yes it is, Papa. See? Federals are all over the place. They are everywhere. Everywhere. I'm burning up! Here drink this tea. Drink it. It's made from crushed fern fronds boiled in river water. It breaks fever. Where are my clothes? I have no clothes on.

I am naked. It's not raining now. The waterfall roars into Lost Creek. Bright rays of sunshine warm my body. Greenberry looks down on me from a great height. A rabbit roasts over the fire. I taste the rabbit broth. Where are the Little People, Greenberry? Did they bring me here? Did the Nun-ne-hi save me from the roaring waters? If they had not found me in time, the stream would have swallowed me up. Listen, Greenberry. Listen to me. I want to live!

Are you not alive? You have Tsa-la-gi blood, ancient blood. The blood in your veins is powerful blood, mixed blood. It is my blood.

Will you stay with me, Greenberry? No, James. I cannot. Where are you, Greenberry? I cannot see you. You do not need me any more, James. The Great Spirit speaks to you in the wind and the sun and the moon and the stars. The answers are there, hidden in every leaf and rock. You must look for them to keep your life in balance.

You will live, James, because you want to live.

BOOK VII

THE STRAWBERRY FIELD

1899-1965

The stars are wide and alive, they seem each like a great sweetness and they seem very near . . . And who shall ever tell the sorrow of being on this earth . . . in a summer evening, among the sounds of the night. May God bless my people . . . oh, remember them kindly in their time of trouble, and in the hour of their taking away . . . Sleep, soft smiling, draws me unto her, and those receive me, who quietly treat me, as one familiar and well-beloved . . . but will not, oh, will not, not now, not ever, tell me who I am.

—James Agee
A Death in the Family

The beauty of the world, which is so soon to perish, has two edges, one of laughter, one of anguish, cutting the heart asunder.

—Virginia Woolf

ONE

On the Great Wagon Road

White County to Huntsville
August 1899

Vennie stopped and looked back at the cabin one last time. She was glad her cousin Asa had been willing to buy the farm. Henry and Clary would have been happy to know she had sold it to a member of the Fraley family. Vennie wondered what James would do when he returned and found them gone. She knew she had to forget about James. She still loved him, but she had to leave him behind. James's drinking habit was something none of them could take anymore. He had caused them nothing but misery, and she could see no end to it. She couldn't help James anymore.

She had sometimes wondered if his problem was that he carried too much pain from the war and simply could not turn it loose. Maybe, she thought, it would have been better if Greenberry had not told him he was part Indian. Nobody who was part Indian in White County wanted to be Indian. Most of them tried to keep it a secret. In fact, she herself had been careful not to tell the children.

She hoped the two older boys, Sam and Joe, were not exaggerating when they insisted she and the other children could live better in Huntsville. It had not taken much to persuade her. She had come to her wit's end. Every time after a child was born, she had sworn not to allow James to take her to bed again, but despite her resolve, babies kept coming. A part of her had rejoiced in the birth of each child, but she also found herself facing the prospect of another with dread. She wished she could have been happier about the birth of the twins, but all she could think about was how she and the rest would survive with two more mouths to feed. Nine children in eighteen years had taken a heavy toll on her. When she looked in the mirror, she saw a broken-down, worn-out woman of sixty-five or seventy, not the forty-two-year-old woman she actually was. With Clara gone and the older boys in Huntsville, she had been left with only Will and the two girls, Susie and Lillie, to help her with the younger children, and they were barely more than babies themselves.

Vennie held the reins on one of the wagons and Will drove the other. The wagons, one loaded with supplies and the other with children and a few possessions, bumped southward along the well-traveled Old Wagon Road toward Huntsville. They were not alone on their journey. Others in White County who could not make a living as sharecroppers or even as small landowners, had left for jobs in the Huntsville mills. More than once, they passed wagons coming back from Huntsville. Some said they had tried working in the mills for a short time, but found they simply could not stand being shut up all day with noisy machines and bad air. One of the returning travelers said, "I did the same thing over and over, day after day. Might as well go back to the farm. At least on the farm I can work out in the open. I can see the rolling hills and breathe the fresh air. Back on the farm I won't have a boss standin' over me tellin' me what to do."

Vennie and the children picked up a few supplies and staples when they reached McMinnville. By the time they left, the sun promised no more than two hours of daylight. They moved on to an open field near Smartt's Station, where they set up camp for the night on a small hill not far from the road. Will tied up the mules near a stream, and made sure they were fed. When everyone had eaten and bedded down on the ground near the wagons, they lay in silence awed by the darkness and the clear starry sky.

Suddenly Susie shouted, "Did you see that?" A long-tailed shooting star sped across the sky and quickly disappeared beyond the horizon.

"What? Where?" The rest chimed in.

"It was a shootin' star," said Susie, "but it's already gone. You missed it. Papa said it's good luck when you see a shootin' star." It was the first time anyone had mentioned James.

There was a moment of silence before Richard spoke up. "I wish I'd a-seen it. Why does she always get to see things I don't?"

"She didn't see it," Will said. "She just made it up. She's all time comin' up with her strange little stories. She didn't see it, Richard, so don't worry about it."

"I saw it," Green piped up.

"You did not." Richard argued.

"When we get to Huntsville we're all gonna sleep in a house. And we're gonna have real soft feather beds to sleep on," Will said.

Vennie was glad Will had changed the subject. "All of you hush and go to sleep," she declared. "I'm tired and we've got a long way to go tomorrow." Vennie's last image before sleep came was of watching the stars with James, and she felt a deep hurt that James was not with them.

On the second night, Vennie and the children camped among some trees off the road near the small village of Manchester. During the night, a storm came up and the rain soaked through the canvas that covered the wagon. The four-year-old twins clung to each other and cried off and on throughout the night. They both got up the next morning with runny noses. Will built a fire, and Vennie made the children strip down so she could hang their damp clothes on nearby branches to dry. Everyone sat around the fire wrapped in strips of sheeting Vennie had pulled from the trunk.

Vennie was preparing gravy over the fire to have with the fried hoecakes and the salt pork she had bought in McMinnville when a man and woman appeared in the clearing. The woman wore a dress made from coarse cotton flour sacks, and on her head she wore a broad-brimmed bonnet tied around her wrinkled face. The man wore dirty overalls, a brown cotton shirt, and brogans so badly worn that some of his toes were exposed.

The woman spat out a dark stream of tobacco juice from the snuff she had lodged in her jaw, and asked, "Where y'all headed?"

"Huntsville," Vennie answered.

"Ain't you got no man around?" the old man asked.

"Yep, me!" Will answered.

The old man looked Will up and down and asked, "What's your name, son?"

"Will, Sir. Will Preece. This is my mother and my sisters and brothers."

"Glad to know ye, Will Preece. We're the Poseys. She's Coralee and I'm Herman. And y'all is a-trespassin' on our land."

Coralee Posey ambled up to the twins. "Am I seein' double, or is you girls jist alike?"

"They're boys," Susie corrected her.

"We don't see many children anymore, specially not cute little twins like them." The old woman smiled at Green and Richard.

"Yessum, they was born just a few minutes apart," Susie volunteered.

The twins stood stock still while the woman walked all around them and then back to the old man. "You know, Herman, I allus heard it was good luck to be around twins. Why don't y'all bring them babies and come home with us. You can dry out and have a good meal and rest a little while."

She took the twins by their hands and headed over the hill toward a ramshackle cabin. The twins dropped their wraps of cotton sheeting and toddled off unclothed toward the cabin with their hostess. "Now y'all come on. Bring your wet clothes and we'll dry 'em by the fire," she said.

Vennie quickly put the food she had been preparing back in the wagon. They could eat it tomorrow. Tucking their sheeting tighter around their bodies, the others grabbed their wet clothes and followed Coralee Posey to the cabin.

"Herman," his wife ordered, "feed and water them mules."

"I guess it's all right for y'all to camp here tonight," the old man said, as if there had been some question in his mind about whether or not to let them stay.

Coralee arranged to sit between Green and Richard. "I declare I ain't never seen nothing' like it. They're like two peas in a pod. Y'all bow your heads, now. I aim to turn thanks." Coralee bowed her head and prayed, "Dear Lord, thank you for leadin' these sweet little twin boys and their family to our table. A-men."

"A-men," said Herman Posey. Then Will said, "A-men." "A-men," Vennie echoed. She nodded to the others and they all said "A-men," even the twins.

"Best beans I ever ate." Will said. Susie wanted to tell him he was a big fat liar, but she held her tongue.

"Have y'all ever eat beans for breakfast?" Coralee asked. "They're real good with a spoon of sorghum molasses stirred in." She passed Vennie a jar of sorghum.

Vennie gave Susie and Lillie a hard look that said, "Don't you dare say anything." She hoped the rest of them would keep quiet. Sometimes she couldn't contain Woodard, Marian, and the twins. They usually said whatever popped into their heads. Vennie smiled at Susie when she changed the subject and told Coralee her johnnycakes were the best she'd ever eaten.

Vennie was proud of the way her children had behaved around these strangers. She appreciated the generosity of the Poseys. They were good, caring people, and she needed to know there were people outside Lost Creek Valley that cared. Maybe she could go back there someday and repay them for their kindness. She smiled as it crossed her mind that she might have been in danger of losing the twins to Coralee, who kept eyeing them with longing, even as they climbed aboard the wagon and pulled onto the Great Wagon Road toward Huntsville.

In the late afternoon of the second day, they stopped just outside Fayetteville and joined a group of travelers who had permission from a farmer to camp overnight. Vennie and the children could smell the stew cooking in a big black pot over the fire.

"Where ye headed?" One of the men wanted to know.

Will, who had decided to act as head of the household since he was at the moment the oldest boy, replied, "We're headed for Huntsville to find work in the Dallas Mills."

"Well, that's where we're headed too. You're welcome to travel with us," the man said. "We ain't got much, but we'll share what we got."

"We'd be much obliged," Will said.

"That is, if y'all belong to the right church. What religion are ye?"

Will shot Vennie a nervous look. "Well, my folks is all Methodist," she said.

"We're Baptist," he said with a broad grin, "but I reckon if you can put up with us Baptists, we can put up with a Methodist or two."

Vennie couldn't sleep that night. After the fires had burned low and everyone was bedded down, she lay wondering about James. One part of her wanted to turn around and return to Lost Creek Valley. She thought of finding James and trying to persuade him one more time to rid himself of his drinking habit. But she knew it was too late. Life would be better for all of them in this new place, this big town where Joseph and Samuel said they wouldn't have to plow and plant and watch the drought wipe out their labors. They could all work in the mills and have money to buy clothes and shoes and food. Samuel had even said the younger children could go to school right there at the mill. Yes, she decided, they had done the right thing to leave Tennessee.

The mules picked up their pace as they rolled into Alabama. They seemed to know they were nearing their journey's end. As they crossed the Tennessee line and headed south into Madison County, stopping to rest and water the mules at a place called Hazel Green, Vennie began to notice the change in landscape. She wondered if she could ever get accustomed to this flat country. She would miss wondering what was just around the next bend and over the next hill. The old wagon road had become the Meridianville Pike, which lay ahead in a long straight line, disappearing at a point in the distance. Cotton fields separated by woods of oak and cedar lined the road.

Monte Sano rose at some distance to the left of the road. "Sam says it's the only big mountain around these parts," she said. "When you see it, we'll be almost there."

Vennie's first impressions of the Dallas Mill Village gave her hope that what was to follow would mean a good life for her and the children. Streets were curbed and guttered. Cows grazed at the back of small cottages, and on the edge of the village, she noticed vegetable gardens where green beans, pumpkins, watermelons, and tomato plants grew. Some of the cottages had front porches. She imagined they could sit there in the evenings after working in the mill all day.

Marion and Woodard sat at the back of Will's wagon with their legs hanging over the rear edge. Lillie and Susie sat beside Vennie in the other wagon, with the twins squeezed in between their mother and sisters. Nobody spoke. Everyone was agog at the sights. Presently, Lillie began waving at the passersby and they waved back. When a horseless buggy approached, chugging and tooting its horn for them to move over, the twins mimicked its sound, making everyone laugh.

Susie wasn't sure she liked this new place. The houses were too close together and there was too much noise. Like her father James, she liked to roam the fields and woods, and she wondered where the fields and woods were around here. She missed her father. She missed hearing him tell stories about his explorations in the caves. She knew she was the one in the family who looked most like him. Touching her straight black hair, she remembered Uncle Thomas saying, "You're the spittin' image of your daddy!"

"Is my Papa a Indian?" Susie had asked her mother one day. "I remember Aunt Clara calling him a half-breed one time when she was mad."

Vennie was determined to spare her children the anguish of being called Indian. "Oh, honey," she said, "You know how Aunt Clara was. Don't give it another thought. Clara was as apt to say one thing as another. It don't mean nothing."

TWO

The Homecoming

Elkwood, Alabama
July 23, 1965

A small funnel cloud skipped over the cotton fields and hopped back and forth across Meridianville Pike. Hetty could see it in the rear view mirror a good distance away. It was gaining on her. Her hands began to sweat on the steering wheel. Wouldn't you know it! The day I come back to the farm, a tornado challenges me to a race. She pushed down hard on the gas pedal and roared through Madison Crossroads. She wished she had worn something else. She had gained a little weight lately and her Jacqueline Kennedy tight dress hugged her hips, causing it to move above her knees when she sat down. Grandma probably won't like the way I'm dressed, she thought. When she dared look again, the tornado had turned and was headed west away from her.

When was it I saw Grandma last? Two or three years ago, the summer of '63? I have so many fond memories of being here at Grandma's, but I always felt there were secrets the adults in the family wanted to keep from us children. They were all so secretive, the whole bunch of them! Did they think we would never find out? Sometimes when they sat drinking iced tea on hot afternoons we could hear them talking softly, and when we came near, they would hush. More than once I thought I heard whispers about Indian blood in the family.

I should have asked Mama outright if we have Indian blood. But for now, I'll have to start with Grandma. Some people say the long-ago memories come easier for old people. I hope that's true for Grandma Susie, and I hope I haven't waited too long!

Some people I know brag about having Indian blood. They claim to be one-fourth or one-eighth or even one-sixteenth Cherokee. It seems to be the style these days. If the truth were known, we're all mixed-bloods—Indian, white, and black. That thought would probably drive some people crazy!

Susie watched the car dust rise on the sandy road that led to the big house. She was glad the storm cloud had passed her by. It was late July. She hadn't seen her oldest granddaughter in almost three years, and she could hardly contain herself. The last time Hetty was here, she thought, I was still living in the old house. I don't know if she'll like staying with me in my new place. It's so tiny.

When Hetty turned into the lane, she noticed how the tall cedars that lined the narrow road made a cool shady tunnel almost to the house. She couldn't believe how small the old house had become. Peonies and rosebushes struggled to survive under the sagging windows, and the house needed a coat of paint. Where cotton fields used to be, rows and rows of green soybeans grew. The stormpit, covered with green moss, was still there, and she wondered if it were still in use. The orchard stood fruitless, the well was covered over, and the barn was gone. She was glad to see the swing still hanging on the front porch.

Grandma Susie, now in her late seventies, stood on the porch of the new cottage waiting. Susie's face was wrinkled and sagging, but she still had a mischievous twinkle in her eyes. Her graying hair was pulled back into a doughnut bun with her old bone combs to hold it together. Hetty noticed she was wearing the white cotton dress with purple flowers—the one Hetty always admired. It was a bit faded, but still just as pretty. Grandma still orders her shoes from Sears Roebuck, Hetty thought. It's the same black leather lace-up shoe she remembered Grandma wearing all through the forties when Hetty was a child.

Susie looked Hetty up and down. "Law, child, you ain't changed much. Just a little rounder. Not much though. How long has it been? Two, three years?"

Yes, so little time left and so much to learn, Hetty thought. She had lots of questions for Grandma, and this time she wouldn't leave until she asked them.

While Grandma Susie busied herself making supper, Hetty sat at the little dinette table in the kitchen waiting for the right words to begin her questions.

"Grandma," she ventured, "I'm hoping you'll tell me about your life, yours and Grandpa's, and anything you can remember about the family."

"Law, child," her grandmother said, "there ain't much to tell. Why would you want to dig up the past, anyway? What happens now is what's important, don't you think?"

"I want to know who my forebears were and where they came from. And I want my children to know, if and when I have any children."

"Oh, you'll have children, don't you worry," Grandma Susie laughed. "But don't forget, you gotta find a husband and get married first. That's the way most people do it."

Hetty had often heard the story about her grandma's wedding day, and it seemed to her this would be a good place to start. "When was it you got married, Grandma?" Her grandmother had always been ready to talk about that. "How old were you?"

"Aw, I don't remember exactly. I reckon it was 1903, in March. I was almost sixteen. My birthday was in June and I was from June 'til March over fifteen."

"Boy, were you young! Grandpa was a lot older than you, wasn't he?"

"Well, he was thirty when we married. Yeah, he was fifteen years older than I was." Susie was looking out the window at the old house. Hetty wondered if her grandmother had forgotten she was there.

"Man, he beat that mule, he whipped that mule! He was runnin' that mule just as hard as he could. You'll kill that mule, I told him." She was rambling now.

"Who?" Hetty asked.

"John. The day we got married. He run that mule plumb from Huntsville to Hazel Green so hard he beat a streetcar."

"Surely not," Hetty chimed in, hoping she would tell more.

"It's the truth. I've never seen anything like it. Man alive! That mule could pick up and go. And it was his daddy's mule, you know." She paused, her mischievous look turning into something more somber.

Hetty had the feeling she was about to change the subject. "You were running away from home, weren't you?"

"Yeah, and he was afraid of Will. I knowed what Will was like, and I knowed if ever they met, they would do one another harm. Well, we got there in Judge Hawkins's office and we had to sit there. Just had to sit there and wait for Hawkins to come in. Seemed like hours."

"Weren't you afraid Will would get there first?"

"I could just hear Will's big old brogans a-bumpin' up the steps. I could imagine, you know, that shotgun he was carryin'. I was just scared to death.

Will got there too late, though," she chuckled. "We was already married. There was nothing Will could do. But he threatened John that if he ever hurt me, he would kill him."

"Grandma," Hetty said. "Do you remember that summer I stayed with you when I was fourteen, and I went to spend the weekend with a friend, and you thought I'd run off and got married?"

"Aw, I reckon it crossed my mind," Susie said

"I guess now I know where you got that notion," Hetty laughed.

Susie stopped and stood in the middle of the kitchen shaking her head. "My Mama nearly had a fit. She threatened to whup me. Never did forgive me for runnin' off. But she had no idea how bad it was for girls working in the mill."

"The mill in Huntsville?" Hetty asked.

"Yeah, it was hard, and a girl had to be careful, you know. The older boys weren't bringin' in enough for us to live on, so when I was thirteen, Mama agreed to let me work. She had Lillie, Woodard, Marion, and the twins to think about. She couldn't work. There was even some younger than me a-workin' in the mill. I would get up at five o'clock, eat me some breakfast, and head off with Will to the mill to get there before the 5:15 whistle blowed. I'd work all day, from 5:30 in the mornin' 'til 6:15 in the evenin'. That's when the whistle blowed for quittin' time.

"I remember the first morning I worked. Will left me with this man who was gonna teach me how to work the spindle. I almost cried. I kept thinkin' I was gonna get lost if I left that machine. Man, that mill was big! It was a big red brick buildin' about five stories high, and it was dirty and hot in there. And it smelled awful. The sweat and the oily smell from the machines was almost more that I could stand.

"The mill owners weren't supposed to let children work, but they didn't pay no attention to that. And when the government inspectors questioned them about it, they said we was all just mountain dwarfs, that we only *looked* like children."

"How awful!" Hetty said.

"We didn't make a whole lot either, only about half what they paid the grown-ups. And they was always havin' accidents. Mama worried all the time about that. And when she heard about a man getting his hand cut off, she said I couldn't go back. But I did. Aw, it didn't matter to them mill owners. All they wanted to do was make money. Will and some of the older men tried to get all the mill hands to go to the owners and demand better pay. Will said the company owned us—lock, stock, and barrel. He said we was no better than slaves. But it didn't do no good. People was too afraid of losin' their jobs. Them owners all lived in fine houses over in Twickenham. One of them, old man Reisen, had a mansion on top of Monte Sano.

"Aw, I recon' I was lucky. I stopped workin' before I got the brown lung disease like some did." She paused and looked out the window. "I shoulda listened to what Mama told me. He's too old for you to marry, she said. Drinks too much. But I was tired of workin' in the mill. And I was scared."

"What were you scared of?" Hetty ventured.

"Men. They wouldn't leave us girls alone. They was all time sayin' nasty things about our bosoms, and sometimes they would even pull our petticoat straps when they passed. One of them once called me his little Injun Princess and said he'd love to get into my teepee. I told Will what he said, and he whupped the livin' daylights out of him. He told him if he ever come around me again sayin' anything like that, he'd kill him. Will had a temper. Nobody fooled with him. He promised Mama he'd watch out for me. I always figured I could take care of myself, but I was glad Will was there."

Hetty watched her grandmother move once more to the window, gazing into the distance. After a long moment, Susie said, "I was sick and tired of working in that mill and I reckon I would've done anything to get away. When John come along and promised to get me out of there, I was ready to go with him. Aw, I guess if I hadn't gone to the strawberry field that day, it wouldn't have happened." She stopped suddenly, as if she hadn't meant to say it.

"*What* wouldn't have happened, Grandma?" Hetty asked.

"I used to get these bad headaches," Susie said. "And I always used to have this dream over and over about pickin' strawberries in the cold wintertime in a frozen field. I'm standin' in the upstairs window in the old house, holdin' tight to the white lace curtains. I can see long icicles hanging from the roof. Then I'm out in the snow in that frozen strawberry field, and a tall old man walkin' with a stick is coming at me over the frozen ground. Ravens are flyin' over and divin' down at me. I try to run, but my feet are stuck in the frozen ground. Then the old man chases the ravens away with a big cedar stick. In my dream, I think if I can blink my eyes, it will all go away. But I can't move my eyelids. Finally, I do blink, and the ravens and the old man are gone. Funny, I remember always wakin' up to the smell of cedar. I used to tell Lillie about my dream, 'cause she was always with me when we went a-lookin' for strawberries. Thank goodness it finally went away, my dream did. I can still remember it, but I don't dream it anymore. And my headaches went away. You know, Lillie died a few years back. I sure do miss her. We used to tell each other everything."

Susie turned toward the stove. "I'm a-thinkin' that cake must be done by now. Lord, a-mercy, it's so hot! The windows in the bedroom need to be up. There's nowhere a-body can go to get away from this heat."

"When I was younger," Hetty said, "I had a dream. I dreamed it over and over for a long time, like you did. In my dream, you warned me about the old well we used to draw water from."

"Yes, I had it covered over after it went dry a few years back."

"Well, in my dream, you warned me not to lean too far over the well. And, of course, I didn't pay any attention. In my dream, I wanted to know if I could see myself in the water at the bottom of the well. So I reached over into the well to feel the cool, mossy stones on the walls. But I was leaning too far over and I began to fall. And, in my dream, you caught me just in time and pulled me back."

"Dreams have meaning, you know," Susie said. "What do you think it meant?"

"It means I always knew I could count on you. Now tell me what your dream meant."

Susie was silent.

"What does it mean, do you think?" Hetty pressed Susie gently. "About the frozen strawberry field?"

"Lord, Lord!" her grandmother went on. "I've got to do some work on the old house one day soon, and I'm going to buy the stuff, and if that man that's livin' there with his family and not payin' me no rent don't fix it, I'm gonna skin him." She laughed. "I got to buy windows, you know, and fix it up this fall. It's dowdy around the windows. I always do that to the house—fix it up in the fall. I used to paper and paint that whole house by myself. I liked doing it. Sometimes John would help, but mostly he had his own work to do. I'm gonna let that man stay just like I told him I would. Aw, he's just as poor as Job's turkey, and he's got a big family to take care of—five of 'em in school. Right big boys—all redheaded."

That's just like Grandma Susie, thought Hetty. She's always doing something for somebody. As far as Hetty could remember, her grandmother had never complained about anything. She was the comfort giver, the one the family depended on when anyone was in trouble. She was the one who made sure the church house was clean and ready for services every Sunday morning.

"Do you still set out the bread and grape juice at church?" Hetty asked.

"Why yes, honey. Reckon that preacher over at Reed's Chapel couldn't get along without me," she laughed. "Anyways, he claims he couldn't get along without my fried chicken of a Sunday. You couldn't preach if I didn't fix for you, I tell him. He says he'd marry me if he didn't already have a wife. I ain't studyin' no marriage, I tell him. I already had enough of that. But if you was a Mormon and not a Methodist, you could have all the wives you want." She laughed. "Aw, I don't mean nothin' by it. Just gotta have my fun. I couldn't stand it if I couldn't have my fun now and again.

"I reckon a body can stand most anything if a body can laugh about it," she went on. "We had to put up with a lot when I was a girl. I don't know how my mama stood it, living on the street in them two wagons with all us children. People nowadays don't know how lucky they are to have a house to live in with a roof over their heads."

"Where did y'all live on the street, Grandma?"

"In Huntsville, at the Dallas Mills. We camped out on Meridian Street for months a-fore we moved in with Joe and his wife on Hume Street. The mill owners claimed they was building more cottages for the mill hands, but as soon as one was built, the foremen moved in. Mama used to build a fire by the road and cook our food. She would take Lillie and me down the hill to the Dallas Branch to wash our clothes. It was awful living there. Richard and Green had no place to play. Before I started working, Mama put Lillie and me in charge of watching 'em. We use to get into all kinds of fights with Marion and Woodard playing marbles. They thought they was too big for us to watch. Sometimes we would go fishing in Dallas Creek and try to catch something for supper. People used to pass in wagons and buggies and stare at us. We didn't pay no attention. We got used to it.

"One time these rich people from Twickenham, you know right across from Dallas Mills Village, came by and asked Mama if they could adopt the twins. They thought the boys was the cutest things they'd ever seen, and they said they could take better care of 'em than she could, and they'd send 'em to good schools. It made Mama real mad. You can bet Mama told them where to go. Them Twickenham people looked down on all us millhands. They called us lint-heads because we had this stuff in our hair and all over us, little bits of cotton fibers from the sheetin' we made, you know."

"Why didn't y'all go back to Tennessee, Grandma?"

"Aw, I guess we had it better than some. A lot of people lived in the shantytown around the mill, some with only a piece of canvas to protect them against the weather. But it wasn't all bad. If you got sick, you could see a company nurse. On Sundays sometimes we'd all ride the trolley car into town, or take a picnic up on top of Monte Sano. The boys loved to go fishin' or just catchin' tadpoles in the branch below the mill. Sometimes there was square dances and cake walks and box suppers. All the mills around Huntsville had ball teams, and we loved to cheer for the Dallas team.

"One time we got to go to the train depot to see President McKinley. I was only about fourteen I guess, but I got to shake his hand. I thought that was really something, to get to shake the president's hand. He was comin' through Huntsville 'lectioneerin' for his second term. But it didn't do him no good. They shot him just a few months later.

"We didn't have much time for foolishness. Our time was mostly taken up with workin' in the mill, and we was generally too tired to do anything on our day off."

"Did you ever wish you had stayed in Tennessee?" Hetty asked.

"Mama was the one that missed Lost Creek Valley the most," Susie said. "Seem like she spent a lot of her time wishin' she could go back. But we never did. She worried about storms a lot. We didn't have no storm pit at Dallas Mills like we had in Lost Creek and like I do here. But if a storm come up durin' the night, she'd still wake us up and make us put our clothes and shoes on. There was no place for us to go, so we'd just sit there and wait for the storm to pass. The little kids would giggle about it, but Mama didn't think it was funny."

"Yeah, I remember sitting in your storm pit right over there many times waiting for a storm to pass over," Hetty said. "Us kids didn't worry about the storm either. Not the way you grown-ups did. But I was scared to death of snakes and spiders. I remember listening to git-ye stories and playing shadow games on the wall. I remember Grandpa telling us to hush so he could hear the thunderclaps and tell how far away the lightning was. Us kids didn't mind daytime storms because we got to stay home from school."

"Aw, I wished I had gone to school," Susie said. "But I couldn't. We needed the money. Everybody my age and even younger had to work. Woodard, Marion, and the twins did go to school for a while though. They learnt readin' and writin' at the company school. Woodard use to read out loud to me at night. He tried to teach me how, but I was just too tired to learn.

"Supper's done. Let's eat."

"Grandma, where's your Bible, the one that used to lay on the mantle in the bedroom?"

"It's over there in a drawer. I got it when I joined the church over at Reed's Chapel, and my sister, Lillie, helped me put down the date John and me married. The dates when all my children were born are in it. Susie pulled the Bible from a desk drawer in the little sitting room. "Here it is," she said.

"Are there any other family Bibles around, Grandma? Did your Mama Vennie have one?"

"I think she had Grandma Orpha's, but I believe Uncle Brennan over in Memphis took that one when she died."

"What about your papa's family? Did they have one?"

"If he did, I never saw it. That side of the family, the Preeces, was awful closed-mouth. I never knew a lot about them."

Hetty had noticed that in all Susie's rambling about her past, she had not once mentioned her father. During supper, she asked, "What happened to your papa?"

"Aw, he drank too much, so we left him in Tennessee. Mama said the war left him wounded in the head. Not really hurt, like somebody had knocked him in the head with a hammer or anything like that. Mama said that after his own pa was killed in the war, he was never able to get hisself back together. And he saw some awful things in the war when he was a boy. This Indian man used to take him on trips to hunt for caves, and I think he was happier when he was doing that. He even went up to Kentucky with this Indian to explore the Great Mammoth Cave.

"Did I tell you what he did just before Mama died? After we left Lost Creek, he moved off down to Marshall County below Huntsville. When Mama knew she was dyin', she asked me to find him and bring him to her. She was livin' with me then, over there in the big house. That was in 1924. I remember it because I had just brought her up here to live because she needed somebody to take care of her. But I didn't get to take care of her long before she died. I buried her over in Hazel Green at Plainview Cemetery.

"Well, I sent my cousin Monroe to find Papa. Monroe said he found him runnin' a bakery business in New Hope, just southeast of Huntsville, and he had lots of women and girls workin' for him. Anyway, Monroe brought him back up here.

"I never saw anything like it. Papa got down on his knees beside Mama's bed and asked her to forgive him. And she did. I heard him tell her he had quit drinkin' a long time ago, and that he still loved her even after all those years. Course, he'd been livin' with this woman somewhere around New Hope and they had raised me eight half-brothers and sisters. He brought one of them with him, a big old strappin' boy bout thirteen years old. Looked just like him.

"About four years ago, I decided to make a trip to Marshall County to find my half-brothers and sisters. And I did, too. They was real nice folks. Put me up for two or three days, and treated me like I was one of the family, which—bless goodness—I was." She laughed.

"That's the oddest thing I ever heard," said Hetty. "If I figure right, your papa must have been the daddy of about seventeen children. And I just don't know if it had been me whether I could have forgiven him after all those years."

"Yep, but my mama never stopped lovin' him, and I loved him too. I was glad to know he was alive. He said he tried to bring hisself to come back after he stopped drinkin', but so many years had passed, and I guess he was just afraid he would interfere with people's lives. Nobody knows what other people have to live with. So I couldn't fault him. But it makes me sad, even today as old as I am, that Mama had to live without Papa all them years. I think she wished her whole life long she had stayed in Tennessee with Papa."

After supper, Hetty and her grandmother sat in the swing on the front porch, watching the sun disappear behind the woods. They watched the blinking fireflies. A comet shot across the sky.

"Did you see that shooting star?" Hetty asked.

"Yes, I saw it," Susie said. "My papa always used to say that seeing a shootin' star was good luck. I saw one night before last, and I knew it was a sign. I reckon your comin' to see me was my good luck."

"And mine, too," said Hetty.

"Honey, before you leave tomorrow, remind me that I have something I want to give you," Susie said.

"I won't forget," Hetty said, then added quietly, "Grandma, I've been thinking about your dream. That dream about the strawberry field. Can't you tell me what you think your dream means?"

After a long pause, Susie put a finger to her lips and whispered, "Hush, child, and just listen to the guinea hens in the high oak tree settlin' for the night."

THREE

The Outrage

Dallas Mills Village, Huntsville, Alabama
July 23, 1900

*W*e just wanted to pick strawberries in the strawberry field, Mama.
You're the only one I will ever tell. We went to pick strawberries for
you, but they was all gone. They're a—comin' across the field from the brickyard.
One of 'em is Isaac. I don't know that other one. Don't be a-scared, Lillie. It's just
Isaac. You know him. He's that colored boy that brings milk from the dairy. He's
always wavin' and smilin'. But he's not smilin' this time. Him and that other boy
is a-comin' straight towards us across the field. Somethin' ain't right. He's got a
knife in his hand. Run, Lillie, run. Run home and get Mama.

Oh, Mama. I'm a-hurtin' bad. I hear Mama's voice: Is she okay? My neck
and head hurt. Who's touching me? It's okay, Mama says. They're doctors. Will
she be all right?

Is this the man? My eyes are shut tight. I can't look at him. Lillie says: yes, he's
the one. Lillie is cryin'. He had a knife, she says. I feel dirty. Mama is washin' me.
I hear her cryin'. Mama, I say, I'm all right. Where's Will? Mama asks. Don't tell
Will, I say. Tell me, Susie, you can tell me what happened. I can tell you, Mama.
You're the only one I'll ever tell.

I scream. I fight. He bangs my head hard on the ground. The briars in the
plum thicket hurt. I see them black birds a-circlin' overhead. They come closer
and closer. They're a-peckin' at me. He's chokin' me. It hurts. I can't tell you any

more, Mama. Tell me the rest, Susie. He says if I move, he'll kill me. It hurts. It hurts so bad. It's dark. I open my eyes. I see him, the tall Indian man standing there. He's wavin' a cedar branch over me, chasin' the black birds away. They're gone, he says. They won't bother you anymore. You're dreamin', Mama says. She says I'm out of my head. But I say the tall Indian man was there. I know he was. I can smell cedar. Hush and just rest, she says.

Vennie was worried about Susie, but she was also worried about Will. She could hear the loud voices of the men at the end of the street, and she was sure Will was among them. She knew they were getting ready to go after the man who attacked Susie. The sheriff came to the house on Hume Street.

"I need to talk to your little girl," he said to Vennie.

"The doctors are here with her now," Vennie said. "She's in no shape to talk to anybody."

"We need to know who did this," Sheriff Fulgrum said. "We got to go after him." Moving to the foot of Susie's bed, he asked, "Who did this to you, child?"

"It was Isaac. Isaac Chambers," Susie whispered.

"Are you sure?"

Susie began to cry. "Ask Lillie. She was there."

"Stop badgering her," Vennie said. "She's barely able to talk."

"These two boys come after us," Lillie told Sheriff Fulgrum. "Susie told me to run. I didn't know one of 'em. He run away, but the other one was Isaac. He had a knife, and he told me to git on home. He said if I told, he would kill me."

"Don't you worry," the sheriff told her. "He won't hurt you. We'll find him."

The two doctors continued their examination of Susie. "She's been ravaged," Dr. Burwell told Vennie. "You need to wrap cool wet cloths around her neck to keep down the swelling and you need to keep her quiet. He nearly choked her to death. She's a lucky girl. It'll take awhile before that big bump on her head goes away. She's lucky to be alive. I think she's going to be fine, but it will take time."

Dr. McKelby told Vennie he had known Isaac since he was a child. "As far as I know, he's always been a good boy. It's hard to believe it was his fingers that left these bruises on the child's neck. He's only about nineteen or twenty, and his father and mother are hardworking Christian people. He's been working with his father on a farm near the Monte Sano Dairy, and he sometimes drives one of the wagons for the dairy." He shook his head. "I can't imagine what got into him."

Vennie was worried. The minute Will heard what had happened, he ran out into the street with his gun. "I'll kill that son-of-a bitch," he said. "I swear I will!" He ran through Dallas Village calling for help to go after Isaac Chambers. Within minutes, most of the men of the village had taken up arms and gone with Will.

Vennie had been concerned for some time there would be trouble at the mill. It was just waiting to happen. The mill workers were bitter. "They work us like dogs and they don't pay us a decent wage," Will had told Vennie. They only needed an excuse to vent their anger, Vennie thought. And now Will and the others had a reason to explode. Isaac Chambers had violated Will's sister, and now the men had poured out of the Dallas Village on a rampage looking for him. If only I had known the girls were going to the strawberry field, I could have told them there wouldn't be any strawberries in July. Then this would never have happened, she thought.

On Wednesday, July 25, two days after the rape, the headlines of the *Weekly Tribune* in large bold print read: "Huntsville Afflicted with a Mob Today." The next line, in slightly smaller type, reported: "The Most Intense Excitement Prevailing from Early Morn till Evening." Then followed line by line, in even smaller type, what the reporter considered the main events of the day:

"Sheriff Fulgram Valiantly Held the Jail against the Great Odds. Stood Like a Hero at His Post."

"The Crime Was Heinous One, Most Repulsive. The Community, a Unit for the Death Penalty, but the Better Element Want the Law."

"Fire, Brimstone, Tar, and Feathers Were Used to Smoke Gallant Fulgram from His Barricade—The Dynamite Fiend Was Also in Evidence. The Defaced Walls of Jail Showing Its Handiworks."

The first few sentences of the article that followed read: "Negro is lynched shortly after five o'clock. At 4:45, mob has gained entrance to cell door where negro is. Negro will be lynched in short while. Men with sledgehammer at door, entrance nearly effected. Negro will be burned."

The paper reported that Jailer Connally had "kept his stand in the jail; so did Mrs. Connally until the jail door was broken in and she was carried out. She did a heroic thing," the paper said, "trying to suppress mob violence by pleading with the enraged men, but it was ignored." The paper further reported that "others—ministers and citizens opposed to violence—tried to address the crowd, which by the time of the lynching, had grown to six thousand. They pleaded for them to wait for justice, but no one listened."

Vennie later learned that a Dallas Mills man, James Cornell, was the mob's leader. It was reported he was not a local, but from the state of Texas. He demanded the prisoner be turned over, and when the jailer refused, the men used a sledgehammer to break into the jail. They set fire to barrels of oil and sulfur and feathers in an attempt to smoke out Sheriff Fulgrum and his prisoner. When the sheriff refused to turn over the keys to the mob, they laid sticks of dynamite under the jail and threatened to light them.

If the sheriff doesn't give over, Vennie thought, he could lose his life, or at the very least, his job. How long will it be before he pays the price for trying to protect his prisoner? Cornell and the other mill hands should have let the law take its course. Then Isaac Chambers could have been found guilty in a court of law. Why couldn't somebody have put an end to this madness?

Vennie learned that Judge Speake had tried to convince the mob to wait. He promised a speedy trial, but they refused to listen to him. According to the newspaper, Judge Speake did impanel a grand jury under the special term of the court ordered by the governor of Alabama and promised the trial would take place two days later. But the mob was not interested in listening to lawyers. The men wanted blood.

One of the mill hands told Vennie that Isaac Chambers was crouched in the corner of his cell when they got control of the jail. "They put a plow line around his neck," he said, "and dragged him down here to Dallas Village and on over to Moore's Grove." She noticed that the millhand talked about the lynching as if he hadn't been part of it. The paper stated that no one had been arrested or held accountable for the lynching. The reason given: there were no witnesses. Vennie noticed Will didn't want to talk about it either.

FOUR

Moore's Grove

Dallas Mills Village
July 24, 1900

I *despise that bastard. What made him think he could get away with rapin'* *Susie? She's my little sister, for God's sake. And I don't care what color he is,* *I despise him. I shoulda been there. If I hadn't been off messin' around, throwin'* *a few balls and tryin' to impress Polly, maybe I coulda saved her. She ain't but* *thirteen, for God's sake. She's a baby. Mama won't say it, but I know she blames* *me. I'm supposed to be watchin' out for her. That's what Mama told me when* *she let Susie start workin' in the mill. Will, you watch out for Susie, she said. If* *I'd a-been there when they found him cowerin' under his cousins' feather bed, I'd* *a-blowed his brains out right then and there. Oh, I woulda done it, all right.* *Wouldn't a-had to go through all that mess with arrestin' him and tryin' to get* *him a trial. He's guilty. Susie said it was him. He's admitted it. Look at him settin'* *up there on that horse like he was somebody. I reckon he's a scared somebody right* *now. The boys say I oughta be the one to put the noose around his neck. They* *want me to do it 'cause it was Susie he raped. I guess that's nothin' but right.*

*   *   *

Didn't mean to hurt her. She just kept yellin', Git away, don't touch me. I *just wanted her to stop yellin'. That's why I pulled my knife. Didn't aim to use it* *on her. Just meant to scare her and git her quiet. I seen her lotsa times, struttin' and actin' all high and mighty, like she was better'n me. She quit talkin' to me. Said her brother told her not to. Who's she think she is? She ain't nothin' but a half-breed lint-head.*

Somebody oughta take her down a peg or two. I'm just the one to do it, I told Albert. Albert run off when she set in hollerin'. The little 'un was a-hollerin' too, and I run her off. Told her to git on home. That was pretty dumb. I'll kill you if you tell, I told her. I knowed she'd tell. Gotta get outta here. Run for the woods. Make Ben and Bob hide me. If they catch me, boys, they'll kill me. You don't want 'em to shoot me dead, do ye? They're a-comin'. Hear the dogs? Sheriff says I'll get a fair trial. Them mill men done set the jail a-fire. Nearly smothered me to death.

What's he doin' with that rope, slingin' it over that tree limb? Sweet Jesus, please get me down from here. Dear God, I can't hardly breathe. Don't leave me a-danglin'. Please don't! Oh, God. I'm a-chokin' to death. Lord Jesus, don't let me die. Mama! Daddy! Come git me down from here. Please . . .

*   *   *

Poor bastard. I don't want to see you swing. Don't want to see your face. Don't want to smell your sweat. Man alive! Just listen to that crowd holler. I'm a-gonna throw up. Gotta get outta here. I'm a-goin' somewhere they don't know me, somewhere I don't have to think about it anymore. Good God, Mama, it was awful.

*   *   *

In the *Weekly Mercury's* issue of July 25, 1900, the headlines read: "Isaac Chambers, Negro Rapist, Taken from Jail and Hanged." The first paragraph described the hanging:

> At the hands of a quiet and orderly but determined mob of one thousand men, Isaac Chambers, a negro boy twenty years old, last evening paid the extreme penalty for a criminal assault upon a white girl Sunday afternoon. The negro was taken out of jail after the sheriff had been overcome by smoke, carried to the girl and identified, and then taken to the Moore's Grove near Dallas and swung to a limb, his body being riddled with bullets. The body is at this late hour tonight swinging to a limb in a deserted grove

and stands as a warning to other negroes who may have an idea of committing this crime.

The *Mercury* described how men with guns had searched for Chambers during the night. Sheriff Fulgrum's deputies had captured him in bed with two cousins near Meridianville. According to the paper, they were attempting to conceal him by lieing on top of him. The paper further reported, "When the news spread about the arrest, the male population of the Dallas Mill suspended work, causing nearly the entire mill to shut down. The men brought rifles, shot guns, and pistols with them."

The *Mercury* further stated that "when Sheriff Fulgrum realized he could not contain the mob, he asked the Mayor to request Governor Johnston to send troops, and the governor ordered the Decatur Company to come on a special train. But the troops never came. On August 1st, the *Mercury* reported that "Governor Johnston received a telephone message from some unknown person in Huntsville informing him the soldiers weren't needed. The message doubtless was sent by someone in sympathy with the mob."

Vennie wondered how they would get through the days to follow. "Susie needs time to get well," she told the others. "We'll keep quiet around Susie 'til she's better." They all agreed not to tell Susie about what happened with the lynching, and not even to talk about it where she might hear.

Vennie kept her in bed and fed her soup and tea. "Here honey, drink this," she told Susie, holding the cup to her lips. "It's sassafras tea. My mama used to give it to me when I was sick."

Well-wishers and curiosity seekers from Dallas Mill Village came by with flowers, and she received notes from people all over Huntsville. Woodard read her a note printed at the bottom of the front page of the Huntsville *Weekly Mercury*: "We wish little Susie a speedy recovery and hope she is up and around soon."

Susie first thought they were all being quiet about what happened in the strawberry field because they were too embarrassed to talk about it, but she soon sensed there was more. She knew Will had not been home since it happened, and the rest of the family had stayed away from the mill. Finally, Susie forced Lillie to tell her what had happened.

"They caught him and then they hanged him," Lillie told her. "Over at Moore's Grove. They hanged him from a tree over there." Lillie knew Mama Vennie would be mad. She knew she would get a thrashing for telling.

"Why did you do it?" Vennie asked. "Why did you have to tell her about the hangin'?"

"She kept on botherin' me," Lillie said. "She said she wouldn't speak to me ever again if I didn't tell her ever'thing."

Susie didn't speak to anyone for days after she learned they had hanged Isaac. "It's my fault," she whispered to her mother. "I ought not a-told on him."

"Of course you shoulda told," Vennie said. "You did the right thing. You didn't do anything to him. He did it to hisself."

Vennie wished there had been a trial instead of the mob taking matters into its own hands. She definitely didn't want Susie to hear about the lynch mob. She especially didn't want her to learn it was Will who put the rope around Isaac's neck. "Susie needs time now to heal," she said to Lillie. "We all need time to heal."

Vennie couldn't forget what the sheriff's deputy said Isaac Chambers had told him when asked why he did it. "I didn't think nobody would care. She was just a mill girl, and I didn't think it'd matter." Did he really say that, or had the deputy made it up? Why would Isaac think nobody would care?

It was true the law seldom paid attention to what went on in Dallas Mills Village. Vennie knew that time after time, the police had ignored reports of girls being molested there. They claimed they had no jurisdiction over the mill workers. And the mill owners would never let anything interfere with turning out cotton sheeting, Vennie thought. What's more, the sheriff generally didn't bother with the village. After all, don't he depend on the mill owners to keep him in office? And what about Twickenham? Most of the men who run this town live there. They certainly don't care. We're just lint-heads to them, she thought. They was right there, all high and mighty, watching the lynching and doing nothing to stop it?

There ought to have had been a trial, Vennie thought. Then the jury could have heard from his own mouth what was going on in his mind when he raped Susie. Maybe if there had been a trial, Will wouldn't have joined the lynch mob. Had they really said Will was the one who put the rope around Isaac's neck? Had he done that? I would've given my life if he hadn't done that, she thought.

What must Isaac's mother and father feel! Vennie asked herself. At least my son is alive. Even though he has to live with what he's done, at least he's alive. Did they actually say Isaac's parents refused to claim his body and bury it? Were they afraid of the mob? Is that why they didn't come for the body in Moore's Grove? How awful not to be able to bury your own son. Nobody knows the burden of sorrow another carries.

Moore's Grove! She would never be able to go there again. No more picnics or games among the cedars in the grove. From now on, the only peaceful place in all of Dallas Village would be known as the place of the lynching.

If I could turn back time, Vennie lamented, I would. If only I had been more watchful about where the girls went that Sunday. Sooner or later, Susie can't help but learn all about the lynching. It'll just add to the pain she already has to live with. The most painful thing for a mother, she thought, is to watch her children suffer. If only I could have stopped Will when he came for the gun. But Will is his own person and always has been, Vennie thought. He's got a mind of his own. After all, he felt he was protecting his sister. What did I do to my children when I brought them here from Lost Creek Valley, from the mountains where they could live off the land and hunt and fish and breathe clean air? They've all become expert weavers and spinners, but at what a cost!

For several days, Vennie sat by Susie's bed holding her hand, sometimes staying with her into the night. The red marks on her throat were beginning to turn yellow and purple. It will be a long time before she gets over this, Vennie thought, if she ever does. And while people are sending her get-well wishes and flowers now, I'm afraid that later, they will convince her what happened in the strawberry field has made her a ruined woman. I've seen it happen. People can be so cruel and unforgiving sometimes. But I can't worry about that now. I have to help Susie get well. Vennie wished she had her mother Orpha and Aunt Clara there beside her. She could just hear Mama Orpha saying: "Don't worry, honey, we'll get through this. We have to."

FIVE

The Secret

Elkwood, Alabama
July 24, 1965

Hetty woke to roosters crowing. It was hazy outside, a hot murky day. She wanted it to be one of those cool June mornings she remembered as a child when everything was crisp and clear. The guinea hens would be marching across the yard with their babies and everything would be alive and moving. She wished she could hear the crunch of the leaves in the fall as she walked beneath the hickory nut tree. If she could just be there when the first snow of winter quickly came and melted away. What wouldn't she give to smell again the newly plowed fields in the spring and watch the small green cotton shoots rise above the sandy red earth. If only she could sit dreaming under cedar shades, as she had as a girl.

As was her habit, Grandma Susie was up early and already moving about the kitchen preparing breakfast when Hetty arose.

"I have to leave soon," said Hetty. "I have to stop by Mama's on the way home, and then catch a plane in Nashville."

"You have to stay and eat breakfast," Susie insisted. "I have to show you what's in the trunk."

"Grandma, how do you stand being here all by yourself? Aren't you lonesome?"

"Aw, sometimes I get down, thinkin' about my children all gone now. That's one thing a mother never gets over—takin' care of her children, and then one day they're gone. Even though they're on their own now, I still worry and fret over them. But I like the peace and quiet here. It gives me time to crochet and do my little bit of gardenin'. See them dried-up daffodils over yonder? They was the prettiest things this last spring! I put 'em out the first year John and me married. I remember that. Me and the daffodils are still here." Grandma chuckled. "And they'll be here long after I'm gone."

"Grandma, what do you think about God? I've never heard you say."

"Aw, I don't know, it's all a mystery to me. I can't decipher it. I sometimes wonder, but they ain't no way a-knowin'. I used to wonder a lot about how we come to be here, but I've never found any answers to suit me. Yep, it's all a mystery to me.

"I believe the closest I've come to knowin' is when I'm sittin' in the swing just before the sun sinks down behind the woods. The birds stop their chirpin' and the guinea hens settle their wings in that big oak tree. The cowbells stop ringin'. It's in that quiet time when long shadows creep down the path to the house, and day gives over to night. It's when the first faraway stars come out. Sometimes I watch 'em for a long time. And sometimes, if I watch long enough, I'll see a shootin' star. And I get this feelin'. Aw, I can't name it, but it's this feelin' that tells me to hush and watch and listen.

"You know, it's all bigger than me, and it'll be here long after I'm gone. Life is so short, ain't it? What matters to me now is spendin' these few hours with you, and us rememberin'. I remember you skippin' down the lane to the mailbox when you was little, and I'll remember us watchin' the stars together.

"Aw, when I get down and out, feelin' sorry for myself, I just sit myself down and remember how Mama Vennie, with all the sorrow and pain she carried, forgave my papa after all those years. Some things you never forget. I remember that like it was yesterday. I thought then, if there is a God, that's what God must be like. Did I ever tell you it was my papa taught me to watch the stars?"

"Grandma, I've never heard you talk about heaven or hell. An awful lot of people worry about that."

"Aw, I can't worry about that. There's a awful lot of hell right here on earth," she chuckled. "And there's a lot of heaven here too. It's all around us." Grandma Susie stopped dead still for a moment, and then she laughed. "Aw, I drove my mama crazy sometimes. You know, I was a jokester when I was younger."

"What do you mean, *when you was younger*?" Hetty chuckled. "You still are."

"Why, when John and me first married, I would stand behind the door when he come from the barn and jump out at him. He said I was gonna give him a heart attack, but he really liked it. Aw, we had a good time, I reckon. I was only fifteen, you know." She laughed a devilish laugh.

"I guess I was just bored to death sometimes. He would go off and play cards and booze it up with the men, and I would be there waitin' for him to come home. Do you know what he did on our weddin' night? His cousins come and give us a shiveree. They banged on tin pans the first part of the night and then they rode John off on a rail. He said they played cards and partied all night long. I didn't see him again 'til way up in the morning.

"One thing he was good about, though. When I told him I wanted to have my name on the paper that said who owned the land, he went to the courthouse and put both our names on it. You know women couldn't own land in their own names in Alabama in them days. It had to be in the name of both the man and wife. Then he told me I could take care of half the cotton fields and half the milk cows. Yesiree, that's what John did. I had my own cotton fields, and my own cows to milk. We had different cans that the milk company picked up every morning at the end of the road, and both of us got separate checks from the company. I always wondered what the milk carrier thought."

She stopped to check on the corn bread. "He was good to me, John was, and when he died, I thought I couldn't live no more."

"Remind me when he died, Grandma."

"Aw, it was in 1953. He was seventy-three when he died and I was fifty-eight. I didn't know how I was going to run the farm without him. All that land to take care of. But I did. I hired a tenant farmer and his family to help me.

After breakfast, Susie pulled the old trunk into the middle of the sitting room. "This was Mama Vennie's trunk," she said. "She give it to me just before she died."

The first thing she pulled from the trunk was a faded photograph in a large oval frame. "This is Mama Vennie. It was taken in Huntsville in December 1901. I know because she let me go with her to get it made. The boys wanted us all to give it to her for Christmas. They had it set in this gilded frame. I don't remember how much it all cost, but I know it was expensive."

Hetty studied the photograph. A tired-looking little woman in long, black satin dress stood by a chair. She wore a matching turn-of-the-century hat, round and black. Her left hand clutched the back of the chair. There was a hard, determined look on her face.

"I need to hang this in the front room." Susie said. "And here's that old quilt Grandma Orpha and Aunt Clara made." Susie said, unfolding it to show Hetty. "See how they quilted these bright yellow daffodils on it?"

"This must have been made during the Civil War," Hetty said.

"I reckon so," Susie said. "Mama Vennie said the War Between the States was the awfulest war there ever was. Did I tell you what the women did when the bushwhackers came?"

"Yes, Grandma," Hetty said. "You've told me." And every woman in the family has told that story over and over, she thought. Bushwhackers come. The women cut their hands off with a butcher knife. They run off bleeding."

"I ain't decided who I'm gonna leave this quilt to. I think I'll just let 'em fight over it." Susie cackled, laying it aside. "Close your eyes and hold out your hands, I want you to have something."

Hetty felt like a child again. "What in the world is it?" she wanted to know. Susie placed a small deerskin bag in Hetty's hands.

"It's a flute, a Indian flute." Grandma said. "It's little carryin' sack keeps it from the elements. Open it and take it out. It's made out of cedar wood. Smell its good cedar smell."

Hetty took the flute from the deerskin bag and gently ran her fingers over the smooth surface. It looked a little like the recorder she had played in grammar school.

"Where did you get this, Grandma?"

"Play it for me first and then I'll tell you," her grandmother said. "You're the music maker in the family."

Hetty's hand hovered over the six holes. She made a tentative sound with all the holes open. Then she began to play a mountain tune Grandma Susie had sung to her when she was a child. Someone had taken great care in creating the flute, shaping it to bring out the best possible sound.

"How did you get this flute?" Hetty asked.

"It was Papa's flute. Mama said when he asked her to marry him, he didn't have a ring to give her, so he give her this flute. Papa said this Indian man carved it from a cedar limb up in the Tennessee mountains when he was a boy. It's real old. Mama said Papa would play this old Indian tune over and over. He used to play it for me when I was little. I think I can still remember it." Susie closed her eyes and hummed.

Hetty began playing, trying to match the music to her grandmother's humming.

"Do you think the music is tellin' a story?" Susie asked. "When I was younger, I used to think so."

"Well," said Hetty, "let's try to figure it out. I think it tells a story of this Indian boy. He's sitting on a rock by a stream in the mountains. Maybe he's playing his flute. It's summer, a clear day, not a cloud in the sky. Here's where you have to help me, Grandma. What does the boy see?"

"Well, he sees tall cedars and oaks and pine trees, and maybe wild laurels and rhododendrons. He can see way across the valley between the high mountains. Oh, and I remember smellin' honeysuckles bloomin' up in the mountains," Susie said.

"So we'll say in the song he sits among white laurel and pink rhododendron and honeysuckles and the rest," Hetty said. "What would he be thinking, Grandma?"

"I thought *you* were writin' this story," Grandma said.

"It's our story, ours together." Hetty said.

Susie looked out the window. "Oh, he'd be thinkin' about his girl, I guess."

"Yes, and wouldn't he have wished his girl could be with him and they could stay there forever?"

"Yes, I guess so," Susie said. "But sometimes we don't always get what we wish for. I'm afraid he'll have to leave the place."

"That must be what makes the music sound so sad!" Hetty added.

"Tell me about the girl," Susie said.

"Well, I think they've taken her from her mountain home, and she wishes she could go back."

"What's she look like, do you think?" Susie asked.

"Like you when you were younger," Hetty said.

Grandma Susie laughed. "You're a good 'un at telling stories, Hetty."

"I couldn't do it without your help, you know," Hetty said. "It's your music that tells the story." Then after a moment, she added with a gleam in her eye, "Could we add a part about picking strawberries in the snow?"

"I know what you are. You're a jokester!" Susie laughed.

"Yep, wonder who I got that from?" Hetty chuckled.

Susie smiled and closed the trunk.

"Grandma, my whole life long, I've heard whispers that we might have Indian blood. Once Herbert told me that when he was about fifteen around 1945, he was here when this Indian drove up asking about you. He said he was driving a fine car, looked well-to-do. Looked like a lawyer. He said the man went into the house to talk to you, and after he left, nobody would tell him anything about it. Can you tell me about it?"

"Law, child, I don't remember. That was a long time ago."

It was clear to Hetty her grandmother had nothing more to say about the subject. And what about the dream of the strawberry field? Hetty thought. Maybe there'll always be things I'll never know. Maybe, as Grandma says, it's better just to let things be.

"Before you go," Susie said. "You have to brush my hair like you used to. Let's sit out in the shade where it's cooler."

Under the shade of the cedar, Hetty brushed her grandmother's long straight hair.

"It used to be coal black." Susie said. "But now it's got these ugly gray streaks all through it. Sometimes I think I'll splurge and go to the beauty parlor to get me one of them permanents. Maybe I'll dye it all black. Do you think I should?"

"I like it just the way it is," Hetty said. "You've earned every one of those gray hairs. And I like it when you roll it back into a bun. You have pretty hair, so straight and long." She paused, then leaned over her grandma's shoulder and whispered, "Tell me, Grandma, do we have Indian blood?"

"Honey, hush, and plait my hair like a Indian."

EPILOGUE

Ocean View, Delaware
2004

Somewhere in the back of Hetty's mind, she had known it would come. Some secrets cannot be kept forever. Somehow, someone, for whatever reason, allows secrets to escape that hidden place where secrets are kept.

She could tell by the sound of her cousin Herbert's voice on the telephone that he was upset. "I have something I must tell you. It won't be easy to hear."

"Well, tell me what it is."

"Did you know that our grandmother was raped when she was a girl?"

"What are you talking about?"

"She was raped by a black man, and they lynched him, and it caused one of the worst riots in Huntsville history. It happened in a strawberry patch near Dallas Mills."

Hetty sat stunned. Herbert's words were like an arrow shot straight to her heart. So this was what Susie's dream of the strawberry field was about. This was the secret she had taken to her grave!

"Won't you tell me about your dream in the strawberry field?" Hetty could hear her grandma's voice: "Ah, it's better to just let some things be." Hetty wished she could take back her careless prodding about what the recurring dream of the strawberry field meant. How could she not have sensed her grandmother's pain?

"Are you there, Hetty?" Herbert asked.

"How did you find out?"

"A friend just happened to call and ask me if I had read this book about lynchings in Madison County. Can you imagine how I felt when I was reading along and all of a sudden there she was, our grandmother, in this book?"

No, she could not imagine how he felt. But he must have been shocked, just as she was. Herbert must be struggling to understand how something like this could have happened. Snapshot memories from her childhood flashed through Hetty's mind.

Grandma, can I go with you to the milk the cows? Hold the teat just this way, she says. We'll wait until the hens are gone before we collect the eggs. Here's two eggs for you to exchange with the peddler. You can swap 'em for a Baby Ruth bar. Tie my string to my June-bug, Grandma. Hush, child. Your grandpa's takin' a nap. Be careful of them briars in the cotton pile, and stay away from that well. And that poor colored family a-pickin' John's cotton needs help. You take 'em these apples.

Never in a hundred years would I have guessed such an outrage could have happened to my grandma, she thought. One never knows the sorrow another carries. Never.

"I'll send you a copy of the book," Herbert said.

Hetty meticulously and painfully followed the story in the book. In the middle of it all, she realized that only part of the story had been told. The book was, after all, about lynchings in Madison County, not about Susie herself. It didn't tell anything about her life, either before or after two days in July 1900. In fact, according to the book, she and her family simply disappeared after the lynching.

Why did Grandma never tell anyone? How could she keep such a secret her whole life long? Could she have pushed what happened in the strawberry field so deep into her mind that she had no conscious memory of it? Could her recurring dream have been her mind's way of remembering and not remembering? If she *did* remember, how did she hold it inside all those years?

Later at the municipal library in Huntsville, Hetty pored over the newspapers for July 1900. The two white newspapers, the *Weekly Mercury* and the *Weekly Tribune*, provided more detail than she cared to know. The one black paper, the *Weekly Journal*, had provided fewer specific details.

In the excruciating process of sifting through the various accounts, Hetty discovered a number of discrepancies. Political editorializing and racial prejudice tended to shape much of the reporting. Much was written about the heroism of the sheriff, and questions were raised about who would pay for the rebuilding of the jail. One of the papers suggested the mayor should investigate who made the call to stop the state militia from arriving. The paper stated he could have looked through the telephone records and found out who told the governor the troops weren't needed. If the order hadn't been cancelled, the mob could have been dispersed and the lynching prevented.

Few words were written about the injustice of the lynching or about punishment for the vigilantes. The men who put the rope around the neck of Isaac Chambers went free. The black paper, the *Journal*, questioned whether justice was served since there was no trial. "The lawlessness will be handed down to posterity. The jail could have been protected. Huntsville should hang her head in shame," the paper stated.

Hetty wondered how the citizens of Huntsville, as one of the newspapers reported, could go about their business as usual. How could anyone have ignored the rape of a child and the mob violence of a lynching?

In August, four cousins—Hetty, Shannon, Renee, and Herbert, all great-grandchildren of Vennie, and two of them, Hetty and Herbert, grandchildren of Susie—sat under the shade of an old cedar tree in the cemetery at Hazel Green where Vennie and Susie were buried side by side.

"I wonder what Susie would think about her secret being revealed?" Renee said. "Would she be upset or angry, or maybe relieved?"

"I'll bet she wouldn't want it told the way it was," Shannon said.

"Do you want to hear something strange?" Hetty said. "The rape took place on July 23, 1900, and the lynching happened the next day. I remembered my last visit with Grandma Susie was in 1965, three years before she died. I knew it was in the middle of summer, and something told me it was in the month of July. I went back through my old journals, and, sure enough, there it was. I was with Grandma on July 23 and 24, 1965. Don't you think it's strange we were together on the exact same days so many years later? Don't you think it's weird I was pushing her to tell more about her dream just at that time?"

"I think it's a sign," Renee said. "She wanted you to know, but she just couldn't bring herself to say it. By telling you her dream, she was reaching out to you. She wanted you to know what happened. And now we all *know* what happened."

"I think she wants you to tell her story," Herbert said. "Not just the part revealed in the book about lynchings or in the cold newspaper accounts."

"I think Herbert's right," Renee said. "You need to tell about her later life. After all, she lived to a ripe old age."

"Yes, but you must also reach back to tell her whole story, Hetty," Herbert said. "Her story—and ours—goes back a long way."

HELEN LAVINIA UNDERWOOD

Yes, I *will* tell her story, Hetty thought. But I will need to tell Vennie and James's story, Orpha, Clary and Henry's stories, and Claracy and Hannah's stories. And I will have to tell Fannie and John and Lillie's stories, and Elizabeth and Johnny's. But I must begin, she thought, with Analeha and Greenberry. Yes, that's where I will begin.

260

AUTHOR'S NOTE

When Susie died in 1968, she left her farm in Elkwood, Alabama, to her four children—Ivy, Serena, Alvie, and Ruby Mae. They, in turn, left it to their children. In 2005, Susie's oldest grandson, Herbert, purchased the entire farm and preserved it as a park, lining it with young crepe myrtle trees. Susie would have been proud. What once had been cotton fields and woods was now a place where her grandchildren and their children could play under the oaks and cedars. Herbert renovated the little cottage as a guesthouse to be used by family members who wished to visit the old home place.

I was struck by how appropriate Herbert's actions were. Our Indian heritage, though difficult to prove, was showing through. He chose to be a Keeper of the Land. Certainly, the Greenberry in my story would have approved. My mother Ruby, who had feared the home place would be lost to high-rise office buildings and condominiums, would have been pleased.

Telling Susie's story became an obsession for me. Each time I sat down to write, Susie was sitting beside me urging me on. The impetus, which led me to begin this book, has reminded me that I must not forget where I came from, and that I have a responsibility to those who come after me.

I hope my children and grandchildren will take on their ancestors' struggles against discrimination and injustice. I hope they can sit, as Greenberry did, high on a mountain under cedar shades and see the white laurel and pink rhododendron bloom. I hope they can experience, like Analeha, the roaring water cascading over rocks. I hope they can rejoice in days of clear, blue skies, and in cloudy days that bring thunderstorms and rain. And at night when the sky is clear and bright, I hope, like Susie, they will gaze in wonder at the stars. Like the *tsa-lah-gi*, I hope they will remember that all humans, animals, birds, trees, and even rocks are sacred. Finally, I hope they will all be Keepers of the Earth.

For Mark

ACKNOWLEDGMENTS

O ver the four years it took to complete the novel, I was fortunate to have an expert critic and editor in my husband, Joel. He was ever ready to listen, read, and comment and gave invaluable advice throughout the process. He kept me on task, and at times, when I was ready to shelve the project, he prodded me on in his gentle manner. What a great time we had visiting the places I wrote about, and spending hours together doing research in libraries and museums all over the country. I owe him mountains of thanks for his patience, guidance and love.

And to two women who gave the manuscript a careful reading just prior to publication, I owe a special debt of gratitude: Gail Tate King, President of the Alabama Chapter of the Trail of Tears Association and Executive Director of the Southeastern Anthropological Institute, whose reading for historical accuracy was critical, and Deanna J. Bennett, Leader of the East Lake Community Library Writer's Workshop in Palm Harbor, Florida, whose comments and wise counsel proved invaluable.

It was during the writing of this novel that I first met four second cousins: Renee Priest in Huntsville, Alabama; Shannon Adcock in Charlotte, North Carolina; Lynn Little in Elizabethton, Tennessee; and Leigh Hutchinson in Hazel Green, Alabama; all of whom were looking for our mutual ancestors. My first cousin, Herbert Batt, and his wife Carolyn in Huntsville joined us in the search, providing moral and financial support. All were my steady supporters, and I owe them each a debt of gratitude.

I owe special gratitude to Josephine Sack and her husband, Dr. Bradley Sack, in Baltimore, Maryland, for reading through at least two redactions. Jo's was the voice that called me to task just when I needed prodding. Thanks as well to my genealogy group in Delaware: Dr. Frances Wimbush, Joan Brower, and Patricia Frensilli.

I especially appreciate the research help I received from White County genealogists Geraldine Pollard and Bill Colley of the White County Archives and Genealogical Historical Society, Sparta, Tennessee; genealogist Carol Morgan and librarian Gail Meadows at the White County Public Library; genealogist Brad Walker and librarian Mary Robbins of Magness Memorial Library in McMinnville, Tennessee; and Donna Beck, librarian, Burritt Memorial Library, Spencer, Tennessee.

I owe special thanks to my brother-in-law, Barry Underwood, in McMinnville, who read chapter by chapter as I was writing and gave me immediate feedback over the phone. Joel and I loved hiding away in his cabin on the Collins River near the setting of the novel while I was working on the manuscript.

Thanks to my children and their spouses, David and Anastasia Underwood, Lydia and Michael Horan, and Jay and Maureen Underwood for listening to my readings of selections at various stages of the process.

I want to thank the following other family members for their encouragement: my sister Joyce and her husband Dan Jewell, my brother Larry and his wife Judy Greenway, my sister Barbara and her husband Anthony Wheeler, my sister Sandra and her husband Peter Wallin, my nephew Shane and his wife Amy Greenway, my Aunt Hallie Mae Terry, and my cousins Pauline Walker, Cynthia Chitwood, Earlene Garcia, Evelyn Adcock, Richard Adcock, Barbara Greenway Bowman, and Jonathan Letson.

I am especially grateful to the following persons for granting me invaluable interviews: Ed Chastain on Rock Island history, Joe and Sue Davenport on the Trail of Tears in Woodbury and Cannon County, Thelma Hibdon and her mother Ida Pearl Underwood Davis on basket-weaving, Bill and Agnes Jones on Van Buren County genealogy and the Trail of Tears in Tennessee, Kathy Jones on the Amonsoquath Cherokees in Arkansas, Gail King on the Trail of Tears in Alabama, Linda Mackie on coalmining in Bon Air and Ravenscroft, and Marion Smith on Tennessee caves.

Thanks also to good friends who encouraged me: Robert and Mildred Downer, Steve and Jan Hitchcock, Richard and Eleanor Perry, Jeanne Zipke, Susanne Fox, Jeff and Ivy Mask, George and Colette Kokinis, Marian Tambarrino, Steve Elkins and Murray Archibald, Nicholas and Brigitte Fessenden, Helen Fessenden, Brooke Bognanni, Shirley Herndon, Marco and Kimberly Hernandez, James and Alba Logan, Thelma Felker, Jack and Kathy Shigo, Rolf Taylor, Pam Edmonstone, Wanda Eason, Judy Chilton, Jesse Reed, Virginia Monahan, Lois Kinsler, Jack and Regina Rahilly, Chuck and Dona Lewis, Patrick and Patricia Stern, and Bill and Karen West. Special thanks to Dolly Youssef of Bread for the World for sharing her expertise in Microsoft Word.

Many thanks also to the Baltimore Third Saturday Group for listening and responding: Brad and Jo Sack, Charlene Reinke, Henry and Bunny Mosley, Louise Carlson, Brent and Ann Mathews, Pat Collins and Charles Richter, Ron and Janet Oaks, Nate and Diane Pierce.

I owe a special debt of gratitude to the Mullins Restaurant and the Dallas Mills Deli in Huntsville for their generous provision of space and time for the "Cousins' Group" meetings, and David Pound of the Fog House Bar and Grill on the Caney Fork River near Rock Island, Tennessee, for his generosity in slaking the thirst of some weary travelers in off-hours.

And thanks to Savannahs Landing neighbors in Ocean View, Delaware, who spoke words of encouragement as they passed my porch on their morning walks.

RESOURCES

Indian Removal

Banks, William H., *Plants of the Cherokee*

Blankenship, Bob, *Cherokee Roots, Vol. 1: Eastern Cherokee Rolls Guion Miller Roll "Plus"*

Cannon County High School Students, "Old'uns' Stories Told to Young'uns," Woodbury, Tennessee, March 2005

Cherokee Phoenix—September, 2005

Cherokee Removal, *The Journal of Rev. Daniel S. Butrick, May 19, 1838-April 1, 1839,* The Trail of Tears Association, Oklahoma Chapter

Crouch, Arthur, *History of McMinnville*, Chapter Six: "Trail of Tears"

Duncan, Barbara R. & Brett H. Riggs, *Cherokee Heritage Trails Guidebook*

Ehle, John, *Trail of Tears: The Rise and Fall of the Cherokee Nation*

Ellis, Jerry, *Walking the Trail*

Forman, Grant, *Indian Removal: The Emigration of the Five Civilized Tribes of Indians*

Garrett, J. T. and Michael Tlanusta Roger, *The Cherokee Full Circle*

Greene, Gary, "Tales From the Enchanted Land of the Cherokee" (CD-ROM)

Hackett, David, "Yuchi Indians" (yuchi.org)

Harjo, Joy, *She Had Some Horses*

Jahoda, Gloria, *The Trail of Tears*

King, Gail, *Tuscumbia Railway Company and the Tuscumbia, Courtland, and Decatur Railroad*

Indian Land Cessions in the American Southeast, Annual Report of the Bureau of Ethnology to the Secretary of the Smithsonian Institute, 1884 (USGenNet)

Mankiller, Wilma and Michael Wallace, *Mankiller: A Chief and Her People*

Mooney, James, *Myths of the Cherokee*

Nicols, Roger, ed, *The American Indian*

Perdue, Theda, *Cherokee Women*
  The Cherokee Nation and the Trail of Tears, with Michael D. Green

Rozema, Vicki, *Footsteps of the Cherokees*
  Voices from The Trail of Tears

Satz, Ronald N., *American Indian Policy in the Jacksonian Era*
  Tennessee's Indian Peoples from Contact to Removal

Seybert, Tony, *Slavery and Native Americans in British North America and the United States: 1600 to 1865*

Sharpe, J. Ed., *The Cherokees Past and Present*

Speck, Frank G., *Cherokee Dance and Drama*

Starr, Emmett, *History of the Cherokee Indians*

Stiggins, George, *Creek Indian History*

Studi, Wes, "The Trail of Tears: Cherokee Legacy" (DVD)
  "Black Indians—An American Story" (DVD)

Swann, Brian, *Native American Songs and Poems*

Two-Hawks, John, *Good Medicine*

Vest, Jay Hansford C., "Native, Aboriginal, Indigenous: Who Counts As Indian in Post Apartheid Virginia"

Walls, Billie Ruth, *Speak Cherokee Now*

The Melungeons

Callahan, Jim, *Lest We Forget: The Melungeon Colony at Newman's Ridge*

Goodspeed's History of East Tennessee: Hawkins County

Federal Writers Project, "Manuscripts from American Life Histories: 1936-1940"

Johnson, Mattie Ruth, *Melungeon Heritage: A Story of Life on Newman's Ridge*

Kennedy, Brent, "Ties That Bind"

Nassau, Mike, *What is a Melungeon?*

Ursic, Alessandro, "American Gypsies: A Journey through the Lands of the Melungeons"

Huntsville

Betts, E. C., *Early History of Huntsville, Alabama, 1804-1870*

Carney, Tom, *Portraits in Time: Stories of Huntsville and Madison County Old Huntsville: History and Stories of the Tennessee Valley,"* Nos. 149, 156, 162 and 177

Jones, Virgil Carrington, *True Tales of Old Madison County*

The Nebraska State Journal—Lincoln, Nebraska, Tuesday Morning, July 24, 1900

Simpson, Fred B. with Mary Daniel and Gay Campbell, *The Sins of Madison County*

The Weekly Journal—Wednesday, July 25, 1900—Huntsville, Alabama

The Weekly Mercury—Wednesday, July 25, 1900—Huntsville, Alabama

The Weekly Tribune—Wednesday, July 25, 1900—Huntsville, Alabama

Jonesborough

Alderman, Pat, *The Overmountain Men*

"America's Quilting History," The Romantic Double Wedding Ring Quilt" (TNGenWeb)

Colletta, John P., *They Came By Ships*

Cox, Joyce and W. Eugene (Editors), *History of Washington County Tennessee*

Dixon, Max, *The Wataugans*

Fink, Paul M., *Jonesborough: The First Century of Tennessee's First Town*

Goodspeed's History of Washington County

Kennedy, Billy, *Scots-Irish in the Hills of Tennessee*

McRae, Ann Cameron, *"Weaving in Washington County, Tennessee in Mid-1800's*

Sproul, William W., "The Sproul Families of early western Virginia" (sproulfamily.net)

Sproule, Robert James St. George, *The Ancient Spreulls* (www.cindy.spruill.com).

Warmuth, Donna Aders, *Legends, Stories and Ghostly Tales of Abington and Washington County*

Wigginton, Eliot, and Students, *Foxfire*, Vol. 1 and 2

Williams, John Alexander, *Appalachia*

White County

American Philosophical Society, "Bernard Romans" (amphilsoc.org)

Bon Air Hustler, "Community News," Dec. 4, 1917, to Nov. 5, 1920

"Civil War in Van Buren County," (TNGenWeb)

Colley, William, White County Tennessee Genealogy (CD-ROM)

Crouch, Arthur Weir, "The Caney Fork of the Cumberland" (TNGenWeb)
    Great Falls Cotton Mills, Warren County, Tennessee (TNGenWeb)

Dudney, Betty Jane, "Civil War in White County, Tennessee 1861-1865" (TNGenWeb)

Gates, Henry Louis, Jr., Editor, *The Classic Slave Narratives*

Glebe, Iris, *Brief History of the Coal Industry of White County, Tennessee, 1882-1936*

Goodspeed's History of White and Warren Counties (TNGenWeb)

Francis, Frankie Passons, "The Charles Caffery Martin Family" (TNGenWeb)

Frazier, Eula, "Journal of Eula Frazier" (TNGenWeb)

Higginbotham, Julie S., "Four Centuries of Planting and Progress: A History of the U.S. Nursery Industry," American Nurseryman Association Journal

Huehls, Betty Sparks, *Mining on the Mountain*

Rains, Maj. George. W, "Notes on Making Saltpeter from the Earth of the Caves," *Augusta, Ga., Steam Power Press Chronicle and Sentinel*, 1861

Rogers, E.G., *Memorable Historical Accounts of White County and Area*

Seales, Monroe, *A History of White County* (TNGenWeb)

Smith, Darlene S., "Great Falls Cotton Mill Historic Structure Report" (TNGenWeb)

Sparta Expositor, *Souvenir Supplement*

Sparta Magazine, "200 Years Legends, Legacies: White County, Tennessee 1806-2006"

VEC Powerlines, May-June 1995, "Recalling the Bon Air Mountain Mines"

Walker, Hugh, "Tennessee Tales" (TNGenWeb)

White County Heritage Book Committee, *Heritage of White County, 1806-1999*

White County Retired Teachers Association, "Trips Into White County History"

Williams, Coral, Legends and Stories of White County, Chapter V. (TNGenWeb)

Wilson, Susan Douglas, "Transportation in Early Middle Tennessee," (TNGenWeb)

Public Libraries and Genealogy Centers

Burritt Memorial Library, Spencer, Tennessee
Huntsville—Madison County Public Library, Huntsville, Alabama
Little Rock Public Library, Little Rock, Arkansas
Magness Memorial Library, McMinnville, Tennessee
Maumelle Township Library, Maumelle, Arkansas
Muskogee Public Library, Muskogee, Oklahoma
Nashville Tennessee State Archives
National Archives, Washington, DC
Pinellas County (Florida) Library, Oldsmar and East Lake branches
H. B. Stamps Memorial Library, Rogersville, Tennessee
South Coastal Library, Bethany Beach, Delaware
Washington County Public Library, Jonesborough, Tennessee
Washington County Visitor's Center, Jonesborough, Tennessee
White County Public Library, Sparta, Tennessee

Museums and Historic Places Visited

Big Bone Cave, Van Buren County, Tennessee
Blythe's Ferry Site—Cherokee Memorial Park on Tennessee River
Brainard Mission Cemetery, Chattanooga, Tennessee
Cherokee Removal Memorial Park, Decatur, Tennessee
Chieftain's Museum, The Major Ridge House, near Rome, Georgia
Cumberland Caverns, McMinnville, Tennessee
Cumberland Gap, Bell County, Kentucky, on TN, VA, KY lines
Embree Stone House, Telford, Tennessee
Etowah Indian Mounds, State Historic Site, Cartersville, Georgia
Five Civilized Tribes Museum, Muskogee, Oklahoma
Fort Cass Cherokee Internment Camp area, Charleston, Tennessee
Fort Loudon State Historic Area, Fort Loudon, Tennessee
Giles County Trail of Tears Memorial Park, Pulaski, Tennessee
Jonesborough Historic Site, Earliest town in Tennessee
Lewis Ross Home, Charleston, Tennessee
Mahala Mullins homeplace, Newman's Ridge, Hancock County, Tennessee
Museum of the Amercian Indian, Suitland, Maryland
Museum of the Cherokee Indian, Qualla Boundary, Cherokee, North Carolina
Nancy Ward Grave Site—On the Ocoee River near Benton, Tennessee

New Echota State Historic Site, Calhoun, Georgia
Oconaluftee Indian Village and Living History Museum, Cherokee, North
  Carolina
Old Stone Fort Archeological Park, Manchester, Tennessee
Plain View Cemetery, Hazel Green, Alabama
Roan Mountain State Park, Roan Mountain, Tennessee
Rocky River Crossing, Trail of Tears Site, Van Buren County, Tennessee
Red Clay Historic Park and Visitor's Center, Red Clay Tennessee
Rock Island State Park, Rock Island, Tennessee
The Rock House, Sparta, Tennessee
Ross' Landing Plaza, Chattanooga, Tennessee
Sequoyah Birthplace Museum, Vonore, Tennessee
Sequoyah Home, Sallisaw, Oklahoma
Shellsford Cemetery, Shellsford Baptist Church, McMinnville, Tennessee
Smithsonian Institution's Museum of Natural History, Washington, D.C.
Sunset Rock, Sparta, Tennessee
Sycamore Shoals State Historic Area, Fort Watauga, Elizabethton, Tennessee
Tahlequah Cherokee Museum, Tahlequah Oklahoma
Tuscumbia Landing, Tuscumbia, Alabama
Unicoi National Millenium Trail, State Park and Turnpike
The Vann House State Historic Site, Chatsworth, Georgia

Online Resources

Ancestry.com
Crowe, Elizabeth Showell, *Genealogy Online*
Cindislist.com
FamilySearch.org
Nara.gov
RootsWeb.com
TNWeb.com
USGenWeb.com

THE TRAIL OF TEARS ASSOCIATION

The Trail of Tears Association (TOTA) is a nonprofit, membership organization formed to support the creation, development, and interpretation of the Trail of Tears National Historic Trail. So designated by Congress in 1987, the Trail commemorates the forced removal of the Cherokee people from their homelands in the southeastern United States to Indian Territory (present-day Oklahoma) in 1838-1839. The mission of the Trail of Tears Association is to promote and engage in the protection and preservation of Trail of Tears National Historic Trail resources; to promote awareness of the Trail's legacy, including the removal stories of the Cherokee, Chickasaw, Choctaw, Muscogee (Creek), and Seminole; and to perpetuate the management and development techniques that are consistent with the National Park Service's trail plan. For membership information, contact www.nationaltota.org. Jack Baker is President and Jerra Quinton is Associate Director. Address: Trail of Tears Association, 1100 N. University, Suite 143, Little Rock, Arkansas, 72207, (501) 666-9032. The Association offers chapter membership in the nine (9) states where the trail is located: Alabama, Arkansas, Georgia, Illinois, Kentucky, Missouri, North Carolina, Oklahoma, and Tennessee. Contributions to the Trail of Tears Association are tax deductible under section 501 (c) (3) of the Internal Revenue code.

The author is a member of TOTA, including the Alabama and Tennessee chapters.